JEREMY KLINE

and the LOST TRIBE

Ray Wenck
Glory Days Press
Columbus, Ohio

Ray Wenck

Glory Days Press
Columbus, Ohio

Book Layout © 2016 BookDesignTemplates.com
Cover Design by Mibl Art
Lost Tribe/ Ray Wenck. – 3rd ed.

ISBN 978-1-7360350-8-5

Dedication

This book is dedicated to all those who can open their hearts and minds to see and absorb the magic that surrounds them.

Author's Notes

As with any work there are always many people to thank for their assistance or contribution to the project. The Jeremy Kline series has even more than usual. Many people contributed to this production though not in a way you might think.

It has long been my practice that when I meet someone whether at a book show, a conference, or even a server at a restaurant, which has happened three times now, and find they have an unusual name, I adopt it for use at some further date for characters in stories. Since the Jeremy Kline series has so many characters I have used up almost my entire list of names.

Thank you goes out to Biatta, Jerricka, Gwenydd, Jno, Nika, Neveah, Allyra, Gianna, Retta, Chase, Favyan, Aric, Olivianna, and Delphina. I appreciate the use of your names. Although the character in the story does not necessarily represent you it is still nice to have your name in a book.

Special thanks goes out to my editor, stand-up comedian Jodi McDermitt. You can catch her on tour at various clubs around the Midwest.

The Jeremy Kline series has been a fun distraction from my normal genres. As of now it is scheduled to be a trilogy. However, if enough support is generated for a sequel I might be able to be convinced to do another. That's up to you.

Until the next volume: Read all you want, I'll write more.

Ray

Prologue

"We're surrounded," Rhylie said barely able to keep his voice below shrill. "They have closed in our escape route."

Rowan noted how hard the man fought to hide his concern and remain calm. But this was war. How many were able to keep composed during battle? Well, himself, of course, and Tarney, but Tarney was still in recovery and not here to add his considerable power to their defense.

He glanced around. The small force of a dozen had come to seek the aid of several wild wizards who lived in seclusion in the mountain range a hundred miles from the city. The venture had been a failure. But even as the circle closed in on them and perhaps led to their last moments, Rowan's thoughts returned to the strange inviting communication he had received from those wizards mere hours before. It was clear now that it had all been a ruse to catch them in the open and whittle down their already depleted numbers. He readied a spell but his mind was elsewhere. Only one explanation existed for their current predicament. They had a traitor in their midst.

Overhead, a fireball descended toward them, but most of his group were busy fending off other magical attacks and did not see death falling from the sky. Rowan shook aside the offensive spell he was ready to unleash, losing some of the important cached energy he had drawn into himself, and switched to a defensive shield. He readied and cast it in seconds with a few intricate weaves of his fingers and the activation word, "Deflectus."

In a blueish flash, a shimmering half shell of light formed over the small band of wizards. Still, he was too late. The shield formed, slicing through the fireball and deflecting a large portion of it, sending a shower of sparks and flame against the rocky mountainside. The portion that sheered off beneath the forcefield exploded on the ground in the middle of four young wizards, incinerating three and leaving the fourth alive but face down with the back of her body charred black.

The sight sickened Rowan. He had been too slow, and the others were too inexperienced to be aware of multiple attacks or cover each other. They would all perish on this remote mountain if he didn't do something.

He needed time. He straightened his arms with his palms to the ground. In a slow circle, he drew energy from the Earth. His arms tensed and he drew them upward with tremendous exertion as if lifting a heavy weight. Then he bent his elbows, pulling his arms in, and recited words he had learned ages ago.

"Energeasee. Boltoreadous. Expulosaea. Maximosus."

With all the rage he held, and with every bit of strength, Rowan pushed his arms straight out like shoving someone from his path. A stream of ten expanding bolts of power ripped from each finger and spread in a powerful arc of concentrated light down the sloping mountainside, tearing rocks, trees, and humans from the ground. The massive amount of debris fell and rolled hundreds of yards from where he stood.

Before the shattered rock, splintered trees, and broken bodies stopped rolling, Rowan began a second chant.

"Evoctoris. Spoutourous. Smokilaterolea."

Tiny wisps of smoke began pouring from the ground wherever Rowan extended his hands. He made a slow circle. By the time he finished, his surviving team was covered by a wall of smoke.

"Quickly. Rhylie, gather everyone to me." He would have gone to them but after a dual release of that much energy, he was barely able to stand, let alone walk. As two women, two girls, and four men arrived, Rowan asked Rhylie, "What about Landa?"

The man shook his head. The charred young woman was dead. So much promise, so much energy, so much heart, cut down decades too soon. Rowan shrugged off his anger and guilt. There would be time enough for that later if they survived.

"Rhylie, I need your assistance. Give me your hand. Everyone gather close. Hold on tight to each other."

Rowan once more absorbed energy, praying he could hold enough to get them all to safety.

"Sir," one of the men said. "The smoke is thinning."

Rowan ignored the comment. He needed his full focus. He ripped the energy from Rhylie, pulling it down the man's arm and up his. Rhylie, screamed and arced back his face aimed toward the sky. *"Evoctorum. Acceleracoreum. Transpolocatious. Maximosus."*

In a flash of light, a rush of wind, and a feeling of weightlessness, the group crashed to the ground. They cried out in surprise and pain. Most fell or stumbled over each other. As they regained their equilibrium and untangled, one of the girls cried out, "Billy! Billy!" Her voice increased in volume and panic until she was in a full shriek. "Billy!"

But the boy was gone.

One of the young women said, "He was holding my hand but as we began to move, he let go."

Rowan Vandalue lay staring at the sky miles from the mountainside. He was too weak to rise and too aggrieved to speak. They had lost another prodigy, making it five on the day. As much as it pained him to admit it, they were losing this war. Bradenbaugh was always one step ahead, and it was costing valuable lives. While his numbers were being eroded one by one, Bradenbaugh seemed to have an endless variety of minions to send against him. He had to find a way to out-maneuver his enemy before he had no one left to stand against him.

Bradenbaugh would pay with his life for all he had done and all he had taken from this world. Rowan shifted focus. First, he had to find a traitor and deal with him.

Back on the mountainside, a large form exited the smoke, wiping it from his shoulders like it was snow. Initially stunned from the abrupt fall, Billy shook his head to clear his mind, then scrambled to his feet. He took three running steps before someone clotheslined him and sent him crashing to the rocky ground. He moaned. Strong hands lifted him and set him on his knees in front of the hulking shape.

"We found one, General Perva," a man in a dark uniform said.

General Perva lowered his bulk toward the man and glared. "Where have they gone?"

"I-I don't know. They were just gone."

"Ah, and they left you behind? How sad. Where is their hideout?"

"I-I don't know. I have never been."

"You don't know much, do you?"

He shook his head vigorously. "N-no, sir."

General Perva straightened and eyed the slowly clearing ground. A woman appeared at his side.

"They're gone."

"We almost had him."

The woman displayed an evil smile. "What will you tell our master?"

Perva's eyes flashed from fear to annoyance. "That we cut their numbers down and will proceed with the plan and keep the pressure on."

"What about our cute little friend here?" She spoke as though talking to a puppy.

"He's all yours, McGrew."

"Oh goodie!" she beamed with delight and gave several light claps.

Billy looked from her to the general. As his gaze switched back to the woman, he caught movement followed by sharp pain. His mind was confused for a moment before going blank. His body toppled to the ground and lay still as his head bounced down the slope like a rock.

Mad Madelyn McGrew watched the head bounce and roll until it came to a stop near a rock cropping. As she watched a gleeful smile stretched across her face. Without taking her gaze from the head, she said, "If you keep disappointing our master, one day that may very well be your head tumbling down a mountain." She shrieked with delight and began the long hike back to the mountain top.

General Perva stared a long while at the discarded head.

Chapter One

Three days had passed since the strangers moved into Jeremy's house. Jeremy considered them strangers not only because they were unknown to him, but their behavior was rather strange and unconventional. He was still struggling to understand what had happened and how he had allowed them to live with him.

Though he was adjusting to this new living arrangement, he fretted about the day Chandra arrived at his door. Her reaction to his new house guests would not be pleasant. They were already at odds over all that had occurred during his guest's previous visit.

The bathroom door opened and Biatta exited with a towel wrapped around her lithe body and another around her head. "It is wonderful to have hot running water again. I always feel so much better after a shower." She sat on the stool at the kitchen counter and blotted her hair with the towel.

"Ah, shouldn't you get dressed?"

She stopped drying her hair to study him. A twinkle lit her eyes. "Does my near nakedness bother you?"

He cleared his throat. "It's inappropriate. Besides, what would the neighbors think if they saw you sitting here like this?"

She went back to her drying. "When was the last time a neighbor came to the door?"

He cleared his throat again. "That's beside the point."

"Do you not find me attractive?"

"Irrelevant. I'm old enough to be your father."

"How old are you, Jeremy?"

"Some days, older than others."

She smiled. "I don't want you to feel uncomfortable about us being here." She slid off the stool.

"Why *are* you here? You seem to avoid that topic each time it is brought up."

She padded toward her room, Chandra's old room, then stopped and faced him holding the towel on her head with both hands but leaving the body towel unattended. "Shall we talk now?"

He swallowed hard and was unable to respond. Instead, he shook his head.

She laughed lightly, the sound filling the room like music. "Give me a moment to get dressed, and we shall have that discussion."

She disappeared into her room and Jeremy let out a long, slow breath. He poured another cup of coffee and sat at the kitchen table staring out the window without seeing outside. So many thoughts raced through his mind. They started with his first encounter with Daria, the second guest in his house. He followed the mental memory trail to the village that was supposedly invisible, yet he could see it plainly. How? He pushed the question aside for the moment. He settled back into the timeline.

Then there was his second visit to the village and subsequent encounter with a myriad of beings straight out of a fairy tale. Somehow, he had managed to stop a massive charging boar dead in its tracks without ever lifting a finger against it. He should have been impaled and killed. Instead, the beast, which had to have weighed at least five hundred pounds, had its neck broken. Again, how?

It all had something to do with the strange way Biatta looked at him. She suspected something about him. Whatever it was made both of them nervous. *What* it was was a major question he inserted at the front of the growing list right behind *who* were these people? What did they want from him besides a place to stay and food to eat?

His thoughts shifted to Chandra, his daughter. He didn't have the energy to go there. One crisis at a time was all his old brain and body could handle.

He heard the bedroom door open. Biatta exited, dressed in clothes she borrowed from Miranda's closet. Miranda. His deceased wife. They were much too old for her. He should take Biatta and Daria shopping, but how much would that cost him? Did it really matter? He had more than enough to live on. Of course, if Chandra caught wind of his shopping binge…No, no. He wasn't exploring that avenue of conflict.

Biatta poured a cup of coffee and joined him at the table. Her hair was still damp. He studied her as she sipped and stared out the window. Did she see the same things he did? She had hit the mark on one thing. He did find her extremely attractive, though more in a fatherly appreciation than anything remotely romantic. She was tall and lean with long brown hair, rich and bright green eyes, and a soft, unlined face that made her appear younger than she must be. Her features ethereal in nature and quality, gave her an almost angelic appearance. Almost.

She sat back and crossed her slender legs, Miranda's pants riding up her calf, still staring out the window. She had to be aware of his scrutiny. She held the mug in front of her lips and blew across it absently. Elegant. That was the word that best described her. He looked away and swallowed a gulp of his now tepid brew.

They sat in silence for a minute, then Biatta said, "Jeremy, what do you know about your family?" She never took her eyes away from the window. The question was asked simply and out of the blue like she was asking about the tree in the front yard.

"My family? I know my parents and my grandparents."
He cocked his head to look at her. "Why?"

She didn't answer immediately. Her mind appeared to
be elsewhere. She turned her soft eyes to him. Though no
hint of emotion displayed within them, he felt as if they
bore through his skull and into his brain in search of
answers. She smiled without sincerity.

"You have no idea where your family originated from?"

He met her gaze and held it, tired of playing her one-
sided game. "You know, I'm not as dense as I may
appear. You want information but never provide any
about yourself. Maybe it's time for you to reveal *your* real
purpose here."

An amused look touched her flawless face. She thought
him funny. How old was she? Though she looked young
to him, perhaps mid-thirties, she carried herself like
someone with decades more life experience. What did
they call it…having an old soul?

The twinkle in her eyes faded, leaving an almost
sorrowful gaze. No matter what she was thinking, he
knew he was tired of the back and forth, or more the lack
thereof. It was like playing a tennis match without a ball.
The heads swung from side to side with no action to
follow.

He offered a polite smile, then stood. Finally, a reaction.
His movement caused confusion. Good.

"I have errands to run. Try not to destroy the house in
my absence." He picked the keys off the counter and
moved toward the door leading to the garage. His hand
touched the knob and Biatta spoke.

"Jeremy. Please." She motioned to his chair. "Sit."

"Not if it's going to be more of the same."

"What I have to say is not easy. It will sound quite
foreign and strange to you, but I think it will be extremely
important because of what is to come."

"And what is to come?" he asked moving behind the chair.

She shook her head and glanced away. "So much—I'm not sure where to start."

"I hear the beginning is a good place."

She smiled, this time with warmth. "Please. Sit."

Jeremy hesitated, then sat. He folded his hands in front of him and waited.

"I know this may not be how you want me to start, but if you will please oblige me for a minute and allow me to ask a few questions I will have a better understanding of where the beginning is."

Jeremy was tempted to stand and go about his errands but decided to give her a few minutes.

"First, can you remember a time when something happened either to you or a family member that was beyond explanation?"

The question took him by surprise. "How so?"

His question seemed to frustrate her. "I don't know. Just anything out of the ordinary. A sudden dimming, flaring, or flickering of the lights. Something that appeared to float or fly without a source of propulsion? Or perhaps a noise or voice that sounded very close when no one was near?"

What was she getting at? "Are you talking about things like those that happened at your village?"

"Yes, or any other time in your life."

Jeremy noted tension in her jawline. A fluttering of nervousness in her body like a vibration one felt through the feet when a train passes nearby. Then he made a discovery. *Weren't her eyes green?* They were a sharp steel gray now.

"This is very important, Jeremy. Please think back. Can you recall any odd occurrences or behaviors that you had, or maybe your father?"

Oh, this was too much. He was about to say so when she waved a hand in front of him like she was saying farewell. A distant memory flashed and the image came back.

He was a boy of perhaps six. They were throwing a football. His father was teaching him how to catch. The ball slipped through his fingers and smacked point first into Jeremy's forehead. It bounced away and he gave chase out to the street and into the path of a speeding car.

When he noticed the car, he froze. Everything around him became a slow motion movie with him as the star. In the distance, he heard his father shout his name.

"Je-re-my!"

The sound was long, like it came through a long tunnel. Then the car took flight, clearing his head by inches. The force of the backdraft knocked him to the ground. The car bounced twice, hit a tree broadside, and wrapped around the trunk like a blanket.

His father raced in, scooped him up, and hurried into the house. He was placed in bed and covered with a blanket, and his father sat on the edge of the bed and spoke to him in words he didn't understand. The next morning, he woke and told his father about the strange dream he'd had about a flying car.

But that was all it was. A dream. Wasn't it?

Jeremy snapped from his fugue and stared at Biatta.

"You do remember something, don't you?"

"I'm—no. It's not...I don't know what I remember. It was a long time ago and as far as I remember, it was nothing more than a dream."

She nodded sagely, as if she had been there. "Tell me anyway."

He began to recount the incident, but when he came to the part about the flying car overhead, she stopped him.

"Close your eyes and picture the car over your head. Not just picture it. See it."

He closed his eyes and pulled up the images.

"Slow, now. Take in the details you missed as a child. What do you see?"

Jeremy was suddenly there, an old man mind in a six year old's body. It was a two-door sportscar. A Mustang with a convertible top. The car lifted off the ground and flew above him. He could feel the rush of the wind the car created. Could feel the heat from the engine and smell the exhaust from the muffler.

Six-year-old him fell to the ground on his butt and smacked his head on the blacktop. Sixty year old him watched the car hit the blacktop, bounce and turn sideways, bounce again, and hit the large, thick tree trunk. The passenger was sent flying, ejected like from a fighter jet. He went head first through the windshield of an oncoming truck. The driver covered his face against the body and the sudden barrage of flying glass. With his hands off the wheel, the truck veered off the road and slammed into the tree, pinning and crushing the Mustang into a flattened slab of metal. It was clear neither man survived the impacts. Blood erupted everywhere.

His father carried him, blocking his view from the violence and the gore, but Jeremy saw it all as if it just happened.

The next image was of him in bed. His father was speaking. The words were clear now and yet still not understandable. Jeremy focused harder. It wasn't that the words all that time ago weren't clear. They weren't English. What language was his father speaking?

He heard a snap and the scene faded. He was back in his kitchen sitting at the table. Biatta had her elbows on the table and rested her chin on the top of clasped fingers. Her now sparkling blue eyes glimmered. Her breathing slightly rapid.

To his surprise, he found a thick line of perspiration had formed across his forehead. He tried to speak but had to swallow twice to lubricate his throat. "Wh-what just happened?"

With awe in her voice, she said, "Magic."

Chapter Two

Daria choose that moment to stagger from her room as she fought an evenly waged battle between sleep and awake. They watched with amusement as she bumped into the wall, having misjudged where the door was before disappearing into the bathroom amidst a flurry of grumbles.

The instance passed, bringing them back to focus on the still unbroached subject and explanation Jeremy craved. They remained silent long enough for Daria to stumble out of the bathroom and stand in the hallway, undecided which direction to turn. Her head swung toward them. With slitted eyes she took in the room. Her head turned toward her room. Her arm lifted and pointed toward the room as if guiding her which way to go. She followed her arm, seeking the comfort of her bed over conversation or breakfast, both of which required consciousness.

Biatta smiled in a motherly fashion as the door closed behind Daria.

"She's a good child," Jeremy said.

"Yes," Biatta said with pride and a touch of sadness. "She certainly is."

"You seem fond of her."

"Of course, I am. I'm found of all our students."

"Is that all it is?"

She stiffened and her eyes narrowed. The gray darkened and hardened. "What does that mean?"

He shrugged, picked up his mug, and studied her over the rim. "Just that your affection appears to be more motherly than teacherly. Is there more of a relationship there?"

"What are you implying?" Her tone held no anger but was firm.

"Nothing." He sipped the coffee. "Just an observation."

"Your observation is speculation and nothing more. She is a student whose safety has been entrusted to me."

"Why her?"

"Why her what?" An annoyance crept into her voice.

"Of all the students I saw at your village, why choose her and only her to protect? It's obvious there were more students than staff. Why does she deserve one on one protection and the others don't?"

Her eyes flashed a dull red. The suddenness of the change and the unusual hue made Jeremy flinch.

Biatta noticed and in an instant, change came over her. She set the mug down, placed her palms on the table, and stood. Jeremy could see the tension in her arms, as if the move took great effort to control.

"My relationship with Daria or any student is none of your concern. Do not make assumptions about things you know nothing about." She turned to leave.

"That's kind of the point though, isn't it? I know nothing about anything where you are concerned, hence the reason for my initial question of why you are here. A question you once again appear to be about to sidestep."

She sighed. She looked away, then back at Jeremy. "You deserve an explanation. It's time. Let me check on Daria, and I promise we'll have that talk."

"I look forward to it," he said, but as she turned toward her room, he thought, *And to whatever the reason you duck it.*

"Yes," Jerricka said. "This will do nicely. She scanned the grounds of their new haven. It was a small farm with a large five-bedroom house and three outbuildings. The elderly woman who owned the house would allow them to stay in exchange for maintaining the house and grounds, looking after and harvesting the crops, and feeding the livestock, which consisted of four chickens, two goats, and a cow.

The woman had lost her husband a month earlier and was unable to keep up with the demands of the property. A bargain was struck. The students and staff agreed to handle the chores in exchange for room and board and no questions.

"Have the wards been set?"

Jno, her head of security and longtime confidant said, "Yes, Mistress. They have been set, enhanced, and backups were positioned. There is a lot more ground to cover here."

Jerricka nodded as she continued to inspect their surroundings. "Yes, but the wards take less energy and are easier to maintain than the mass invisibility spell used to hide the village. Check them three or four times daily and adjust them as needed."

"The ground is much more open," Jno said, his concern coming through.

She faced the tall older man and offered a reassuring smile. "True, but we'll be able to see anyone coming and be ready to react accordingly."

"We are also close to others of this world. We risk exposure by staying here."

Though they were surrounded by woods on three sides, this new retreat was closer to the local population than the previous village. Jerricka was still undecided whether that was a benefit or a detriment to their safety. Would Bradenbaugh send his minions to openly attack them in view of so many witnesses? A stupid question. Of course, he would. He wouldn't think twice about the risk being seen by or killing them. They meant nothing to him or his plans, but then, life meant nothing to him, unless it was his own.

"Jno, we will make the best of this place. Who knows how long we will be here but until forced to move again, we will adapt. Making friends of a select few of the local population may be beneficial. We'll discuss this all later." She pivoted and walked toward the farmhouse. Jno followed.

"Have we heard from the others?"

"Nika's and Retta's groups have checked in."

"And Biatta?"

He frowned. "Nothing, Mistress."

As expected. Biatta had her own agenda. She wished her friend success with whatever it was she sought and prayed it wouldn't be the undoing of them all.

"I want to meet with everyone in the barn. Give them time to get settled. An hour. Have food brought in. We will eat as we make plans."

"As you wish, Mistress." As he turned to go, a hand shot out and grabbed his arm. "Thank you, Jno, for everything you have done and for all that you do."

He blushed at the intimate moment and touch. She gave his arm a warm squeeze and released him. He left without a word.

So much had happened in the few short months of their self-imposed exile. Though for the most part their stay in this world had been quiet and peaceful, the events of the past few days weighed like a harbinger of challenges yet to come. How long before Bradenbaugh's minions found their trail and came hunting? With their numbers now split into three factions…well, four counting Biatta…they might be harder to locate. However, if one of their groups was discovered, her people may no longer have the strength to fend off an attack. Splitting was an enormous gamble. One she prayed she wasn't forced to regret.

She reached the wide wooden steps of the farmhouse and paused with one foot on the bottom step. Jerricka allowed her gaze to wander over the large structure. It brought back memories of her childhood. She was raised on a farm in a house much like this one, only two bedrooms fewer. She was the youngest of five children; as many as once lived here. Her childhood house had a large front porch and this one had a wraparound porch covering three sides. Her house had also been wood construction, but this one was better cared for and did not look its age, which she was sure was more than a hundred years old.

Her mood darkened. That time had been too short. Not enough memories remained. After being expelled from her family home she had been forced to live on the streets. That was where Vandalue had found her. That moment had changed her life and led to this moment. For better or for worse? That was still to be determined.

Not for the first time she reminisced about what her life might have been like had her—no, this was not a time for looking back. Now was the time for looking ahead and planning on how to keep them all alive. For whatever reasons, her past had brought her to this moment and she vowed she would not fail those entrusted to her care.

At the top of the stairs, she turned left, the sound of her heels clopping on the painted wooden planks reminding her of her mother. Each morning after breakfast, her mother gathered up the vegetables and potatoes to be used for the evening meal and took them to the porch. There she sat on a glider and peeled, cut, or shucked while staring off across the fields.

Jerricka sat on a similar glider now. Despite her desire to push the memories from her mind they persisted.

When Jerricka was old enough, she would join her mother on the porch and help. The warm memories of what felt like generations ago washed over her. How long had it been before it all fell apart and she ended up on the city streets begging or stealing food? How long between then and the first coming of her abilities when her warm and loving parents had turned her away from the family?

The comforting memories burst like a soap bubble. Anger rose from the depths where she had long ago hidden the remembrances away. Jerricka allowed the fury to percolate for a moment before letting it go like exhaling a long breath. She only wanted to remember the early years. Nothing after the change. It took a long time to get over the sudden abandonment, and a longer time to trust. She had forgiven her mother years ago. She would not be the woman she was today or wield the power she possessed, had her mother not banished her from the family home.

The outer door cracked against the frame and snapped her from her thoughts. The old woman, Elsbeth, came around the corner of the house carrying two large bowls, each filled with potatoes, carrots, and onions. She stopped when she spotted Jerricka.

"Oh! I didn't see you there, dearie. That's my working chair. Would you mind moving to the next one?"

Jerricka smiled and stood. "Of course, Elsbeth. Can I help you with anything?"

"I'm just getting things ready for dinner. There's a lot more to feed now, so thought I'd get a head start."

The old woman backed up to the glider. When her calves touched, she lowered as best she could and dropped the last few inches, causing the glider to slide back to its fullest extension. She set one bowl down and extended the second toward Jerricka. "If you are serious about helping, these carrots need peeled."

Jerricka smiled, took the bowl, and sat on an old wooden rocker next to the glider.

"I was just reminiscing about when I was a girl on our family farm. I used to sit on the porch with my mother and do the same thing." She found a metal peeler in the bowl and smiled. Elsbeth had been prepared for assistance. She picked up a carrot, and went to work.

"Where was your farm?"

"Oh, a long way from here."

An hour later, Jerricka stood in the barn facing her remaining staff and students. Spread out on hay bales were twelve students, ten girls and two boys, ranging in age from ten to seventeen. Though they had been through quite an ordeal over the past month, they displayed little concern on their young faces. The resiliency of children, she thought.

"This will be our new home. How long we will remain is unknown, but we shall treat it like home. Ms. Elsbeth is to be given the proper respect she deserves. Any who dare treat her otherwise will be the recipient of my wrath." She glared at them to reinforce her words. Several of the younger students leaned back, perhaps fearing something painful might shoot from her eyes.

"We will adhere to a strict schedule. You will rise early and perform your assigned chores. We will break for morning meal, then return to finish your chores. After a short break, you will meet with your instructors and resume your curriculums.

"After the evening meal, we will meet for an evening lecture before heading off to bed."

A low grumble escaped several of the children. Jerricka fought back the urge to shout at them. After all, they were children. But even as that thought entered her mind, her anger flared anew. "I will not tolerate any further outbursts. Your lives may depend on how well you learn to follow a schedule and learn your lessons. This is not the academy or your own world. We are in a strange place facing many unknowns, while being pursued by people who would much prefer you dead. Your survival depends on how well and how fast you can learn to protect yourselves and your friends. Look around you. Would you want to be responsible for one or more of your friends to perish because learning your lessons was too much work?"

Jerricka drew in a long breath to calm her voice. Two of the students had their had bent crying softly.

"I am sorry, but you are going to be required to grow up much faster than is normal. You will have the next few hours to yourself before the evening meal. Afterward, we will meet back here before bed. Your schedule begins tomorrow. Staff, I will speak to you once the room is cleared."

She turned and moved to the corner of the barn as a few last minute directions were given and the students vacated.

When they were finished, the staff joined around her. With twenty other students occupying a more rustic location twenty miles to the north and a third batch being fostered in local homes, the staff was limited to two instructors in the arts, Nika and Retta, and two male defenders, Chase and Martine. Jno was the head of security and went wherever Jerricka did.

"We are going to have to work hard to train the students. They will be split into three groups. Retta you will teach basic offensive spells to those who can handle the power and are mature enough mentally and physically. Do not get fancy. Simple is best. Nika, you will see to their defensive spells." She spoke over the younger woman's protests. "Even though some of them are not ready, they must have a rudimentary knowledge. Their lives may depend on it." She eyed Nika, waiting for acknowledgment. When she nodded her acceptance, Jerricka turned her attention to the men. "Chase, you are to teach them hand-to-hand skills. Teach whatever they can absorb and customize the lessons toward each student's strengths."

"Am I allowed to teach knife skills?" Chase asked.

"If any are advanced enough." To Martine she said, "Teach them how to gather food, herbs, and other ingredients safely. If separated, they need to know how to feed themselves and find spell ingredients. Each student will do two of the three classes each day. Each session will be two hours. Nika, make up the schedules, please."

She looked at each face, then added, "Jno will assist where needed, as will I. I will give the evening lectures. I need not remind you what is at stake. Teach as if their lives depend on the knowledge you impart because they do. Keep them close and keep a watchful eye on our surroundings. Danger may come from any direction and at any time. We are all that stands between those children and survival. They need to know how to protect themselves and each other and survive on their own, should we fail."

Chapter Three

Biatta found her starting point. "It was almost ninety years ago. Before..." she hesitated, "both of our times. Few people know the story and fewer know the truth."

"How do you know your version is the truth?" Jeremy asked, interrupting.

Biatta smiled. "For the moment, and until I'm sure of what I surmise, let's assume it is."

Jeremy blinked a few times then nodded.

"In our world, magic exists. If you can accept that, then what I have to say will make sense."

She waited, watching him.

"I'm still listening," he said.

"Okay. As I said, magic exists in our world. Few people have the ability to use the art and even less can do so with any skill. That's why our academy exists. So we can find and train those with talent in a way to keep them and the general populace safe.

"Throughout our history, tales have been passed down about magic, magicians, and the feats they have performed or the savagery and devastation they have caused. Over the generations, our kind have survived several cleansing attempts by non-magic users. Those usually occur after some magician unleashes an evil upon the world that destroys the fragile bond between magic wielders and non-magic folk. Each time, the general public has risen up and wiped out any of those suspected of having magic ability. Many were killed just for being different, though they never displayed any form of magic."

"This sounds like the Salem witch hunts."

"I'm not sure what that is, but if you see a correlation, then yes, like that."

Before Biatta continued, a loud knock on the front door drew their attention. For the briefest of moments, Biatta paled. Then in a burst of motion, she was out of her chair and down the hall. Jeremy watched her go, unsure if he should answer the door. The knock came again, followed by a weak voice.

"Dad?"

A sharp pain lanced at Jeremy's heart, a mix of fear and elation.

"Nick?"

He shot from his chair, sending it bouncing into the wall and hurried to the door. Without looking, he unlocked the door and pulled it open.

Behind him he heard, "No! Don't!" but the door was already open. He ignored Biatta as his eyes focused on his son. He hadn't seen the boy for several years and though the time had not been kind to Nick, he had no doubt who stood on his doorstep.

Distantly aware of running steps behind him, Jeremy flung the door open and stepped onto the porch.

"Nick." He wrapped his son in a tight embrace. "Oh, my boy, it is so good to see you." Warm tears flowed down his face. He fought back sobs and squeezed tighter. It took several moments to realize Nick was not hugging him back.

"Jeremy," Biatta said. "Quick, bring him inside." Her hand touched gently to his shoulder. "Hurry."

Jeremy stepped back and held Nick at arm's length. Nick's head lolled to the side. His eyes were barely open and unfocused. *Oh no. Is he on drugs? Has he overdosed?* Nick looked so thin and weak. Jeremy scooped up his almost thirty-year-old boy and carried him inside.

Biatta cupped Nick's head in her palms to keep it from drooping. Jeremy set him down on the sofa and knelt beside him. "Nick. Nick, can you hear me. It's your dad. Nick."

Biatta knelt next to him, her hands roaming his body. She slid to the side, nudging Jeremy out of the way. She placed one hand on Nick's forehead and the other over his heart. She mumbled something Jeremy did not understand. He became aware of a soft blue hue peeking out between her palm and Nick's head. He wanted to speak but didn't want to break her concentration. He had no idea what she was doing but found he trusted that it was not detrimental to Nick's well-being.

Biatta arched backward, her faced tilting toward the ceiling. Again she mumbled words that sounded nonsensical to Jeremy. She took a deep breath, shuddered, and slumped low to the floor.

"Daria, bring me my bag. Hurry."

Jeremy was unaware the child was behind them. Without a word, she bolted down the hall.

Throat constricted by worry, Jeremy was unable to ask questions. He watched as Biatta hiked up Nick's dingy t-shirt and probed his torso with her long slender fingers.

Daria returned. She had the bag open and rummaged around inside. When she withdrew her hand it held a small glass vial with a white label around its circumference like a prescription pill bottle. Biatta turned toward Daria, saw the vial, and read the label. A smile flickered across her face.

"Well done, child."

She turned her attention back to Nick and plucked the tiny cork from the vial. Once more she chanted, this time over the vial, then she gripped Nick's chin, pulled down his jaw and tapped one drop of a thick amber liquid into his mouth. She closed his mouth, handed the vial back to Daria without looking, then clamped both hands over his mouth.

Biatta straightened to her full kneeling height and pressed her weight down on her hands. Before Jeremy could object, Nick's eyes flew open wide, his body convulsed, and he screamed against her hands. His body bounced on the sofa like he was being dribbled by an unseen basketball player.

Panic stricken at the sight of his long-lost son in what he perceived as death's embrace, Jeremy lunged for her arm to break her hold. Biatta turned to him her face unrecognizable as the beautiful woman he just had coffee with and spoke in a deep voice that had him thinking she was possessed. "No." The voice seemed to rumble off the walls.

Jeremy balked at the tone and the horrid sight. Daria rushed to his side and gently guided his hands away. "Trust her, Jeremy. He will be all right." A full minute later, the convulsions subsided and Nick slumped back.

Biatta removed her hands and sat back on her haunches. Her shoulders rounded like she was exhausted from a great effort. She drew in three deep breaths, then placed her fingers on either side of Nick's head at the temples. Again she closed her eyes, chanted, and worked her fingers as massaging to relieve a migraine. After several minutes, strain showed on her face. Lines appeared on her forehead as the effort of whatever she was doing intensified. Then, in a rush of exhaled air, she slumped back, her fingers trailing along Nick's body, then fell off.

"What-what just happened?" Jeremy asked.

Before Biatta replied, Nick's eyes opened. They were clouded, watery, and almost colorless.

In a weak voice, he said, "White lady. You're the white lady." Then his body stiffened and a deep, rumbling demonic voice erupted from his throat. "They are coming. They are coming. They are coming." His body went slack. His head lolled to the side and his eyes closed.

"Nick!" Jeremy shouted, pushing Biatta out of the way. He shook his son. "Nick! Wake up! Nick. Can you hear me?" Desperately, Jeremy tried to get a response. When none came, he started to rise. "I have to call 911."

Biatta placed a weakened hand on his arm. He barely felt it. Daria said, "Jeremy. Wait."

Perplexed, confused, and frantic, Jeremy swung a wild unfocused gaze her way.

"Biatta is trying to tell you something." She ran to him and took his other arm and shook it. "Listen to her."

Jeremy glanced down at Biatta. Her face was pale. She appeared on the verge of passing out. She spoke but it was so soft he could not hear. Her grip tightened on his arm and she pulled him closer. "He is fine. Resting. Trust..." her eyes rolled up. "...me." She slumped to the floor.

Jeremy was too overwrought to react. Daria stepped in front of him and bent to Biatta. "Help me lower her to the floor."

"What?"

"Jeremy. Help me."

"Oh, oh! Of course."

He bent down on one knee and the two of them straightened her out. Daria snatched a throw pillow off the sofa and slid it under her head.

"Go in her room and get a blanket," Daria said.

Still confused and unsure of what was happening, Jeremy went to do as ordered without a word. He returned with the blanket from her bed and handed it to Daria. The young girl took care to place it over her teacher's body before standing.

"Daria, what is going on?"

Daria glanced from Biatta to Nick. "They are both fine. They just need some rest."

"Are you sure I shouldn't call an ambulance?"

She bent over Nick, licked her finger and put it beneath his nose. "He's breathing. He will wake when he's ready. Like Biatta said, trust her."

Jeremy didn't know what to do. He placed his hands over his face and peered through the spindles of his fingers. Daria took his arm and guided him to the kitchen table. She sat and said, "I'm starved. Got anything to eat?"

He looked at her, nodded, and in a daze went about making her breakfast. As he worked, his mind wandered back to the last time he saw his son. It was at Miranda's funeral. He thought he'd caught sight of him in the distance. He came to say goodbye to his mother but didn't want to get too close. That had pained Jeremy since he was responsible for chasing Nick away.

Afterward he searched for Nick, but Chandra had not seen him and didn't believe he was there. She had given up on her brother a long time ago. She had witnessed his slide into drug induced darkness and though she initially supported and defended him, when he stole from her, that was over. She was done with him and didn't want him anywhere near her children.

Jeremy recalled the last time they had spoken in person. They'd had a terrible fight that night. Miranda was ill and showing the first signs of the then undiagnosed cancer that eventually took her. She was in bed, in pain, and upset. Jeremy took out his worry on his son in the form of anger.

"You're a drug addict. You see how that is affecting your mother?"

"Dad, you don't understand. I don't *want* to take drugs. I *need* to take them."

"That's the definition of an addict."

"It's because of the voices. I can't shut them off. The drugs help. Otherwise, I can't sleep."

"If you are going to continue taking drugs, you can find somewhere else to sleep."

And he had. After a lot more arguing and yelling, Nick left. Initially, he stayed with Chandra. Three days later, feeling worse, Jeremy took Miranda to the hospital where she was diagnosed with breast cancer. Jeremy wanted to keep it from the kids, at least for a while, but Miranda insisted and he called Chandra. The next day, Nick was gone without a word. Not to him, which he understood, but not to his mother either.

Did he blame himself for his mother's condition? He called Miranda periodically to check on her health, but she never saw her son again. That had hurt her right to the end. Jeremy carried the guilt of that denial all these years later. It had been his fault that Nick left. But what could Jeremy do? The boy refused any offer of help. All he had tried to do was scare his son into at least trying to get off the drugs, but he never accepted. Why? Because of voices in his head. What kind of voices did he hear? Maybe Jeremy should have found out more rather than chase Nick away.

Well, he was here now. This time he would listen. He turned his face upward.

"He's back, Miranda. This time I'm going to help him. I promise. I'll make it right."

Chapter Four

Nick slept most of the day. Jeremy kept watch over him with growing impatience for him to wake. He debated calling Chandra to tell her the news and twice had his phone in hand to do so but decided against it until he spoke with Nick. He also wanted to finish his aborted discussion with Biatta but she remained in her room where they had moved her, apparently recovering from whatever it was she had done to Nick.

Was it truly magic like in the books and movies? If so, how did it exist? It all seemed too farfetched for his old, tired mind. And what was her interest in his ancestors? She still hadn't established why she was here. He wanted answers. He knew they had to be right in front of him, yet they were just out of reach.

He focused on Nick's last words before succumbing to unconsciousness. *White lady.* Did he mean Biatta, who Jeremy had come to know as the lady in white? If so, how was he even aware of her? Had she done an internet search and reached out to him? Unlikely, but how else to explain his sudden reappearance?

And what about the other part? *They are coming.* Who is coming? What did they want and more importantly, why did Nick sound so afraid when he said it? Too many questions. He had half a mind to stand up and scream for everyone to wake up. Where was Daria? Maybe she had some answers. He glanced around but she was not in sight. He couldn't remember the last time he saw her. It was sometime after moving Biatta to the bedroom. Was she hiding in her room avoiding his questions?

He checked the wall clock for the hundredth time. A little after three. Nick had been out over six hours now.

Jeremy stood, intent on rousing his son, but as he looked down at the calm sleeping face, he couldn't bring himself to do it. His color looked better, his face looked younger than it had when he arrived. He brushed loose strands of hair back from Nick's face. A feeling of calm settled into his core. He paced the room several times before stopping at the front window.

A low light-gray sky hung over the area, reminding him of impending snow even though they were a good month away. Perhaps it was an omen. Maybe that's what Nick was warning them about. *They are coming.* Maybe *they* were early snowstorms.

As if Jeremy's thought had connected with Nick's subconscious, he began chanting, "They are coming. They are coming. They are coming."

Jeremy hastened to his son's side. He was still out. His body was shut down but his mind was working overtime.

"They are coming. They are coming. They are coming." The cadence increased in speed.

Down the hall, a door swung open, hitting the inner wall of the bedroom with a loud smack. Running footsteps brought Biatta to the front room in seconds. Her face was wan, making her look much older. She pulled a green sweater around her slender frame as she stopped to gaze down at Nick.

"They are coming. They are coming. They are coming." The words came faster and louder.

"What does it mean?" Jeremy asked.

She shook her head but did not take her eyes from Nick. Was that fear in her eyes? Jeremy stepped in front of her to wake Nick, but she gripped his arm with more strength than he thought she could possess and kept him back.

"We must hear this through," she said.

"They are coming, they are coming, they are coming."

"Daria," Biatta called.

"Here," the girl replied and stood next to her mentor.

Faster the words poured forth, running together in one long word.

"Theyarecomingtheyarecomingtheyare—"

He stopped with an eerie abruptness. They released a collective breath, waiting for what was to come next. Then, in a slow clear and calm voice, Nick said, "They are here."

Biatta turned to Daria, "Quick, child. Shield. Like I taught you."

They both began reciting words that made no sense to Jeremy and waving arms, hands, and fingers in bizarre patterns.

Then the front door exploded inward, ripping from its hinges, and flew across the room where it crashed against the wall. Jeremy shouted from surprise then fear but remained calm enough to drop to the floor and cover Nick with his body. Unable to see from his position, he became aware of a thundering roar like a high-speed train had just rumbled through the living room. Shades of light and dark flashed overhead like combatants on some strange virtual reality battlefield.

He glanced up and could see the strain on Daria's and Biatta's faces as they continued their strange dance. At one point, the room was so filled with smoke that he lost visual connection with everything including his son, who he was laying across. Light flashed like lightning behind heavy clouds. Then came a rumble, a flash, and a scream, followed by the odor of cooked meat.

He had no idea what was going on only feet from him but knew it wasn't somewhere he wanted to be. He slid off the sofa to his knees pulling Nick toward him and lifted him over his shoulder. Jeremy tried to stand but lost his balance, bumping into a leg. He placed a hand down to stabilize and felt the coffee table. With a push he stood but stayed in a crouch, then walked blindly toward where he thought the hallway must be.

With an outstretched hand he found the wall and slid along it until he found the gap leading to the bedrooms. Visibility wasn't much better there. He kept his hand on the wall for guidance and kept moving past the bathroom and into his bedroom. He closed the door. Though hazy, the interior of the room was at least visible. He set Nick down on the bed as gently as possible, then searched for a weapon. He had none but made a mental note that if he survived this attack and Biatta and Daria continued to stay here, he would get one.

With the same suddenness the assault began, it ceased. The ensuing silence created even more tension than did the sounds of battle. If someone other than Biatta or Daria came through that door, he wanted something to defend with. His eyes settled on a lamp on the nightstand. He moved fast, tore the cord from the wall, and lifted the wood and glass lamp. He hefted it and faced the door, ready to strike anyone who entered. An image of Miranda flitted through his mind. It took months of searching and deliberation before she'd settled on these lamps and here he was, ready to destroy one in a violent moment.

Voices he didn't recognize traveled down the hall. He wanted to call out but if whoever the enemy was had won, he didn't want to draw their attention. Soft footfalls padded closer. He took a step toward the door and raised the lamp. His muscles vibrated with nervous energy. He held the heavy lamp in a swinging position, poised and ready. The doorknob turned, or so he thought. The haze in the room made it difficult to be sure.

Whispered voices were outside the door. If it was Biatta or Daria, wouldn't they call out? He slid another step to his left for a better swinging arc. The door swung open. A moving cloud filtered around a large dark shape. Though not clear, the form was too large to be Biatta or Daria. What had happened to them?

The dark shape let out a cry and lunged. Jeremy swung for the head with all his might. The figure ducked the swing. Jeremy spun in a circle. Panicked over the miss, he tried to adjust for another swing. The shape hit the floor with a loud thud. Jeremy whirled around, tripped over the body, and fell on top. Frantic to avoid a physical conflict, Jeremy scrambled away, got to his feet, and readied to strike again.

"Dispersio."

A breeze blew through the room. He glanced behind him to see the window was shut and the curtains still. When he looked back, the smoke was gone. Biatta stood in the doorway breathing hard. In her hand was a knife that glowed with a blue hue. Face down on the floor was a large body of what he did not know, with a bubbling wound in the center.

Too astonished to speak, Jeremy felt the lamp slip from his hands. It landed with a thud on the back of the dead man's head. On the verge of collapse, Biatta leaned against the doorjamb. Jeremy forgot all that was around him and rushed to catch her before she fell. He picked her up in both arms and set her down on his bed next to Nick. Nick hadn't moved an inch through the entire ordeal.

He reached to take the knife from her hand but it was gone. A quick search of the floor did not locate it either. As long as it wasn't still in her hand where it might cause her harm, finding it was not a priority.

Biatta looked so small and frail, like an eighty-year-old with concerns of osteoporosis. She looked almost skeletal. She fought to open her eyes.

"Daria."

"It's Jeremy. I'm here."

A thin smile turned the corners of her lips up a fraction with his misunderstanding. "Get Daria." Her voice was but a whisper, yet it rang throughout his mind.

"Daria. Of course."

Jeremy hurried to the front room. He found Daria in a defensive stance in the middle of the room, arms extended to each side with fingers pointing at the front doorway and the rear patio door. Another body lay smoldering on the dining room floor. Shattered glass from the destroyed patio door littered the floor. The room appeared to be in the middle of demolition.

Jeremy slowed upon seeing how taut Daria's features were. Her young features had matured so much in the short time he knew her. The meek, scared, somewhat unsure young lady he first saved from charging boars was gone replaced by this strong, determined, and apparently lethal, warrior.

"Daria," he said in a soft voice. The girl twitched with new tension. "Biatta wants to see you."

Daria glanced at each portal, then nodded and slowly backed away. Jeremy stood amidst the furniture carnage and scanned the room. What would Miranda think? What would Chandra say? Each thought saddened him. What was he going to do now? This new arrangement had gone too far. It had to end before something else happened.

As if in answer, sirens sounded in the distance.

Chapter Five

With Nick still unconscious and Biatta too weak to move, they had little chance of leaving before police arrived. Between Daria and Jeremy, they got Biatta on her feet and all but carried her through the shattered patio door to the shed. Jeremy unlocked the door and ushered the two of them inside. Once situated, he locked them in and hurried back to the house. His mind raced as he searched for a story to tell, but the first police car pulled to a screeching halt seconds later, driving any chance of forming an explanation from his mind.

The first officer came to the door in a crouch, gun leading the way.

"What the hell?" Jeremy said to himself upon seeing the damage. The officer spotted Jeremy and began barking commands. Jeremy followed each, trying to interject comments between orders.

Finally, Jeremy shouted, "I'm the homeowner! These men broke in."

The officer relaxed a fraction before two more policemen entered. Between the three of them one kept him under a gun at all times while they searched the house.

"Got a body in here!" one yelled from down the hall. "Another on the bed, but he's alive."

"That's my son," Jeremy said, turning to move to his defense.

"Don't you move!" the first cop shouted. "Get those hands behind your head."

Jeremy did, adding, "My son's ill. I was about to call for an ambulance when these men broke in."

A firetruck, an ambulance, and two more cruisers drove up. One of the police cars held a supervisor. He took charge and began issuing orders. He called for a detective and had Jeremy sit on one of the two intact kitchen chairs and began a dialogue.

"What's your name, sir?"

Jeremy told him, then verified he was the homeowner.

"Are you injured?"

"No. Just scared."

"What happened to your son?"

"I-I don't know. He showed up at my door looking ill. Once inside, he fainted. I put him in my room and was about to call an ambulance when the doors crashed in and these men entered."

Another man entered, saw the supervisor, and joined them. The supervisor and the detective conferred, then the supervisor left and the detective took his place.

He introduced himself. Detective Don Vasili glanced at the body in the front room. "Did you do that?"

Jeremy glanced at the body and quickly turned away. "No. I never touched them."

"Then how are they both dead?"

"I-I don't know."

Vasili stared at Jeremy for a long while and had him repeat his story. When finished, Vasili asked again if Jeremy had killed either man. When the answer stayed the same, he said, "Look, you're not in any trouble here. You have a right to defend yourself. If these men threatened harm to you or your son, your actions are justified."

"I'm telling you the truth. I never touched them. When they crashed through the doors, I ran down the hall and tried to barricade myself in the bedroom."

Vasili took that in. Before he could speak, an officer interrupted. "Sir, the EMTs want to transport the man on the bed."

Vasili thought about the request. He asked Jeremy, "What's he on?"

"Excuse me?"

"Drugs. What drugs are your son on?"

The question took Jeremy by surprise. "He's not on any drugs."

"You know once he gets to the hospital they'll do a blood test and find out, so you might as well tell me now."

"I don't know about any drugs. He didn't take anything while he was here. He arrived, then collapsed. That's all I know."

"But he has a history of drug use, right?"

The questions about Nick's drug use annoyed Jeremy and it showed in his tone. "I haven't seen my son for a long time. I have no idea what he's into."

The officer said, "They tried Narcan but he didn't respond. They fear he may not make it if they don't transport him now."

Jeremy stood. He wanted to go to his son.

Vasili said, "Sir, sit down. We're not done." To the officer, he said, "Tell them to do what needs done to keep him alive."

Jeremy didn't know what to do, but if Nick's life was in jeopardy, he was going with him. He started to move away from the table.

"Sir, sit down until we're through."

"They are transporting my son. We are through."

"I have two dead bodies that need an explanation."

"Then follow me to the hospital."

A noise at the door drew their attention. Two paramedics lifted a folding gurney and carried it down the hall. Jeremy tried to follow and a hand clamped around his wrist. "We will do this here or at the station, but either way it is going to be now."

The two men eyed each other. Though Vasili's gaze was hard and determined, Jeremy's was at critical mass. Pressure built behind his eyes. The image of Vasili faded to an undefined dark image that only vaguely resembled a man.

As the EMTs wheeled his son outside, Jeremy tore his arm free, pulling Vasili over the table. He slammed both palms down on the table on either side of the cop's head. In a voice unrecognizable as his own, he said, "Two men broke into *my* house. I took my son to the bedroom." Vasili appeared to be having trouble breathing. "It sounded as though they were destroying *my* house. As you can see, they were." Vasili clutched at his throat. His eyes were wide with fear. "When the larger man smashed open the bedroom door, I was ready to crush his skull with a lamp but instead of attacking, he fell where you see him. Another figure behind him fled. It was not one of the first two to break in. That's my story. I'm leaving." He turned to leave.

The room got brighter. It began to spin and for a moment, Jeremy feared he might pass out. He placed a hand on the kitchen counter to stabilize himself and glanced around the room. Vasili gasped, hands still clutching at his neck. Breathing was ragged but airflow returned. The other cops stared at him with shocked expressions. Two had hands on their weapons.

Jeremy straightened and walked on rubbery legs toward the garage door, snatching up the car keys as he went. He was backing down the driveway before sufficient air flow eased the pressure throughout his body. No one stopped him as he drove toward the hospital.

Across the street, hidden behind a car in the driveway, a dark-skinned man observed the target's house. The men and women in uniform were a problem. Though he didn't fear them and was quite certain he could eliminate them all, until he knew where the other two targets were, it was best not to announce his presence. He sent two minions in to find out if they were all inside. He saw the man as he passed in front of a window but had no idea where the other two were. If they were inside, they were keeping out of sight.

He expected the sudden appearance of the two beings to elicit a reaction. He thought it might chase them all outside and into his arms but he never considered the women to be powerful enough to eliminate the intruders. Clearly, at least one of them was more powerful than he was led to believe. He'd have to form a new plan that allowed him to take them one at a time.

His mission was to capture one or both of the females. The younger one was deemed the more important. Then he was to discern the connection between the women and the man. After that, the man could be forgotten or eliminated. Of the two, he much preferred elimination.

If he had learned one thing over his years, it was that no plan worked perfectly. He knew now the women were inside. The man had driven off. He wasn't important. The women, however, were inside with the uniforms. Should he go get them or wait?

One of the cars took a uniform away. Ten minutes later, the bodies of his minions were carted out and driven away. Perhaps they were all leaving. Could he allow the bodies to be examined by the inhabitants of this world? Unknown, but his gut told him why take a chance. He was sure their anatomies were sufficiently different from those in this world to create curiosity as to their presence. That might increase interest enough to keep the investigation into the attack a priority thus inhibiting his mission. No, that couldn't be allowed.

With a few words and the flick of his wrist and snapping of his fingers, the two bodies encased in zippered black bags burst into flames. The people handling the gurneys leaped back as the sudden flames consumed bodies within seconds. The foul stench of the burnt flesh caused many to run for clear and cleaner air.

Firemen rushed to douse the flames but before they could bring their hoses to bear the flames faded and extinguished on their own. What remained of the bags were opened by men in full body covering suits to find nothing but ash.

The unfortunate side effect of the erasure of evidence was the increased amount personnel and the length of time they stayed to discuss what just occurred. That frustrated him and drew his patience to their end. After much internal debate, he opted to wait, though not for long. The time stretched on as one by one, other vehicles drove away until an hour later, one car remained. It was time to move. Before he did, an older woman exited from the back door ten feet away. Astonished to find him there, she stammered, "What-what are you doing in my yard?" A horrified look fell over her face. Hands flew to her mouth. She turned to go inside. "I'm calling the police."

Annoyed at her sudden appearance and without giving it much thought, he swept an arm toward her and sent her slamming into the door. Her plump body folded beneath her and she slumped to the ground. Seeing an opportunity, he stepped over her, clutched her head in one massive hand, and dragged her into the house. He dropped her as he passed through the kitchen, snagging a banana from a bowl. He stopped at the large front window and peeled and ate the banana as he watched the house across the street. Fifteen minutes later, the last man exited the house.

As if sensing someone was watching, the bulky dark-haired man scanned the houses. Though he doubted the man could see him, he stepped back behind the heavy flowered drapes. When the man drove away, he flipped the banana peel over his shoulder and exited through the front door. With a casual gait, he strode across the street.

Without hesitation, he stepped up on the short front porch. What remained of the door had been set in place but was no longer attached to the hinges. He lifted it out of his way and stepped through.

Chapter Six

In the shed, Daria rocked nervously on the floor. Her knees were drawn up and her hands clasped around them. Biatta lay unresponsive on the floor next to her. Daria had done what she could but her knowledge of the healing arts was limited, and her experience even less. She was only a first-year student and a struggling one, at that. With only a basic healing spell in her repertoire, and that having been learned from a friend well before coming to the Academy, there was little she could do. Besides, Biatta showed no outward signs of injury. No blood. No cut. No bruise or lump. Whatever had happened to Biatta was internal and well beyond her trivial capabilities. She couldn't very well open her up to find the damage. Still, every hour, once her energy was restored, she cast her meager spell and prayed it did some good.

Her legs were cramped and her back ached. Daria needed to move. She stood slowly to avoid crying out in pain and stretched. Where was Jeremy? Why hadn't he come back for them? Were the police still in the house? Afraid to leave but too curious not to look, Daria crept toward the lone small window on the side. With only had a partial view of the shattered patio door, she saw no movement but couldn't be sure.

She watched for another minute, which felt like twenty, then decided to test the door. It was locked. That worried her. What if Jeremy didn't come back or forgot about them? He was old, after all. He might forget. Knowing the door was locked made her more determined to get out.

She backed away a step and searched her mind. Opening things was a rudimentary spell. Even at her beginning level, the spell was taught, but she hadn't been very good at it. She came up with the words and was reminded of a TV show she had watched at Jeremy's house. It was something called a cartoon. The colorful thief made a gesture with his hands and said, "Open sesame," and the entrance to a cave appeared. She was still confused as to why anyone felt the need to open a sesame.

She found the proper words and repeated them a few times to herself. Then, sure she had it right, activated the spell. Nothing happened. Had she said the words wrong? Placed the emphasis on the wrong syllables? Or did she have to be facing the lock from the proper side of door? She might be better off using her lock picks. That was something she *could* do, but she had to be able to reach the lock and her picks were inside the house.

Maybe she could get Jeremy's attention. Once more, she went to the window, this time pressing her cheek against the glass to try to see better. She found the broken glass door and someone was standing there. She strained for a better view. Her efforts were rewarded with a complete image. Her body shuddered and she leaped back. That sure wasn't Jeremy unless he'd grown long curved horns.

Jeremy sat in the emergency waiting room. He was growing more agitated and concerned by the minute. He had already been up pacing four times and was about to start his fifth circuit when a nurse called his name. He glanced around and found a tall black woman standing next to the admittance desk. Long strides carried him to her. He scanned her face as he approached for signs of good or bad news.

"I'm Jeremy Kline."

"Your son is Nickolas?"

"Yes. Is he all right?"

She offered a quick emotionless smile and turned. "Follow me." She led through double doors that opened automatically as they neared and stopped at a smaller waiting room. "Wait here, please. Doctor Burgess will be with you shortly." She was gone before Jeremy could ask a question.

With dismay, he slumped into a cushioned chair for what was sure to be another extended wait. At least the chairs here were more comfortable than those plastic ones in the other room. He was gratified that two minutes later Doctor Burgess entered carrying a clipboard and sat across from him. Burgess was of medium height and build and looked too young to be a doctor. His smile was genuine. "Mister Kline, I have finished a thorough examination of Nick and can find nothing wrong."

Did he just say nothing was wrong?

Burgess chuckled at the perplexed expression on Jeremy's face. As if reading his mind, he said, "You heard right. We found nothing wrong. He does not appear to be on any drugs, illegal or otherwise. He is not intoxicated. He does have a mild fever and is slightly dehydrated, but…" he skimmed through the chart, "I see nothing here to indicate any sort of medical condition." He looked up and met Jeremy's eyes. "That doesn't mean that one doesn't exist, but if so, it's deeper and will need more tests. For now, I'd like to keep him overnight for observation. That way, we can be sure something wasn't missed. He is still out, which is a concern, but…well, I'd rather have him here just to be on the safe side. In the morning I'd like to do a scan of his brain to eliminate any problems there."

"Okay…" Jeremy said with hesitation. "You're not holding anything back?"

Burgess smiled. "No. I promise. I told you what we know and I'll tell you everything we find out. Any other questions?" He stood.

"Can I stay with him?"

"He will be transported to a room shortly. You should be able to stay with him until visiting hours are over. It's up to the nursing staff on the floor to determine anything beyond that."

He stuck out his hand. "I'll be talking to you tomorrow."

"Thank you, Doctor."

Burgess left. Jeremy collapsed in his seat. He covered his face with his hands and said into them, "He's all right, Miranda. The doctor says he's all right and," he choked up, "he's not on drugs."

A short time later, the tall black nurse entered and said, "They're transporting your son. Would you like to follow him to his room?"

"Yes. Thank you."

She brought him to where Nick's bed was waiting at an elevator. A husky young man in blue scrubs stood with his hand on the bed rail. He nodded at Jeremy when the nurse announced who he was. Jeremy entered the elevator behind him and they rode to the sixth floor. They wheeled to room six fifteen. A pleasant nurse came in and helped get Nick situated. The transporter handed a hospital bag of Nick's clothes and belongings to Jeremy, said goodbye, and left. The nurse took some initial readings, made notes on a portable computer, and introduced herself as Jessie. She explained what was to come and walked out, saying she'd check back later.

Jeremy put the bag into the small closet and pulled up a chair. Nick slept through the entire ride and exchange but appeared to be comfortable and breathing freely. He stared at his son a long time, pulling up memories from Nick's childhood. Christmases, school events, special family moments. With each he smiled fondly and wondered where that happy little boy had gone.

What had brought Nick to his door in such a heightened and drained condition? What happened to him from the time he'd left wherever he was until he reached the house? What were those ramblings about *they were coming*? And how did he know? Were those men chasing Nick?

If not for Biatta's quick aid...oh dear God, Biatta. He left her and Daria locked in the shed. He stood abruptly, needing to leave but looking at his son. How could he? Was there someone he could call? Chandra? No. That would never work. Besides, she wasn't talking to him at the moment. Maybe the cops were still in his house. He could call the house phone, but no, that meant Biatta and Daria would be questioned. He had no choice. He had to drive home to let them out.

Though he didn't know if Nick could hear and understand, Jeremy explained, then went out to the nurses' station, found Jesse, and gave a more detailed explanation to her, omitting the part about letting two captive women out of his shed.

"If Nick wakes, please tell him I'm coming back."

He hurried down the hall and into the elevator. As he drove home, he wondered if the police were still there, if the bodies were still there, and thought about the mess he'd have to clean up if they were all gone. He made the drive faster than the legal speed limit and drove up the driveway but did not pull into the garage. The door was closed. Someone had made an effort to at least prop it up in place. He fumbled for the house key before realizing he didn't need it. Instead, he found the shed key. The door needed to be picked up and moved since it no longer hung. Glass still covered much of the floor. Before he returned to the hospital, he had a lot of cleanup and repairs to do.

Jeremy walked straight through the house and through the broken-out patio door. He was two steps out the door when something big and strong grabbed him from behind. He screamed as he was lifted off his feet. He squirmed and kicked but the grip around his torso only tightened, making it difficult to breathe.

His shouts for help grew fainter as the pressure increased. With wild flailing kicks, one of his feet connected between his assailant's legs. An explosive foul breath blew past his face, reminding him of an animal. The grip relaxed and his feet touched the ground. He whipped his arms until he broke free and started to run, but his attacker was faster. Strong hands clamped down over his shoulders, stopping him with a sudden whiplash-like jolt. The hands spun him around. Before the lights went out, Jeremy caught a glimpse of a large two-legged beast with a huge forehead and large red eyes. But what sent him into hysterics were the two large curved sheep horns on each side of the head.

The head descended in a snap. The contact from the headbutt drove consciousness a long way from Jeremy's body.

Chapter Seven

Daria heard the commotion and bolted to her feet. She didn't need the sharp angle to see the men grappling on the patio. Jeremy was lifted off his feet by the horned man. Daria kept up a running commentary.

"Get away, Jeremy! Let him go, you horrid creature! Oh, good kick, Jeremy! Now run. No! Let him go!"

Then her jaw dropped and hands flew to her face as she witnessed the goat head strike Jeremy. Jeremy slumped like he was dead. She stifled the scream and held back at slamming on the window or the wall. Her indignation at what befell Jeremy would not serve them well if they were captured too. Besides, even if she broke out of the shed, what could she do against whatever that creature was?

As she watched, the creature slung Jeremy over his shoulder with little effort. He shot a curious glance toward the shed before spinning and marching off. *Did he have a ride?* Daria wondered. Otherwise, how did he expect to get Jeremy away from here without being seen? Someone was sure to call the police.

She whirled and looked at Biatta. Somehow, Daria had to wake her. She would know what to do and more importantly, have the skill to do it. Arms extended to her sides, Daria turned a slow circle, drawing as much energy into herself as she was able to hold. When she felt on the verge of exploding, she knelt, placed a hand on each side of Biatta's head, and called out in a deep, strong voice.

"Healoniasous, advantageous, intenacious, criticolius."

An electric current ran down her arms and created tiny arcs between her fingertips and Biatta's head. Daria could feel the power flow from deep within her. It was more power than she had ever released at one time. Her body began to shake, then bounce on the shed floor. She was losing control. Afraid of the damage she might do Biatta and herself, she struggled to hold the flow steady. As she realized her effort was not good enough, she fought to break the connection. Her vision clouded. She thought Biatta's body bounced, but a haze filled the tiny space and obstructed her view. As the power waned, her eyes rolled up, and she gasped for air. The flow weakened, having been drained of its energy source. As the connection fizzled, Daria slumped to the floor and slipped into a cold darkness.

Visions assailed her. Biatta healing. Biatta flying. Biatta as an owl morphing into a full winged, glowing angelic figure. Then her face contorted into a horrible demonic visage. Claw-like hands reached for her. The mouth opened, baring three-inch-long fangs sharpened to knife points. The hands clutched her. The horrendous face lowered toward hers. The teeth sunk in, spouting blood. Her blood. She screamed.

"Daria," a voice called from a distance. Her body was being shaken apart. "Wake up, girl. Daria."

A stinging pain cracked against a cheek. She gasped, screamed, flailed, and her eyes opened. An image sat in front of her. It had her in its claws, shaking, rending. A second smack echoed and her eyes cleared.

Biatta sat in front of her, hands on her shoulders. Concern ran deep behind her pale eyes.

"Daria. Are you all right?"

Daria sucked in a breath and held it as her muddled thoughts cleared and vestiges of the images she saw in her mind faded. Recognition came and Daria threw herself into Biatta's arms. She held tight and sobbed. Biatta allowed it for a few seconds, then shoved her back.

"Are you with me?"

Daria nodded.

"Speak."

"Yes. I am with you." Her hand went to the still-burning cheek. "Did you slap me?"

"I will if you don't come to your senses. What has happened in the time we were put here?"

Daria glanced around as if needing a reminder of where they were. Then it came back in a rush. The intruders. Jeremy. The shed. The horned man.

"Oh, Biatta. They took Jeremy."

"Who took Jeremy?" Her eyes narrowed to slits. What was visible appeared to pierce Daria's mind. Something happened inside her brain. *Is she reading my mind?* As if in answer, Biatta clutched the sides of Daria's head, pressed her fingertips into the thin skin, and chanted rapid words like Daria had never heard before.

It felt like a flying bug had entered her head and bounced against the interior in search of a way out. A minute later, she released the hold and Daria slumped and moaned.

"What-what did you do to me?"

"Later. We must find Jeremy before it is too late."

"How do we do that? We're locked in the shed."

Biatta gave an annoyed look. Then with a wave of her hand, the shed doors flew open. Daria's jaw dropped, then snapped shut. "Show off," she murmured.

"Quick, child. We must be away."

With a burst of energy, Biatta ran from the shed and leaped through the broken back door. Daria followed but was not as confident in her skill to avoid catching a jagged glass shard, so she slowed and stepped through the opening. By the time she was inside, Biatta was racing back from her room carrying a worn leather satchel. She ran for the pegboard mounted to the wall between the refrigerator and the garage door. In one motion, she snatched up a ring of keys, pivoted, and sped for the front door.

The door was on the floor. As she ran through the doorway, she shouted over her shoulders, "Set the door up!"

Daria slowed and looked at the door, then at the fleeing Biatta. "It's too heavy."

Biatta skidded to a stop, glanced back at her, and shot a deeper look of annoyance at Daria. She motioned with her hand and the door lifted from the floor. It swatted Daria from behind, chasing her from the house, and slammed into place.

Daria looked at the door as she held both hands across her bottom. She looked at Biatta, ready to make a comment, but her mentor was already inside the car. Daria frowned and hurried to the passenger side. As she slid onto the seat, Biatta was studying what was in front of her.

"So, the key goes in here." She inserted the key in the ignition and twisted. The engine roared. "Then he did something with this stick thing."

Daria rolled her eyes. "You don't know how to drive?"

"Never had the need."

Finally, something she knew more about than Biatta. She had watched Jeremy work the vehicle and thought she knew how to handle it. "You move it until that little red arrow points at the letter D." Biatta shifted as Daria realized her mistake. "No! Wait!" But it was too late. The car shot forward and crashed into the garage door. The metal crumpled around them. Biatta let out a squeak of surprise, then glared at Daria. "You said D."

"Yes, but when you want to go backward, you move the arrow to R."

Biatta's mouth narrowed into a straight line. "That was important to know three seconds ago."

Daria felt her own anger rising. She opened her door and got out then walked around to the driver's side.

"Get out. Let me do it."

Biatta started to object. "You will get us killed. Now, get out."

Biatta wasn't happy about being spoken to in that tone, but grudgingly vacated the seat. Once they exchanged places, Daria said, "Now fasten the seat belt, or the car will yell at you." It was obvious Biatta was fighting back a retort but she snapped the belt in place.

Daria shifted and tried to push down gently on the gas pedal. Not being used to the operation, her touch was too strong and the car shot backward. The car flew toward the street. Just in time to avoid slamming broadside into a delivery truck, she jammed her foot down on the brake. The tires caught and screeched. The truck honked and swerved, and their bodies were tossed forward then back, hitting the headrests hard. They both rubbed the backs of their heads.

"Can you do this or not?" Biatta snapped.

"Yes."

"I hope so. Jeremy's life may depend on you being able to maneuver this thing."

Daria drew in a deep breath and released it slowly. When the air was depleted, she eased her foot off the brake and the car rolled into the street. The tires hit the curb on the opposite side before she braked, but the car stopped. She shifted into drive and tapped the accelerator then the brake, jerking them back and forth. After several attempts, she got the car rolling and let it go. It was still going at the end of the street.

"Were you supposed to stop?"

"Where?"

"At that red sign that said *Stop*."

"Oh! Ah, I guess I missed it."

"Do you know where you are going?"

Daria suddenly realized she didn't. "No."

Now it was Biatta's turn to breathe in and out slowly. "Keep going in this direction."

Daria reached the end of the road and remembered to stop this time. She waited for two passing vehicles, then turned left.

"Wait," Biatta said. Daria braked and they jerked forward again. "You are going to concuss us both."

"Well, you can't give me last second directions like that."

"Why are you turning when I said go straight?"

"Am I supposed to drive through those buildings?"

Biatta looked across the street.

Daria said, "We have to follow the roads."

"How does anyone get anywhere in these things?"

Behind them, a horn blared, startling them both. Daria pressed down too hard again and the car shot forward. The car behind them continued to blare its horn. Biatta made a gesture and the sound of a crash reached Daria's ears. She glanced in the mirror and saw the car had leaped the curb and smacked into a tree.

"Did you do that?"

Biatta displayed an innocent expression. "Me? Dear child, I don't cause problems."

"No, but you sure solve them."

"Precisely."

Chapter Eight

Daria got used to handling the car, though making turns almost resulted in three head-on collisions. If not for the quick reactions of the other drivers, their journey would have been short. After more than an hour, they reached a section parallel to their goal. Woods lined one side of the road and assorted buildings lined the other.

"We need to get in there."

"I don't see any place to turn to get there," Daria said.

"Then create one."

"Create one?"

"Your ears are working. Now see if you can follow directions."

Daria was as annoyed with Biatta as the woman was with her. "You want a way in? Fine!"

She whipped the wheel hard. The car made a sharp turn in front of a line of other cars. It struck the curb, jarring them both. The front wheels bounced up and landed hard, digging into the soft ground. A loud metallic screech ensued as the undercarriage scraped across the cement curb. The car groaned but kept moving until the rear wheels hit.

On the street, a series of minor crashes occurred. Daria fed gas and the wheels climbed the curb until all four wheels had purchase. The car shot forward as a host of people shouted at them. The car zoomed ahead for twenty yards before coming to a wall of trees. Daria hit the brakes but did not allow for the softer surface. The car skidded, coming to a stop after contacting a trunk. The contact tossed them forward, straining against their seatbelts. Explosions fired rough material into their faces, slamming them backwards.

They sat stunned for several moments. Biatta shook her head and turned to see a dazed Daria rubbing her face.

"Well," Biatta said, "that was interesting."

She undid the belt and opened the door. Daria did as well but had to lean against the car to keep from falling. It was then she noticed several people running toward them from the road.

"I think we should be going now."

Biatta looked and without a word broke into a run, disappearing into the forest. Daria caught up fast. When stride for stride alongside, Biatta extended an arm behind her.

"*Fuegosius smoktatious.*"

She kicked into high gear and pulled away from Daria. Daria risked a glance behind and saw a wall of smoke develop obscuring the trees. She smiled and murmured, "I've got to get me one of those."

In a minivan fifteen miles away, Connor was having difficulty staying awake. Harper sat in a car seat next to him chatting away to a doll. His mother had just picked him up from school. They had been discussing what he'd learned that day, when he suddenly went quiet.

Chandra glanced in the mirror and saw her son's head bob. She smiled. Whatever he'd learned had drained him of energy. He was taking a nap.

They drove for another minute and his faint voice reached her.

"Mommy. Mommy. Mommy."

She glanced back to see if he was all right. His eyes were still closed but his face looked strained.

"Harper check on your brother. Is he all right?"

Harper never looked at him. "He's just being weird again."

Chandra's first reaction was to smile at her daughter's statement until she remembered other strange behaviors Connor had exhibited lately. Just before she moved her gaze to the windshield and the road, Connor's eyes flew open. The sight was unnerving. Gone were her son's soft, kind eyes. They were replaced by the older, harder gaze of a stranger.

In a voice that did not belong in her now six year old boy, she heard, "Mommy. Pe-pop's in trouble."

"What? What are you talking about?"

"Pe-pop. He is in trouble."

She hated to ask. "How do you know?"

"I can see him. Mommy, the man with the horns is carrying Pe-pop away."

"Connor it is just a dream, honey. I'm sure Pe-pop is fine. We can call him when we get home, okay?"

"Mommy. We have to help him."

If her son's words and entire persona had not already caused her severe anxiety, his next sent icy tentacles squirming through her veins.

"We have to go now or he will be gone."

This couldn't be real. There was no way Connor could know any of that. It had to be a dream. But having witnessed all the strange occurrences and behaviors of the past week, did she dare take the chance that her father was safe at home? She reached for her purse on the passenger seat and dug for the phone. She hadn't spoken to her father in several days since his involvement with that Jezebel and her sinister offspring. If anything was wrong with her father, those two were surely at the core.

With growing concern and pressure in her chest, she fumbled the phone from the purse and scrolled for the number, surprised it was so far down in the log. She pressed the last communication and was connected. Her father's phone rang and rang but went to voicemail.

"Ah, Dad? It's…ah, Chandra. I haven't heard from you in a while. Ah, when you get a chance, call me back please. Just want to make sure you're all right. Okay. That's it. Bye. Love you."

She ended the call and rubbed the edge of the phone over her teeth as she tried to decide what to do. She made the turn onto their street. The high-priced homes and the area felt suddenly unsafe. She pulled up the driveway and looked in the mirror. Both children were looking at her.

"Mom," Connor said.

She was surprised at the use of the shortened version. He sounded so old, so grown up.

"Pe-pop's in trouble."

Harper added, "Yeah, big trouble." Then she went back to her dialogue with the doll.

"Old man," Chandra said to herself, "you better not be in trouble." She backed down the driveway and headed for her father's house.

Though the distance wasn't that great, there was no direct route. On a good day without traffic it was a thirty minute drive. Today, of course, because she was worried, every obstacle possible appeared in her way. She called his phone at least ten times with no answer. Forty-five minutes later, she parked in the driveway, stunned.

The garage door had been rammed in. The car did not seem to be inside. She turned to the kids, and in her best authoritarian voice, said, "You do not leave this van." She pointed a finger at each and made eye contact to emphasize her words. "Do you understand me?"

Wide-eyed, they nodded. She got out, took the keys, and locked the doors. First, she examined the garage door, then climbed the front steps. Something looked wrong with the door. She inserted the key, twisted the knob, and pushed. The door opened then toppled to the floor with a loud crash.

"Oh. My. God." As she glanced around the destruction, Connor's words hit her hard. *Pe-pop's in trouble.* She had little time to analyze how he knew. Instead her mind raced with what could have happened and what she should do about it. She hurried through the wreckage to examine the bedrooms. The bathroom, her bedroom, and Nick's bedroom were fine, but her father's bedroom door had taken some serious abuse.

She stood in the doorway shocked, confused, and frightened. What had happened here? Where was her father? And what happened to those two women? Were they the cause of all this damage?

Her eyes stopped on a dark stain on the carpet. Oh, dear Lord. Please don't let that be blood. She backed down the hall on the verge of hysterics. When she heard the voice, she almost hit the ceiling.

"Who are you?"

She screamed, whirled, and held the keys in front of her like a knife.

A dark-haired man stood in the front room. "What do you mean, who am I? Who are you? Why are you in my father's house."

"Your father? Jeremy Kline is your father?"

She didn't respond, suddenly concerned about giving out too much information.

"You have any idea where he is?"

She ignored the question. "You need to get out of here now or I'm calling the police."

"That's a good idea." He raised a hand to an ear. "Hello, police? I need some assistance." Then he shoved a badge toward her. "Wow. How's that for response time?"

"Wait. You're a cop?"

"At your service."

"Why are you here? What do you want with my father?" About to lose control, she shouted, "What happened here?"

The man held up his hands. "Okay. All right. Take a breath. Come on over here and sit down and we'll talk."

He motioned to the kitchen table. Chandra started forward then stopped. Her backbone steeled and all emotion except resolve fled.

"I want answers. Let me see that badge again."

A mild look of surprise crossed the man's face. He stuck out the badge and Chandra snatched it from his hands.

"Hey!"

"Your name?"

"Vasili. Detective Vasili."

"All right, Detective Vasili, tell me what went on here."

He motioned with his fingers for his badge. Chandra hesitated, then handed it over. "Miss, I'll ask the questions if you don't mind."

Before he could continue, Chandra blurted, "I do mind. I want to know what happened here. Where's my father?"

"That's what I'd like to know."

"Well if you don't know, then you are of no use to me." She walked toward the door. Vasili grabbed her arm.

"You aren't—"

Chandra whirled, ripped her arm away, and swung her purse. Though not the heaviest of her bags, it had enough force to knock him back a step. Chandra stepped outside, leaped down the three steps of the porch and went to the van. Both kids were out of their seats and standing at the sliding door watching.

Vasili exited behind her. "All right. All right. You win."

Chandra froze then pivoted.

"Let's talk," he said. "Come back inside."

"I don't think so."

"I was only thinking about your kids. You want to have this discussion in front of them?"

Chandra thought about that. She looked at the nervous and concerned faces of her kids and walked to the sliding door. She didn't open it but talked through it. "Everything is all right. I'll be right back. You stay there."

Both children gave tentative nods.

She walked up the steps and stopped inside the door where the kids could see her. She crossed her arms and waited.

"You got a lot of spunk, I'll give you that, but you ever strike me again, and kids or no, I'll lock you up." If he expected Chandra to blanch or offer an apology, he was wrong. "First, one question. And this is important. Do you know where your father is?"

She hesitated.

"I only ask because as you can see, he may be in danger."

She softened a bit. "No. I haven't seen or spoken to him in several days."

"Okay. Any idea where he might go? You know, to be safe."

Chandra was out of patience. She gave him her best mom glare and turned toward the door.

"Okay. Okay. God, you're a hard nut. We're still putting the pieces together but it looks like someone broke into your father's house. An altercation ensued, and the two men—"

"Two?"

"Yes, sorry. Two men broke in. Whatever happened, both men ended up dead."

"My father wasn't…" Her throat went dry, preventing the completion of the question.

"No. The last I saw of your father, he was fine. He was racing off to the hospital."

"Hospital? But you said he was fine."

Vasili put up his hands again. "Easy. He was fine. He was going there to be with his son. Your brother, I guess."

"What? My brother? Nick was here?"

"Yeah, that was the name. You didn't know?"

She shook her head. Her defiance slipped away. "I haven't seen or spoken to my brother in years. Not since my mom's funeral. He—"

"He what?"

She shook her head.

Vasili eyed her for a moment then said, "Evidently, he was in some sort of coma. I have to be honest. I thought it was drug-induced and all this was because of some drug deal."

"And it wasn't?"

"You sound surprised. Anything I should know?"

Again, she shook her head.

"Didn't think so. Here I'm being so cooperative, but you're giving me nothing."

She sighed. "My brother had some trouble before. I'm not sure about now."

"Drug related?"

She nodded. He took that in.

"You'll be happy to know the doctor says he had no drugs in his system."

Chandra perked up. Her eyes showed her surprise.

"Yeah, surprised me too, which leads me back to the current situation. Any idea who might have had a beef with your father or your brother?"

She averted her eyes, fearing something might show in them. If she had to bet, whatever happened here had to do with those two women.

"Was anyone else involved?"

"Now, that's an interesting question. Who else was staying here?"

She looked away again, but this time he caught a look.

"Look, it's obvious someone else was living here. If not your brother, who apparently just arrived and fell ill, then someone else. In fact, two someones, since both extra bedrooms are being used. Both have women's clothes and accessories in them. Could this have anything to do with them?"

She felt her body tense.

"Oh, finally a reaction I can use. Tell me about them."

She drew in a deep breath. "I honestly don't know what to say. I don't know either of them. They appeared suddenly in my dad's life. Next thing I knew, they were living here. I suspect they are either freeloading or playing a con on my dad and trying to take him for whatever they can. It's a source of conflict between my dad and me and the reason we haven't spoken in a while."

"Can you tell me their names and give a description?"

She felt guilty, as though breaking her father's trust. Truth was, she wasn't sure if they were trouble. They seemed protective of her dad. Still, what other reason would two younger women have for moving in, other than to take advantage of her father?

"Yeah. One is named Biatta and the other, Daria. I have no idea if those are their real names. I never knew their last names. Biatta is tall and willowy, with pale skin and dark hair. Maybe in her thirties. Daria is skinny and young, maybe sixteen. She has long brown hair. If neither one of them was here, it'd be my guess they were either involved or someone was chasing them."

"Did your father ever serve in the military?"

"No…" Chandra said with obvious surprise. "Why?"

"Well, that's where I'm having a problem. Both intruders are dead. Your father says he never touched them. That brings up a lot of questions. Did they kill each other? Did these two women kill them, then flee? Or, as your father posits, did a third intruder kill the first two? He also says they didn't break in to get at him or your brother. They broke in as part of an ongoing fight between the two intruders."

"Huh!" Chandra said in complete puzzlement.

"No thoughts on any of that?"

"No. Ah, you said my brother was taken to the hospital?"

"Yeah. Your father said he was going there to be with him. I checked at the hospital. He was there for a long while, but the nurse I spoke with said he left to get some things from home and if your brother woke, she was to tell him your father would be right back. I waited a while. When he didn't return, I came here, and that's where we are now."

Chandra said, "I'm going to the hospital to see my brother. Anything else?"

"When I think of it, I'll let you know. He's in room six fifteen, your brother."

"Thanks. Are you staying? If not, I want to set the door up so no one breaks in."

Vasili laughed. "A little late, but here, let me help you."

Once the door was in place, Chandra walked to the van with Vasili close behind.

"I do have one more question."

Chandra stopped with her hand on the van door.

"Any idea how the garage door got mangled?"

She looked from him to the garage door and back again. "You mean it wasn't like that before?"

"No. That's new since I was last here."

"This whole thing is such a mess."

"Ain't that the truth."

She got in and he closed the door for her.

"I know it might not be the thing to do but if your father contacts you, have him call me, please. If this happened afterward someone may still be pursuing him."

Chandra nodded, started the car, and once the children were secured in their seats, backed down the driveway and drove away.

"Oh Dad, what have you gotten into now?"

Harper said, "Yeah, Dad. What?"

Vasili watched the attractive young woman drive away and wondered if she knew more than she said. If so, the shocked expression on her face was Oscar worthy. His phone rang in his jacket pocket. He slid it out and looked at the screen. The office. "Vasili." He listened and jogged to his car. With the information given and the call ended, he tossed the phone on the passenger seat, hit the lights and sped away.

According to witnesses, a large beastlike man was seen running toward the woods carrying a man over his shoulder. Without any other details his gut screamed this event was somehow tied to Jeremy Kline. If so, this case had become more confusing and intriguing. He hoped he could reach the beastlike man before he disappeared into the forest. He also hope if Kline was involved he was still alive when he found them.

Chapter Nine

Jeremy woke as the breath was bounced from his lungs. As consciousness returned and his vision cleared, he discovered he was being carried. Slung over a shoulder like a bag of flour. Though he wanted to move, a memory surfaced that prevented a reaction. It was a quick and painful blur of a man with a goatlike head ramming into his head. The memory caused a recurrence of the initial explosive agony inside his brain. Maybe he had a concussion.

He glanced around in his upside-down position. The constant bouncing was becoming too much to handle. They were running through trees. Lots of trees. Perhaps a forest. Was it the one where he'd first met Biatta? Had to be. It was the only one close.

Biatta. His thoughts returned to her and Daria. Were they still locked in the shed? Were they all right? Then came another flash. Oh no. Nick. Had he woken? He had to get back to his son. The man…creature…or whatever he was slowed. He bent and dropped Jeremy to the ground. Though his feet hit first, they were unable to hold him upright. He fell backward and dropped hard to his butt.

"I could feel you awaken," the goat-man said. The deep voice rumbled as if it came from the ground. "You can walk from here. Any effort to escape will result in pain." He lowered his massive reddish head with the high forehead and black eyes close to Jeremy. "Severe pain."

He glared unblinking for several seconds to emphasize his words, then straightened. "Get up. It's not much farther."

"Where are we going?"

The creature sneered. "We're going for a visit. Someone wants to meet you." He reached down with one mighty hand and yanked Jeremy to his feet.

"Move."

Jeremy had no choice but to do so. It was obvious he couldn't fight the man-thing, and he doubted he could outrun him. That left only one option. He had to outthink him. His mind raced, scanning for options and possibilities, but in the end he was left with needing luck or a miracle.

Ahead through the trees, he spotted open ground. A large, unusual gray shape was at the far end. As they reached the tree line, Jeremy could make it out better but still had no idea what it was. It appeared to be rotating in a circular pattern like a vortex depicted in a science fiction show. Perhaps thirty feet long and ten feet high, the strange, out of place oddity was their apparent goal. It had to be a creation of some other world. He thought about Biatta and the aborted conversation. She and Daria had come from another world. She also spoke of abilities like magic. Was this conjured from her world? Perhaps a passage? If so, Jeremy had to avoid passing through it at all costs. But how?

As they neared the shape, Jeremy could now see the inner portion. It was circular, like a tunnel. The interior spun in opposing directions like something you might see in a carnival funhouse. The closer they got to the shape, the more it pulsed like a beating heart excited to see them.

No. This can't happen. Jeremy panicked and bolted to the left. The man-thing must have anticipated a last minute escape attempt. He reached him before he got two steps away. As the claw-like hand touched him, Jeremy whirled and lashed out with a fist. He had never been a fighter and doubted he had the power to do much damage, but the strike took the goat-man by surprise and staggered him back a step. The hold on Jeremy was broken. He wasted no time. As fast and hard as he could, Jeremy sprinted for the trees.

His only plan was to make it to the trees. His only hope was to somehow lose the beast inside the trees. Neither had a chance. He was grabbed by the back of the neck and lifted from the ground so fast that his feet still churned as if making progress.

"So, the little man has a bit of spirit after all." The creature gave what might passed for a smile. Then his head snapped at him and everything went dark again.

Biatta pulled up. Daria started to, but Biatta grabbed her arm and slung her forward. "Keep going to the clearing. I need to move faster." Daria didn't argue. She knew what that meant. Though she wanted to witness the transformation, Jeremy's life was at stake. She ran harder.

It was good Biatta was taking a different path. The older woman was slowing her down. Without having to run slow for her to keep pace, Daria was now able to cover ground in a hurry.

A full minute later, she heard the flapping of wings and a shadow passed overhead. She glanced up in time to see the large white owl fly past. It was easily four times the size of a normal owl. Biatta would get there before she did, which might be good. Not only was she better suited to fight the creature, but with it occupied, Daria had a better chance to sneak up and either make a surprise attack or whisk Jeremy away to safety.

She began organizing her slim array of spells into defensive and offensive categories, then into order of strength and proficiency. Sadly, that didn't take long. She could pick a lock if she was looking at it from the front. She could perform minor heals. She could create a personal shield around herself but could only maintain it for a short time. Her best offensive weapon was the ability to create sparks, which, depending on the situation and available fuel, could grow into a fire and she could propel an enemy back, though not far. That was her limited arsenal. With luck, Biatta would have the situation in hand by the time she arrived.

Minutes later, she burst from the trees and into the clearing. It was the same one that held the portal she used when she'd first entered this world. The portal was ahead where it had been the last time she saw it. Biatta stood in front of the opening in human form.

Daria slowed as she neared.

"I fear we are too late," Biatta said.

"How do you know? Maybe they haven't gotten this far yet."

"The coloring of the portal. It turns a lighter gray during transfer."

Daria didn't know anything about a portal other than it took you to another world. "What do we do now?"

"We go after them."

Those words scared Daria more than the horned man did. You-you mean, me too?"

"Of course, child. I can't leave you here by yourself."

"What if I prefer that?"

"Don't be a *child*, child. Besides, I will need your assistance once we're through."

"*You* need *my* help?"

"There is much you have to offer. Now, come."

She extended her hand and wiggled her fingers. Daria hesitated and glanced at the trees. What would happen if she made a run for them? She knew she could outrun Biatta—though not her magic. She sighed, took the hand, and side by side they entered the portal.

Daria remembered the sound like being underwater. She wanted to hurry and had pressed ahead, but Biatta squeezed her hand and kept her back. It took less than five seconds to complete the transfer. On the other side, Daria's nerves fired in rapid sequences, making her jittery.

"Relax, child," Biatta said, but swept her gaze in a complete arc and did not relinquish her hand. "Okay. Let's move.

This world looked and felt different from the one they'd left. The air felt and smelled heavier, moister. It had an older appearance. They were on the fringes of the city. The buildings, though well-cared for, looked generations old. The stone had a worn and somewhat dingy appearance. The rough square edges had been rounded by time and the damper weather. Even the sky looked different somehow. It was grayer and the sun appeared dimmer.

Biatta led out of an alley to the street. No one was in sight. She studied the buildings, especially those across the street that had a line of sight to the portal. Her constant surveillance increased Daria's nervousness.

"Where do we go from here?"

"I'm not sure. I must get a message to the headmaster. Perhaps he will have an idea where to start."

"Do you know how to contact him?"

"Of course, child. I'm not a complete fool."

"Oh. You mean by magic?"

Biatta smiled down at her, conveying that whatever the contact was, Daria was not going to like it. She was right.

"No. You are the contact."

"Me? How? Why?"

"Relax. There is no danger. Well, hardly. Besides, you have me to protect you."

Biatta could read the concern on her face. "No one knows about you. You can walk the streets unnoticed and without drawing attention. I will be spotted in an instant. Regardless, we cannot stay here. Let's move." Biatta turned and walked down the street, keeping her head down. Daria followed a few steps behind.

With each block they covered, the streets became more active. That was both good and bad. Good because it gave them others to blend in with as well as to be witnesses, should anything untoward occur. Bad, however, because now there were eyes that might see and recognize them.

They advanced toward the heart of the city. It was a large, heavily populated city constructed generations ago in the center of a beautiful valley. Surrounded on three sides by mountains, the city had grown and spread to the point it was now at the foot of the mountains on two sides. They walked through the oldest and most congested section. Because of the amount of bodies they were forced close together.

Along the way, Biatta purchased a scarf from a street vendor and covered her head. Where she got the money, Daria had no idea. She walked backward with a delighted

smile on her face. "How does it look?" she asked, then
proceeded to bump into a man coming from the other
direction.

"Watch where you are going!" the man admonished
sternly.

"Oh, I am so sorry, sir. Forgive me please. Yes, I will
take better care of where I am going."

It was then Daria understood where the money came
from. Biatta, her sweet and wonderful teacher, had picked
the man's pocket. It all made sense now. She had bumped
into another man before she purchased the scarf.

She put an arm around Daria and discreetly handed her a
wad of bills. "Get something that conceals your face."
She shoved her toward another cart.

When Daria made her purchase and found Biatta, the
woman's eyes widened with horror. She snatched the
bright purple ski beanie with full ear coverings from
Daria's head and tossed it in a trash bin.

"Hey!" Daria said.

"I said conceal, not shout, *Here I am*"

"But I liked that hat."

"You are not adding to your wardrobe. It is nothing
more than a tool, not a fashion statement. Must I teach
you everything? You wasted the little money we had. I
don't need to be picking everyone's pocket up and down
the street for you."

She moved in front of a cart, scanned the contents, and
made a purchase. She tossed it to Daria. "There. That will
work."

Daria held it up and made a face. It was an old worn
sweatshirt with a hood. It had been washed so much that
the designer name across the front was unreadable.

"Stop analyzing it and put it on."

Daria did. It hung down to her calves.

"Pull the hood up and look like the slovenly teenagers you saw in the other world."

Daria settled on an image of what Biatta meant. Strangely, the idea offset the loss of the purple hat. She left the jacket unzipped and sank her hands deep into the pockets. Yes, this felt like her.

They walked for another few blocks before Biatta stopped and pulled Daria into an alley.

"What is it?" Daria asked.

"Shh." Biatta eyed an area of the street ahead then scanned behind them. She stiffened then whirled on Daria. "You stay right here."

"But—"

"No!" Biatta snapped. "Stay here. Give me your word or I swear, I'll stick you ten feet up this wall and leave you there." She gave another second's hard glare, then pivoted and left the alley

Chapter Ten

"Our people are reporting a lot of movement on the streets," Professor Wilden said. "Not sure yet what it means, but something is brewing."

Rowan Vandalue stood in front of a heavy lead window with one-inch-thick bars running up the outside and stared at nothing. His hands were clasped behind his back. He had needed a moment away from the madness, if only to refresh his overworked and stressed mind.

They had lost contact with the students now located on the other world. Had they been taken? His people found the vacated village. There had been signs of a struggle and they'd found the burned body of the harpy. Though he had no way of knowing for sure without seeing the body, he was told she had died from the use of black magic. Had she accidentally done that to herself or had it been done to her? If the latter, who?

He long suspected that Jerricka had roots in the forbidden art, but over the nearly twenty years that he had known her, she had never exhibited the signs that were normal to black arts practitioners. Was she that good as to be able to hide it from him?

Regardless, if she had been the one to use black magic, it had been in defense of the students. He would not mention it to the others until he had the chance to speak with her. He pushed that aside for more pressing and current concerns.

He turned to face the other four in attendance. "Define movement."

Wilden cleared his throat. "Those that we have identified are moving to another location. We have yet to determine their final destination but have narrowed it down to three possibilities." He went to the citywide map spread out over the conference table. With a red felt tip pen, he made three little Xs. "Here. Here. And here." He recapped the pen. "We were aware of these two locations but not of the third. I have people watching it now, but so far they have been unable to get close enough to see what is going on."

"When did all this movement begin?" asked Tarney. He was still recovering from injuries sustained during an encounter near the portal. He sat back in a deep cushioned chair with his legs propped up, his head back, and his eyes closed.

"Earlier today."

"Was there any catalyst to this sudden movement?"

"None that we witnessed," replied Wilden.

"What are you thinking, Tarney?" asked Rowan.

"If there doesn't appear to be a reason for the sudden activity, perhaps the activity alone is the reason."

Wilden released an exasperated breath. "Enough of your riddles, man. Speak clearly for once."

Tarney opened his eyes to gaze at Wilden. "Meaning that perhaps the only reason for moving is to see who is watching."

"You think it's a trap?" Rowan asked.

Tarney placed the tip of his finger on his nose and closed his eyes.

Rowan turned to a younger man standing near the door.

"Get word on the street to be alert. Have a few of our better surveillance people follow our watchers to see if they spot any tails."

"If they do, sir?"

"Evasive actions. Reorganize and take down as many of the enemy as possible without drawing attention."

"Yes sir." He left the room, closing the dark, heavy wooden door behind him.

Wilden said, "Do we have the manpower for such a wide spread effort?"

"No," Tarney said, "but it still needs to be done. If this is indeed an attempt to draw us out, there is a reason for it; one we need to know, and fast."

A knock at the door stopped them from further discourse. Tarney sat up. Wilden moved to the left of the door along the wall. They both nodded at Rowan.

"Come," Rowan said. The door opened slowly and a head poked inside.

"Sorry to disturb you, sir, but we got word that a young lady is looking for you and wishes a meeting."

"A young woman?"

"Yes sir."

"Did she give a name?"

"Daria, sir."

The name brought Rowan to attention. "Daria?"

Tarney said, "Is that the small young girl we sent to the other side with a message for Jerricka?"

"Yes." To the head at the door, "She isn't here, is she?"

"No, sir. We're running surveillance on her."

"Is she alone?"

"Unknown, sir, but on the surface, yes."

"Any sign of the enemy on her trail or watching her?"

"Not currently, sir. She did have a message, though."

"Out with it, man," Tarney said, his patience at an end.

"She said to say Bradenbaugh has a member of the lost tribe."

Tarney exploded from his seat, then howled in pain. Wilden hurried from the wall to Rowan's side. "What does this mean?"

"It means," Tarney said, hobbling on one leg, "we now know the reason for all the sudden movement."

"It means," said Rowan, "we have a rescue mission to plan." To the head at the door, he said, "Continue surveillance. When you are sure it is safe, take her and bring her here. Go."

The door closed.

They were silent for a moment, each lost in thought, then Rowan said, "Professor, find Kanter for me, please. Tell him why."

"Right away." He turned and left the room.

"My God, Rowan. Can it be true?"

"If so, we have to send everything we have to take him from Bradenbaugh."

"And if we can't?"

"We cannot allow them to have such a powerful ally."

Tarney nodded his understanding and approval.

Daria stood on a side street near a corner and leaned against a brick wall. "It will make you look like a hooker," Biatta had said.

"What?"

"Relax. It will draw less attention than you hanging around on a corner. Keep your head down but your eyes active. Beware of anyone who approaches you." Biatta had been all action and nerves when she had returned. All she would say about her side venture was it had been informative and they were not alone. She took out her last coin, covered it with both hands and cast a spell on it. Then, she handed it to Daria. "Keep this close but out of sight. If someone comes near you, glance at the coin. If it glows blue, it's someone safe. If it glows red, run. Don't look back. I'll cover you. You will be safe. You understand?"

She nodded that she did, but her stomach was doing flips.

"You remember everything I told you to say, right?"

"Yes."

Biatta cocked her head challenging her answer."

"I promise. I've got it."

"You know who the headmaster is. You will recognize him, yeah?"

"Yes. I know who he is. He was the one who sent me to you."

"Okay. Good. A message has been delivered. If you aren't being watched, you will be soon. I have to go now. My presence places you in danger. I must play decoy and lead them away. I'll be around. Don't worry. You won't be out of my sight. Now go."

And here she was, still waiting almost an hour later.

She shifted her position, bending one leg and placing her foot flat against the brick wall. A man in a tan overcoat turned down the street. A smile crossed his face as he spied her. It wasn't a comforting smile. She stiffened. Her first instinct was to run but she tried to stay relaxed. Other than his smile that sent chills through her, the fact that he wore an overcoat on such a warm day was a warning blaring in her head. Something was wrong with this man.

She slid her hand from her jacket pocket and glanced at the coin. It did not glow red but it didn't glow blue either. The man stopped four feet in front of her and squared up. "Well, well. What tasty little morsel do we have here?"

She looked at his eyes and thought, *Weasel.* With his hands in his pockets, he pulled his arms to the sides. The upper portion of his coat parted. In practiced slow motion, he revealed his bare chest.

"Oh, please, no," Daria muttered and reassessed him as a perverted weasel.

"Oh, you like what you see, don't you?" He stepped closer. "Want to see more?"

"No."

"Of course you do. No need to be shy. I'm not."

The coat separated down to the waist. He wore no shirt. Daria feared he wore nothing at all under the coat. He stepped closer and the coat separated more. She did not want to look but her eyelids were slitted open just enough to see. In her pocket she wiggled her fingers and began to draw energy.

The man was loving her flustered reaction. He stepped to within one foot of her and opened the coat all the way. She pulled her hand from her pocket and shoved it toward his manhood as she finished the last word of the spell. Sparks shot from her fingers. The smell of burnt hair wafted upward. The man's eyes went wide and he screamed. He danced away down the street, patting his body with the flaps of his coat.

She breathed easier but looked at her hand. Had she actually touched him? She didn't think so but made a note to scrub it the first chance she got. She glanced down the street. The perverted weasel had gone around the corner. She smiled with satisfaction, then glanced the other direction. A tall black woman stood there eyeing her. Uh-oh, she thought. The woman advanced toward her. The smile on her face was more genuine.

"Nicely done," she said. "I might have been a bit more forceful, but you did well."

Daria didn't know what to do. "Ah, thanks."

"You should come with me now before someone less easy to dissuade arrives."

"Why would I do that?" She peeked at her hand. The coin glowed blue.

"I'm going to take you to a mutual friend."

"Is that so?" Daria glanced at the coin again. It was still blue. She was safe. Just before shoving it back in her pocket, she caught a glint of red. She looked again. The coin throbbed a reddish color. She looked at the woman. Seeing her expression, the woman went on the defensive.

"What? What did you see?" She whirled, ready to fight.

Before she got the chance, a thin bolt of light shot from a man on the corner. It hit the woman in the chest and burst out her back. She crumbled to the ground. Shock froze her joints. Daria was slow to react. She turned to flee in the direction of the weasel and ran into his arms.

"It's payback time, little girl." If possible, his smile was even more disgusting.

Without hesitation, she drove a knee up into his crotch. He yelped and doubled over. She took off running. Behind her, two men gave chase. She didn't need to see the coin to know they were not friendly. Daria turned the corner and put on speed. She had no doubt of outrunning her pursuers. They would not catch her.

One thought raced through her mind. Where was Biatta? She promised to have her back. Did something happen to her?

She glanced back. She was well ahead. The lead man was already struggling. The second man, however, had stopped and was making hand gestures.

No. He was going to use magic. Out in public. Did he not care if the normals saw him?

Something hit her legs. A broom handle. She went flying. The impact with the ground brought immediate and severe pain to her palms, knees, and arms as she rolled across the paved ground. She rolled to a stop, dazed by the sudden and painful change of events. The two men ran toward her. The perverted weasel was twenty yards behind.

She got to her feet but was only able to hobble. Her one leg hurt bad. Her jeans were torn and blood oozed through the gap. The men closed on her. She couldn't outrun them. The only thing left was to fight. She turned to face them. From nowhere a man and a woman appeared in front of her. They faced the charging men, said a few words with combined choreographed hand gestures, and a quick, blinding flash detonated in front of them. It was as if a hundred flash photographs had been taken at once.

Daria was forced to blink her eyes several times before her vision cleared. The two men pursuing her were gone. In their places were two dark marks engraved into the pavement. The weasel, seeing what happened to his partners, turned and fled. Her two rescuers faced each other and smiled. Then they did rock, paper, scissors. The woman smiled, then spoke one word. A fine line of energy sprung from her finger, trailed after the man, and caught him as he reached the corner. His body stiffened, danced a few seconds, and then in a poof, disappeared.

Daria was stunned at the exhibition of magical skill and power, no longer concerned about who might have seen. They turned and looked at her. She had no hope of survival if they were the enemy. Her only thought was to check the coin. To her relief, it glowed blue. She collapsed back to the ground.

Chapter Eleven

Jeremy woke with a severe headache and wondered if he had a concussion. It hurt to open his eyes but he had to know what was going on and where he was. He cracked one eye and adjusted until he reached a balance between acceptable pain and sight.

He was in a circular room with light wooden paneling. Small windows were on three curved sides with a door on fourth. Rows of shelving followed the curved walls from one side of the door to the other. The volumes they held appeared to be leatherbound and old. He had been placed on a cushioned seat with his feet propped on a matching ottoman. Several other chairs were spread out around the space, making Jeremy believe he was in a reading room.

The door opened and a pleasant young man entered carrying a polished wooden tray. He smiled.

"Ah, you are awake. Marvelous. I shall inform the master." He walked to a small round table a few feet from Jeremy and set the tray down. "I was instructed to bring you some tea and sandwiches. I also noted the rather large lump on your forehead and brought some pain pills. How is your head?"

Jeremy cleared his throat and croaked, "Hurts."

He walked closer to examine the knot. "Yes, well, I don't doubt it. Rondovian can be a bit brutish in his behavior. Most like he gave you a mild concussion. Well, a bit of rest and some refreshment will go a long way in easing your discomfort. I'm going to leave the bottle of pain pills. Take only what's necessary. I don't need you ill. The master is not very forgiving."

He smiled, turned, and walked toward the door. "You have some time before the master will be able to see you. He is quite busy with other things. Take the time to recover."

"Where am I?"

The man stopped and looked over a shoulder. "You are safe. That is all that matters. Relax. Be cooperative with the master and all will be well. I'll be back in a bit to clear your tray."

With that, the man left. Jeremy heard the extra click at the door, indicating it had been locked from the outside. He made an effort to sit up but dizziness struck and the room swam about him. He was in a dilemma. Several dilemmas, actually. His head hurt too much to rise but he needed the pain pills on the table to ease the pain.

After giving it some thought, he rolled off the chair and crawled along the floor. His head throbbed and nausea built, enforcing his self-diagnosis of a concussion. He reached the table and stretched an arm up but was not close to the tray. Each attempt pained him further, having an accumulative effect. Finally, he decided to risk the extra pain and rose to his knees. The pain was blinding but he persevered, grabbing the pill bottle and the small ceramic tea pot.

He slumped to the floor, gasping and unable to open his eyes. He lay on his back, breathing fast and shallow as he fumbled to open the bottle by feel. It was not like the childproof caps he was used to. This one twisted off with ease. He slid a finger inside and worked two pills into his palm. It was then he realized he did not have a cup for the tea. He opened an eye a slit and looked at the table. It was so far away. He had no desire to reignite the slowly receding headache, so he put the pills in his mouth and tipped the teapot spout toward his lips.

He wrapped his lips around the spout and poured. The tea was scalding. He cried out and the hot liquid dribbled down his chin. The heat was enough to melt the pills, leaving an acrid taste in his mouth. Not wanting to waste the pills or try again, he steeled against the upcoming pain, and swallowed. The tea burned down his throat all the way to his stomach but the pills were down. He prayed they worked fast.

Jeremy didn't remember much after that. The next thing he heard was a voice saying, "Oh, bother. What has happened here?"

He was dragged from the table but not lifted. A pillow was placed under his head and a blanket over his body. A cold hand pressed to his forehead.

"Dear me, the master will be most upset."

Daria was ushered through the streets and into an old building in the middle of a block of similar buildings. They went up the stairs and into an old fashioned elevator complete with operator. The elderly uniformed man did not speak but exchanged slight nods with the two escorting Daria. He closed the metal security frame and then the door, and moved the golden handle three times, ringing a series of bells.

Though the lit numbers on the panel showed they were traveling up, the sensation was of going down. She looked with concern at her two minders but their faces did not reflect similar concerns. She withdrew the coin from her pocket. It was still glowing blue. She replaced it and looked up. The woman was watching her. Though her lips did not display it her eyes glinted with a smile.

The elevator settled and the operator opened both doors and stepped aside. The man led out. The woman gave Daria a gentle push and followed her into the hallway. The hall was dimly lit by caged fixtures strung along the wall. Each wall held five doors aligned across from its opposite number.

They stopped at the end of the hall and looked at a section of wall. The man made a hand gesture at the wall and tiny specks of bluish dust floated from his fingers and attached to the wall in a rectangular pattern. He then touched a spot on the rectangle with his pointer finger and a doorknob appeared. He turned it, pushed, and entered a short eight-foot-long by six-foot-wide space. At the end of hall he repeated the process this time with green dust.

The door opened onto a large room filled with desks, file cabinets, and other office equipment. Twenty people were inside and they all stopped as if frozen in place by a spell. Their eyes tracked Daria and their heads swiveled as they watched her progress through the room. Being the center of attention made her feel self-conscious and nervous.

They passed without comment and into another hallway, this one running left and right. They turned right. This hall was also lined with doors, but spaced out farther than the previous ones and were more ornate.

The woman rapped lightly on the third door on the left.

A voice from within said, "Come."

The man opened the door and motioned with an arm for Daria to enter. She did. The woman followed but the man closed the door and stayed out. The woman went to one of the four men in the room and whispered something. He nodded, made a comment to which she replied, then she turned and exited.

Daria recognized the man as Headmaster Vandalue. She did not know the other three. One was a professor and looked the part of a professor with his wire rim glasses, his tweed jacket, and his paunch. She did not know his name but had seen him at the academy. He taught upper level classes. He watched her with curiosity. There was a medium height, trim black man with a kind and calm face. He studied her with deep probing eyes, but she did not feel threatened by him. The last man was stretched out on a recliner. He was slovenly in appearance but had the physique of a bear. His gaze was the most intense of the group and did convey concern.

The headmaster stepped forward. "Daria, how good to see you again. I'm so glad you are here and are all right. I heard about your ordeal earlier. Rest assured, all threats have been dealt with. You are completely safe here."

Daria did not know what to say. She looked at him in silence, which made her more nervous the longer it stretched on. In a jolt, everything came rushing back to her. The words exploded from her mouth.

"Quick. Do you have roof access?"

"What?" Vandalue said.

"Don't be rude, young lady," the professor said.

"Roof access. Do you have it here?"

"Whatever are you blathering about?" the reclined man asked in a harsh and challenging tone.

"This is very important."

"Sir," the professor said. "You will refer to the headmaster as sir."

"Quiet!" she yelled. She took a long step toward the headmaster that made his eyebrows rise and the reclined man sit up in his seat. "It is extremely important we get to the roof immediately. If they find she is here, her life will be in danger."

Vandalue raised a hand to stop further protests from the men. "Who, child?"

She had come to hate the word child. Her annoyance showed.

"Biatta, *sir*." She snapped off the sir and shot a glance at the professor. "Now, can we get to the roof or not?"

The reclining man said, "Biatta? Here?"

The professor mumbled something under his breath. The black man looked amused.

Vandalue rushed toward the door. "Professor, with me. Tarney, you and Kanter keep the girl safe. They ran from the room, leaving the door wide open. The man and the woman who escorted her ran after them.

Daria bristled at the use of the girl as an identifier. "My name's Daria, not *child* or *the girl*," she muttered. That brought a snicker from the black man. He smiled.

"Daria, please come sit with me."

She felt the heat rise up her cheeks. *Had he heard her?* The words were barely audible to herself. Daria moved and sat in the chair he motioned to. Once seated, the black man leaned forward. "Would you care for some tea?"

"Yes, please."

"Allow me to pour." He did not pour, however. The large silver pot rose in the air on its own, tipped, and poured in one fluid motion without spilling a drop. The cup and saucer slid across the table and settled in front of her. Though simple, to her it was an amazing display. She beamed.

"Thank you, ah, sir."

"You are most welcome. Now, please tell me about your journey."

Rowan rushed to the end of the hall. With a sweep of his arm, a panel slid back, revealing a staircase going up. He took the steps two at a time. From the thundering footfalls behind him he knew a large group was following. He ran the entire three flights to the main floor then through another hidden panel into the main lobby of the building.

He reached the normal stairway and continued up at high-speed, drawing much attention from those around him. He didn't have time to worry about who might see or what they might think. Getting to the roof was too important. On the fourth floor, he rounded the banister and sprinted to the end of the hall. Another sweep of an arm and the last door on the right swung open to reveal a custodian's closet. At the back of the closet bolted to the wall was a steel rung ladder that led to the roof.

He stopped near the top and cast a dispel spell to remove the wards protecting the access hatch. Then, he cast another spell to open the set of three locks. Without touching the hatch, it rose, flipped, and crashed onto the roof. He was through in a flash.

He stood on the roof, ready to either attack or defend, and slowly panned the area. Few places were available to hide. He wanted it that way. If an attack came from the roof, the enemy had nothing to use for cover. That also made it easy to see that no one was there. As the others filed out behind him, he felt a twinge of concern for Biatta. Where was she? Had something happened to her?

The group spread out, but there was no place to search. "I need four of you to stay here and keep watch. Report to me the moment anything happens. I mean *anything*." He whirled and started for the hatch.

A concerned voice called out, "Sir."

Rowan whipped around and spotted a large pure white owl sweeping across the rooftop. "Do not attack!" he shouted.

The owl blew past and shot through the hatch. Rowan ran toward the access and stared down. He didn't see anything. Without hesitation, he leaped in the air, drew his limbs in tight and dropped from sight. He floated to the floor and hurried through the door into the hall. Biatta stood there patting her hair back in place.

Chapter Twelve

Jno rushed into Jerricka's room without knocking. Though he'd been doing that a lot lately, she kept her anger in check. If he did not follow proper procedures, it was usually for a good reason, and that reason usually meant trouble.

"Mistress, the man I sent to check on Biatta has returned. The house they were in has been attacked."

Jerricka stood abruptly. "Casualites?"

"Unknown. Neither Biatta nor Daria nor the man they were staying with were there. They found a strange man and a woman outside having a heated discussion. While they were outside he crept around back. The glass door had been shattered. The interior showed signs of a struggle. He found a large blood stain in one of the back rooms, but no one was inside, alive or otherwise."

Jerricka's mind raced, searching for possible explanations. She shook them away. That line of thinking was unproductive. "Could he sense the use of magic?"

"I'm sorry, Mistress. He has no abilities."

She was upset at not knowing what had happened and frustrated she was powerless to help. What were the options? Biatta and Daria were dead. Biatta and Daria had escaped. Biatta and Daria were captured. Biatta and Daria were injured. Solutions to each. Dead. Nothing to be done other than verify.

Escaped. Where would they go? Neither knew the area outside the forest that well. However, if the man Jeremy lived, he would know where to go. She set that option aside for the moment.

Captured. Would they be prisoners here, or would they be taken back through the portal? That could be verified.

Injured. Two choices: medical assistance or self-healing. Either was possible, but the latter more likely. Biatta was a powerful and experienced healer. Unless she was incapable of doing so, in which case the man might escort her to their local medical center.

Decisions made, she looked at Jno. "Find the local newspapers and check for possible related stories. Send someone to the portal and report back the exact shade of color. Send people to the medical centers in case they were wounded." She paused. Was there anything else to be done? She sighed. Their bodies would not be immediately buried. "Send someone to find where bodies are held. That's it. Wait. Send word to the others to be on the lookout for them and on the defense in case they've been compromised. Go now."

"Headmistress, you realize there are only three of us, right?"

Jerricka stared at him, openmouthed. She had forgotten. Flustered by the lack of resources, she said, "Do the best you can, Jno."

Jno gave a slight bow and exited, leaving Jerricka to her thoughts. It was hard to get ahead when Bradenbaugh kept the pressure on. He was taking them out one at a time, dwindling their numbers and their overall strength. They had to go on the offensive before it was too late. But how did you attack when you didn't know where the enemy was or have nothing but students to attack with? Still, something had to be done, and that started with knowledge. She rose and left the room.

At this hour, no one was in the house. They were all outside finishing up the chores. She exited the house and strode toward the barn. The girls were doing various tasks within. She studied each and rated them on their abilities and levels, and God forgive her, their expendability.

She eliminated those without a basic knowledge of the city. It was too easy to get lost and end up in trouble if you didn't know where to go. She then rated physical abilities like running, climbing, and fighting, then guile. Whoever she sent had to be quick-witted and able to see and avoid situations as well as work her way out of them.

She settled on two. One was an upper-class young lady, the other in her first year. As hard as she tried to be cold and distant and to make the choice without emotional baggage, the thought that she might be sending either one of them to premature and possible violent and painful death was too much to bear. Her head slumped in defeat.

Jerricka turned from the barn, but a sudden resolve steeled her. Before she allowed thought, guilt, and emotion to alter her mind, she whirled and called, "Gwynedd!"

The young dark-haired girl lifted her head. Her bright, childish smile locked on Jerricka, further lancing her heart. She extended a hand and waggled her fingers in a 'come here' motion. She plastered on a warm smile, something she had used and practiced over the years for just such occasions.

The girl skipped to her. "Yes, Headmistress?"

Such a sweet child. A sob caught in Jerricka's throat. She swallowed hard and placed a tender hand on the girl's cheek. "I have a special mission just for you."

Gwynedd beamed with pride.

"Are you interested?"

"Oh, yes, Headmistress."

"Good. Come with me." She glanced up and caught the eye of Gwynedd's teacher, Nika. The woman held the gaze for a moment. Then, as if she knew what Jerricka was doing, glanced away. Had that been disgust she saw in the other woman's eyes, or had she assigned that title to the look because of her own guilt?

Biatta sat and accepted the cup of tea. She wrapped her hands around the cup as if fighting off the cold and inhaled deeply. It was heaven. Good tea was one of the things she missed most about the other world.

"Biatta," Rowan said. "Please."

She sighed, knowing by the time she got to enjoy her tea it would be tepid at best. "Yes, of course." With longing, she set the cup and saucer down.

"You mentioned the lost tribe," Professor Wilden encouraged.

"Yes. Bradenbaugh sent henchmen to attack us. Though we managed to fend off the initial attack, my young ward, Daria, watched a horned man knock our host out and take him away."

"Horned man?" Wilden asked.

"That would be Rondovian," Tarney said. "He was once a minor player who wanted more. Once he had a taste of power, he was obsessed with attaining it. Since he had only limited ability, he made a deal with the dark one and was granted greater power and ability. However, he was pledged in servitude to the dark one for eternity or his death and was turned half goat to ensure he didn't try to disappear from the dark one's service."

"But-but," Wilden stammered, "that was generations ago."

"Precisely," Kanter spoke for the first time. "He was dispatched during the dark one's first attempt at world domination. His head and fingers were removed. Evidently they have been reattached, a feat someone only as powerful as the dark one could manage. Which leads one to assume he has nearly risen."

"Nearly?" asked Wilden.

Tarney answered. "Otherwise, he would be wandering about, causing havoc and have little use for Bradenbaugh."

"But he is close," Rowan added. "We are running out of time."

"Tell me, Kanter," Tarney said, "How is it you know some much about Rondovian?"

"I was his mentor."

Wilden gasped. Tarney nodded as if getting verification of something expected.

"I am also the one who brought him down."

"Obviously, the next time," Tarney said, "you may want to separate the head and fingers rather than bury them all in the same place."

"Yes, that was a mistake. One I will have to rectify. I know for a fact he didn't get all of his fingers back."

"Why is that?" asked Wilden.

Kanter reached down his shirt and withdrew a metal chain. On the end was a withered finger.

"I kept one as a memento."

"You should be able to track him with that," Biatta said, All eyes swung her way.

"Oh, tell me you haven't already thought about that," she said.

The others looked blank eyed. All except Kanter. "I have but until now I was unaware he had made his escape."

"You should be careful," Biatta warned. "It's his finger. He'll be tracking it to you as well."

They looked at Kanter for a moment. It was clear he hadn't considered that possibility.

Tarney broke the silence with his annoyance. "We are getting off track here. Tell us about this man and why you think he has a connection to the lost tribe."

"His name is Jeremy Kline," Biatta said. "I have no proof that he is connected, but I do have a strong suspicion. He is an unusual man in his early sixties. Mild mannered and completely unaware of what may lie within."

"Speculation aside," Tarney said clearly losing patience, "What has sparked this suspicion?"

Biatta flashed a mischievous smile intended to drive Tarney up the wall. "When we first discovered Jeremy, he was tailing Daria. She had run into some trouble when coming through the portal and Jeremy rescued her. Concerned for her well-being, he followed her all the way to the village. Our combined talents were melded to create an invisibility cloak that enveloped the entire village, yet he walked right through the shield and saw us all.

"When we wiped his mind of any knowledge of us, he found his way back. Then, when Angwella attacked, she brought her hunting boars. Somehow he managed to kill one, though apparently never even touched it. I doubt he even knows how or that he did it. He has no training and no knowledge of magic and little of his past. I sense something in him that he is unaware of."

She leaned forward and called up long percolating thoughts. Though the world has the ability to have magic we are not as powerful there as here. As far as I can tell, magical ability or the thought of using magic is pure fantasy to those In that world. If any have the ability it use magic they are unaware."

"Tell me," Rowan said. "Would Bradenbaugh know of this possible connection?"

"I don't see how."

Wilden said, "Why do you suppose they took him, then?"

"My guess is they saw us with him and are trying to find the connection. They may also think he knows where the students are."

"Does he?"

"No. I'm not even sure where they are."

"Biatta," Rowan said, "we have been starved for information. How are the students?"

"As far as I know, they are fine. They were the last time I saw them. Jerricka and the staff developed a plan and the students were split into several groups. Daria and I went to Jeremy's house so I could explore the possible connection. We had only just begun the discussion when we were attacked."

She reached for her tea, then stopped as something that had been bothering her for a while resurfaced. "Perhaps even more curious is Jeremy's son. He seems to be exhibiting telepathic skills. He doesn't understand them or know how to control the power. I think it is driving him mad. When he arrived, he was feverish with long contained overload, and I was forced to go deep into his mind to heal him."

Her eyes went distant as she recalled the horror and the pain within Nick's mind. "He may not last long unless someone can teach him how to handle his latent ability. He has been suffering for a long time. He was the one that gave us the warning that someone was coming." Her eyes refocused and she glanced around the room at what was perhaps the last remnants of a magical gender. If Jeremy was, in fact, a member of the lost tribe of Salemnon, it would generate new hope for the dwindling magical menfolk.

"Yes, I do believe they are related and have long hidden abilities that need to be explored, managed, and taught," she said.

"With our declining numbers, he may well be our last hope."

"Which brings up the next subject," Tarney said. "How do we find and rescue him?"

Chapter Thirteen

Chandra entered the hospital room with tentative steps as if afraid any sudden move or sound might dispel the illusion of her brother laying on the bed. She stopped and studied him. He was so thin, so drawn; almost skeletal. Her throat constricted and a hand rose to her mouth as she thought, *He looks dead already*. But no, his chest still inflated and deflated in a steady rhythm. She hadn't seen him in such a long time that she still wasn't sure it was him.

She approached as tears welled and stared down at her ill-looking yet peaceful brother. She wished he was awake so she could tell him how sorry she was for the way she'd treated him the last few times and the final time they had been together. She wanted desperately to hug him and tell him she loved him.

"Please, Nick. Be all right."

She reached down and took his hand. It was cold, which concerned her. She checked to make sure he was still breathing and the monitors displayed a heartbeat.

Nick's eyes flew open. He sucked in a harsh breath as if he had been underwater and resurfaced with only a second to spare. His body arched and his hand squeezed tight around Chandra's. Startled by the suddenness of the noise and action, Chandra screamed and backed away.

Nick pulled her close and turned his gaze on her. Eyes completely rolled back, showing almost all dingy white, a voice bubbled up from somewhere deep within his core that she did not recognize.

"They've got him. They've got Dad." The bed began to shake like an earthquake erupted beneath them. "Must save him. Must—" His body relaxed and his grip slackened. Then the room returned to normal.

Chandra shook loose from the hand and backed away. Before she got out of reach, Nick's hand snaked out and latched on as if it had sunk fangs into her wrist.

"Connor. Connor can help."

His eyes rolled down, color returned to his cheeks, and for a moment, he was just Nick, her long lost brother.

"Chandra." The voice was warm and loving. Then his color drained and he released a breath, slumping back on the bed.

Alarms blared. Lights blinked. In the hall, she could hear running footsteps. People rushed into the room, shoving her to the side. One of the last people to enter, the nurse who had pointed out Nick's room, grabbed her arms and escorted her from the room.

"You don't want to be in there right now. Let them work."

She didn't hear anything else. She stared through the open door as a multitude of hands worked on her brother's body. Then the door closed and he was gone.

She paced the hall for what felt like an eternity reciting prayer after prayer for her brother. It wasn't fair. She just got him back. He couldn't die. She had too much to say— too much to atone for—too much lost time to make up for.

Her mind reeled from the possibility of losing both her brother and her father all on the same day. Speaking of her father, where was he? She took out her phone to call. He needed to be here. Now. No answer. With growing frustration, she screamed in her mind with such length and violence it made her head throb.

She tried again. As it reached the end of its ringing string, she formulated a message.

"Nick is in cardiac arrest. He may die. If you care at all, get your ass here."

She jabbed at the end button, missed, which infuriated her further, and hit it the second time. Her anger boiled to the point of overflowing. She drew her arm back to pitch the phone against the wall. Whether she was so far over the edge to have done it, she'd never know. The phone rang as her arm was already starting forward in the throw.

She halted its progress, managing to prevent the phone from releasing under the force. Without looking at the number, she slid her finger across the screen to connect the call.

"Dad. Come quick. It's Nick."

"What about Nick?"

She froze. That was not her father's voice. She looked at the screen but did not recognize the number.

"Chandra."

Whoever it was knew her name. Afraid something dreadful might come through the phone, she cautiously placed it against her ear.

"Chandra. Are you there?"

Vague familiarity kindled.

"It's Detective Vasili. We have your father's phone in evidence. Are you there?"

The detective. At first she bristled, recalling their conversation, then she remembered her brother's warning. "Detective. My brother is being worked on at this moment. He crashed and they are trying to resuscitate him. Before he crashed, he told me they took my father."

"Who took him?"

"I don't know. He went down before he could explain. It might be those two women."

"You're still at the hospital?"

"Yes."

"Stay there. I'm coming over."

He disconnected. Chandra lowered the phone to her side and stared at the wall. She replayed the conversation in her mind. After completing the process twice, she decided to fully cooperate with Vasili. Her father's life may be in danger.

She faced Nick's room. How did he know something happened to Dad? Did he see who took him? But he also said something else just before he crashed. *Connor can help.* How could a six year old boy help?

She toyed with calling to speak with him. Upon learning of Nick's return, she called their usual babysitter and dropped Harper and Connor off before coming to the hospital. She was still debating when the door opened and a stream of medical personnel exited. From still inside the room, a female voice said, "Nice work everyone. You are the best."

Was that good or bad news?

The nurse from before spotted her.

"Come."

She turned and went back into the room. Chandra followed. They stopped behind a woman making a note on a chart. When she finished, the nurse said, "Doctor Warner, this is Chandra, the patient's…ah," she looked at Chandra, "…sister, is it?"

Chandra nodded

After the introductions were completed, Warner said, "He had a heart attack. Not sure of the damage or the cause yet. I've ordered tests to find out what's going on. He's too young to be having these problems. Is there a history in your family?"

"Not to my knowledge."

She nodded thoughtfully. "He's stable for the moment. Hopefully I'll know more later and be able to make a game plan. Until then, it's important to let him rest and avoid anything stressful."

Chandra asked a few questions, and then the doctor was gone.

The nurse said, "He is going to be moved to ICU, so give me a number to call and I'll let you know where he is." The nurse took down Chandra's number and left to attend to other patients.

She called the babysitter, explained the situation, and asked how the children were doing.

"Oh, they're as sweet as always. Harper's playing and humming to herself. Connor took a nap. Oh, sounds like he is awake now. I hear his little footsteps."

"Can I speak to Connor?" When he came on the line, his voice sounded weak and distant.

"Uncle Nick is sick, Mommy."

"Yes, Connor. How did you know?"

"I saw him."

A chilly draft washed over her. "How did you see him?"

"In my head, Mommy. He said Pe-pop is in trouble and I have to help find him."

The chill turned icy. She swallowed hard. "Can you find Pe-pop?"

"No, Mommy."

To her surprise, those words brought a sense of relief.

Then he said, "He's not on this world," and she slid to the floor and cried.

What was going on? Where was her father? And who was this person posing as her son?

"That brings up another problem," Kanter said. "If they don't know he is important now, they certainly will once we attempt a rescue."

"That's true," said Wilden. "But can we afford not to?"

Tarney said, "Bradenbaugh will have the means to extract information if he suspects there is something to be learned."

"It is certainly a tricky situation," Rowan said. "To make a rescue we will have to commit a good number of people. That will out many of them who have been able to stay off the radar."

"Not to mention the losses we may suffer," Wilden said. "Is this man worth all we will endure?"

"It may be a moot point," Rowan said. He pushed off the desk, sunk his hands deep in his pants pockets, and walked toward the window. "We have no idea where he is. By now, he may already be used up and buried."

"Well, fortunately, that's what you have me for," Biatta said, standing. She glanced at her tea with sadness, then walked toward the door. "Gather whatever force you deem necessary for the rescue. Give me a few minutes and I will have your location." She left the room without a glance at them but knowing she was leaving them with their jaws dropped.

Chapter Fourteen

The strange man was back tapping his cheek gently to bring him awake and alert. "I'm sorry, but it is time to rise. The master wishes the pleasure of your company."

"I don't feel well," Jeremy said, and rolled onto his side.

"No, no, no. You are not allowed to go back to sleep." He grabbed Jeremy's arms, straddled him, and pulled him to a sitting position. He placed both hands in one of his to keep Jeremy upright, then reached behind him for the pain pills. He opened the top with one hand and expertly shook two tablets into his palm. "Open your mouth."

Jeremy did, but the pills had to be pushed in. The man reached for the now cold teapot, poured a small amount in a cup, and placed it at Jeremy's lips.

"Drink."

Jeremy was unresponsive.

"Either drink or chew." His tone was no longer friendly. "It doesn't matter to me but one way or another, you are getting up and meeting with the master."

It took great effort on both their parts but Jeremy got to his feet. With the man holding him up, they left the room, walked down the hall, and started down a well-worn winding marble staircase. Twice Jeremy staggered and had to be pressed against the curved stone wall to prevent serious injury from a fall down the hard steps. Once at the bottom, the going became easier.

Jeremy found it difficult to concentrate. The steady thumping in his head was distracting. He did not feel like himself. Thoughts were muddled and when the man spoke to him, he only heard about every third word.

They reached a set of heavy ornate double doors. Jeremy was propped against one side as the man opened the other. He was ushered inside and two brutes stepped to each side and carried him to a seat at a dinner table long enough for twenty people. He was seated and immediately slumped onto the table.

A loud voice broke through the fog in his brain, but the words were unclear. He kept his head on the table because it felt better resting there while he worked to clear his hearing.

"What is the meaning of this? I told you to have him ready. I need to get information from him. Is he even capable of speech?"

"Master, my apologies, but I warned you he was concussed. Rondovian was too aggressive with him. Look at the bump on his head. You're lucky he is even alive. I doubt he will last long under interrogation."

"Has there been any movement or retaliation in regard to his abduction?"

"None, master. A girl of interest was spotted earlier in the city, but she was whisked away before we could secure her. We believe she was one of the students that crossed through the portal."

"Why would she come back?"

"Unknown. She may have been separated from the others and this was the only place she knew."

"Send teams out to find her."

"Already done."

"I want those students. With them in our possession, we will have the leverage to bring this stalemate to an end."

"Do you believe Vandalue will sacrifice himself for untrained students?"

"Oh, he will. That's one of his many weaknesses. He cares." He shot an angry look toward Jeremy.

Through slitted eyes, Jeremy could make out the blurred image of a man with a long, narrow ratlike face. Then everything went dark again.

He woke back in the room on the cushioned chair. The tea service and sandwiches were gone. It took a moment to realize his head didn't hurt as much as before and his thoughts were clearer. He decided to keep that to himself until he knew more about what was going on. The light through the windows was fading. How long had he been here? He had to get home. He had to see Nick. To call Chandra. To free Biatta and Daria. To—to what? Whatever was going on was too overwhelming for him to comprehend, especially in his current condition.

He wanted to rise but didn't want his attendant to walk in and see him. He decided to test if getting up was even possible, considering the pain still throbbing in his head. He grabbed the edge of the cushion with his fingers and pulled to a sitting position. His head hurt, but not as bad as before. The nausea was gone.

He probed the bump on his forehead. It was tender to the touch and caused a wince. It felt enormous. He listened for a moment but doubted he could hear anyone coming over the pounding in his head. Jeremy chose to take a chance on being discovered and got up. He stood for a moment until his equilibrium settled, then moved toward the nearest window. The land stretched out for a long way. Though no other buildings could be seen except for those on the immediate grounds, he did see smoke rising in the distance, perhaps from a chimney.

He thought about checking the farthest window across from him but if the man entered, he would know Jeremy was awake and alert. He settled back on the chair, leaned back, and closed his eyes.

His thoughts traced back through this current ordeal to Biatta, Daria, and Nick. He hoped they were all right and prayed he would see them again. Then, unbidden and uncontrolled, his mind shut down on its own and drifted.

Was he asleep? Was he dreaming?

A strange glow appeared in the distance. Mesmerized, he watched as it grew and moved ever closer. He flinched, drew back, and pressed his eyelids tighter as it threatened to engulf him. Nothing happened for several seconds, long enough to increase his angst to a point his body shook.

Then, a voice called to him. At first, he thought the man returned to bring him to whoever the master was, but no, the voice wasn't his. It was vaguely familiar in a distant memory sort of way. It called again, closer this time.

"Jeremy."

The sound of his name made him jump and whimper. Who was calling him? He desperately wanted to know but was too afraid to open his eyes.

"It is time, boy."

Time? Boy? Who—

In a sudden flash of recognition, his fear vanished.

"Grandfather?" he said.

"Yes, boy. My time is limited. You must listen."

Slowly, fearing some sort of trick, he slitted his eyes and peered through the narrow gap. The glow had surrounded him. In the center was a dark form still too shrouded for the details to be clear. It moved closer, but the identity remained hidden. The haze within the glowing sphere swept across the face like a moving mask.

"Grandfather?"

"Listen."

"But-but," he swallowed hard. "You're dead."

Memories assaulted him like a flash flood. An image of his grandfather, tall and lean, with a kind face but hard eyes. He could be so warm and caring and in an instant, turn angry and cruel. A vision appeared and held. Jeremy was but a boy and his grandfather had taken him for a walk in the woods.

"I have something to tell you," his grandfather said. "There are things you should know about our family. About our history and where we come from."

Before he could continue, a large black bear appeared on the path. Jeremy had never seen a bear up close before. The sight both enthralled and terrified him. His grandfather gave his hand a reassuring squeeze.

"He will not harm us as long as we are not a threat to him."

The bear growled and advanced. Jeremy began to get nervous. He looked up at his grandfather. He had cocked his head at an angle and studied the bear.

"Ah, I see. You are not a real bear, are you?"

That statement startled and confused the young Jeremy. Not real? He looked real enough to him.

"Why are you here? What is it you hope to achieve?"

The bear did not answer but did move closer. Its unwavering focus was on his grandfather.

"Perhaps the better question is who sent you, friend or foe? Good foe or bad foe?"

The bear roared and charged. Jeremy remembered wondering how his grandfather could remain so calm when his own heart threatened to burst from his chest. Shouldn't they be running?

His grandfather released his hand. Jeremy wanted to flee, but his terror of the monstrous bear had him frozen to the ground. His grandfather lifted both arms, spoke foreign words and…and what? What happened next? Why couldn't he remember?

"Fight through the block," his grandfather's voice encouraged. "You can do this. Concentrate. The block I put on you that day was never intended to last forever. Push. Remember what happened next." The voice urged him on like a sports parent at a soccer game.

The haze around the dark form cleared for just a moment, revealing his grandfather's face. He nodded at Jeremy the last bit of encouragement needed. Like a veil being lifted, the rest of the scene returned. The battle resumed. The bear raced closer, its powerful limbs digging and pushing, gaining speed and momentum.

Then something red and fiery streaked across the space between them. The sudden bolt startled Jeremy. He traced the fiery streak back to his grandfather. His mouth gaped. The fire had come from his grandfather's hands. Though he stood only a few feet away, he could feel no heat from the blaze. The twin beams struck the bear in the chest as it leaped for his grandfather. The force of the contact propelled the bear backward. Jeremy remembered the smell of singed hair, the sudden snap of bone from the whiplash created from the sudden reversal of direction, and the cry of pain released from the animal. But the cry sounded more human than animal.

The bear smashed hard into a thick tree causing more cracking sounds both from the tree and the body. The bear stayed pinned against the tree six feet off the ground by the continuous lances of fire emanating from his grandfather's hands. He held that position for another few seconds before lowering his arms. The bear slid down the tree, smoke rising from its charred fur.

But there was something else, something that remained out of view.

"You are almost there, boy. Keep pushing. You must see and believe to understand."

See? Believe? Understand? What was his grandfather talking about?

The dark form swept an arm to the side.

"See."

Whatever obscured his mind's eye came clear. The bear lay in a heap at the base of the tree. Smoke still poured forth.

"Believe," his grandfather said.

As the words faded, the bear shimmered and faded as well but didn't disappear. It morphed into a man with two reddish rimmed black holes bored through his chest.

"Understand."

But that was beyond Jeremy's ability. "No. It's a dream. It never happened," he said.

"Yes, it did. You know it did. Search your mind and your heart. You will discover the truth of the event and begin to comprehend who you are, and with that revelation, your destiny."

Chapter Fifteen

Biatta returned wearing a look of frustration.

The men looked at her with curiosity.

"I placed a tracing spell inside Jeremy's mind."

"Well, what are we waiting for?" Tarney said, hobbling to the table. "Let's go get the man."

"I dare say, let's," Wilden said. "I am most anxious to delve deep inside this man's mind to discover the truth."

"Here's the thing," Biatta said. "I can only track him when he is awake. For some reason, when he sleeps, his mind becomes protective and interferes with the signal."

"Huh," Tarney said. "Another sign he is indeed from the lost tribe."

"How so?" asked Rowan.

"If he has an inert ability, it might not show when he is awake and is less restricted when he sleeps. Its self-preservation allows whatever his talent to become active."

Kanter stood. "Enough wasted time on discussion. Let us rescue this man before he is not worth rescuing."

In a surprised voice, Tarney asked, "You're accompanying us?"

"Of course. I'm not going to allow you all the fun."

Rowan said, "Biatta, do you have a location on him?"

"General at best. He has been asleep a lot."

"Not dead?" Wilden asked.

"No. There would be no signal at all. He is a good distance northwest of this location. I hope to have the exact location soon."

"I suggest we move now to be closer once the location is known," said Rowan. "Professor, see to our transportation. Tarney, gather a few reliable and skilled people. Mister Kanter and Biatta, lets discuss plans."

"Sir, I have had a report of unusual activity in the city."

Lord Drewmore sat in a lounge chair, his legs crossed, and a finger inserted between pages of the book he had been reading. He studied his aide. The man, George Carpenter, one time colonel in his majesty's army, knew his duties and knew better than disturb him without good cause. He assumed that was the purpose of this interruption. He gave a nod for the man to continue.

He stood at attention as his long heralded military service had taught him.

"An altercation occurred outside a shopping area near midtown. Reports say a man and a woman abducted a teenage girl after first eliminating her minders."

"Certainly there is more to this story to warrant this intrusion?"

"Of course, sir. Witnesses only vaguely remember the events, suggesting their perception of the situation had been altered. What they did recall to a person was the beam of light that appeared to shoot out from the woman. The target the beams were aimed at vanished in a puff."

"A *puff?*" Lord Drewmore said.

"Yes sir. The witness's words, not mine. The man and woman ushered the girl down several streets where they entered a building located at fourteen twenty-six Chelsea Lane. Our people entered shortly after but found no sign of any of the three. Subsequent inquires gave no hint of where they might have gone, which suggests everyone in the building is part of their network or there is a secret way out of the building.

"Or both," Drewmore said.

"Yes sir. The building is owned by a corporation that is owned by a conglomerate. I have people researching the lineage of ownership now." Report concluded, he stood at attention awaiting his assignment.

Drewmore set a gold bookmark into the book in place of his finger and sat digesting the report. He came to both a conclusion and a decision and set the book down on the table next to the chair. "Beams of light, eh. So what? some sort of laser weapon?"

"That'd be my guess, sir."

Drewmore took another minute to consider then said, "Carpenter, assemble a small but experienced team to raid that building. Have them search every room. Have a document created giving them authority to…ah, let's say hunt for an escaped murderer. That should offer cover and cooperation. Have them report straight to you with any findings."

"Yes sir." He performed a perfect about face pivot and started for the door. "Oh, and Carpenter. Have the assault team go to standby."

"At once, sir."

Once the door had closed behind his aide, Drewmore ran possibilities, solutions, and outcomes through his mind. Then, he picked up the telephone and called Lords Fontworth and Barnabus. They would want to be kept apprised.

Finished, he reached for his book but stopped shy of contact. He debated for a moment, playing pros and cons against each other before picking up the phone to make another call.

"Let me speak to him," he said when the call was answered. He didn't have to say anything more or identify himself. The man on the other end was one of his. A spy. His so-called affiliate came on the line.

"To what do I owe the honor of this call?" Bradenbaugh asked.

The man was a pompous ass. A pretender. However, he had his uses. Once those uses had been consumed he might have to eliminate the man just on principal. Before his end he'd want the fool to know it was because he dared presume to be Drewmore's equal.

"I have news you may be interested in."

Bradenbaugh set the phone down and leaned back in his chair to think. So, Drewmore had associates watching the city as he did. The man was a pompous ass but did have his uses. He was going to assault a building Bradenbaugh didn't even have suspicions about. His own people were slacking. Perhaps the man was onto something.

He called to his man. "Quinton."

The man entered seconds later. He stood to the side but made no comment.

Bradenbaugh said, "It appears or compatriot, his pompousness Lord Drewmore, may have discovered Vandalue's secret lair. Send two of our people to fourteen twenty-six Chelsea Lane to assist in the assault. If they do not find anything, have them wait until Drewmore's team leaves and then go back in and perform a magical search. If they find something, they are not to engage. Just report back. Understood?"

"Yes master."

"Good. See to it, then. Oh, and rouse our guest and bring him to me. I tire of these delays. I will learn of his importance. Now." As Quinton left, Bradenbaugh called after him. "And send for Madelyn and that fool Perva."

Regardless of what was discovered at the building, it was time to increase the pressure. The best way to end this conflict was to either cut off the enemy's head, meaning Vandalue and his council, or capture the students in the other world. That seemed the more attainable goal. This time, instead of sending small forces through the portal, Perva would lead an army.

Gwynedd stared with apprehension at the rotating tunnel. If anything, it looked even more intimidating than when she first crossed through. Then, she had been with the other students and her instructors. It was less threatening when going in numbers. Now, her only companion was Martine.

Ever since the headmistress had taken her into the house and explained the special mission, Gwynedd had felt fear like she had never known before. Still, lives depended on her. The lives of her friends and fellow students, of her instructors, and possibly all those left in their world and did not cross with them. However, she was just one girl, and an untrained girl, at that. But the headmistress had told her she had nothing to fear. It was a simple mission. One with important implications but was not dangerous. A strange thought entered her mind. Would the headmistress lie to her?

Before she discovered an answer, Martine called out, "It looks clear. Come on!" He motioned with his hand. Gwynedd left her hiding place and ran toward him. He was only to guide her to the portal. However, he told her he didn't feel right about leaving her so far from friends and alone so would take her on the first leg of her journey. Once in the city, they'd separate and she'd continue on her own.

"You ready?" he asked her.

Unable to speak, she nodded. He dropped to one knee in front of her. In a soft reassuring voice, he said, "Hey, you will be just fine. I will be close in case there is a problem. I wish I could take you all the way to your destination but I'm needed back at the farm." He smiled. *If she was going to be just fine why was her body shaking so much?*

He took off a ring from his left ring finger and held it in front of her. "I want you to take this. It will be too big for your fingers, so clutch your fist around it so it doesn't slip off. See this part here?" On the surface was the engraved image of a fire. "If trouble comes and you can't get away, point this portion at your target and say *Flamioso*. Can you say that?"

She nodded.

He smiled. "Say it for me."

"Flamioso." Her voice was almost too faint to hear.

"Gwynedd. I know you are afraid, but if your life depends on this ring, you have to say it with conviction. With power behind the word and in your voice. Say it again."

She swallowed, and this time yelled out, her voice rising in pitch to squeaky. "Flamioso."

"There you go. Much better." He slid the ring on her left ring finger and closed her hand around it. "Do not say that word unless you absolutely need to. Make sure the image on the top of the ring is pointing at your target. Otherwise, it either won't work or will shoot back at you."

He stood, glanced around the clearing then through the portal. "Are you ready?"

She nodded. He offered his hand and she took it. Jerricka had instructed him to see her through then return to the farm. It was obvious that Gwynedd was too frightened to go through alone. The headmistress would just have to get over it. If Gwynedd's task was that important, she would forgive him, he hoped.

They entered the portal. A loud roar filled their ears like the steady drone of rolling thunder. They vanished inside. Seconds later, they emerged into their world. They had only a few hours of daylight remaining to get where they were supposed to go.

Martine exited first and swept her behind him in a protective manner. Once sure they were alone, he stepped to the corner of a building and cast his gaze down the narrow confines of the alley. A man and woman walked past the entry by the street but no one appeared to be watching or waiting for them. He motioned Gwynedd forward.

"Stay behind me and to the side closest to the buildings."

He walked through the alley and she followed. She held the hand with the ring against her chest with her other hand wrapped around it. They reached the street, and after Martine checked, they exited and turned left.

There were not many people on the street until they moved three blocks. The streets were more crowded there and the noise from the bustling horde grew noticeably. They came to an open market where the crowds were thick. Martine took Gwynedd's hand and held her close as he scanned for a contact.

Unable to locate whoever he was looking for, he guided Gwynedd to the side.

"You see this vendor? He has a wide variety of books. Stay here and peruse the titles while I search for a contact. You understand?"

"Yes."

"Do not leave this booth."

He stood and melded with the crowd. Gwynedd turned her attention to the stacks of old hardbound books.

After a few moments, the proprietor took the book she had been reading from her hands. "This is not a library. Either find a book to purchase or move along."

"I'm still looking," Gwynedd said.

He eyed her up and down. "Do you even have any money to purchase a book with?"

"I do not, but my guardian does. He told me to pick a book out and he will purchase it when he returns. Now, if you do not mind, I'd like to continue my search."

The proprietor narrowed his gaze then said, "Do proceed, then." He backed away but kept his eyes on her as if he suspected she would slip away with books in her hands.

Gwynedd lost track of time. She picked up a lot of books and read the back covers, then set them down. The proprietor came back. "Your guardian has yet to return, I see."

Gwynedd bit her lower lip. "Yes, that is a concern. He told me to stay here and wait for him, but it has been a while."

"I will give you a few more minutes to browse, but then you will have to leave whether your guardian is here or not."

Gwynedd turned her attention from the books to the crowd. She was not tall enough to see over the milling throngs. Minutes later, Martine still had not returned. She feared the book vendor would force her to move on. She stepped to the side between the book stall and one selling various dried herbs.

Through the swarm of bodies, a hand appeared. There was something wrong with it. It wiggled around legs like a snake except it was two feet off the ground. She watched, amazed at first, but then with growing concern as it appeared to focus and advance on her. She backed away but bumped into the pole holding up the tent over the book vendor's booth. She had nowhere to go. The hand seemed to be aware of that and squirmed closer. Was the hand attached to an arm that was connected to a body? If so, where was the person it belonged to?

It stopped a foot away, crooked a finger and motioned for her to come. Was it Martine? She didn't think so. Martine had no magic. The hand snapped fingers at her, then pointed toward the ground for her to come. She shook her head. The hand became more adamant. When she continued to refuse, it shot forward and latched onto her arm. It pulled hard.

Gwynedd dug in her heels and fought, but the hand was stronger. As she was dragged, she reached back, grabbed a large hardbound book, and slapped it down on the hand. The hand released and retreated.

The proprietor saw her a few feet away from his booth holding a book and shouted at her to return it. She moved to do so when something grabbed her leg and yanked. Her feet were pulled out from underneath her and she was dragged through the swarm of legs. She kicked with her free leg but could not break the grip. She began to scream then. The crowds parted to avoid being knocked down, but for the most part ignored her.

What was wrong with them? Why didn't they help?

The proprietor ran from his booth and grabbed the book. With his grip pulling from the other direction, Gwynedd's progress was halted. She clung to the book with all her might, pulling it down to her chest. The hand squeezed harder.

The book vendor grunted and shouted, "Thief! Thief!"

This appeared to get a reaction from the crowd. Several people bent to assist him. Her fingers were bent back and the book pried from her grasp.

With no further resistance, the hand dragged her through the crowd. Desperate to get free Gwynedd remembered the ring. She lifted her hand, aimed it toward the hand, and shouted, "Flamioso!"

A gout of fire shot from the ring face, except she hadn't turned it around. The fire shot backward, striking the book vendor's booth. Instantly the front table ignited. Flames rose toward the tent and began to spread down the line of booths. People screamed and ran in all directions at once. As the panic grew several of them stepped on the hand pinning it for the moment to the ground and breaking the grip. Gwynedd scrambled to her feet and fled. She followed the crowd as it fled away from the fire.

She kept moving until she found a short street to the right. With all the speed she possessed, Gwynedd bolted down the street and emerged onto the busy main street they had come down when they first arrived. There she stopped and looked both ways in search of Martine.

Confused and frightened, she turned right following the direction she last saw her watcher going. She made it two blocks before a woman with wild dark hair abruptly appeared in her path. The sinister sneer on her face told Gwynedd all she needed to know about her objective. Gwynedd stopped, screamed, and turned to run. However, something grabbed and lifted her from the street. She was pulled through the air. Her hands found whatever held her but only by feel. It could not be seen.

She kicked and thrashed, then lunged to latch on to a passerby. None of the people around her appeared to be aware of her predicament. They acted as if they didn't see her at all. The only person who showed any inclination of her presence was the one person Gwynedd didn't want to see her.

The evil woman pulled hand over hand on the invisible thing that secured her like she was pulling something with a rope. She was reeled in like a fish. Just as the woman reached her hands to take control of Gwynedd, the woman arched back, her head looked at the sky and her eyes rolled into her skull. She fell, revealing Martine and another man. The other man held a short, polished shillelagh with a rounded head on one end.

He smiled, doffed his bowler, and said, "Pleased to meet you, miss."

Chapter Sixteen

Martine rushed forward, scooped her up, and turned to run. Whatever concealment spell the evil woman had used evaporated when she fell unconscious. People noticed her on the ground and saw Martine running away with Gwynedd and began shouting for help.

"That man kidnapped this woman's child!" another woman shouted. A buzz ripped through the crowd and several men gave chase. The man with Martine got in their way and tangled feet and legs with his. His legs looked to be everywhere at once. He fell under the pursuers but took them all down with him.

Martine kept her pressed against his chest as if trying to keep her from seeing. He rounded one corner, raced down and across the street, and went down a side street. There he stopped, set Gwynedd down, and took her hand. He pulled more than walked with her several more blocks before stopping at a sidewalk café. A waiter appeared and he ordered tea for two and some scones. He was tense. Though his head didn't move, his eyes made a constant sweep of the street.

When the pot of tea and scones arrived, he sat back. Though more relaxed, he continued his vigil to ensure their safety.

A short time later, the man with the shillelagh arrived and pulled up a chair. He had a scrape on one cheek and a streak of dried blood under one nostril. He smiled pleasantly.

"Well, that was a bit of fun now, wasn't it?"

The waiter brought another cup and the two men spoke in whispers. While Gwynedd finished her scone, Martine said, "Gwynedd, this is Mister Archibald Weatherly. He will take you to where you need to be."

"Are you leaving me?"

"Yes. I was never supposed to come this far."

"Good you did, though," Archibald said. "We might have lost her."

"Still don't understand how they found her."

"That is a mystery," Archibald said, sipping his tea. "I shall have to be extra careful. We have a long way to go, as the party in question just left the city."

"Oh?" Martine said. "Is there a reason?"

"Of course, but not one I can discuss. Do not fret. I will keep her safe."

Gwynedd slid the ring off her finger and handed it to Martine.

"No. You keep it," he said. "You may need it."

"I did need it. I said it like you told me. The fire shot out, only—"

"Only what, child?"

"She sighed. "Only I forgot to point it forward. The flame shot out backward."

"What? You are lucky to be alive."

"Yeah, but I kind of set the book vendor's booth on fire"

"My word. She is a firecracker, isn't she?" Archibald chuckled. "Don't worry, child. We shall see the man is compensated for his lost inventory."

Martine took the ring. "It only had the one charge in it."

Archibald said, "If it was made properly, it can be refilled like a prescription."

Martine nodded. "I best be off."

The two men clutched hands and exchanged unspoken words. Then, Martine was gone.

"Looks like it is just you and me against the world, Gwynedd. You up for it?"

She hesitated, unsure of how to respond.

He smiled. "Of course you are. You are a firecracker, after all."

Three blocks from where they sat, a group of black clad, armored, and armed men entered the building at fourteen twenty-six Chelsea Lane. They dispersed as they went, two men entering each office and announcing they were looking for an escaped felon. They went about their search in efficient and professional manner. The chaos they created spread throughout the building like a fire. It reached several people who passed the invasion on to others, who in turn sent it further up the chain of command until it reached Tarney.

They were in a helicopter flying along the countryside outside the city. "It appears our bunker has been discovered."

Rowan's eyes widened. "The actual bunker or the building?"

"So far, just the building. My people are not sure who the intruders are. They are dressed as a military or police assault team. They say they are searching for an escaped felon but offer no proof or paperwork to that effect. It appears they are searching more for something rather than someone."

"You think they followed Daria into the building?" Rowan asked.

Biatta glanced at Daria, who looked afraid all of a sudden. "Don't worry, child. It is not your fault." She turned to Rowan. "She was brought in by your people. It is more likely they were seen. Not many would know Daria."

Rowan nodded. Tarney didn't look convinced. "At any rate, we left just in time."

"Make sure everyone there stays calm and takes no action," Rowan said. "I'm not sure who these people are but once they've gone, have someone follow."

"They may belong to the same people who sent the snipers to the portal," Tarney said.

Rowan gave that some thought. "That makes sense. We need to establish whether they are independent or connected with Bradenbaugh."

Tarney relayed the information.

Rowan asked Biatta, "Anything yet?"

"No, not a peep. I'm beginning to wonder if he has been drugged. That's the only reason I can think why he has been asleep for so long."

Rowan started to speak. Biatta sat forward, alert to something, and held up her hand to silence him.

"There he is. Have your pilot alter course a few degrees to the left. I'm locked on to him and the signal is growing stronger."

Jeremy was shaken awake. His vision cleared slowly. The man would not allow him to fall back asleep. "No, no. No more sleep for you. The master wants to speak with you and will not be put off any longer. If you are smart, you will cooperate. The level of pain will be drastically reduced."

The words came through but comprehension was delayed. He was lifted onto his feet and guided toward the door.

"That's a good pigeon. Cooperation is key."

The door opened and he was ushered into the hall. The crisper air helped to revive him.

A voice called to him from far away. "Jeremy. Jeremy, can you hear me?"

"Yes. I can hear you."

"Wonderful," said the man. "That's the spirit."

"It's Biatta. Don't let them know you can hear me."

Brain still fuzzy, he said, "Okay."

"We are coming for you. Stall."

"Okay."

They reached the stairs and started down. The man pinned Jeremy to the stone wall to keep him from falling. His mind began to clear but he was unsure of what he had heard. Was it real or in his mind?

They reached the bottom. This time he was led down the hall from the large dining room to a smaller sitting room that was a larger version of the one he was locked in. He was pushed into a larger chair.

"Lord Bradenbaugh will be with you in a moment."

A fire burned high in the stone fireplace twenty feet to his left. He scanned the room slowly, trying to take in and make sense of what he saw. A door opened in front of him, not the one he entered through. The same man he met with over dinner entered. He was dressed in a black suit and black shirt. His slightly too long black hair trailed behind him as he walked briskly across the stone floor. His footsteps echoed off the walls. His dark eyes fixed on Jeremy, gaze intensifying with each step he drew nearer. He stopped ten feet away.

"You and I need to have a long overdue conversation. Answer my questions and our discussion will remain friendly. Don't, and pain will come for you. So you understand…" He lifted his hand said something, and tiny pinpricks of pain ran up and down his body. He screamed. His body contorted. His muscles twisted into hard knots. It lasted for mere seconds but left his body in excruciating agony for much longer.

As his muscles relaxed and his rapid breathing slowed, his mind cleared. He glared at the man. In his mind, a concerned voice said, "Jeremy. Are you there? Are you all right?"

"Yes," he growled through clenched teeth.

Bradenbaugh eyed him with curiosity. "Yes? Yes what?"

"Yes, I'm still here."

He gave a derisive laugh. "Good to know. And now you understand what will befall you should you displease me. Now, shall we begin?"

"Jeremy, we are setting down now. We are minutes away. Stay strong."

"I will."

Again, Bradenbaugh eyed him. His eyes narrowed as if understanding was working its way through his head. He was about to speak when the door he entered through opened and a man rushed in.

"Lord, forgive the intrusion, but we have a situation. The wards to the east have been triggered."

As the man explained in a voice too low to be heard by Jeremy, Bradenbaugh swung his hard eyes on him. Jeremy thought, this can't be good.

Finished with his report, the man stepped back to await orders. An evil hatred brought about the image of a fiery demon skull on Bradenbaugh's shoulders.

"What have you done?" he asked Jeremy. He whipped a hand out and the fire erupted over Jeremy's body, devouring him like a dried branch.

Jeremy writhed and slid to the floor. He didn't feel the impact through the all-consuming pain. Bradenbaugh strode toward him and used his foot to roll him on his back. Jeremy kicked in spastic response to the agony. Bradenbaugh released him and squatted.

"Who are you? What importance do you have that someone would risk a rescue?"

Unable to speak the pain came again. This time, the pain lingered longer. Bradenbaugh stood.

"Quinton!" Bradenbaugh shouted. The name reverberated around the stone walls.

Quinton rushed in.

"We have visitors," said Bradenbaugh. "Bring him downstairs. I am not finished with him."

Chapter Seventeen

The helicopter set down outside a line of trees. They disembarked and hurried through the trees. On the far side was a massive stone mansion. The assault team immediately began casting detection spells.

"They have a shield in place," Professor Wilden said.

"Everyone, concentrate on the same area," Rowan said. "We need to get through fast. They may already know we are here."

The group stood side by side and aimed hands in front of them. Daria stood back and watched with awe. She had never witnessed such power before. Though she had nothing to contribute, she could feel the pull of drawn and expended energy. Everyone was engaged in the assault except for her and the old black man. She had never seen him before today but heard the others call him Kanter. He was watching her in a peculiar way that made her nervous.

She met his eyes and held them to show she was not happy about his attention. His lips curled into a bemused smile. He nodded at her, then shifted his gaze toward the assaulting group. She saw his lips move. His eyes closed. His body appeared to grow larger and hover a few feet off the ground. His arms lifted to his side. Long white tentacles stretched from the ground to his hands and crackled with raw power. The air around him sparked with current ready to expel.

In slow motion, his hands curled into fists, then his arms rotated forward. His hands and eyes opened at the same time. His fingers caught fire and ripped through the air. A backdraft of intense heat washed toward her, curling around her like she was a stone in a water stream disrupting the flow.

In a blinding flash, it all disappeared and the shield disintegrated. The concussive blast knocked her to her butt. She rolled forward. A few of the others were also rising, but the core group was already on the grounds. As Daria stood, she caught sight of a massive four-legged creature bounding toward the side of the mansion. A huge white owl flew overhead followed closely by the largest black bird she had ever seen.

She looked around and realized she was the only one still on the edge of the trees. She moved forward as a three-foot-wide electric bolt came from the mansion. It struck one of the armed men and disintegrated him in a flash. The sight gave her pause. She had as much defense as that man did against deadly magic. She crouched and moved deeper into the trees.

Daria peered out from around the largest tree she could find. Explosions of magic and ordinance rocked the ground and sent bright sparks into the air. She saw another man fall but not disappear. She wanted to do something, to somehow contribute, but she wouldn't survive going toe to toe with an experienced mage.

The battle intensified for a few moments, then faded. She no longer saw anyone outside the mansion. Periodically she caught sight of flashes inside the mansion like a bright light was turned on and off. It was then she risked leaving the safety of the trees and moved in a crouch toward the mansion.

She was halfway across the grounds when she noticed several large silhouettes exit the trees near the back of the property. They stopped and waited; some on two legs, and others on four. Red eyes glowed. A pair landed on her. She could hear the deep growl from where she stood. A quick glance in front and behind showed she was midway between the trees and the mansion. She doubted the trees would offer safety from these creatures, but staying where she was surely invited a gruesome death. She started for the mansion. At least hope, if not protection, was inside.

Every cell in her body screamed for her to run, yet she feared to do so would draw an immediate reaction from the werewolf creatures. As she neared the mansion, a group of twenty ran from behind the building toward the creatures. One man was being dragged. The sight drew her up short. It was Jeremy. Panic swelled her heart. She looked from the mansion to the group.

If she ran for help, Jeremy might be gone. What else could she do? She did not have the skill to prevent them from escaping. Without thought, she found her legs taking her toward the enemy group. Her mind reeled, doing battle within itself. Run? Fight? The battle raged. She found herself drawing in energy. The run side of her brain screamed *Why? What can you possibly do?* The fight side rebutted, *Fight.*

Though the poorer of the two choices, she still moved toward the enemy and her most likely demise. Several members of the group climbed on the backs of the beasts and were carried away. Two of the party morphed into their own beings and flew or loped from the mansion. As Jeremy was lifted to the back of one of the wolflike creatures, Daria shouted, "No!" and broke into a sprint.

A man dressed in dark clothes saw her and pointed. The creature who had spotted her initially bounded toward her on all fours. The sight brought reality back into the equation. Though she had no chance of outrunning or defeating the beast, Daria whirled and ran for her life. Knowing she had no chance of reaching the mansion, she continued drawing in energy and readying the only real offensive spell she possessed.

The beast ate up the distance between them in seconds. With its explosive breath heating her back, she spun, raised her hands, and shouted, *"Igniseo!"*

A small gout of fire shot from her fingers. They struck the beast but other than singe the fur-covered hide, it had little stopping power.

As the creature leaped for Daria, she raised her hands in a last attempt at protection, turned her head, and closed her eyes. Fire erupted in a ball in front of her. She was hit and driven backward in a rolling ball of flames. Air exploded from her lungs. Her next inhalation scorched her throat. Pain enshrouded her. Then just as fast, the fire extinguished. The creature was lifted by unseen hands its blackened body dropped twenty feet away.

As her vision faded and her brain sought refuge, she caught sight of a large black bird lighting beside her. The beat of its wings brought a waft of air, which in turn brought relief to her overwhelming agony. She saw nothing else.

Jeremy was hustled down a hall then downstairs to a basement. He was forced to run down the lower hall to another set of downward stairs. The voice returned.

"Jeremy. We are here. Where are you?" He was now sure it was Biatta somehow in his head.

"In the basement. Descending."

Quinton stopped propelling him for a moment. "What did you say?"

"Nothing," Jeremy replied, fear creeping into his voice.

"Were you talking to someone?" Quinton didn't give him a chance to answer. "Who are you talking to?"

He pressed forward, grabbing Jeremy by his shirt front, lifting and slamming him against the circular stone wall. "Answer me."

"Okay. Okay. I'll talk. Just give me some room to breathe."

Quinton eyed him but backed a step. As he did, Jeremy shoved forward, knocking the man back. His grip released and Jeremy ran at him, shoving him into the opposite wall. He then flung the man sideways down the stairs. He didn't look to see if any damage was done. He turned and bolted back up. Quinton followed and caught him at the top of the stairs. He tried to slam Jeremy headfirst into the wall, but he managed to get his hands splayed out to prevent contact.

He pushed back. Never much of a fighter, he still knew what to do. Whipping around, he struck Quinton's face with his fist. The contact staggered the unsuspecting man but also sent excruciating pain up Jeremy's arm. He shouted and shook his aching hand, then remembered to run. He didn't get two steps before being tackled. He went down and Quinton climbed up his back. His hair was grabbed and his head yanked back, then his face was driven into the floor. An explosion of pain spread across his face. Blood spouted, breathing became difficult, and several teeth felt loose.

Quinton repeated the move and all resistance left him. Barely able to focus, he was lifted forcefully from the floor and marched toward the stairs. His feet did not respond to every step and he tripped and was dragged down the remaining steps. At the bottom, Quinton recruited another man to aid him and their progress increased. He thought he heard Biatta's voice calling to him but was too dazed to make a connection. Cool air revived him somewhat and told him they were outside.

He was lifted onto the back of a large foul-smelling furry creature. It bent lower as Quinton climbed on behind him. With a jolt, they bounded away from the mansion. Still too dazed to have a clear idea of what he faced or where he was, he caught sight of something descending toward them. It was large and white and emanated an aura of peace and tranquility. He was lifted from the back of the beast. Something heavy clung to his legs, threatening to pull him back to the ground.

A calm voice broke through his foggy thoughts. "Jeremy. I need you to lift your free leg and kick downward. Can you do that?"

"Yes."

The hands gripping him began to move up his leg. Instinctively, he knew that was bad. He raised his leg and snapped it downward but felt nothing but air. He tried again, and again met no resistance. Taking every bit of effort and focus he could pull together, he ran his foot down along his other leg until he found a solid object. Then, he brought his foot up as high as it would go and drove it downward. This time, he connected. He heard a grunt and repeated the action twice more. After the last kick, a scream faded beneath him and the weight was gone.

Chapter Eighteen

Mad Madelyn McGrew walked along the hallway a full two minutes after the assault team had entered. The heavily armed and equipped soldiers were not in sight, having moved to other floors to continue their search. But Madelyn doubted if anything was there to be found. Those muscle heads had little chance of making the discovery. This was something that took more finesse…and a bit of magic, of course.

"Do a quick sweep of the rooms on this level," she said to her partner, Angry Agnes Muldoon. The woman wasn't necessarily angry; she just had one of those faces where the lips curled down, giving her a constant sneer. She did not answer as she veered off into the first room.

Madelyn proceeded down the hall, ignoring the excited voices protesting over the way armed men had just invaded their world. Their whiny voices irritated her. One such biddy with an annoying squeaky voice barely took a breath to interrupt her diatribe. As Madelyn moved past the open doorway, she flicked a hand in the woman's direction and a stapler lifted off a nearby desk and attacked her face, stapling her lips together.

Madlyn stopped at a T-section of the hall and glanced each way. In front of her was an old-fashioned elevator. She smiled and pressed the button, hearing a ringing bell somewhere above her. She waited as the car descended, settled, and the operator opened the doors.

"Good afternoon, miss," the old man greeted her. "What floor?"

She entered and looked around the ornate car as the operator closed the outer door and then the inner gate. "I'm not sure. How many floors are there?"

"Six, miss. If I may, who or what are you looking for?" he asked politely.

"I'm looking for an old friend. Rowan Vandalue. What floor is he on?" She studied him. There it was. The tell. The briefest of hesitations. He put on a perplexed thinking expression.

"I'm sorry, miss. That name does not ring a bell. Are you sure you have the right name? Or for that matter, the right building?"

She smiled. He was very good. "Why don't you take me to the level that doesn't appear on your dial?"

"Beg pardon, miss?"

"Oh, come now. We both know there are secret floors here. Take me to one of those."

A bell rang from somewhere above and a light winked on the panel, displaying floor three. "I'm sorry, miss. I have a call. Will you be riding up or would you prefer to get off here?"

"I'd prefer if you told me where to find Rowan Vandalue."

"I've already told you, miss, I do not know that name."

"Yeah. Yeah. I heard you. If you can't tell me, then I have no use for you." She stepped forward as if to leave, muttered a word, and drove her hand toward the man's chest. He was quicker than she gave him credit and caught her hand in both of his and bent it to the side. A smile widened across her face.

"I knew it," she said. While he struggled with her hand, she slammed her other palm against his chest and said, *"Currencio explosiona."*

Electric current ran through her fingers and into the man's heart. He struggled but the pain was severe. He arced backward against the panel. As strength was sapped from him, his body bounced and vibrated against the wall. In seconds it was over. He slid to the floor and Madelyn broke the connection.

The smell of charred flesh filled the little car. She studied the panel, took hold of the control handle, and swung it to the left opposite the floor numbers. Nothing happened. Above her, the bell rang repeatedly.

"Shut up!" she shouted, and sent an energy bolt through the hatch blasting up the shaft.

She moved the handle back in place and studied the various buttons on the panel. Besides the floor numbers, there were three other buttons. One for emergencies, a call button for help, and the middle one depicted a fireman's helmet. She looked at the three, pushed in the one with the fireman's helmet, then shifted the handle. The car lurched and began its descent.

With a satisfied smugness, she faced the elevator door, wondering what or who she might encounter. Numbers to the left of the normal floor numbers appeared. The number one passed. When the number two lit up, she stopped the elevator and opened the inner gate. She stepped out. She had no real reason for choosing two over one or three, only that it made sense. Level one would probably house staff and a few managers. Level three would be for storage, or perhaps a dungeon. That thought excited her. She was sure, if Vandalue was here, this was the floor to find him.

She advanced down the long hall that stretched in front of her. Six doors filled the walls, three on each side. Two doors on each side were closer together than the third. Those were the two rooms she wanted to check first. Her skin tingled with anticipation. If she was the one to kill the Dark One's nemesis, her rise to favorite status would place her above Bradenbaugh. That thought made her want to skip down the hall.

She took her third skipping step when the third door on the right opened and a man poked his head out. Disappointing, but the look of sheer surprise made it acceptable. She gave a little wave.

"Hi. I'm collecting for the Wizard's Benevolent Society." She flicked out her hand and sent two darts with six inch long points toward the man.

He slammed the door, but not before one of the darts got through. The second imbedded in the door. Inside, she heard something heavy hit the floor and smiled.

"I am sooo good."

She skipped toward the door. As she arrived, red blinking lights told her the man had survived long enough to set off a warning. She paused for a moment and cast a spell. A loud alarm that only those with magical abilities could hear was ringing. Damn! If Vandalue was not here, he'd be warned against arriving.

She reached the door, placed a hand on the knob, and turned it. The door didn't open. If the man had any magic at all, he would have used it when he first spotted her. Since few men had the ability to cast spells, the odds were good this man didn't either. Still, it paid to be cautious. She unlocked it magically then stepped to the side and shoved the door in. Instantly, a streak of highly concentrated energy shot through and carved a deep hole in the opposite wall.

Her eyebrows rose, impressed with the power and at her own intelligence for recognizing the possible trap. She poked a head in and withdrew it. Nothing happened. She repeated the move, holding longer in the door. The man was slumped over a desk on the far side of the room. An unadorned wooden wand was held loosely in one hand. He did not move as she entered.

She withdrew a knife, muttered a few words over it, and tossed it in the air. It hovered a moment, then with a flick of her wrist, the knife took off like it had been caught by a strong wind. It flew toward the man and buried deep into the top of his skull.

Madelyn mused, "If he wasn't dead before, he sure is now."

She scanned the room, finding an object that intrigued her. She picked it up and examined it closely. It was a triangular shape about three inches high with polished silver sides and no seams. She could find no way to open it. Each of the four sides bore a symbol she didn't recognize. She had never seen anything like the object before and had no idea of its purpose. Madelyn swept a hand over it and it gave off a faint glow. It was definitely magical, though whether it contained magic or was made of some magical material, she could not say. As she held the triangle it began to hum. It was faint, but she could feel the tingling sensation in her palm. She slid the item into a pocket. Since Vandalue wasn't there, it was time to go. Madelyn wanted to search the room more closely to see what other rare items she might discover, but with an alarm sure to bring those who wished her dead, leaving wasn't the most fun thing to do but it was the smartest and safest. Besides, she had confirmed what she came for. This was indeed a Vandalue property.

She paused at the door, thinking about a parting gift. A wide grin split her face as one came to mind. She reached deep into an inner pocket and pulled out a small dried item that resembled a raisin. She recited words over the tiny thing and blew on it. It dissolved in her hand and spread out across the room like dust mites. With a quick sniff of the air, she was satisfied.

She moved down the hall to the elevator. The operator's body was still there. She rode to the second floor above ground. From there, she unlocked a door of a vacant office with the wave of her hand, walked to a rear window, and peered out. It faced an alleyway, as she anticipated it might. Madelyn climbed out and hung by her fingers from the sill. She spoke the words of a spell and let go. For a moment she plummeted, then she slowed and settled gently to the cement below.

A quick look up showed the window was vacant. She skipped to the street and then across without looking. Vehicles slammed on brakes and honked horns. She blew kisses to each driver and continued down the street, melding with the crowds of people leaving their jobs after a hard day's work and heading home.

Archibald Weatherly led Gwynedd down a long street then left. Ten minutes later, they entered a large building in the middle of a block. As soon as they were in the hallway, the man paused and his friendly face morphed into one full of concern. With an arm he guided her behind him and slid his hand down the shillelagh, gripping it like a club. His muscles tensed and he moved with caution.

Gwynedd sensed the change but knew better than to ask questions. She stayed behind him and glanced back in case someone tried to sneak up. They reached a T-intersection in the hallway. Weatherly peered both directions, then took a quick step forward and pressed the button for the elevator. It did not come right away, causing Weatherly to mumble to himself and ring for the car again. He heard the motor engage as the car moved. A minute later, the outer door opened but the inner gate remained closed.

Archibald scanned the halls again before pulling the gate to the side and stepping across to peek inside the elevator car. Slumped to one side was Gordon, the elevator operator. Weatherly turned and pointed at Gwynedd.

"You stay there."

Terrified, Gwynedd froze where she stood. Weatherly bent to examine the fallen man. Moments later, he returned and stared down the hall. His eyes shifted to Gwynedd. He motioned to her with his fingers. As she entered the car, he guided her to the opposite side of the body, placing himself between her and the dead man. Though she had no direct line of sight to the dead man, she had been through enough with the other students to have witnessed death before. Enough so that she made no effort to view the corpse.

Weatherly closed the doors and worked buttons and a handle. The elevator started down. When it bounced to a stop, he opened the doors and ushered her down the hall.

"Stay here."

He started back to the elevator, but the doors slid closed before he reached them. He swore, then returned to Gwynedd. He stopped outside the third door on the right, staring nervously at a blackened hole in the opposite wall. He rapped on the door. No one answered. He tried again, then opened it himself. Inside, the body of a man was slumped over a desk. A foul odor wafted through the door, causing them both to gag.

Without pause, Weatherly snatched Gwynedd's arm and pulled her across the hall to another door. He held the shillelagh in front of him like it was a shield. Then, standing to the side, he pushed the door open. Whatever he was expecting did not happen. After peering inside, he pushed Gwynedd in.

"You stay here. Do not leave this room. I have to check out the rest of the facility. I will be back in a few minutes. If I don't come back in ten minutes, assume I will not be returning, and hide."

"For how long?"

"Until someone friendly comes along."

He backed from the room and closed the door, leaving her to face whatever it was alone.

Chapter Nineteen

"I just received a report!" Tarney yelled to be heard over the helicopter. "The base has been hit. We took several casualties. The lower level was breached."

Rowan was stunned by the news. "Bradenbaugh?"

Tarney shrugged, a gesture unusual for him. "There was at least one wizard, but unless he has recruited a military assault team, we may be dealing with whoever set the snipers outside the portal."

"You don't think Bradenbaugh capable of doing that?"

Tarney frowned in thought. "It is possible, even smart. I just can't see Bradenbaugh using what he considers to be inferior people. He is too vain to use normals."

"Still, it's something we need to look into. If he has, it brings us to an entirely different level in our conflict."

"He will be looking for some serious payback now that we have breached his base. At least we are on even footing in that regard. We both need to find new quarters."

Rowan said, "I am concerned that he has control of such beasts as lycanthropes and got them there so quickly."

"Not sure how close they were, but I'm sure the property had protective wards before we reached the shield. They had enough advance warning to be on the move before we breached."

"Still, he seems to have an unending array of creatures at his beck and call to wreak havoc. It leads me to believe that we need to create our own arrangement with like-minded beings."

Tarney said, "That may go to your point of him not using military normals. If he has these creatures to call on why use normals?"

"Yes, a fair point. We need to assign a team to track down whoever is sending them. With things heating up between us and Bradenbaugh, we can't afford to be blindsided by an unknown."

"I'll see to it," said Tarney, massaging his wounded leg.

"Do we know where Biatta and Kanter went?"

Wilden said, "I saw Biatta snatch our quarry from the back of one of those lycanthropes but did not see Kanter."

Rowan sat up with a start and glanced around the interior. "Has anyone seen the girl?"

"Daria?" Wilden said. "No. We lost two men during the fight but once we engaged, I did not see her. She was to stay with the helicopter."

Rowan slumped back in defeat. What had happened to that poor girl? Was she dead, or worse—in Bradenbaugh's clutches? "I hate to say it, but we may need to plan another rescue."

Silence settled over the interior of the helicopter as each man pictured how that might go.

Biatta landed a mile from the mansion as the weight of carrying Jeremy eroded her strength. She settled with as much control as her depleted reserves allowed, but he was still bounced hard off the ground. She released him and he rolled. He groaned but did not move. She morphed back into human form and dropped to one knee, exhausted from the effort.

She raised her head and called, "Jeremy! Can you hear me?"

He groaned again but did not respond. She noticed red streaks staining his shirt on his side. *Oh no.* Unable to stand, she crawled forward and rolled him on his back. She lifted the shirt revealing two long furrows gouged into his side, one deep enough to expose a rib. It took a moment to understand that her own talons had been the cause. Blood ran freely from the wound, and Biatta knew if she didn't do something fast his chance of surviving was slim.

Depleted as she was, Biatta had no hope to draw in enough energy or strength to heal him. However, she hadn't risen to her level without the experience and knowledge to plan ahead. She twisted the top of a ring on her left pinky, flipped the lid open, and deposited a pill into her palm. Holding the pill between thumb and forefinger of each hand, she snapped it in half. She placed the halves inside both wounds, covered them with her hands, and recited a string of activation words. The pills began to dissolve. Then, she closed the lid on the ring, twisted the top in the opposite direction, and pressed it into each furrow, reciting the words again.

The dissolving pills solidified, creating a bandage that prevented further bleeding. She did not possess the strength to perform a heal as yet, but at least he wouldn't bleed to death. She sat back and looked around. She had to find someplace to hide. They weren't far enough away from Bradenbaugh's mansion to feel secure. If they were discovered now, she was beyond able to defend. Hiding and recovery was their only hope.

She pushed to her feet, aware of how weak she was and how much effort it took to do such a simple task. How did she imagine moving Jeremy? She looked around again, spotting an old barn about two hundred yards away. She grabbed Jeremy's arms and began dragging. The distance was too great to consider, so she sent her mind elsewhere to a more pleasant memory and submerged deep within that joyous time.

She was a child wandering the countryside with her sister on a grand adventure. They had no idea what a grand adventure entailed, but that didn't matter. They ran, skipped, jumped, and explored. They created games, discovered imaginary friends, and all was wonderful until they heard the faint cry of a cat.

They followed the mewing and approached with caution. The sounds came from under the low branches of a pine tree. Her sister warned against getting too close; that a wounded animal was a dangerous one, but Biatta only heard the anguished cries. She crawled on her belly beneath the branches to discover the bloody body of a raven black cat. Its battered head lifted to eye her but did not have the strength to keep it up. It settled back and cried out.

"Oh, you poor thing. How can I help?" She crawled to its side and gently examined the multitude of wounds. It was apparent the cat had been on the losing end of a fight. She had no idea what to do but touched the wounds, trying to ebb the flow of blood.

A tingling sensation settled over her body and a voice entered her mind.

"You can help."

Though startled, she did not flee. To her amazement, Biatta felt calm.

"You have the skill. It is untrained and faint, but it does reside within you."

"Who are you?"

"It does not matter. I will be no one without your aide."

"What can I do?"

The voice did not respond, and Biatta feared she was already too late. When it returned, it was clear that time was short.

The voice whispered, "Come closer."

Without hesitation, she knelt.

"Biatta!" her sister called from beyond the trees. "I'm scared. Are you all right?"

Biatta turned to reply, and a sudden lance of pain raced up her arm. She jumped back, ready to crawl away, but the desperate voice said, "No. Please. I just need a few drops of your blood inside my wounds. Please. I need to absorb your energy or I will die."

Biatta paused, unsure whether to run or stay. She looked at her forearm. Droplets of blood were formed rising from two punctures.

"Please. I am out of—"

The voice cut off. Panicked she had delayed too long and caused the death, Biatta slid forward, and squeezed her blood into each wound. When it appeared her blood had clotted and the wounds were not producing, she scratched them with her fingernail. Once each of the cat's wounds had received a few drops, she covered the punctures with her hand, slid back, and watched.

"Biatta, please answer me," her sister pleaded.

"I am fine. Give me a few minutes."

The cat still did not move, but she became aware of an itch on her arm. She removed her hand and to her shock found the two puncture wounds enflamed. The reddish circles had puckered.

A sound drew her attention to the cat. One paw moved. Elation flooded her, the wounds forgotten. She scooted forward and leaned closer. Over the next few minutes, the cat's body moved and twitched. It cried in pain and Biatta feared whatever she had done had not been enough. She thought about reopening the wounds and adding more blood but when she went to do so, tiny red lines had spread in both directions from each puncture on her arm. She probed one and winced. It was tender to the touch.

Her cry of pain brought more pleas from her sister. Branches moved. "No!" Biatta shouted. "Do not come in here. I am all right."

The cat's eyes opened. The head lifted and the gaze locked on hers. The voice came back.

"Thank you. You have given me enough strength to survive." The cat's eyes fell to the infected arm. Biatta followed the gaze, alarmed to find it swollen and the lines advancing at a surprising rate. "I am sorry for what I have done to you. It was the only way to ensure my survival. You do have the ability to heal yourself, if not the knowledge. You must lay down and go deep within your heart and mind. Concentrate and call the skill forward. If you can tap into your energy you will heal, be well, and thank me. If not, I am truly sorry."

The cat rose on shaky legs and darted from the tree. Biatta made it home but was in anguish and had developed a high fever. She collapsed and fell unconscious, and just before she succumbed, found the hidden source. As she tapped into the energy flow, slowly she began to fight off the poison coursing through her. She learned and grew stronger until she fully healed. It was the start of who she was now.

And the memory was long enough that when it ended, she was in the barn.

Chapter Twenty

Daria was frightened. She had been in this situation before when she was captured by the Harpy, but back then she knew she was in enemy hands. Right now, she wasn't sure. The massive bird had swooped down and saved her from being mauled by that monstrous wolf but was this one of those out of the pan, into the fire things?

The only reason she hadn't made an effort to escape was because she saw the black bird flying alongside Biatta's owl toward the mansion. It had to be someone on their side, didn't it? Also, unlike the Harpy, this bird had taken care not to pierce her with its talons. From the looks of those sharp things, they were more than capable of running through her body with more than enough to spare coming out the other end.

Daria glanced down at the ground as it swept beneath her. If not for the unknown of who had her, she might enjoy the feeling of flight. She wondered if she would ever attain a level to allow her capable of flying on her own.

She did not recognize the ground below but then the bird flew so high, details were unclear. They had been flying for more than an hour and had passed over villages, a lake, a lot of farmland, and now, this untamed land. In the distance was a mountain range. She knew of none this size near the city.

She craned her neck to see the black bird. It looked much the same as any other bird, except much larger. Its body was longer than she was tall and the wingspan was twice her length.

"Hey. I'm getting tired. Can we set down for a while?"

The bird ignored her.

"You must be getting tired too. You've been flying for a long time."

Perhaps the bird couldn't hear her or didn't understand her. She thought about using her flaming ability to scorch the underside of the bird like she had done to escape the Harpy. But that time, they were flying lower and there were trees to break her fall. They were much higher now and there were rocks below. There would be no surviving a fall.

The bird flapped its expansive wings hard and they rose. The sudden shift both startled and frightened her. Weren't they already high enough? Large rocks rushed toward her. She screamed and tried to draw up closer to the bird. They cleared the rocky pinnacles by only a few feet. Now she understood why the bird soared higher. They crested several more mountain peaks before the bird ceased flapping and began a long slow glide toward the ground.

Though Daria was relieved to be closer to the ground, she wondered what awaited her once they did land. Beneath her, trees grew larger and dangerously close. They flew over a large forest sandwiched between two mountain ranges. Once clear of the trees, the bird angled toward the ground. She saw buildings. Perhaps a small village? She thought the bird was about to land, but while still moving and ten feet off the ground, its claws opened and she was falling.

She screamed and flailed in a desperate attempt to slow the speed of her fall to no avail. She landed in a haystack. Though the softness cushioned her fall, the speed and momentum were not curtailed enough to prevent her from busting through the hay, then hitting and skidding along the ground, eventually rolling to a stop on her stomach.

"Oh! Well done!" a voice shouted.

"You better check to make sure she hasn't broken her neck," a second person said.

Daria was afraid to move. Though shaken, she was still alive and alert. Slowly the aches and pains of her landing made themselves known. She heard something close and opened her eyes. A hoof was inches from her face. Hands touched her and she jumped and shouted.

"Easy there, youngster. Just checking to see if anything's broken."

She stiffened but made no effort to stop the exam.

"Okay. Everything seems to be in place from this end. Let me roll you over now to check the front." She did not resist but drew in energy. She was surprised at how much was readily available and reached her limit fast.

"Best be watchful, Drumford. I think she just enhanced."

"Do tell. Is that right, little lady? You preparing to cast a spell at me, though all I'm doing is trying to help?"

Daria was rolled onto her back. The sight of her two rescuers—if that's what they were—widened her eyes and forced a yelp of fear from her throat.

"What? You've never seen a Gelf before?"

The short man had a lean frame, large round eyes, and a greenish-blue tint to his skin. His long, thin fingers probed her ribs.

"I should feel insulted that you think my appearance so repulsive as to make you scream."

"Maybe she's not friendly enough to waste time on," the other voice said.

Daria turned her head and followed the hoof up to a horse body with a man's torso. Though once again startled by the sight, she at least recognized this creature—er, person as a centaur. Much had been written about the ancient race, though she never believed they were real.

"I'm sorry. I just didn't expect to, ah…"

"What?" the blue man asked. "Be saved? Rescued? Treated with respect?"

He was angry. He finished his examination and stood. He glared down at her, as if daring her to rise.

"I don't feel any breaks. Other than some scrapes and bruises, you should heal fine." He pivoted and walked away.

The Centaur stood over her. His long beard hung low enough to cover much of his large muscular chest. "You insulted him. That wasn't very kind."

Daria sat up, afraid to stand. "I am sorry. It was all so fast…so sudden…so unexpected."

"Don't apologize to me. Apologize to Drumford."

The Centaur moved away, catching up to his friend. Daria stood, groaned her way past the aches, and dusted herself off. With a shielding hand over her eyes, she scoured the sky for the bird, but it was gone. In a slow circle she scanned her new surroundings. It was a farm. Crops were to the left, two barns with animal pens were in front of her. To the right was a large farmhouse, and beyond that a row of smaller houses. Behind her was a massive field of golden wheat stretching farther than she could see.

The farm and village were surrounded on two sides by mountains and a third by a deep forest. The final side was the one with the wheat field.

Her gaze stopped on the centaur and the…what did he say? Gelf? They appeared to be in a heated discussion. With nowhere else to go, she strode toward them. The least she could do was offer an apology. She needed information and friends were a better source than enemies.

"She just doesn't know any better," the centaur was saying.

"Ah, look. I'm sorry if I offended you. I was whisked away from my home, dropped in a strange place, where I was confronted by—"

"Strange people," the Gelf finished.

Daria sighed. "Let's go with strangers, okay? I had no idea if I was in the middle of friends or foes. I just came from a battle, and—"

"A battle?" the centaur asked. "Where? Against whom?"

"Ah, some evil guy named Bradenbaugh. He chased us to another world and has been trying to kill me and my friends."

The two beings exchanged knowing glances but did not speak.

"Wait," Daria said. "You know this guy?"

"For the moment, we prefer not to say," the Gelf said.

Daria was instantly on guard. "Oh. Okay. I, ah…I should be going now." She backed away, eyeing them expectantly.

"You going to stop her?" Drumford asked.

"What do you want me to do, shoot her?"

It was then Daria noticed the bow and quiver of arrows strung across the centaur's shoulders.

"Well, we can't let her leave. She might be the enemy."

I don't think so," the centaur said. "He never would have dropped her here if she was a threat."

He? He who? She had lots of questions, but her survival instincts overwhelmed her desire to ask them. She whirled and ran with no destination in mind, other than getting away. Mountains loomed in the distance in front of her. She veered left, aiming to lose herself in the endless wheat field. She ran hard. Behind she heard footsteps coming fast. She angled away.

A voice called, "We mean you no harm! Stop!"

It didn't sound like they meant no harm. She drew in energy and readied her spell. The centaur pulled up next to her. "Stop so we can talk."

Still running, she shoved her arms across her body, spoke the launching word, and a short gout of flames shot from her hands.

The centaur reacted in an instant and dodged the path. Though she didn't score a hit, the spell gave her some breathing room and a chance to get more distance. The wheat field was closer, yet still a distance away. The centaur pulled up abreast of her but kept more distance. "You have to stop. I cannot allow you to leave the valley. If you don't stop, I will be forced to shoot you. I do not miss. It will be a shame for you to die when it is unnecessary."

She continued to run as her mind swirled with endless jumbled thoughts, possibilities, and solutions.

"Very well. You leave me no choice. The person who brought you to us will be extremely disappointed. Obviously, he sees something in you worth risking his life for."

The centaur dropped back from sight. Daria's mind reeled, anticipating an arrow driving into her back at any moment.

"Last chance. Please. Don't make me do this."

Something he said sparked a thought that led to a question. Who had brought her here, and why was his life at risk? She slowed with the wheat field ten feet away and turned. As she did, she sensed the arrow already in flight and closing too fast to avoid. She shut her eyes, threw up her hands, and fell back, knowing it was too late to dodge. She could not keep her eyes closed. The iron-tipped arrow hit something inches from her face. Sparks flew and the arrow deflected away.

Daria fell back, hitting the ground hard. In an instant she was up on wavering legs, frightened beyond control after yet another near-death experience. Her mind was no longer able to comprehend what had happened. Her body shook, her legs gave way, and she collapsed in a quivering heap.

Somewhere in the back of her mind, she saw a beautiful dark-skinned woman descend toward her as if gliding on a breeze. Her smile was brilliant and blinding like a flashbulb. Warm fingers touched her forehead.

"Sleep now, child. We'll talk later."

Chapter Twenty-One

Jeremy woke with a start. Wherever he was, it was dark. Did that mean night had fallen, or was he someplace without light? Though a chill was in the air, he did not have the feeling of being outside. He moved and something crunched beneath him. He reached out to feel what it was.

Straw? Was he in a barn?

He looked around as his eyes adjusted. He could make out shapes but other than guessing, he had no idea what they were. A few feet away was a dark shape curled in a ball. Not wanting to disturb who or what it was, he moved away. The movement caused a sharp pain in his side. He winced audibly and grabbed at the pain. Two ragged raised welts, each about eight inches long, stretched across his left side. Though it hurt when he moved, it did not when he touched the puckered skin.

Slowly, he rose to his knees, to one foot, and eventually to standing. Though his breath was taken away twice from the sharp pain, once he stood, it subsided. He did a circle to get an idea of the space around him. Sure now he was in a barn, he moved forward toward a dark shape with tiny streams of light filtering through. His outstretched hand touched weathered wood. He moved along what he thought was a door until he reached the first of the light sources. He placed an eye to the opening. It was as dark outside as it was inside. The light source was a full moon. The bright beam allowed him to make out treetops. He scanned left and right but saw no other shapes that might be buildings. He appeared to be in or at least near yet another forest.

He turned to gaze toward the other end of the barn. How had he gotten there? It took a moment to recall the sequence of events that led him to this place. He remembered being taking prisoner by the goat headed man. The image of a room and another man cleared before his eyes. He was taken to another man who was in charge. Then, Biatta was there. No, not Biatta. Her voice. Somehow, she was inside his head. But where was she?

The next memory was of him struggling with the first man. He was mounted on a towering wolf man. Then in a whoosh, he was lifted into the air. His hand went to his side. *Ah, that's how I got these.* It was a large white bird. The rest was blank. How had he arrived at this place?

Something stirred in the hay. A rat? Something else? He didn't want to know. He slid sideways to get away from the light. Jeremy had no desire to be spotted by whatever was there. He felt an obstacle to the side. He had reached a corner. He squatted and waited. Whatever it was moved more now. Thirty feet away, a dark form rose. The beam of light hit the thing and highlighted something golden. Fur? Hair? Wait. Hair. Biatta had golden hair. He thought about calling out but if it wasn't her, his position would be known.

A whispered voice called out, "Jeremy? Where are you?"

He recognized the voice. "I'm here, Biatta."

Her voice conveyed relief. "Oh, thank goodness. How do you feel?"

"Sore. Tired. Okay. You?"

"The same."

"How did we get here? For that matter, where is here?"

"We have to be careful and quiet. We are still close to Bradenbaugh's mansion. He may have things out hunting for us."

Bradenbaugh? "Things?"

She offered no reply. She stood, then cried out and fell back down. Jeremy left his hiding place and rushed to her side. He found her by feel. "Biatta, what's wrong?"

"Jeremy, I'm hurt. I'm weak. I don't know if I can stand."

"What's wrong?"

"That foul creature swatted at me as I lifted you off its back."

"Where? Let me see."

Her unseen hands caught his and held them. "No. It wouldn't be proper."

"Not proper. I just want to help."

"He caught me across the butt."

"Oh," he said, unsure what else to say.

"I have gouges in my skin and I'm still bleeding. I'm sure I've developed an infection as well. There is nothing you can do for me. I am still too weak to heal. I need rest, but I don't think this is the place to stay."

"Can you move?"

"With your help."

He rose, about to help her up, when he stopped. "Are you sure it isn't better to rest here?"

"No, we should go."

"I was thinking it might be better to rest here rather than get caught out in the open."

She sighed. "A good point." She settled back down.

"Are you bleeding?"

"Yes."

"Then you need a bandage."

He began removing his shirt."

"Jeremy, no. It is too cold, and you aren't completely healed yourself."

"Nonsense. The threat is greater for your health than mine. You cannot afford to lose too much blood, or we may never be able to leave this place." He gripped his shirt and attempted to tear it down the middle, but he didn't have the strength. It always looked so easy on TV. He put the hem in his mouth and gnawed and pulled until he had a small tear. Once that happened, the shirt ripped all the way to the collar.

"Okay, roll over so I can wrap it."

"No, I don't think so."

"Oh for heaven's sake, Biatta. Yours isn't the first female bottom I've seen."

"Maybe not, but you've never seen mine."

"It's too dark to see anything. Is there something strange about yours compared to others?"

"It just isn't proper."

"You know what isn't proper? Allowing you to bleed to death. Now roll over before I roll you over."

With reluctance, she did.

"Undo your jeans."

"Jeremy, I—"

"Just do it. We've already wasted enough time."

He felt her wiggle then heard the zipper. He put his fingers inside the waistband and slid them down. She winced several times. It really was too dark to see much else other than a pale form. Once he had enough exposed, he touched gently with his fingers until he found the wounds. She flinched at the contact.

He moved to adjust the bandage. When he did, the beam of moonlight his body had been blocking settled on her butt, illuminating it. He paused, then flushed with embarrassment. He decided to save her that same feeling by not mentioning the spotlight on her.

He wrapped the sections of shirt around her, having to slide his hands under her hips three times to complete the wrap. He tied it off as tight as possible, then retreated and turned his back so she could redress.

"Thank you, Jeremy."

"You are welcome."

"Also, thank you for being a gentleman."

A sound outside cut short his reply.

"Quick," she said, and moved to a stack of hay bales. Jeremy followed. "Help me move this corner a bit but do it slowly."

He moved next to her and together they inched the far corner of the stack away from the rear wall.

"That's good," she said. "I'm smaller. Let me slide in first."

He stepped aside. She moved as the door creaked and moonlight flooded the center of the barn. Jeremy froze, afraid to move for fear of making noise. Instead, he leaned so his torso was behind the stack. To be seen, anyone searching had to come inside and move to the corner of the stack. Only his legs were in view at that point.

Nothing moved, but he caught the faint sound of someone or something sniffing at the air. Straw crunched under a heavy footfall. Whoever was there had entered the barn. Jeremy judged its progress by the straw. The sniffing at the air led him to believe whoever was there was not human.

In the distance far from the barn, something howled. The sound sent shivers through Jeremy. The beast in the barn grunted, then bolted, leaving Jeremy with raised flesh.

"One of them must have caught our scent from where I dragged you here."

"You dragged me? That explains the condition of my clothes."

"That's not important." She got up and pushed past him. "It won't take long for them to realize the trail leads back here." She reached the barn door and peered out. "They are close. We need to move now. I'm still weak, but a little more rested. Turn your back."

"Huh?"

"I'm going to heal a bit and it works best skin on skin."

Jeremy wasn't quite sure what that meant but turned his back. Seconds later a faint white glow emanated from behind him. Startled, he turned. "Hey."

"Oh, sorry."

The glow was coming from her. That shouldn't have been a surprise. He witnessed her doing that same thing to Nick. A minute, later the howls sang out in a blood-chilling chorus.

"They sensed the magic. Sounds like three of them. They are close. We must leave now."

She grabbed his arm and yanked him toward the door.

"I used most of my reserves healing. I'm not sure how far I can go, especially carrying you, but they won't be able to get our scent and track us in the air."

Jeremy was confused but knew enough not to speak. With the sound of terrifying howls fast approaching, speech was not something he could do anyway. Before his eyes, Biatta's body shimmered, then altered. When the vision settled, the beautiful woman was replaced by the elegant lines of a white owl. He stood dumbfounded. The owl hooted at him, but he was too shocked to move.

The owl moved fast, snatching him off his feet with its claws and expanding its huge, powerful wings. In three muscular strokes they were at tree height. Jeremy glanced down and his heart leaped to his throat. Until that moment, he had no idea he was afraid of heights. The barn got increasingly smaller and before it disappeared, Jeremy caught sight of three large animal forms entering. Even at this height, the sound of their angry howls reached him.

For the moment, they were safe.

Chapter Twenty-Two

They flew on into the night. They had been in air for less than thirty minutes before Jeremy felt the first problem. The owl gasped and they bounced as if hitting turbulence. Seconds later, their height decreased. The owl used her wings less often, taking to gliding.

He knew there was a problem when they were even with the treetops. The owl Biatta was fighting to stay airborne but was losing the battle. The only question that remained was whether they would land or crash. Biatta juked left then right in abrupt moves that had Jeremy's body snapping from one side to the other. He realized she was searching for a place to land. They were still forty feet up. Falling from there would hurt but he thought Biatta had a better chance of landing safely if not carrying him.

"Biatta, let me go." She did not respond. Maybe in this form she couldn't understand his words. "Biatta. Listen to me. You can't land safely if I'm still here. Let me go. The fall isn't too high. I'll be fine."

The owl craned her neck to face him. She can understand me, he thought.

"You know it's the right thing and the safe thing to do." They were still gliding downward perhaps thirty feet above the ground. "I don't know how much room you need to land but when you get to that point, let me go."

They glided lower.

"Biatta, do you understand? It is more important for you to be unhurt. If those creatures come after us, I can do little to protect you. Our only chance is if you are able to do what you do." He began to squirm, trying to get free. "Now, let go."

Instead, the claws closed tighter around him.

"Biatta, think."

The ground was rushing toward him, cutting off any further pleas. Ten feet above the ground, Jeremy extended his hands and feet in anticipation of the touchdown. The owl slowed, hovered for a moment, then Jeremy was falling. A short cry of surprise left him. He touched the grassy surface, tightened his muscles against a face plant, and managed to slow his body enough to only mildly impact the ground.

Though the contact might have been much worse, it still stunned him for a moment. Then, he heard something else hit the ground. He lifted his head to see the owl laying in a heap ten feet away.

Jeremy pushed to his feet, took a moment to make sure he could stand, then hurried to Biatta's side. As he approached, her body began to shimmer again. He paused for a moment until the glow faded, leaving Biatta's human form in a ball. He dropped to his knees next to her, but unsure of her injuries, did not touch her.

"Biatta, are you all right?"

Her rapid, heavy breathing was audible, but she did not speak. He wanted to ask again but decided to give her a minute to regain some composure.

It was the right move. Moments later, she lifted a hand and touched his arm.

"I'm fine, Jeremy. Just very tired. I need rest but getting to safety is more important. Please help me up. I have a good idea where we are. I know a place we can hide until morning."

Jeremy took her arms, stood, and hauled her to her feet.

"This way," she said. She had only gone a few steps before she leaned against him. "I hope you don't mind. I need the support."

"No, not at all."

He put an arm around her. They walked on in silence. A few minutes later, she said, "Jeremy, I am sorry but I need to rest for a few moments. It is farther than I thought."

"That's all right." He released her and she sat on a tree stump. "Take all the time you need."

He waited for her to get settled before saying, "I've been thinking. Maybe it's better if I leave you someplace to recuperate and continue on myself." He raised a hand against her immediate objection. "No, listen. They are hunting for me. If I'm not with you, you'll be safe. You can rest. Get your strength back. The only reason you are in this predicament is because you had to rescue me from whoever that guy was. If I go, you won't have to spend your valuable time and energy on me."

She tried to smile but the effort was a further drain. She inhaled deeply.

"That's not going to happen, so put the thought out of your mind."

"Biatta, you are not thinking. I'm a no one. I'm not important. I am not going to have you get hurt because of me. Besides, I may not look like it, but I can take care of myself."

Despite her weariness, she did smile that time. "I have no doubt you are capable, but even a hero needs help when the odds are stacked against him. You do not know what you face here. Once they figure out who you are and what importance you may be to either side's struggle, you will never be safe. They will hunt you until they have you, and then they will try to use you."

"Is that what you're doing? Using me?"

"Don't be absurd. I'm trying to protect you. Now that I know you better, there is no way you would willingly work for the dark side. You are a good man. Believe it or not, you have the ability within you to prevent anyone from ever using you. I'm not sure it can be reached or tapped, but it is there, buried deep from generations of unuse and lack of training and knowledge."

"You keep hinting at something beyond my understanding or belief, but never explain what you mean. I want to know. Tell me why I'm so important that you would risk your life to save me."

She stood slowly and stretched. "I promise to tell you all I know once we get someplace safe."

Jeremy was tired of being put off.

"No. Tell me now. Telling me later is something you've said too often. Later never comes. People are trying to kidnap me, kill me, threaten me. I've been carried away by a goat man, a giant wolf, and an owl. My life has been forever changed since you and Daria entered it. I think I have a right to know what I've gotten involved in."

"Yes, you do. I owe you that. But Jeremy, the story is long and best told someplace safe where I can take the time to explain and answer your questions. Please be patient with me. I will tell you, if only for your own protection. Just not here."

She began walking, leaving him staring after her and feeling a long overdue anger building within him. He followed, rehearsing everything he wanted to say…no, unload on her.

He heard barking. He froze. Was that a dog or one of those wolf things? If Biatta heard, she did not show it. She continued walking. He hurried after her. They reached a house with a fenced in front and backyard. A minute later, another house came into view. They had reached a populated area. He thought about running up to a house, banging on the door, and asking for help. But banging on the door at night in a neighborhood he was not familiar with was not a bright idea.

More houses appeared. When he saw the first storefronts, Jeremy knew they had reached a town or perhaps were on the outskirts of a small city. He began looking for someplace to hide or seek assistance. If Biatta was doing the same, she gave no indication.

They reached a street full of businesses that led to the downtown area where a wooden placard on the corner of the town square proclaimed, *Welcome to Lithglo.* He had never heard of it but thought they were somewhere up the east coast. Perhaps Maine. If so, they were a long way from home but at least he had an idea of how to get back.

Biatta's pace slowed by the time she turned down an alley three blocks past the town square. The backs of businesses were on the left and backyards of houses were on the right. Midway down the alley, her steps faltered. Jeremy rushed to catch her before she fell. He caught her and pinned her against the wall to keep her upright.

"I am okay. Thank you."

"You need to sit down. We can't go any farther until you get your strength back."

"Don't. Have. To." Between each word she paused for a breath. "We. Are. Here." She lifted an arm and pointed to a narrow passageway between two buildings. "Help me."

She tried to walk but he carried her more than she supported her own weight.

They slid into the passageway single file in the tight space. He went first, fearing Biatta might fall forward and he wouldn't be in position to catch her. He held one hand and she placed the other on his shoulder. They moved a third of the way down its length before she said, "Here."

Jeremy glanced around. "Here? There's nothing here."

"Shh," she said raising her hand.

She placed a hand on a brick darker than the others. At first Jeremy, thought she needed support. Then she mumbled a few words, and a fiery line appeared and raced to create the shape of a rectangle. Its task complete, the line vanished, leaving behind a door. The door had no knob or handle or even hinges. Biatta tapped out a pattern on the four corners of the door and a whoosh sounded.

The door slid into the wall about six inches, then swung inward.

Jeremy gaped. Biatta lifted a weak arm, placed a gentle finger under his chin, and lifted his jaw closed. Then she stepped through the doorway. Jeremy followed, still amazed at what he was witnessing. Once through, the door closed and slid back to its original position, blocking off all light from the night sky.

A flame flickered then grew into a light bright enough to erode the shadows. They were in a small room, perhaps a vestibule. The walls were unadorned and the room completely empty save for three doors on the right. Biatta chose the one in the middle. She placed her hand in the center of the door, recited words, and an audible click sounded. She turned the knob and stepped through.

Inside, steps led down. Jeremy kept a hand on Biatta's shoulder to keep her from falling but also so he didn't lose her. At the bottom of the stairs she turned left. The short hall opened into a large space containing furniture. It was outfitted as a family room and had enough seating for twenty people.

Biatta extinguished the torch and flicked a switch that turned on the lights. "You can stay here if you want. I'm going down the hall to lie down for a while. There is food to the right, or if you're tired, bedrooms are down the hall." She took two steps and faced him. "I made you a promise. We will have that long overdue talk when I awake."

With that, she moved down the hall and disappeared inside the first room on the right. Jeremy looked around the space. What the hell was going? Where was he? Who were all these strange people he was now involved with? The questions were unending. Unfortunately, no answers were coming.

He sat down on a sofa and stared at the wall. He didn't remember curling up on the sofa. He didn't see the lights wink out. He didn't see or remember anything after that except for strange dreams.

Chapter Twenty-Three

"What do you mean, you didn't find anything?" Lord Drewmore said. "How thoroughly did you search?"

Carpenter stood at ease in black military special ops gear.

"Sir, we searched everywhere. We did find two secret compartments, but neither had anything inside and from the dust build up, neither has been used in years. The original owners of the building probably had them built to hide their wealth."

"Did you interrogate?"

"Yes sir, but none are residents. We found no evidence that anyone lived there. It is a building that houses a variety of small businesses. They rent space from whoever the owner is. It's like an office building that has undergone renovation to accommodate its current usage. As far as interrogation goes, we did more than twenty interviews, a few by force. No one had any idea what we were talking about."

"They could have been lying."

"Sir, these are working people. None held secrets pertaining to what we were searching for. Most were too cowed to refuse to answer. Most spilled what they knew without hesitation."

Drewmore turned, put his hands behind his back, and paced.

"How could this be?" he muttered to himself.

"There was one curious thing, however."

"Yes. Spit it out, man."

"The elevator operator was found dead."

"Dead? How?"

"Unknown sir, but if I were to guess, I'd say from strangulation. There were witnesses. None to the crime, but several mentioned seeing a strange woman walking the halls."

"Strange. How so? Strange looking?"

"Yes, but also in her behavior. One woman noticed her just before a stapler appeared to float in air and staple her co-worker's mouth shut. We got a very basic description and searched for her, but if she did exist, she was gone."

Drewmore looked aghast, unable to form words. Finally, he sputtered, "Did anyone else see this unusual event?"

"No sir, but a woman did indeed have her mouth stapled shut. One woman said she didn't condone that sort of thing, but she understood why someone would go to such extremes. The woman never stops running her mouth."

"And what was your conclusion?"

The colonel shrugged. "That she deserved it, sir."

Drewmore frowned. "I want you to keep that building under surveillance. You hear me, Colonel? I want to know everything that goes on there, and I want a record of everyone who enters."

"Yes sir." He snapped to attention, pivoted to leave, but was stopped.

"And Colonel, if you find this woman or anyone else whose behavior is strange, bring them to me."

"Aren't we being a little reckless by staying at the school?" Wilden asked.

"Having already driven us from these grounds, it's the one place they won't think to look," Rowan said. "Besides, it's not like we have many options."

"There are places to hide here unknown to those from outside," Tarney said. "Plus, we don't have to worry about protecting the students now."

The small contingent entered Rowan's office on the campus grounds. He walked to a metal spiral staircase and ascended. At the top, he drew a wand from an interior pocket and walked to the back of the staircase. With the wand he drew a sigil, spoke a word of activation, and a section of the floor moved to reveal a similar descending staircase. He walked down the stairs. As the others followed, Wilden said, "Go up the stairs to go down the stairs. How intriguing."

The descent was much longer than the ascension. When they reached the bottom, an entire network of underground passageways presented themselves.

"My word," Wilden said. "I never knew these existed."

"And few others do either. These were built by the original owners, a sect of monks who valued their privacy as well as their valuables. It turned out they were not real monks but a very well-organized group of smugglers led by some very influential men of their time. I discovered them quite by accident when researching the history of the property before buying it. In fact, the possibility that these existed was the deciding factor for the purchase. I've never had the need for them but have explored them extensively and made some modifications. We should be quite safe and protected here."

He entered what appeared to be a large apartment.

"There are rooms to the right for those who need to rest or tend to injuries. I do not have much food down here, but I will make what I can. The downside of being here is that we are out of contact with our people. That must be remedied immediately. Tarney, will you see to that, please?"

The group of six men and five women spread out around the room as Rowan entered the somewhat primitive and ill-stocked kitchen. A short while later, Rowan carried a large wooden platter to the dining table. It contained bowls of soup with beans and canned vegetables. He set them around the table as the others came to join him.

Everyone looked at the meager fare and if they were disappointed in the selection, none mentioned it or refused to take up their spoon. While they ate, Tarney joined them.

"There is a girl in town sent by Jerricka. There have been several attempts to abduct her and she was almost caught up in that assault on our base."

"Are they bringing her here?" Rowan asked.

"No. I figured I'd go out and meet her. If it's safe, I'll bring her here. If not, I'll fall back to another location and send word."

"Any idea as to why she was sent?"

"From what I can tell, she was to inform us about the events of the other world."

Rowan nodded. No one spoke again until every morsel was consumed. As the table was cleared, Rowan sat back and gave voice to his thoughts.

"We need to locate Biatta, Daria, Kanter, and this man who might be from the lost tribe. We need to develop a battle plan that takes into account not only Bradenbaugh, but this other entity that may be stalking us. It is imperative we discern whether any connection exists between them and Bradenbaugh. If not, we must find out who they are and why they have inserted themselves into our lives.

"Next, we have to hear what this messenger has to say."

"And," Wilden interrupted. "Not to make light of your culinary abilities, but we need to stock your pantry with food that will last a while."

"Water is not a problem," Rowan said. "I tapped into the water line a while ago. We will have plenty as long as no one cuts it off."

"We also have to be careful no one is monitoring the usage," Tarney said. "That would be a sure give away someone is here."

"Yes," Rowan replied. "However, when I connected the electricity I ran a separate meter. That bill does not come here. It has an entirely different address."

"Anything else?" Wilden asked.

"We have a lot to do. Word has to be sent to search for our missing people." To Tarney, he said, "When do you go to meet the girl?"

"I'll leave in twenty minutes."

"How's your leg? You want me to come?"

He shook his head. "It's well enough. I can handle it. Better you are here to knock some of those items off our list."

"Oh, it was their base all right," Madelyn said. "Complete with guardians, secret chambers, and wards."

"But other than the two guardians, you didn't find anyone else." It was said as a statement, not a question, so Madelyn did not reply. Bradenbaugh turned to face her. "I doubt they will return, and if they do, it won't be for long once they discover the bodies, but I want someone to keep an eye on the building and report if anyone enters."

He paced and looked at the table where General Perva, Toradon, and Rondovian sat. He had gathered them together to discuss recent events and plans moving forward. He studied the three men at the table, then Madelyn. These were his leaders, his most trusted people. The most powerful people. Why didn't that fill him with confidence?

Perva was a cruel, ruthless man whose heart was evil, but he did not possess the ability to perform magic. Oh sure, he had enchantments and magically enhanced items, but he did not have the talent to replace the magic in them once used. However, he was unreliable and rash and needed to be reminded of his place and whatever mission he was given.

Toradon was a sadist who had magic; one of the few men in his army that did. He was strong, nowhere near his own skills, but formidable. His was a power learned from an ancient time and realm. He was ambitious, but Bradenbaugh did not fear him. The man had to know his demise was imminent, should he ever dare to attempt to usurp his power. Besides, Bradenbaugh was the dark one's only contact in this world. He was careful to cultivate and enforce that connection to ensure his longevity at the head of the table.

Rondovian was not a thinker. Though he possessed power, he more often relied on brawn to achieve his goals. He enjoyed issuing pain. He had no desire to lead, which made him more valuable than the other two men. But unlike the other two, if given a task, he always completed it.

Madelyn was easily the most skilled and powerful wizard in the group…next to him, of course. His only concern was her sanity. Granted, that could be beneficial at times, but his hold on her was tentative at best. She was kept in line by the promise that once the dark one was returned to this world, she would be by his side in whatever capacity he wished.

"We have a more pressing matter at hand. Who is the man we held? Why does Vandalue think he is important? Why did he rescue the man and come himself? I doubt he's been involved in anything magical in years besides lighting a candle or creating pretty designs in the air. This man has extreme value to the enemy, and I need to know why."

"Have you considered that it's all an illusion?" Toradon asked.

"He was certainly real enough. That was no illusion," Bradenbaugh said.

"That's not what I meant. What if he is a mere carrot dangled in view to draw us out?"

"You think it's a trap?" Perva asked with a sneer.

"It is a possibility. Otherwise, where did this man come from? He isn't anyone we know. Think about it. This man appears out of nowhere in the presence of known wizards. We are led to believe he is one of them and in fact, a very important someone. They can't find us any other way, so we jump at the chance to capture him. As soon as we take him, they suddenly appear at our door, at a place out of the way of anything and completely secluded, and warded to the max."

Madelyn moved to the back of one of the chairs. "Then why come with such a small force? If they were setting a trap and felt it had sprung, they would've attacked in force and tried to take you all out. Instead, what did they do? They attacked, found the man, and fled for safety. That doesn't sound like much of a trap. It sounds just like Lord Bradenbaugh said. He is a valued asset, and as such, we need to know why."

Bradenbaugh eyed her with surprise. In the time he had known her, that was perhaps the first time she'd made sense. She was calm and in control. Gone was the absurd, over the top comments and that awful cackle she called a laugh. He liked this side of Madelyn. But then, he realized it also made him nervous. If she was playing roles and was this calculating, what else was she hiding?

Bradenbaugh was positive that although the others might plot to overthrow him, she was the one most capable of doing so. He pushed that thought aside, knowing it required more attention.

"I don't like not knowing. Toradon, you and Rondovian take a team of wizards to the prison site. It is time to break the dark one free, or at least weaken his prison so he is ready once the last key is in place. Use your magic to attack the magic that holds him captive. No matter how strong and deeply woven it is, nothing can last forever under constant barrage. I want to be ready so nothing can stop us."

"As you wish, my lord," Toradon said. He gave a slight bow and left.

Rondovian moved to Bradenbaugh's side.

"My talents are better suited to attack than this mundane task."

"Agreed." He motioned the big man to a more private place. "But two things make me send you there. One, if they are discovered by Vandalue's people, Toradon will need your protection while they continue to work. Two, I need you to keep an eye on Toradon. Make sure his efforts are spent toward our goal and not his own."

The big man grunted by way of answer and left the room.

"Madelyn, there was a report of one of the students being whisked out of the city. Find her and bring her to me."

The woman gave him a sinister smile. "As you command, my lord," she said with heavy mockery in her voice. With a circular wave of her hand she vanished.

That left Perva. He had a special assignment for the big man. One he hoped my take Vandalue y surprise and end the war. The thought brought on a sinister smile of his own.

Chapter Twenty-Four

Daria woke with a start. She sat up fast and looked around, nervous about her unknown surroundings. She was on a small bed inside a room. Was it one of the buildings on the farmland? She was under heavy blankets. She yanked them aside and swung her legs over the edge of the bed. The floor was a surprisingly long way down. Whoever usually slept in this bed must have long legs. She thought that ruled out Drumford.

She slid from the bed and padded to the window. From what she could see, she was in the farmhouse. She crept to the door and opened it slowly, hoping to avoid any creaking. It groaned anyway. She grimaced against the sound and wondered if there was another way to get out of the house. For a moment she considered going out the window, then decided against it. Regardless of how she went outside, they'd catch her before she got far.

Drumford's words came back to her. *We can't let her leave.* Did that mean she'd be a prisoner for the rest of her life? If so, she vowed to run away as often as possible until she escaped for good.

She stepped outside the door into a hall. She saw five other doors. At the far end were stairs leading up and down. She hadn't realized it was a three-story house. Daria moved to the banister and peered over. She did not hear anyone talking or moving around. She stepped with caution to the first stair. A voice called from below.

"We can hear you. Just come down. I'm fixing something to eat."

The thought of food made her stomach rumble loud enough to be heard below. When was the last time she ate? Realizing the futility of sneaking out, she pranced down the stairs, hoping to find food at the bottom. The aroma of fresh baked bread wafted to her, exploding her taste buds in a flood of saliva.

"We're in the kitchen."

She walked through a doorway and to her surprise, found the centaur. He was at the counter working on something. It was a large, bright space and Daria wondered if it had been constructed with his size in mind.

"There you are. How you feeling?"

"Ah, okay, I guess."

"Good. I'm sorry about nearly shooting you with an arrow."

She had almost forgotten about that in her excitement over finding food.

"You tried to kill me."

He placed his hands on the counter and looked annoyed.

"I said I was sorry. Besides, I'm too good a shot to have killed you. I was only aiming to wound."

"But you still shot at me. I'm a defenseless young girl and you tried to pierce my precious skin with your arrow."

"Hey, I said I was sorry. You didn't give me any choice. Oh, and if you try to leave again, I'll try to shoot you again. I won't like it and I will probably be sorry, but I will take the shot."

"Nice to know."

"Hungry?"

"Starving."

"Well, in that case, go out on the front porch and ring the dinner bell."

"There is an actual dinner bell?"

"Of course, though it's not really a bell. It's a triangle. Take the metal striker and bang it around the inside of the triangle. It will be loud and will draw everyone here."

On the porch she found the triangle hanging from a nail in the roof. The striker was tied to the triangle. She took it in her hand and clanged it around the interior of the triangle. The loud clanging echoed off the buildings and out over the fields. Heads popped up above the wheat, then everyone began moving toward the house. How many worked the farm? She counted eleven before she went back inside.

She stood near where the centaur worked. He stopped, wiped his hand on a towel, and extended it.

"We haven't formally met. I'm Declan."

She took his hand. "Daria."

His hand was strong. He crushed hers, but only for an instant before she cried out.

"Wonderful to meet you, Daria. Take a seat on the far side of the table. Breakfast will be served in a few minutes."

As she moved toward the table, voices traveled through the open door. Others entered, all speaking in loud, excited voices. Most quieted upon seeing, her making her feel like the outsider she was. She stood behind a chair, uncertain where everyone else would sit, and not wanting to take their seats, thus further alienating herself. She waited.

A dozen or more people…beings?…whatever they were, ranged from human to…well, she didn't know. Drumford came in and eyed her but did not offer a greeting. There didn't appear to be any seating order, so she pulled the chair out and sat.

Declan brought over two bowls and set them on the table. Another member of their strange family carried two more. In all, seven bowls of assorted foods were passed around. Some contained eggs, others fruit. Assorted breads filled another. The other bowls held contents she did not recognize. She did notice that none of the bowls contained meat of any kind. The table talk began as soon as the food was on their plates. They appeared to be a happy and close-knit bunch. None of them addressed comments or questions toward her, leaving her to feel isolated. She slouched in on herself and focused on the food on her plate. She ate without tasting.

Between bites she sneaked glances at the collective around the table. Other than Drumford and Declan, there were two greenish beings, she thought a male and female, but had no idea what race. A slender man with pointed ears sat at the end of the table to the right. Daria was sure he was an elf.

Across from her was a hawk faced girl with large piercing eyes. Each time Daria looked up, the girl was studying her. The scrutiny increased her feeling of unease. If there had been enough room to do so, she would have gotten up and left the table. She was trapped and had to endure. At least her belly was happy.

The two next to the hawk faced girl looked like humans. A man and woman. They had pleasant faces and were full of happy talk and warm smiles. But for some reason, they made her nervous too. At the end of the table to her left, Declan stood. He smiled at her. She offered a faint smile in return, then averted her gaze. From that point until the meal was finished, she kept her head down and stared at her plate, even when it was empty.

As soon as she heard chairs scraping back, she lifted her head. The group exited and went back to their chores. The hawk faced girl and Declan cleared the table. Daria stood and picked up her plate to carry it to the sink.

The hawk faced girl said in an unfriendly tone, "Leave it. I'll get it."

Not knowing what else to do, Daria left and stood at the outer door. What should she do, hide in her room or go outside and explore? Outside sounded like the better option. Besides, it gave her a chance to look for escape routes.

She walked along a path leading to the back of the farmhouse. Her thoughts flicked from Jeremy and Biatta to the black bird and the floating dark-skinned woman. Where was Biatta? Would she find Daria? What if something had happened to her during the fight? She remembered seeing her fly away in the opposite direction from where the black bird took her. At that point, Biatta was still all right.

She had no idea where she was or how she would get back to the city, or for that matter, the new world. So many questions with no hint at answers. She stopped in the middle of a dirt road heading toward a small town. She turned a circle, searching for direction. She caught sight of a sudden movement behind her. A slight girl ducked behind a wooden wagon. Even with the quick glimpse, she knew it was the hawk faced girl. Had she been sent to keep an eye on her? No doubt.

Daria continued through the town until she passed the last building. Ahead of her was a mountain about a mile away. She could cover the distance in a short time. However, she doubted it was as close as it looked. She sighed. Even if it was closer, she doubted she'd ever reach it before an alarm was raised and pursuit was sent to retrieve her. Maybe the hawk faced girl would fly up and intercept her. As odd as that sounded, she now knew it to be possible.

With fading hope, she turned and started back toward the farmhouse, wondering where her shadow had gone. Halfway through town with still no sight of the girl, Daria turned and spotted her pretending to look at something in a store window. How had she managed to get behind her?

She reached the farmhouse as Declan was exiting.

"Ah, there you are. Ready to go?"

"Go? Go where?"

"I'm to escort you into the mountains where you will meet someone very special."

"If it's not a special person who can take me back to the city, I have no interest in going."

Declan's friendly smile faded. "This is not a person you defy. When I am told to bring you up the mountain, that is what I will do. It is up to you whether you go on your own or be trussed and slung over my back. Your choice. Decide before I decide for you."

Anger flashed deep within Daria. She was tired, frustrated, and scared, but most of all she was sick of being taken and dragged all over two worlds and told what to do without having a say. The energy filled her before she even realized. The word rose to her lips and she spat it out.

"Fuegosius."

Flames shot from her hands, startling her as much as Declan. She moved her hand just in time to prevent Declan from being roasted. The flames shot past on either side. She reined in the fire and it extinguished. Stunned by the display of power, she stared at her hands.

Hoof beats drew her attention. Declan was in full gallop, getting distance from her.

"Declan!" she shouted. To herself, she muttered, "I'm sorry."

Daria glanced around. Those on the grounds either stared at her or ran for cover. She had no idea where to go, but she couldn't stay there. She had just torched any chance of help. She backed away, still stunned at what she was able to do. With a last look around the farm, Daria turned and ran.

Chapter Twenty-Five

The dark form of a large dog stalked through the trees, stopping every few steps to sniff the air. It caught a mixed scent. Sweat, faint cologne, smoke, and fear. From experience, the dog knew the distinct scents came from two people. It followed the scent to a point. Once it knew the location of its prey and that they were not moving, it veered off the direct path, taking a circuitous route.

It crept under low branches until it had a clear view. A tall man with a hat and a walking stick and a young dark-haired girl stood in the small clearing. The man rotated in a slow circle ever watchful, keeping the girl behind him. He looked to be an astute and adept protector. Recognition lit in the back of its mind. The dog waited a lengthy period to ensure no trap was being set that it hadn't discovered. If anyone else was in hiding, he'd have caught the scent unless it was magically obscured. To do that meant they had to know he was coming.

Once convinced no one else was present, Tarney shifted into human form and stepped from the trees. Immediately, the man whirled and presented the walking stick, sweeping the girl behind him. Tension formed between them for an instant like a brick wall, then Weatherly relaxed.

"Ah, it's you, Tarney. I'm so relieved. I was about to move on."

"Trouble?"

"You know me. I take pride in doing a thorough job. I did everything I knew to do but can't shake the feeling of being watched."

Tarney went into a reflexive defensive position. His hands weaved a pattern and his hands glowed.

"Do you still have that feeling?"

Weatherly became wary.

"No. I lost it about fifteen minutes ago. Either I lost them, or they gave up."

"Or they were smart enough to cover their trail and wait you out."

Something happened at the fringe of his magical senses. Someone had cast a spell. He raised his readied energy shield. Something thudded against it. He looked to see the point of a large dagger protruding halfway through the shield.

"Quick! Take the girl and run!" Tarney said. He called forth an offensive spell as a woman stepped into the clearing. She shoved her hands at Tarney and a stream of red shot across the short distance. The shield deflected the blast, but Tarney knew this woman was skilled. The power it took to block the attack drained both the shield and his energy. Even so, he called up a spell, and as soon as the energy stream ended, dropped the shield.

With one hand aimed at the woman and another at the sky, he shouted, *"Currencio explosiona!"*

A lightning bolt struck the woman's head as she moved to cast her own spell. In a zap and a crack, the woman disintegrated in a poof of acrid smoke.

Tarney turned his attention on the surrounding trees scanning for the next attack. None came. A cry of pain was followed by a scream. *The girl.* Tarney whirled and ran as hard as his still injured leg allowed toward the sound. He made far too much noise, but haste was more important than stealth.

As he ran, he cast a ball of light and tossed it up. It floated twenty feet off the ground and ten feet in front of him, illuminating everything close by.

The light created a shadow ahead. The dark form of a woman stood over a fallen man. Her arms were raised above her head, and in her hands was a long knife. She was about to finish Weatherly off. As the knife descended, Tarney shot a desperate energy bolt at the woman. The unaimed shot zipped past her. Though it did no damage, it distracted her enough to abort the death blow. She whirled to face Tarney. For a moment, fear crossed her face. Her eyes flicked toward the girl, who stupidly just stood there.

The woman ran toward the girl, swinging one hand overhead in a circular motion. In a quick movement, she snatched the girl, twirling and cackling maniacally as a whirlwind engulfed her. Tarney readied to fire another energy bolt but held back for fear of striking the girl. The whirling wind picked up speed, obscured the two within it, and then in a loud pop, vanished.

Stunned by such a turn of events and sickened by his failure, he cursed at the sky. His futile words fell back to earth. He raced for Weatherly. The man was alive, but barely. Tarney lifted him and ran. As he did, he recited a long unused spell from a more ancient time. His feet lifted from the ground. The sudden change almost toppled him but he quickly adjusted and found his balance. He rode on a circle of air. He whipped through the trees, directing the path with slight movements of his feet.

He rode the invisible platform until he reached the school. Around back, he dispelled the circle and hit the ground running. Minutes later, he was inside the secret bunker. As soon as he entered, a team of people were waiting for him. They took Weatherly and hurried away, leaving Tarney breathless, angry, and defeated.

Rowan asked, "What happened?"

"Weatherly was followed. He led them to the meeting. They waited until I arrived, then attacked." He paused and met his friend's eyes. Never one to display emotion, Rowan was surprised to see the depths of the anguish in Tarney's eyes.

"I took out one, but…it was Mad McGrew. Rowan, she took the girl."

The words hit Rowan like a hammer. Astounded at his friend's failure and shocked by the loss of the young girl, Rowan fell back into a chair, unable to form complete thoughts.

"Rowan, we have to get her back. We have to do something now."

The desperate plea shook Rowan from his depressed fugue.

"Yes. Yes. We have to move fast or the girl will be lost to us forever."

"And Rowan," Tarney added a note of desperation in his tone, "she may know how to reach the other students."

The realization of Tarney's words sunk like a rock to the bottom of his stomach and threatened an aggressive upheaval.

"Oh, dear God, the students. Does she know that information?"

"Unknown. Having traveled from there, she may."

Rowan pushed from the chair and hurried to the table where an unfolded map was laid out.

"We have to locate them fast. What about Weatherly? Is he alive?"

"Yes, but barely. We won't get anything from him for a while, if ever. We have to puzzle this out ourselves, but where to start?"

Tarney joined him at the table.

"Here's where he was," Rowan said, placing a paperweight on top of the area where the academy was located. "We know he isn't in the city. We've got that locked down. No way he gets in without our knowing."

Tarney pointed at a small mountain range north of the city. "We suspected he had a hideout here, but never had the chance to explore to know for sure. The fact of the matter is we don't have the bodies to watch the city and do a thorough search."

"We need allies," said Rowan.

"The best man for that is Kanter. Have we received word from him yet?"

"No. Also nothing from Biatta."

"Could she have gone back through the portal?"

"Doubtful. We are watching it."

"So, the choices are countryside, mountains, or any number of small towns and villages. We need someone with the ability sensitive enough to detect magic."

They remained silent for several minutes as the two men tried to discern a viable location from the limited evidence. Tarney pointed at the paperweight.

"If he was there and escaped on lycanthropes, their range is limited. That might put them in this area here."

He made a circle on the map with his finger."

"Yes, but they have had a full day now. They may have moved several times. If they stayed with their current mode of transportation, that expands the circle to here."

He adjusted the circle with his hand.

"If the lycanthropes stayed with them as transportation, they would avoid populated areas. Too many witnesses. Word would leak. Most of the population is south of the mansion. They moved off northeast."

He pointed to the mountain range.

"That could have been a ruse to make us think they went that way."

"We have nothing else to try. If they are not in this area, at least we eliminated it."

Tarney nodded. "Let's do it."

"Round up whoever is here and send word to anyone not on assignment to join us here."

He pointed at the map at a small town.

"Lithglo?" Tarney queried.

"Yes. We have a bunker there."

"We do? I never heard of it."

"It's not one we have used recently. With our numbers so low, we abandoned it to staff other more central locations."

"It's in a town, though."

"Yes. When it was first developed, we as a group were less conspicuous. It was easier to move about and hide without drawing curious eyes. We can stage from there."

A knock on the door halted further discussion.

"Yes," Rowan said.

The door opened and a short woman with a freckled nose entered.

"Sir, Mister Weatherly is awake and asking for you."

Rowan hastened through the door with Tarney on his heels. Down the hall and to the right, they entered the makeshift hospital room. Weatherly lay on a wooden table with his head propped up. A large white bandage was wrapped around his torso. His haggard face was bruised.

"Master Rowan, you must save the girl."

"We're discussing that now. You should rest."

"No. You don't understand. She was coming here to tell you where the students have been relocated. She has the exact coordinates."

The verification of their fears formed a hard knot in Rowan's stomach. He glanced around the room. He had to act, but they still had a traitor in their ranks. Though he had his suspicions, he didn't yet have the proof. Hopefully, it was coming. Fortunately, that person was not among them just then. He turned his gaze on Tarney.

"We have to move now."

Chapter Twenty-Six

With no knowledge of the area and fear driving her, Daria just ran. She busted through town, and clearing it, settled into a steady pace, one she felt could be maintained for a while.

A glance over her shoulder showed no pursuit, though if Declan had wanted to, she was sure he could have run her down by now. She focused on the road ahead. It appeared to lead straight to the mountains, the very ones she fought against being brought to. As far as she could see, no other path existed. She was not going back, so straight and up were her only options. Perhaps if she reached the top, she might get an idea of where she was.

Along the journey she kept replaying the flames that erupted from her hands. How had that happened? She had never been able to cause that much fire before. Was it because she was able to pull in more energy from her surroundings, or was she just getting stronger? Most likely both. Even though the urgency of escaping should have been foremost on her mind, her curiosity won out. She had to know what she was capable of. True, she only knew a handful of spells and most of those were basic non-defensive or offensive, like lighting a candle, opening a lock, or making lightweight objects levitate. She learned how to make sparks that could start a fire but never was able to create much of a flame. All she did was utter the activation word Biatta used. She wasn't even thinking about fire. She was just angry and tired of being treated like a child, or something to be moved all over. The fire had happened without thought.

She moved off the path and focused on a lone branch working its way out from between two large rocks.

Energy flowed in. She let it sit for a moment before speaking the activation word. Sparks flew from her hand and died as they reached the branch. Disappointed, she dropped her arms and studied her hands. What happened? Or what *didn't* happen?

She tried again, then a third time before giving up. What was different between then and now? She grunted her anger and stomped a foot. Why couldn't she do this?

A noise made her crouch and duck behind a rock. Loose stones rolled. She got lower as voices came clear.

"You sure she came this way?" It was Drumford.

"I am certain," Declan said. The two walked past, heading up the mountain trail. "And I think this is a mistake. She's too out of control. We might get hurt."

Drumford scoffed. "She's not going to hurt anyone. I'll see to that."

"Still, I think we should let her go. We're all better off without her."

"That may be true, but do you want to be the one to tell the sisters we lost her and didn't want to bring her to them anyway?"

"Ah, that would be a big no."

As their voices faded, she stood. Her mind was so wrapped around what she'd heard that she almost missed the extremely soft steps of whoever followed. Daria ducked behind a cluster of rocks and cushioned her landing with her hands. A jagged edge pressed into her palm but Daria stifled the pain. She peered between two rocks and caught sight of one of the greenish people she dined with and the hawk faced girl. The hawk faced girl glanced in her direction but did not slow or stop or show signs of triumph at spotting Daria.

This time, Daria stayed hidden for much longer. When she finally moved and peeked up the trail, it was empty of hikers. She stood by the side of the path deciding what to do. If she went up, she might run into them. Going back meant going through town and the farm, where she might meet resistance to her attempt to leave. She looked around the gradually sloping mountain and made a decision. She was going up but would make her own path.

She traversed the mountain to the right for a distance before starting to climb. The going was much slower, having to move around and over obstacles, but she made steady progress. By the time the sun was directly overhead, Daria had risen high enough to have a great vantage point over the valley.

The mountain across from her was too high to see over. To the left, the golden wheat field was still too far to see past. They must have a lot of grain on hand. She wondered how many people the farm fed. To the right past the fields was a road. In the distance, at the end of the road was something blue. A lake? A river? Perhaps that was the better route to take away from here. She'd have to steal a boat. It was a thought to keep in mind. What she didn't understand was why she turned and started up the mountain again. If she had an alternative to all this climbing, why was she still going up?

The answer, when she realized it, surprised her. She wanted to know who the sisters were and what they wanted with her. It sounded like a stupid reason to her, but she was the one who came up with it, so she climbed. She was still climbing as the sun was setting. She was nowhere near the top. Tired, hungry, thirsty, sweaty, and filthy, Daria sat on a rock to rest.

A look down as sunlight faded from the valley made her realize she was only halfway up the mountain. No man's land. No way was she going to reach the top before dark. The thought of spending the night in the open on the hard ground was not appealing but as she thought about getting up and continuing her ascent, her body rebelled.

"Are you through with your excursion?"

The voice startled her off the rock in a sudden burst. Her feet hit the rocky slope and she tripped. She reached for a large rock but missed and tumbled. As she came to a stop against a large boulder, pain shot through her body.

Daria tried to scramble to her feet, already calling up her newfound power, but her legs gave way and the energy drained as a lance of pain pierced her back. She gasped.

The voice said, "If you are quite done now, perhaps I can take a look at what ails you, both inside and out."

Loose stone cascaded down the hill toward her. Daria pressed into the boulder as if it offered safety. She pushed to her knees and saw the radiant black woman from before descending toward her. Hadn't she been a dream? Maybe Daria had hit her head in the fall and was dreaming now.

The woman landed a few feet away. Her smile looked genuine, her eyes warm and reassuring. With a start, Daria found herself relaxing and instantly went back on the alert, drawing in energy, though the effort pained her.

"There is no need for that, little one. I am not here to hurt you. Let me help you." She stretched a long, slender hand to her, stopping just short of contact.

Daria hesitated. How did the woman know she was drawing power? Was she a wizard? That was a stupid question, she chided herself. She was just flying. Of course she was a wizard. Her eyes met the woman's and she felt all resistance fade away.

Deep within her mind a voice said, *No. Don't let your guard down*, but she was powerless to prevent it.

As if with a mind of its own, her hand lifted and took the woman's. It was warm and comforting, and her body tingled with elation.

"Let me check your injuries before you rise."

Daria did not resist as long, strong fingers probed her flesh. She winced at the contact with her back as the fingers kept moving.

"It appears you have a broken rib, but otherwise, nothing more than a few scrapes and bruises. Would you like me to treat the rib?"

Daria was unsure. She did not know this person but did not sense malicious intent. However, would she? If the woman was a wizard, it might be a trap.

For what purpose, child?

Wait, that voice wasn't hers. She grew panicked again. How was that happening?

Relax, the alien voice in her head said. *If I wanted to harm you, it would be done already, and your skills are not sufficient to stop me. I am asking if you want my help. It is your decision.*

Daria was frightened but tried hard not to show it. Afraid her fear might be apparent if she spoke, she nodded her approval. The woman smiled, placed a hand over the area of the broken rib, and closed her eyes. If she spoke words to activate the spell, Daria could not hear or see. She felt a rush of heat, a quick jolt of pain, then soothing cool. Then, her eyes closed and she slept.

"Well done, child," a voice said from behind the woman.

"That part was easy," the woman replied. "The rest may be a struggle."

"She is in capable hands."

She sighed and stood. "I am still not convinced this is for the best."

"We shall only know once you complete your task."

"You have always been great at giving non-answers."

The man chuckled. "It is a gift."

"One that is not appreciated."

"I am sorry. Please trust me this one last time."

"Until the next one last time."

He chuckled again. "If I am right, what you do here now may make the difference in how we spend the rest of our lives."

"Either way, I fear we will spend our days with one eye looking over a shoulder."

"Perhaps, but it may prove to allow us the freedom to be who we are without worry of reprisals from any source. It is a gamble I am willing to take."

"You are gambling with our lives, so you best be right."

"Time will tell, dear child. Time of which we have so little. Best get on with your task while you still have the freedom to do so."

Kanter stretched out his arms and his body morphed into a large black bird. He pushed off with several powerful thrusts from his luminescent wings, then banked north and disappeared into the fast-approaching night.

The woman glanced at the sleeping girl. "You had better be right, Father," she said to herself. She aimed a palm at Daria and her body lifted from the ground. The woman turned, aimed the other palm at the ground, and rose in the air. She floated toward the mountain top with Daria in tow.

The next few days were going to be interesting, to say the least.

Chapter Twenty-Seven

Jeremy woke with a start. What had roused him? He glanced around the room. Biatta was not in sight. He stood, stretched, and felt his body ache from every possible place. He stifled a groan in case Biatta still slept. He crept down the hall and found a bathroom. He splashed water over his face, scraped his teeth with a fingernail, and tried to rinse out the foul taste in his mouth.

In the hall, he paused to listen at Biatta's door but heard nothing. Thinking her still asleep, he moved silently into the kitchen and began going through cupboards in search of something to eat. He found a box of cereal, a jar of peanut butter, a sleeve of crackers, and a can of coffee with enough grounds left for one pot with one filter. He set about making the coffee, then spread his breakfast on the table before sitting. Mentally, he took half of the crackers and cereal to leave something for Biatta, then opened the jar of peanut butter. An oily film pooled on top of the off-colored paste. He sniffed, scrunched up his nose, and resealed the jar.

He opened the sleeve of crackers and removed one round disc. He took it between his fingers and broke it. The cracker bent before breaking without the snap of freshness. He sighed and slid the crackers beside the peanut butter. Without much hope, he opened the box of already unsealed cereal. The small wheat squares did have some firmness. He squeezed one between his thumb and forefinger and was rewarded with a mild crack. Still unsure about the freshness, he sniffed, then placed a small shred in his mouth. A little stale, but not as bad as the other two options and certainly better than nothing.

He was busy munching when the outer door burst open and several people rushed in. He froze in mid-munch, almost choking on the previous swallow. He tried to stand but his legs rebelled. A thought entered his mind. *Give Biatta a chance.*

He kicked the chair over as he stood. It hit the floor with a loud bang. Jeremy hoped the noise woke her and alerted her to the invasion.

They entered and spread out. He did not recognize any of them. The lead man approached the table. He appeared as wary of Jeremy as he was of him.

"Where's Biatta?" he asked.

The fact he knew her name gave Jeremy pause.

In a louder voice than necessary, he replied, "I have no idea who that is."

The man's mouth twitched in a crooked smile.

"Yes. Of course." He turned and shouted, "Biatta!"

Jeremy grabbed and lifted the next chair at the table as Biatta's voice answered, "Here, Rowan." She rose from a lounge chair and faced the new arrivals.

How did she get there?

To Jeremy, she looked calm; not ready to defend or attack. But then, how did he know what she was doing? Her eyes locked on Jeremy and she smiled.

"Please don't ruin a good chair, Jeremy. He is a friend."

Still confused, Jeremy lowered the chair as the arrivals took turns greeting and embracing Biatta.

"Are you here to rescue us?"

Rowan answered, "No. We didn't know you were here. Let me rephrase that."

"Yes, please do," Biatta said, folding her arms across her chest.

"We thought you might be in the area but didn't know precisely where. Our visit here had a dual purpose. We hoped to find you, but the more important and urgent reason is that Bradenbaugh has abducted one of the students."

Biatta paled and her arms dropped to her sides.

"You mean one of the students from the other world?"

"I'm afraid so."

"But how? Did he find where they were hiding?"

"No, at least I don't think so. But if not, he may soon. He caught the girl here. Jerricka sent her to give us their new location. She knows where they are. Bradenbaugh has her. So..."

"He will know where they are. We have to find her."

"We are working on that now. While we wait, perhaps you can introduce me to your friend."

Biatta moved toward Jeremy.

"Gentlemen, let me introduce Mister Jeremy Kline. Jeremy, this is Rowan Vandalue, Headmaster of our school. That's Professor Wilden, and that's Mister Tarney."

The man introduced as Rowan Vandalue moved forward and offered a hand. Somewhat overwhelmed by the sudden change, Jeremy accepted the hand with caution.

"I am so pleased to meet you, Jeremy. I can call you Jeremy?"

Jeremy shrugged. "It is my name."

The man smiled but had yet to release his hand. "I have heard a lot about you."

"Sorry, but I have heard nothing about you."

Rowan swept his free hand over the table. "Please. Sit. We have much to discuss."

He let go of Jeremy's hand and sat. Jeremy had a strong urge to examine the hand for signs of anything that might have been left behind but managed not to, at least until he bent to pick up the fallen chair. To his relief, he found nothing. He set the chair upright and sat. Biatta took the chair to his right. The professor took the one to the left.

Tarney stood back with his arms folded his dark eyes boring deep into Jeremy.

Jeremy turned to Biatta. "Perhaps it's time you explained what is going on."

She smiled and placed a hand over his. On reflex, he pulled it back. He saw the hurt and disappointment in her eyes but didn't care. Enough was enough. She would either tell him the entire story now, or he was done. He had no idea where to go since he had no clue where he was, but he vowed to himself to wash his hands of her and whatever she had gotten him involved in and leave.

"As I started to tell you before, we are not from your world. In fact, you are no longer in your world. The being you call the goat head man carried you through the portal to this world. He is a minion of the man responsible for our current situations. He captured you, we think, because of your involvement with me. I doubt he has or had any idea of your importance."

"What is my importance? If what you say is true, and I certainly have my doubts, and I *am* in a different world, how can I have any importance at all?" Jeremy was aware his tone of voice was snappish, but he didn't care. He was angry with Biatta for upsetting his quiet, normal life.

Sensing a problem between Jeremy and Biatta, Rowan took over the narration.

"Jeremy, this story goes back several generations. We have always lived in peaceful coexistence with who we call the normals of this world."

"Normals?" Jeremy asked.

Biatta answered, "The non-magic users."

Rowan continued. "The primary reason was that we never used magic in front of them. To do so might give rise to panic and fear. Those unable to use magic do not, cannot understand it. When facing an unknown, people tend to fear the worst and want it destroyed, so we thought it best to keep that part of our lives hidden.

"We created the school as a means to not only train those with magical abilities but to keep them away from normals who might see them as an enemy. We existed for more than a hundred years before the first rise of serious opposition came. A previous headmaster of the school, Everill Leguine, began experimenting with what we call dark magic. It brought him new, serious, and extremely unstable powers. Those powers eventually eroded his good sense and he began using his magic openly and encouraged others to do so as well. He scoffed at the notion that normals couldn't handle knowing magic existed. He theorized that the more they witnessed magic, the quicker they might come to accept it."

The man introduced as Tarney said, "He also didn't care if the sight of someone performing magic upset them. He had the power, so what did he care? No normal could stop him or stand against him."

Rowan nodded and took over again. "People did begin to notice and did take exception, organizing mass revolts striking down those they suspected as magic users."

"As you said before, much the same way the Salem witch hunts worked in your world," Biatta added.

Jeremy didn't look at her as she spoke.

Rowan went on. "Consequently, a rift occurred between this man and his followers and those of us who wanted to keep the peace and find a way to ease the fears of the normals. As this man became ever more powerful, he lost much of his humanity and declared war on the normals and any who stood against them. A violent and deadly war began that lasted almost ten years before the magic using tribes of our world united and destroyed the evil self-proclaimed lord and his minions. Then several things occurred. One, the most important of those, was Leguine was not destroyed. He had become so powerful that even the combined might of the strongest wizards in our world was not enough to kill him. He was weakened, and rather than risk his recovery, he was imprisoned in a magic vault before he was ended. That meant a possibility always existed that one day he may somehow break free of that prison and become a threat again."

"Has that happened?" Jeremy asked.

The professor responded, "Not yet, but that is the goal of those we oppose now."

"The self-titled Lord Bradenbaugh," Rowan said, "whom you were briefly a guest of, has taken it upon himself to break the Leguine free. That is the conflict you currently find yourself in."

"How nice for me," Jeremy said with an icy tone. "That still doesn't explain how it involves me."

"No, it doesn't," Rowan said, "and to be honest, I'm not sure how you got involved. The only thing I know is what Biatta has told us."

Jeremy turned to Biatta and observed her through emotionless eyes.

"Did you know all along and plot to involve me, or was I just some patsy who was convenient for you to use?"

Biatta recoiled from the words. "Jeremy, I had no intention of using you. I am sorry if you think that. I only got involved when my suspicions were piqued by what you were able to do."

"And what did I do that was so spectacular that you were drawn to me?"

He could see the hurt in her eyes but was unphased. Her presence in his life had caused pain and destruction, not to mention the alienation of his daughter.

"Jeremy," Rowan said. "Your obvious resentment of Biatta is misplaced. I am sorry you were brought into this, but it is not her fault."

"Then whose fault is it? Yours?"

"Hey, bud," Tarney said, taking a threatening step toward the table. "No one here deserves your hostility.

You have no idea what we have gone through just to survive."

Jeremy burst from his chair and slammed his palms on the table.

"Then why don't you explain it to me, because from where I'm sitting, *my* life is the one that has been disrupted."

Jeremy was surprised at the vehemence of his response and the rage that roiled within his core. He had the uncharacteristic desire to lash out at someone. To his surprise, Tarney went wide-eyed and took a step back. As the heat ebbed, Jeremy glanced around the table and saw surprise on everyone's faces.

"I've had enough," he said. "Someone point me toward my home, and I will remove myself from whatever this war is. I want no further part in any of it."

He shoved the chair back and made to move but the gentle calming touch of Biatta's hand on his arm paused him. He looked at the hand then followed it up her arm to her face. A pleading expression filled her eyes.

"Please, Jeremy. Hear them out. If afterward you still want to leave, I promise you will never hear from or see us again. If you want to hate me, I understand. But take your anger out on me, not them."

Chapter Twenty-Eight

The anger faded as fast as it came, leaving him embarrassed and somewhat weak. He blew out a long breath. "All right. I'll listen but make it quick."

He pulled the chair in and sat, placing his attention on Rowan. Biatta slid her hand from his arm and pulled it slowly back across the table like a recoiling snake.

Rowan turned to Tarney.

"Would you ask one of our people to find food and drinks for us, please? Perhaps some tea?"

A red flash lit Tarney's eyes, but he nodded, turned, and left the room. Rowan brought his attention back to Jeremy.

"Anyway, after the war ended, it took a long time to make the normals feel secure. We withdrew from the public eye, determined to let all their fears fade until they were nothing more than myths and fairy tales told to children late at night.

"One of the outlying tribes from the other side of the mountain range was not happy about hiding. Once out in the open, they believed they should stay that way and work to ease the normals' fears and allow them to see us for who and what we were. They…well, their leader thought in time they would come to accept us, and with that acceptance would come peaceful coexistence.

"After much debate it was decided that though the idea had merit, it would be tabled for a time to allow the normals to return to their peaceful and secure lives before an attempt was made to connect with them. However, this leader, Salemnon—"

At the mention of the name, Jeremy flicked a glance at Biatta. She had mentioned that name before; had in fact, asked if he knew the name.

"—was not satisfied with that decision," Rowan continued. "He caused an uprising that had to be quelled before it once again spilled over into the normals' lives, thus setting back any chance to reconcile with them. A short battle ensued and Salemnon and his remaining followers disappeared through a portal that none of us had ever seen before. It vanished, and though much effort was made to find them, we never knew what happened to them. Perhaps until now."

He shot a look toward Biatta, who picked up the story.

"To be clear," Biatta said, "you were not singled out or used in any way. If that is how you felt, I apologize. It was unintentional. When you first discovered Daria, it was accidental. You had no idea who we were, and we certainly did not know you. The first time you stumbled into our village, we thought it a fluke. We erased your memory of the visit and returned you to your world. However, when you found your way back and could see us despite powerful magic that obscured the entire village and everyone within it from the sight of all normals, I became suspicious there was more to you than we understood. That is why I got involved.

"Later, when your actions—even though you weren't trying—caused the death of one of the Harpy's killer boars, my suspicions were confirmed. That is why Daria and I moved in with you. One, to protect you; and two, to learn more about you. During our stay, I discovered your grandson has some raw, untrained power. Then, your son came to the door. He was in the midst of an unsettling vision that sapped my powers and left me unconscious. Though I stabilized him, the effort took a huge toll on me, one that should have never occurred with a normal healing.

"Magical ability runs through your family. It is a part of your being. My conclusion is that you are a member of the lost tribe. The fact that you cannot remember much of your history reinforces that belief. The best way to stay hidden in the new world was to erase memories that might make you noticed. Why Salemnon would want to do that after leaving our world because he wanted to be known is a mystery we may never solve."

She went quiet for a moment, leaving him to digest what she said.

Could any of it be true? No. How could it be?

Yet he gazed from face to face and saw they all believed the story.

"Jeremy," Biatta said, "you are untrained and cannot feel it, but when you were angry and stood, we all felt it."

Confused, he asked, "Felt what?"

"You drew in energy. The energy used to perform magic."

The words shocked him. *What was she talking about?* He glanced at Rowan and the professor. They both nodded in agreement.

He shook his head. "That isn't possible. I didn't feel any different."

"Yet you were," she said. "You remember feeling angry?"

"Yes, but that—"

"Do you remember feeling brave or powerful, like you held no regard for the consequences of squaring up to Tarney?"

He wasn't sure. If he did feel like that, he hadn't noticed.

"Let me answer for you. The Jeremy I know would never have lost his temper like that. You are too calm, too peaceful. Yet, here you were, ready to take on one of our most powerful practitioners without pause or thought."

He had to admit that was not like him at all. Sure, he got angry, but seldom ever let it show. He did remember feeling like he wanted to thrash the man. He also remembered the reflective step backward he took. In Jeremy's entire life he had never confronted anyone with enough venom in his words to make an opponent back off.

Biatta spoke to Rowan. "I wonder if this sudden burst of energy is because there is less power to draw in his world compared to ours. I can still perform magic there but it does take more effort to draw in the necessary energy and expel it."

Rowan nodded. "Does he even know where the energy comes from?"

"I don't think so."

"Hey," Jeremy said. "I'm right here. Don't talk about me as if I'm some child who is beyond understanding."

No one spoke, giving him time to calm and to mull over what he heard. He took advantage of the reprieve to reexamine some of what was said, settling on one key point that had been passed over. He turned his attention on Rowan.

"Earlier, you said *one, and most important* when talking about this Leguine person. What else?"

It took a moment for Rowan to find his place.

"Ah, yes. This part is the reason you are so important to us. Before we were able to trap and seal the dark one in his prison, he went to an even darker, ancient, and evil place, where he found, and cast a spell with such intensity and hatred it would change our world forever. Though I was there to witness the release, we had no idea of the end result until years later.

"You see, in our world, men were the ones who held most of the magical ability. Women had magical ability, but for whatever reason, it was minor compared to men's. It wasn't by design, though many had researched the reason. I digress. Over the next few years, it became apparent that fewer males were born with any magical skill. After a decade, not one was born. Women were still born with power, but not greater power than before.

"As the men died off over the next few years, women stepped in to fill roles traditionally held by men. The more they got involved, the more their power increased until they became the dominant magic users. Over the past three decades, not one male has been born with even a trace of magic. Consequently, only a handful of men who can wield magic are left. However long it took for the evil lord's last spell to take effect, the tribe of Salemnon may have escaped before it took root within the men. If that is true, then it is still possible to reintroduce magic to this world by integrating those members—your family—back into our world."

The professor said, "It might take several generations to make a difference, but it may be our only hope at repopulating our brotherhood and sisterhood."

"So, what do you expect of me? To be some universal sperm donor?"

Rowan smiled broadly.

"Honestly, we haven't thought that far ahead. The first step is to determine if indeed you have any magical ability."

"And how do we determine that without making me an experimental lab rat?"

"It is simple. We want to train you. If you can use spells, it tells us what we need to know and we can go from there."

"And if not?" Jeremy asked.

Rowan shrugged. "Then you don't and we'll help you get back to your world and your life."

"But if I do, you want me to stay and help with your problem."

"Yes, we would like that, but you are not under any obligation to do so, nor will you be forced to. If you are not interested, we may be able to trace your family line and perhaps find others who are willing to help."

Jeremy said, "This all seems so farfetched. It can't be possible. Magic doesn't exist."

"But it does," said the professor.

"I think you have seen enough evidence of that to be a believer," Rowan said.

"It can't be possible that I'm who you're looking for."

"It is," Biatta said. "You have the ability. I am positive. I have felt it within you. You are a member of the lost tribe. As much as you might hate me now and think that I have lied to you or used you, know that much is true. You are one of us."

Her final statement hung in the air as if a curtain of silence. No one spoke until the door opened and Tarney rushed in.

"We've got company coming. A group of armed men are scouring the town. There can be only one reason. They are looking for us."

Chapter Twenty-Nine

With a dozen well-armed and highly trained special operators, Colonel Carpenter felt confident in his mission. As they searched the town of Lithglo in the predawn hours, he positioned his men like he was a football coach assigning search grids to four three-man teams.

One of the three targets they had located and were tracking made a sudden departure from the city. The target met with two others on the road. As it became apparent they had a specific location and a definite purpose in mind, the team was assembled and dispatched. Now they were attempting to locate the three individuals who seemed to have disappeared.

The search area had narrowed to a four square-block grid. Doors were being knocked on and local residents questioned but as yet, they had no leads. The three they searched for were either hiding someplace unoccupied or someone here was hiding them. Either way, they would be found and an example made of them. A message sent. Perhaps he'd even make an example of whoever was aiding them. After all there were terrorists and needed to be put down before they attacked.

One of his men jogged over to him. "Sir, one of the locals, an early riser, noticed some people going down the street to the west at about five this morning."

"How many people?"

"He wasn't sure but thought it was five, maybe six. All men, he thought."

Now Carpenter had a decision to make. Was that the group they were tracking? If so, it had grown, providing the witness was correct, which in his experience wasn't often. Perhaps they had met up with another group, or the witness was trying to throw them off track by sending them in the wrong direction.

"Have you searched the man's residence?"

"No sir."

"Do so and question him again to make sure he is telling the truth."

After the man left, Carpenter contacted his team through the radios in their helmets.

"Be advised. There was a possible sighting to the west. If it is our prey, the group may have grown. Take whatever actions you deem necessary, but I want at least two of them alive."

Three of his team leaders acknowledged.

He called, "Team three do you acknowledge?"

No reply.

He tried again. "Team three."

When nothing happened this time, he felt the rising surge of panic followed by rush of adrenaline.

"Teams one and four, merge on team three's previous location. Team two, on me."

Since they were on alert, he received three clicks instead of verbal responses. He moved toward team three's last known position as team two joined him. "I want you two to go down the next street and move toward team three's location. Watch for anyone. I mean anyone, local or otherwise, moving on the streets. Stop and identify and send them inside. You come with me. We'll take this street."

The first group jogged toward their assigned street but one stopped halfway there.

"Sir, what about the alley?"

"Alley?" Carpenter replied.

The man pointed. "Yes sir. If we each take a block, they could avoid us by coming down the alley."

Carpenter moved to join the man. A narrow walkway ran the distance between the backs of the buildings on the regular streets. "Good catch, soldier. You come with me. You other two continue down your assigned streets."

Carpenter led the way, his weapon at firing ready. His teammate followed eight feet behind, scanning high on both sides with an occasional glance behind. The six-foot-wide passageway was clear through to the far end with no trash cans, dumpsters, and very little trash. The walls were solid. The only windows were at the second-story level.

They came to a heavy metal security door on the right. It had no external handle or knob. He pushed on it, then withdrew a large knife from a scabbard on his belt, slid it between the seam and tried to pry it open. It was sealed tight. He moved on.

Ten yards in front of him something moved. The wall appeared to shimmer then a woman stepped into view. Stunned, he didn't react until he heard his partner scream over his shoulder.

"You freeze right there, or I will riddle you full of holes!"

Carpenter snapped from his shock and leveled his weapon at the startled woman. She backed a step and raised her hands.

"Please don't shoot."

Carpenter advanced. "Where did you come from?"

The woman offered no reply.

Carpenter stopped at the spot where she exited. No door existed. He touched the wall. Solid. How had she managed to get through? In the back of his mind, Lord Drewmore's words came back to him from the day he was first recruited for this team.

Watch yourself, Colonel. They claim to be magicians, wizards, if you will, able to cast spells, as if such things were real. The truth is, they are dangerous and deceitful

*tricksters. Terrorists. Their sole purpose is to breed
mistrust and spread misinformation. Their goal is bring
about disorder and chaos and to destroy our way of life.
You may see things beyond belief, but that is how they
fool you. They rely on illusions to shock and distract you
while they move in for the kill.*

Carpenter thought it was a damn good illusion if this
was one. He looked at the woman. How she managed it
was not important, but he vowed while torturing her he
would get the answer.

"Where are the others?"

"Others, sir? What others? You can see I am alone."

He stepped forward and clipped her on the side of her
head with the butt of his weapon. She bounced off the
wall with a yelp and went down.

"You will tell me, or your last minutes on this Earth will
be filled with pain."

"We took one of their teams out, but they captured
Mia," a young woman said, poking her head inside the
room.

"Is it Bradenbaugh?" Wilden asked.

"They look like soldiers. Two men are in the alley. They
threatened to harm Mia if she doesn't give us up."

With fire in his eyes, Tarney said, "We must act now."

"Agreed," Rowan said, "but not irrationally. I want
some alive. We have to know who is behind this."

"Leave it to me," Tarney said and moved toward the
door.

"Tarney!" Rowan called. Tarney stopped but did not
look back. "Do not get yourself or others killed by your
rash actions."

He left without a word.

Rowan turned to Biatta. "Stay with our friend." To
Wilden, he said, "Professor, set some defenses to keep

this room safe. You others." He motioned to the three that had joined them. "Come with me."

After they were gone, Wilden moved to the door and went through a series of gestures that held Jeremy's attention. Biatta touched his arm.

"Come with me."

She led to the bedroom she had occupied the previous night. Once inside, she closed the door, sat on the edge of the bed, and motioned for him to join her. He hesitated but she gave that look of irritation she used when someone said or did something absurd. He sat.

"This will not be easy for you, but I want to put you through a series of basic lessons that may bring forth some of your innate ability. This will be good to know, should you need to protect yourself."

"What is going on?"

"To be honest, I'm not sure. Now please, Jeremy, this is important. Concentrate. I need you to relax. Take several deep breaths. Close your eyes. Pretend you are going on a journey through your body. Where would you go to find the best memories of your life?"

"My brain. Where else?"

"Shh. Just listen. Go there. Walk through those wonderful memories. They bring joy, satisfaction, warmth. Those are valuable emotions to call on when using certain types of magic."

He opened his eyes and looked at her. She was so serene. She emanated warmth, compassion. Love. She was beautiful. As soon as the thought entered his mind, guilt shoved it to the side.

I'm sorry, Miranda. I didn't mean it like that. I promise.

"Jeremy." She placed her palms on his knees. The warmth seeped through his pants. "You must concentrate. This is for your own benefit. Whatever that last thought was is counterproductive to what you are trying to do."

"I'm sorry, Biatta. I just don't know that I believe in all this talk about magic or that I'm an ancestor of some long-lost tribe of wizards."

She sighed. She closed her eyes, held out her hands palm up. He leaned closer. A tiny seed lay on her palm. She whispered something. Like time-lapse photography, a tiny blue flower bloomed in each palm.

He gasped in surprise. As he watched, the flowers grew, sprouted buds, and bloomed more flowers. Each new one that opened was a different brilliant color. He was enthralled and reached to touch one. He stopped short of contact. If it was an illusion, he didn't want to spoil it.

Then, something changed. The flowers appeared to writhe on her hands as if in pain. He glanced at her face. Gone was the radiant beauty, replaced by a dark-featured, hard-eyed woman with malice on her face. The flowers wilted, dried, and fell away. Vines stretched across her hands, then wrapped around them. One sprung forward, catching Jeremy's hand. In a panic, he tried to shake it free, but it stuck and began to curl around his wrist.

He ripped it free with his other hand, but another vine shot out and snagged his thumb. He reached to tear that away, but the first vine had regrown and now had a hold on his right hand. Before he could break free, both vines wound around him, binding both hands together.

Fear took hold and he fought hard to break free. The vines continued up his arms. His heart raced to almost bursting through his chest. The vines climbed fast, reaching his shoulders, then his neck. As the first one curled around his neck, he screamed.

"Biatta! Stop!"

With a sudden poof, they vanished as if they never existed.

Jeremy touched his neck then his arms. Had it been real, or was it some form of hypnosis?

"Do you believe in magic now?"

No sign of her evil twin existed. The sweet, warm, and caring beauty was back.

Chapter Thirty

A growl and a sudden scream had Carpenter whirling, forgetting about the bloody heap he'd left the woman in. A large black dog or wolf, he couldn't tell which, had his man by the throat and was thrashing its head back and forth. The man triggered his weapon as he died, spraying bullets around the alley, ricocheting dangerously close. Carpenter was forced to duck, which took his weapon off target.

He quickly adjusted as the last rounds pinged off the brick, and he turned his weapon on the beast. The animal turned hateful eyes on him, its bloody maw sending a chill down his spine. It took one step toward him. He pressed the trigger but it broke as a searing pain lanced through his back. He arced backward throwing the shot upward, well off target.

He fell, unable to move but still aware. *Had he been tazed?* The dog crept over him but he had no feeling of the beast's weight. Its foul breath filled his nostrils, creating an urge to vomit. Saliva and the blood of his fallen soldier dripped onto his face. He fought to make his muscles move to bring the gun on target, but they refused to respond. *What had they done to him?*

Another figure came into view. It was a woman with a bloody, slightly misshapen face. He recognized her. She was the woman he had beaten. She stood over him now as he lay unable to protect himself. Her eyes flashed with fiery rage. The beast hopped off his chest, which was a relief. Perhaps the beast knew what was coming when the woman began to huff and puff, inflating and deflating her chest in rapid breaths, and moved for its own safety.

The woman screamed and fired exploded from her mouth like some medieval dragon. The flames licked at his face. Though he did not feel pain, the smell of burnt flesh wafted up, forcing the foul breath farther down his airway. Now he did gag as bile and vomit filled his mouth. He knew he was choking, though he could not feel it. Maybe that was for the best.

Rowan led the other three out onto the street and toward the sound of automatic weapon fire. A gout of flame spewed between two buildings. Black smoke rose into the air. Something was burning.

They rounded a corner and were met by a scream. A man engulfed in fire rolled violently across the ground flailing wildly to put the flames out before they consumed him. Rowan showed mercy and shot a bolt of pure energy into the man's head, stilling him.

"Spread out, but work in pairs," he said to the others.

Two younger women ran off toward the next street while the older of the three women joined him. They advanced down the street. The gunfire had lessened. How many of the attackers were left? If at all possible, he had to keep some of them alive.

He motioned for the woman to come.

"Mara, you take the man closest. I'll take the other. I want them alive."

"Alive?"

"Yes. We need to know who sent them."

Mara did not look happy but nodded. They readied their spells and cast them together. The man Rowan aimed at fell forward, asleep. Mara had a different thought about subduing her target. She slammed his head into the brick wall once, then a second time to be sure he was out. He was. He dropped hard to the ground.

After some instruction, the two men were lifted and carried back to the narrow alley. Before entering the secret doorway, Rowan created a fog to obscure the alley from curious onlookers. By the time it cleared, they were inside.

"Lord Bradenbaugh!" Quentin entered the room in haste.

Bradenbaugh was not happy about yet another interruption. The captured girl was just beginning to give up her treasure trove of information, thanks to the cocktail of drugs and the mind reading spell cast by Madelyn. The woman may be mad, but she did prove useful.

"What now, Quentin?"

"There is a battle being waged in the middle of town."

"Battle? What kind of battle? Our people say it is between a group of soldiers and some of Vandalue's people."

That got his attention. "So, they think to rescue this one, too? Call the wolves and send them into town."

"Do you want me to give instructions about leaving the townspeople alone?"

"I don't care. Tell them to kill whoever gets in their way. I want Vandalue's people killed. Take one of them prisoner. We need to know how everything fits together. Then put a call out for forces to meet at the portal to invade another world."

Quentin turned and hurried from the room.

"How much longer?" he asked Madelyn.

Her wicked smile only added to her overall look of insanity.

"Not long." She grabbed the girl's jaw and squeezed, puckering her lips. "Then you'll tell Auntie Madelyn everything, won't you, sweetie?"

She pecked the girls lips, then released her face. The girl's head lolled to the side. A thin line of drool stretched toward the floor.

"Call me when it's time. I want to see what's going on in town."

The two unconscious soldiers were put on the floor. Another man with a melted face was already there. Tarney exited the bathroom wiping his face with a towel. Biatta was not in sight. Wilden was sitting at the kitchen table. A few others were scattered about the room. One was having a bullet wound tended to.

"Where's Margarite?" Rowan asked.

A woman named Dela said, "She didn't make it, sir."

The news of yet another loss staggered Rowan. He sought the support of a chair and hung his head. "Where's the body?"

"In one of the other rooms. We weren't leaving her behind."

He nodded his approval. "And the others?"

Tarney responded, "I set them on guard duty."

Rowan said, "Did we get them all?"

"Yes," Tarney said. "A total of twelve plus management." He nodded with his chin toward the man with the melted face.

"And their bodies?"

"I vanished them."

"He was in charge?"

"Yep."

"Will he survive?"

"If you ask Biatta to stabilize him."

As if he knew they were talking about him, the leader's eyes fluttered open. He glanced around, the good soldier gathering information, then his face contorted.

"The immobilization spell is wearing off. He's feeling pain now."

"Mara," Rowan said, "Get Biatta out here, please."

The woman went down the hall. A minute later, she returned with Biatta. Jeremy trailed.

"Biatta, I know how sensitive you are about causing pain to others, but I need to question this man." He pointed to the leader. "He will not be able to respond through the increasing pain he will be feeling. I need you to ease his pain, but only for a short time. If he cooperates, you can soothe or even heal him, but I need the information he has to find our missing student."

The girl's recovery, though important, was not foremost in his request. He needed the name of the person who'd sent the soldiers after them. If it was Bradenbaugh, he needed to know where he was. If not, it was important to determine who else was a player in this war before they were taken by surprise. He used the girl and her possible fate in the hands of Bradenbaugh to elicit cooperation from Biatta. He knew how she hated to cause pain even to an enemy.

She eyed him with suspicion. He thought, *She knows what I am doing.*

Still, she knelt at the burned man, placed a hand a few inches over his face, and called up her skills. The palm of her hand glowed. If the man noticed, he was in too much pain to do anything about her being so close. In seconds, he stopped writhing and moaning. The tension in his face eased and his eyes focused.

Rowan dragged a kitchen chair next to the man and sat backward in it, his arms resting on the chairback. He looked down at the man for a minute before saying, "You are in bad shape. For the moment, I am allowing this kind woman to ease your pain, but it will return, and each time will be more severe than the previous time. The level of pain you receive or the lack depends wholly on your cooperation. I need answers. You have them. It's a simple exchange."

Through gritted teeth the leader said, "I'm not telling you shit."

"Well, let's be clear. You will. You'll tell me everything I want to know and add a bunch of things I don't want to know, just to keep from feeling the pain you are about to endure. Your face is melted. I have someone here who can heal you and bring your face completely back to normal as long as you talk. If you don't, you'll look like that for the rest of your life. Your time as an operator will be over. The choice is yours."

"That's crap. Just lies to get me to talk. Not happening. You're nothing but terrorists." He began to fidget

"Ah, the pain is returning. Terrorists. That's interesting. You know nothing about us but have labeled us terrorists. Who told you that's what we are?"

No response.

"All I need to know for the pain to vanish is who sent you and what was your mission."

"My mission," he gasped, "is to kill all you weirdos."

"What defines a weirdo?"

"All you crazies who think you can perform magic."

"You don't believe in magic?"

"Hardly. It's a ruse to so you can destroy our people."

"And how do you come by the knowledge that magic does not exist?"

"This isn't some bloody fairy tale. Anyone who thinks magic is real is off their nut."

"What if I can prove to you magic is real?"

"Never happen."

"You are that sure?"

He grimaced. New beads of sweat formed on his face.

"So, since we are all off our nut, as you say, what were you planning to do with us?"

"Wipe you out."

"Just like that? Eliminate us without knowing anything about us."

"That's right. You're terrorists. A danger to everything we hold dear."

"So, I might as well kill you then, since we are terrorists."

He grunted and was having more trouble controlling the pain. "Do what you must."

"You are quite prepared to die without understanding why?"

"I'm a soldier. I follow orders."

"I understand that. The question I have is whose orders you are following."

He didn't respond.

"So, you don't believe in magic but you are willing to work for Bradenbaugh, a man who uses dark magic. Are you under his spell?"

His pain was too great to speak. He rolled from side to side and groaned in a constant rumble.

"I will ease your pain for one answer."

His voice began to edge into the scream level.

"Can you hear me?"

"Rowan," Biatta said. "Please."

He frowned and nodded. She performed another spell and the soldier's muscles relaxed and his body straightened.

"What are you giving me? Morphine?"

Biatta smiled. "No. Something much less addictive."

In a flash, the man sat up, snatched Biatta to him, and placed a knife to her throat.

"You will let me and my men go, or I will rip her throat open."

Chapter Thirty-One

Bradenbaugh rode the back of the leader of his lycanthropes. Feralto, the biggest and strongest of the pack. There were seven beasts in the pack, five male and two female. They swarmed through the small forest, then raced through the open countryside toward the town of Lithglo.

Two of Bradenbaugh's people were in the town already watching and marking where Vandalue's people were. Once in town, the huge beasts would be difficult to hide, so he decided not to bother. When they reached the outskirts of Lithglo, he would dismount, send them hunting, and then follow to kick through the carnage.

He doubted any of the beasts could take down Vandalue. His power was too great, but all they had to do was keep him occupied so he could do the job himself.

They crested a small rise. Lithglo was in view. He called a halt and hopped down.

"Remember, Feralto. I want a few alive. I don't care which."

Feralto growled his understanding and the pack loped off. Bradenbaugh joined his team of wizards and minions, a group eleven strong. He had no idea how many people Vandalue had with him but from the initial reports, it was far less than he brought.

He vibrated with energy and excitement as he anticipated bringing this war to an end. With their leader dead, the others would fold and flee. If they escaped, no matter. Once he had control of the land, he'd send his people to hunt down the stragglers later. For now, the thought of ending Vandalue had him giddy.

The lycanthropes diminished in size as they neared the town. His group walked on. It dawned on him then that he should have ridden them closer to the town before disembarking. They still had a ways to go. He might miss most of the action if he didn't hurry. Without speaking he increased his pace, knowing the others would adjust and keep up.

Before the situation could be resolved, the door burst open. The soldier jumped, nicking Biatta's throat. A drop of blood formed and tracked down her pure porcelain skin.

"Sir, a pack of lycanthropes is approaching town at a run."

"Quick! Everyone outside!" Tarney bellowed. "Get up high and ready your best offensive spells. They are not easy to take down. Work as teams. Remember your lore. Wolfsbane, decapitation, removing the heart."

One of the others said, "And silver."

"No, you fool. That is a rumor started by werewolves. Silver heals them. Now go and prepare."

They all hurried for the door.

The soldier yelled. "Hey. Hey. No one moves or this woman dies."

Rowan stood and glared at the man. "We don't have time for you." He looked at Biatta. "Are you all right?"

"Yes. Go. I'll join you in a moment."

"What?" the soldier asked. "No, you won't. Wait. I swear, I'll slice her from ear to ear."

"We have more pressing things to deal with than you," Rowan said.

"Are you kidding me? Your life is on the line here and they abandon you? What kind of people are you involved with?" He gasped. His hand jerked but this time, the blade did not prick the skin.

"The pain is returning. It will get much worse unless you let me treat you."

"No. You're my leverage to get my team out of here."

A loud crash dropped the knife from her throat. She turned to see Jeremy standing there holding the remnants of a lamp. "You didn't have to do that. I had it under control."

Jeremy stared, dumbfounded.

She stood and brushed herself off, then glanced down at the unconscious soldier. A thin line of blood traced down his face. "Pick up the knife please, Jeremy."

He did so.

"I must go help the others. You should stay here where it is safe."

He looked around at the three soldiers. "Safe?"

"They won't bother you." She aimed a hand at the two sleeping soldiers. If something happened, he didn't see what. Then she squatted next to the leader and placed a hand on his head. A bluish glow emanated from her hand. He groaned. She lifted him to a sitting position, then stood. After mumbling a few words, his body rose from the floor and stood upright with his feet hovering just above the floor.

"I'll take this one with me. The other two will sleep for a long while. Stay here and practice what I taught you."

With that, Biatta and her soldier escort left the room.

Rowan stood on the tallest building in that area of town. That put him four stories up. A wave of dark fur approached from the west not more than a quarter mile from the outskirts. He feared for his people but more so for the townsfolk. At least his people had a fighting chance. He turned to find the professor, who was standing two buildings over on a three-story level.

"Wilden!"

The older man looked around until he spotted Rowan waving his arms.

"We have to make sure the townspeople are inside and safe."

"Already being done."

That was a relief. Now he could concentrate on the battle to come. He looked around, taking note of the positions of the others. They covered five building tops, no fewer than three on each. He fixed his gaze on the advancing line now only fifty yards from town. Movement farther up the countryside drew his attention. He squinted to make out details. It was a second wave, this one consisting of humans. That meant magic users. Unless his vision was failing him, it appeared Bradenbaugh was leading the way. That made a world of difference. He was sure they could handle the lycanthropes, though not without taking some losses, but with a magical attack to support the first wave, survival was doubtful.

Was this the final battle? What to do to swing the advantage his way? He pulled up a spell and cast it to the wind. He doubted any who received the message would arrive in time, but at least someone will be aware of what transpired. He needed to find a way to slow Bradenbaugh's approach until the wolves were dealt with.

As the wolves disappeared behind the first row of buildings, he glanced around and found Biatta next to him. To his surprise, she had the soldier with her. She was speaking to him and pointing. His jaw had dropped. Rowan assumed she was showing him the wolves.

Howling rose above the buildings as the creatures searched for a scent. Then one shifted to a different tone and the others joined in. They were coming. He turned to Biatta.

"Bradenbaugh is coming. Can you do anything to slow him down?"

She smiled. "If you can look after our guest."

Rowan shifted his gaze.

"He will be on his best behavior." She faced the soldier. "Won't you?"

He seemed incapable of speech. "If you still have doubts, watch. I don't usually do this with people watching. I'm a little self-conscious and for a moment, I'm…well, never mind. Maybe you won't notice. Stay here."

Biatta walked to the other side of the building. Her lips moved as she fumbled something from a hidden pocket. The air around her thickened and swirled. For an instant she stood naked within the small whirlwind before vanishing. In her place was a large white owl. The bird cocked its head and looked at the soldier. He rocked back as if hit by a physical blow.

The owl lifted off and flew ever higher before banking.

Rowan came up next to the man.

"Still think magic is fake?"

"I-I don't know what to think."

"Keep an open mind before you pass judgment on us. Someone has lied to you. Someone is using you for their own gain or purpose. We are not your enemy, or you would be dead by now. All I ask of you is a name. Then you and your man are free to go."

The man was giving that some thought when the first attack began.

Chapter Thirty-Two

Daria woke with a jolt. Unseeing, she said, "Trouble. Wolves. Help."

"Interesting, sister," the black woman said. "She received the same message we did, but in her sleep."

Her sister, an identical twin, rocked in her wooden chair and continued her knitting without pause.

"Yes, quite interesting. She is quite attuned and very sensitive to the stream. I hate to admit it, but our father may be right again."

The other woman laughed. "Don't tell him. He will only gloat."

Daria swung her legs over the edge of the bed. Her eyes were still distant. "Must help." She stood.

"No, little sister. Their fight is not ours," the first woman said. She waved a hand toward her. "Go back to sleep."

"Sleep," Daria said, and lifted her feet back on the bed. She settled and in seconds, the soft rhythmic cadence of her breathing could be heard.

The second woman said, "I look forward to working with her."

"Yes," her sister replied. "But her training has been lax, and she has a strong sense of loyalty to those who do not deserve it."

"She is young and doesn't know any better yet."

"Oh, but she will."

They laughed.

Biatta flew wide of the advancing line of magic users before landing. She couldn't draw enough energy to perform the spell she wished to use while in her alternate form. As soon as her feet touched the ground and her morph was complete, she was moving and drawing energy from the Earth.

She stopped at the tree line to locate her quarry. Before they came into view, she was already weaving the spell. As the first leg of the running line came into sight, she thrust her hands into the ground and released the magic. Her body stiffened as she became one with the living beings that took life from the Earth. They listened, recognized her as one of them, accepted her request, and began to move.

It took several moments for the magical message to spread to the site, but then things happened fast. First the grass in front of the advancing humans thickened, the blades slapping against boots. They had little noticeable effect on the runners other than to slow their pace a fraction. Weeds sprouted next. Rough leaves, and prickly thorns latched onto to pant legs, piercing the material, then the flesh. The runners noticed.

Their speed diminished as a multitude of tiny pinpricks grew into sharper pain. The vines came next. Thin ropes of tough leafy strands raced toward the now slowed forms. As they swatted and ripped at the weeds, the vines overtook them and began to climb their legs.

The group was forced together in a tight circle. Bradenbaugh was the first to react, recognizing the magic for what it was. He cast a spell and a gout of black fire ran in a circle around the group, withering all non-human life it contacted.

Unbidden by Biatta, nature revolted against the attack. Enraged by the loss of its children, the Earth upheaved and tossed the humans to the ground. New life sprung over the dead and dying, crawling over the fallen bodies. The screams rose as grass, weeds, and vines covered the humans faster than they could tear them off.

Bradenbaugh spun wildly, searching for the source of the magic. He spotted Biatta at the tree line and unleashed another bolt of black fire. Biatta was just able to raise a wall of energy before the flames engulfed her. She hunkered down behind the shield as the raw power of the assault drove her steadily backward. The magic was too strong for her to maintain the shield for long but to drop it meant her death.

She called out to the Earth for help but if it heard, it did not respond. To use more of its beautiful nature to save her was to sacrifice their lives for hers. She could not blame nature for choosing its own.

As the edges of her shield began to erode, Biatta knew the end was coming. Then, to her great relief, the flame died. Gasping, she fell back behind a large tree as her shield faded. A quick glance around the trunk showed why she had not died. Vines had risen from the earth and grabbed Bradenbaugh's wrists. He battled with them to keep from being hauled to the ground, where he would be covered and consumed like several others of his team.

Exhausted and unable to do any more, she placed a hand on the tree and sent a message of thanks through the trunk down to its roots and spreading through the ground. She turned and ran then, taking flight as she went.

The first wolf crested the building two away from Rowan. The three wizards there had the beast down and were moving to finish it when two more leaped on top. Though help came from the other rooftops, the three were lost in seconds, their limbs torn from their torsos, then their torsos shredded by the long razor claws.

As they turned to leap for the next building, one lost its head. It bounced on the roof as the body plummeted to the ground. Tarney was the only one he knew capable of such violent magic. Three to one losses. Not good odds. They would all die at that rate. He had to do something. He fired an energy bolt at one werewolf as it was in midair between the two buildings. The blast knocked it backward and it fell short of its landing. The wolf fell back toward the street. Rowan knew the beast would be stunned but it would rise and come at them again. All he could do was buy them some time in hopes of lessening the odds.

He glanced around as he readied his next spell. Bradenbaugh's group was battling something. He could not make out the details from where he stood. As long as they were delayed, it was all that mattered. He cast a look over his shoulder. The soldier was gone. He didn't blame him. Rowan wanted to be gone too.

A wolf bounded over the roof edge, having climbed the face of the building. Before it got two steps forward, Rowan blasted him off the roof. Tarney was in a fierce battle with the lone visible wolf leading Rowan to wonder where the others were.

The door opening startling Jeremy from his practice. He had been focused both in shock and awe at the tiny ember that sat on his palm but when the door opened, the ember sparked, flared, and snuffed like a match blown out by a quick breeze. He had no time to think about it. Biatta stumbled into the room looking like she had fought and lost. Jeremy bolted to his feet but before he reached her, a man entered and caught her from behind.

Jeremy froze, recognizing the soldier with the melted face. Panic ensued and he feared for Biatta. He scanned the kitchen for a weapon, settling his eyes on a block of knives. He ran to the counter and withdrew a silver handled blade, then whirled around to face the soldier. He looked at his weapon to discover he had pulled a long tined fork instead of a knife.

The soldier scooped Biatta up and set her gently on the sofa.

"Are you all right?" he asked, his tone soft and concerned.

"Yes, thank you."

"I...uh, that man...he, uh...said we can go."

Biatta said, "Then you should go while you still can."

Jeremy did not understand why, but the exchange upset him.

"Can you wake up my men?"

"Yes, of course." Biatta waved a hand and the men stirred.

The soldier glanced from them to Biatta then hung his head. "I don't understand any of this."

Biatta placed a hand on his arm. "It is all right. Few people do."

"We were told you are an enemy to this country. Terrorists. They say you should be destroyed."

"I understand. Having seen what you have, what do you believe now?"

"I just don't know."

"Would terrorists allow you to leave let alone live?"

The two sleeping men stood and glanced around, confused.

Biatta said, "You should go now. Get as far away from here as you can."

He nodded and turned to go, but her hand tightened around his arm.

"Wait."

With effort Biatta sat up, then faltered as she tried to stand. The soldier caught her arms and helped her to stand.

"I must fix the damage caused to you. She reached her hands toward his face but he grabbed them.

"Please," she said. "Let me do this. I will not hurt you."

He held her while studying her face, then released her hands. She placed one on each side of his face, closed her eyes, and murmured. The bluish glow rose to her hands and appeared to be absorbed into his flesh. Before Jeremy's astonished eyes the soldier's face altered, the skin firmed, and a more normal shape returned.

Biatta collapsed and again he prevented the fall. He guided her back to the sofa.

"I'm sorry. That's the best I can do."

The soldier touched his face the way a man does after shaving. "Thank you."

"Now go."

He nodded, and the three men left the room.

Chapter Thirty-Three

They were at a standoff. Three wolves were on the roofs, one was dead, three were unaccounted for.

A gunshot jarred Rowan from the spell he was working on. He whirled to see the soldier and his two men standing on the roof. A wisp of smoke swirled from the barrel of a rifle. The other two men opened fire on the werewolf that had climbed up the back side of the building and readied to pounce on Rowan from behind.

Though the bullets did not kill the beast, the force of the impacts against its body drove it back. As it neared the edge of the roof, Rowan blasted it with an energy bolt that sent it over the edge.

He turned to the lead soldier. "I told you to run."

"Couldn't do it, sir. We found our weapons where your people left them and decided to help."

"Your bullets will not kill these creatures. You will die trying."

The other two soldiers were looking from each other to their weapons, perhaps astonished their bullets hadn't done any damage.

"What will kill them?" the leader asked.

"Nothing you have."

Rowan turned his attention to the other rooftop. He sent another bolt across, knocking yet another wolf from the roof. He had a momentary reprieve but it would not last. He glanced to the open ground outside the town where Bradenbaugh was working to pull his team free. An idea sprung to life. The soldiers could not kill the lycanthropes, but they could kill other humans.

He turned to the leader. "How good are you with that thing?" He nodded to the rifle.

"I'm very good."

"Can you hit that man in black out there?"

"These weapons aren't made for sniping. I might be able to, but Corwin here," he pointed at one of his men, "is dead on at any distance."

Rowan addressed Corwin. "If you can kill that man in black, this war will end."

Corwin looked at his leader, who gave him a nod. The man moved to the edge of the roof and lay down. With the rifle propped on the sightly raised roof edge, he sighted on his target. Seconds later, he squeezed the trigger.

Rowan watched with hope and anticipation. Bradenbaugh was reaching down to pull up one of his followers from something that held her to the ground. Whatever it was relinquished its hold as the bullet arrived. Her body was lifted in front of Bradenbaugh, then arced back as the bullet struck. Bradenbaugh let her slip from his fingers. He glanced up to see the source of her death.

"Hurry!" Rowan shouted. "Shoot again!"

Corwin did but before the bullet reached its target, Bradenbaugh was gone in a swirl of dark wind, leaving his remaining people on the ground. Disappointment tore at Rowan's gut. As he watched, seven others extricated themselves from whatever held them and ran back the way they came.

Corwin fired again and a man fell, but the survivors were over a rise before another round was fired. Though upset at missing an opportunity to end Bradenbaugh, Rowan was satisfied that the evil man arrived with eleven and left with six. It also ended the threat of a second wave. Now he just had to find a way to survive the werewolves.

As another beast reached the roof across from him, an idea hit. He turned to the leader.

"Do you have a knife?"

He slid a long combat knife from a scabbard attached to his belt, reversed it, and handed it hilt first to Rowan. Rowan took the knife and walked to the edge of the building. He set it down on the rise of the roof edge, point facing out, then backed away a step. With a wide and animated sweeping of both arms, he recited a spell he hadn't used in twenty years, hoping he still had it right. After speaking the activation word, the knife rose and hovered in the air.

From behind he heard a gasp and a, "What the—"

Rowan focused on the beast still battling a weakened Tarney, then pushed his arms outward. The knife moved toward his target, picking up speed. Rowan narrowed his eyes to a slit for a more exact aim. The knife bore deep into the wolf's throat. It staggered backward, clutching at the blade.

Rowan swept his arms in one direction, then back the other way. The knife sliced through the wolf's neck. It lolled to the side as the wolf fought to withdraw the blade. Its blood-slicked paws could not grip the knife.

Rowan pushed his hands forward, driving the knife deeper, then repeated the side to side arm sweeps. Its head appeared to be hanging by only skin and tendons, yet still the wolf fought on. It reached the end of the roof and Rowan feared it might fall from sight before his task was complete.

Once more, he drove the knife deeper. The wolf turned to jump as Rowan swept his arm to the side that still attached the head. The wolf jumped but its head flopped back and bounced on the roof.

Two down. Five to go.

Behind him, one of the soldiers was getting violently sick. The other one kept repeating, "Oh my God. Oh my God."

Across the way, Tarney dropped to his knees but waved a hand to indicate he was okay. Rowan brought the knife back and reset it, ready for the next target. It came from behind him. The beast cast the two soldiers aside with vicious swipes of its arms. Though he knew bullets would not stop it, the leader fired a continuous burst into its chest. It slowed the beast enough to allow Rowan to set the knife back into action. This time he drove the point into the side of the throat and worked it around the wolf's head in a circle. The wolf spun trying to get hold of the knife. By the time it realized his efforts were futile and better suited to end the wielder's life, it was too late. It rushed at Rowan but two steps away, the head fell. The beast kept running, which forced Rowan to sidestep. The wolf hit the roof edge, tripped, and fell, splatting on the concrete below.

Three down, but his energy level was almost depleted. He might have enough strength left to battle one more, but then they were all in trouble.

"Biatta, how can I help you?" Jeremy asked. He was on his knees next to the sofa.

She looked at him. Much of the sparkle had left her eyes. *Was she dying?* The thought caused a tightness across his chest. Something caught in his throat.

"Jeremy." Her voice was weak. "I am sorry for getting you into this." Each word took longer and came in a softer whisper. He leaned forward to hear her better. "I promise. I'll take you home—"

She faded away then.

No. She had to be all right. His heart ached just like when Miranda—no, he dared not go there. Besides, there was no comparison. Yet the emotions were just as real, just as strong.

A noise drew his attention. *Someone is here to help.* He stood and whirled in one motion, the words already delivered.

"Biatta's hurt. She needs—"

It wasn't help entering the room, but a massive black wolf standing on two legs. It glowered at him through large red eyes, then sniffed at the air.

Is it searching for something? Someone?

Jeremy froze. His heart pounded hard enough to send a message miles away. His eyes bulged to the point of being cartoonish. Not enough saliva existed in his mouth to swallow. His body began to vibrate with complete terror.

The beast took one step inside the room, ducking under the door frame. It stood at least eight feet tall. Drops of red dotted its fur. Blood? Jeremy wanted to flee but he couldn't. He wanted to believe staying put was from a strong and brave desire to protect Biatta, but he knew it was from muscle-freezing fear.

The creature took another step, sniffing the entire time. Then it stopped, took one deep sniff, and locked on Biatta. The sight stirred something deep within Jeremy. Whether from the need to protect as a father would his child or a deeper unknown emotional bond, Jeremy steeled himself to face this beast.

He had little doubt of the outcome but knew deep in his core he would not leave Biatta to this beast. An anger borne of frustration, loss, and years of underachievement and failure rose from an unknown region of his being. His body filled with an alien strength as he threw his arms to the side and shouted in a voice that was not his own.

"No! You—shall not—have her!"

He felt ripping from his body like an organ being torn out. A sound like lightning cracked loudly nearby followed by an enormous boom. Jeremy was thrown off his feet. He flew over the sofa, crashed into the wall, and fell hard to the floor.

His last conscious thought was, *I must save Biatta.*

Chapter Thirty-Four

They met back in the no longer hidden room. Though the invisible magic exterior door was still in place showing a brick wall to the townsfolk, the path to the inner chambers was now open to any who entered.

Rowan stood by the door staring open-mouthed at the charred remains of a werewolf on the floor.

Wilden came up behind him.

"What happened here?

"Someone extremely powerful took out a werewolf."

"I didn't think that possible. Who?"

They looked inside the room and saw Biatta's sleeping form.

Wilden said, "Couldn't be."

"She's the only one here."

"I didn't think she possessed the knowledge to do something this powerful."

"Nor the skill," Rowan said.

At their feet, the wolf stirred.

"Roasted but not fully cooked," Wilden said.

"See to its end, would you, Professor?"

"Of course."

Rowan stepped over the burnt body as Wilden bent to his task. He walked toward the sofa and gazed down at Biatta. If indeed she had performed whatever magic used to fry the werewolf, she would certainly need rest.

He touched her neck to feel for a pulse. The beat was there, though not as strong as hoped. A sound on the other side of the sofa drew him up ready to fight. He heard a groan and Rowan stepped to the side of the sofa to find

Jeremy shaking his head like a dog shedding water. He struggled to rise to his knees and shook his head again.

Rowan saw no blood, wound, or any evidence of what caused his current condition. He moved to the man's side and squatted.

"Here, let me help you."

Jeremy appeared not to notice him at first but when Rowan placed a hand on his arm, Jeremy cringed and threw himself sideways, where he smacked into the wall and fell prone. Once Jeremy realized who it was, he allowed the helping hand. He stood on shaky legs and Rowan guided him to the only surviving kitchen chair. Jeremy slumped, placed his arms on the table, and lowered his head to them.

Rowan took in the damaged room. Furniture was destroyed and black singe marks covered the walls. It hadn't been a fire spell, or the room would have been consumed. Fire spells also did not contain the power to do this kind of damage plus take out a lycanthrope. So what was it? An energy blast? Lightning bolt?

Then he noticed all the damage was limited to one half of the room. The side Biatta was on had been unaffected by whatever caused the damage. It had been a controlled strike, which meant the caster had even more skill than first thought.

They heard the explosion while in the midst of battling the remaining wolves. Within seconds of the blast, the wolves howled in mournful unison and fled. That had been a miracle because Rowan's people were losing.

Wilden joined him.

"He was a big one. Perhaps the leader of the pack."

"That would explain why the others left so suddenly. If their leader dies, that bond is broken. They retreat to decide who leads the pack next."

"Regardless of who knocked the brute down, it happened just in time." He shook his head. "I was losing,

Rowan. I had but seconds left before I faltered and fell beneath that beast's claws."

He shuddered and struggled to hide his emotions. Rowan put a hand on his shoulder.

"Steady old friend. We are still here to carry on. The others must see us as strong to have hope of overcoming all we face."

He turned his face and wiped it, then asked, "How is Biatta?"

"She's alive, but I'm not sure what to do to help her."

"What about our new friend?"

"He must have got caught in the backlash of the explosion. I think he's more stunned than anything."

Others entered the room followed by Tarney. The older man was bleeding in several places. With all he had been through, he still looked strong and ready to fight on. He took in the room but made no comment.

"What's it look like outside?" Rowan asked.

"The enemy is in full retreat. The beasties have been cleared from the streets. Townsfolk are beginning to come outside and look stunned. We did what we could to conceal or repair damage to buildings, but they will notice and wonder what occurred here. By now I'm sure authorities have been called and are on the way. We either need to hole up here or get away before they arrive."

"I'd like to be gone," Rowan said. "We can't be discovered or in hiding without knowing what is going on."

"Agreed," Tarney said.

Rowan looked past Tarney.

"Is this all that's left?"

Tarney's eyes clouded. "I sent two with the bodies. Didn't want to leave them here for the locals to examine. Otherwise, yes. We took heavy losses." He motioned toward Biatta. "Can she travel?"

"She can," Biatta said. She pushed slowly to a sitting position and appeared to notice the room for the first time. "What happened?"

Rowan's eyebrows rose. "This wasn't you?"

She gave him a curious look.

"I was in no condition to do even half of this."

"Who else was here?" Wilden asked.

"As far as I remember, it was just me and…"

She looked at Jeremy's slumped form and all eyes followed.

Tarney cocked his head like a confused dog. "You don't think…"

The question hung in the air. No one had an answer.

Daria stirred and sat up. Her mind was clouded. She struggled to form clear thoughts. Looking around the room did not help. Where was she? She had no memory of arriving here. In fact, she had little memory at all.

A clatter drew her attention to the left where a stunning black woman was setting plates on a wooden table that appeared to have once been a tree trunk. The mostly round surface had been polished to a reflective shine. Something about the woman was familiar, but hard as she tried she could not place from where.

A second black woman entered the room carrying a large steaming bowl. She set it on the table and breathed in the aroma. She looked identical to the first woman. Sisters? Twins? The woman glanced at her.

"Well, look who finally decided to join us." She stretched out an arm and flexed her fingers in a come here motion. "Come little sister, it is time to eat."

Daria hesitated but when the aroma wafted to her, making her mouth water and her stomach rumble, she got up and walked sleepily to the table.

The first woman faced her and smiled.

"Welcome to our table in our humble home. You can sit there."

She pointed to a chair.

Daria pulled it away from the table, surprised at its weight. She sat and looked from one woman to the other. Definitely twins. The first held out a hand without looking at Daria and again flexed her fingers. Daria was confused at first until the second woman spoke with impatience.

"Your bowl."

"Oh."

She picked up the bowl and pushed it into the waiting hand. Soup was ladled into her bowl and returned to her. She set it down, looked into the slightly reddish broth, and inhaled deeply. Then she took up her spoon and was about to sink it into the soup when someone cleared their throat to demand attention. She looked up. The second woman gave a quick shake of her head. Daria set her spoon down.

When both women had their bowls full, a wicker basket with a brown cloth was passed to her. Pulling the cloth aside, she found a sliced loaf of black bread. She removed a slice, recovered the bread, and passed it back. Then she waited anxiously for a signal to dig in. The second woman gave a nod and the three ate in silence.

Daria didn't know why the others didn't speak but her mouth was never empty long enough to start a conversation. Her hand was a blur, shoveling spoonful after spoonful in rapid succession. She tasted potatoes, carrots, onion, tomato, something leafy, and a few other unidentifiable flavors. It made no difference to her what any of it was. It all went down fast. When the last morsel was gone, she lifted the bowl and slurped down the remaining broth.

She set the bowl down hard, wiped her mouth with a sleeve, and tore the bread apart. She stuffed the pieces in her mouth and barely chewed before swallowing.

Finished, she burped and eyed the tureen hungry for another bowl.

The woman on the right ignored her but her face bore an annoyed expression. The one on the left seemed to be having trouble with her mouth, as it twitched constantly. Finally, the woman on the left set her spoon down, picked up a cloth napkin, and wiped her mouth.

"Oh, come now, Oli, you have to admit that was funny."

"I don't have to admit any such thing. The child is rude, uncouth, and untrained. At her age, she should know better. Perhaps she is too dimwitted to be taught."

"Oli, remember when we were her age? Were we any different? I remember Momma smacking us with that wooden spoon every time we did something she didn't like. Most times we left the table with hands so bruised we could barely hold anything."

Slowly, the woman named Oli let a smile stretch across her face, though to Daria it looked to be a painful process.

"Oh. And I remember a time she hit you so hard, she broke her favorite spoon. My, she hit the ceiling that day. You were sent to bed without your dinner."

"You would remember that," the other woman said.

"Sure do, especially 'cause she gave your dinner to me. Yum, that was a good night. The rest of the week I was secretly cheering for her to smack you again. Even thought about putting a little slice in her new spoon to encourage it to break again."

"You didn't?"

The second woman leaned over the table and sounded astonished.

"Sure did. Think about it, that is."

The second woman sat back and looked up.

"Sometimes I really miss Momma."

Oli said, "But not when she had her hand around a wooden spoon."

They burst out laughing. Daria couldn't help but get caught up in the joy around the table. She laughed along with them until Oli stopped laughing and turned her hard glare at Daria.

"What are you laughing it urchin?"

The laughter fled Daria like a frightened puppy. Oli turned to her sister.

"Now, that was funny."

They laughed again. This time, Daria had the sense not to join in.

Chapter Thirty-Five

Daria helped clear the table without being told. It brought a nod of approval from one sister.

Oli said, "At least there's hope for the girl."

When the dishes were done and put away, they sat in the room where a fire danced warmly in the hearth. Cushioned chairs had been set in a semi-circle in front of the fire. Daria's cot was in the corner of the room.

"I'm sure you have questions," Oli started, "but before we get to those—"

Daria interrupted. "Where am I and why am I here?"

Oli glanced at her sister. "Honestly. What do they expect us to do with this obviously deficient child?"

"Give her a chance, Oli."

Oli sighed. "Very well. Let's try again. This time, listen with your ears instead of your mouth. First, my name is Olivianna. My sister is Delphina. You have been brought here because someone wiser than us—"

"Well, at least older," Delphina said.

"Yes, quite. Anyway, someone has seen something in you important enough to require education and training. Unfortunately for us, we have been tasked with performing this miracle."

Daria sat on her hands and kicked her feet since they did not touch the floor. Questions were building and threatening to explode from her mouth. She fought to stay focused.

"Your training will begin tomorrow. Along with the training, you will have daily chores that must be completed. We are passing on valuable information. It does not come for free, so you will work. You will receive two meals a day, which is all we have ourselves. You are responsible for cleaning your own clothes and your bedding. By the way, starting tomorrow, that mess will not be tolerated. As soon as you step foot on the floor, make your bed."

Delphina took over. "The first thing is to learn more about you. Then I want to test your skill and knowledge levels. That will give us a starting point. For the moment that is all I have. Oli?"

"Nothing more. Let us begin the interview."

Despite her best effort, a hand sneaked out from under her thigh and lifted upward. Without waiting to be called on like in school, she blurted, "Can I ask questions now?"

Oli said, "Since you just did, I guess you can."

"How long will this take?"

"Of all the impertinence," Oli said. "It will take as long as it takes. The length of time depends on your ability to learn. From what I have seen so far, that may take several decades."

Unphased by Oli's outburst, Daria said, "In that case, I will have to respectfully decline. I must go. The sooner the better."

Oli was beside herself with anger.

"Decline? Who do you think you are? No one declines us."

Delphina raised a hand to quiet her sister. "Where is it you have to go?"

"I have to find my friends. They are in trouble. I have to help them."

"What help do you think you can give?"

Daria shrugged. "Whatever help I can."

"Child, you do not have the skills to help anyone."

"That's not true. I've helped my friends a lot, and I am getting stronger."

"Friends," Oli scoffed. "You don't need friends. The most important thing to do is look out for yourself."

"I may not be as strong or smart or as skilled as you are, but my strength comes from my friends. I need them and they need me. I will not let them face their problems alone. By standing together we are stronger." She stood abruptly. "I am leaving tomorrow." She turned to stomp toward her cot, then stopped and pivoted. "I didn't handle that very well. I thank you for your hospitality. I would like to stay and learn, but not at the cost of leaving my friends to face danger without me. Nothing you could ever teach me would be able to replace the knowledge that I did not go when they needed me. I am sorry."

"Me too, child," Oli said.

She waved her hand and Daria was flung onto her cot. Before she could react, Oli's fast moving fingers drew lines from ceiling to floor that solidified into bars. Daria gripped them in panic and shook them wildly.

"Let me out of here!"

"Not going to happen. We have our orders and they will be fulfilled. You are better off without friends who put you in danger and threaten your existence. You are here until we say otherwise."

Oli left the room. Delphina stood and approached.

"I am sorry child, but this is for your own good. You have a purpose, an important role to play in what is coming. You have to be prepared to face it. It is our job to get you ready. The quicker you accept your fate, the quicker you will be prepared and the easier your stay will be. Get some rest. We start early tomorrow."

With the flick of her hand, the fire died and light vanished.

Jeremy was still a little groggy even after the hasty departure. He had no memory of the journey and no idea where he was now. He was sitting in a lounge chair with his feet propped up.

Biatta's hand caressed his forehead. It felt cool and calmed him.

"Jeremy, do you remember anything at all about the encounter with the wolf?"

"Wolf?" he repeated and searched his brain. He remembered being put on the back of one and almost riding it until a bird scooped him up. No, not a bird. An owl. The biggest owl he had ever seen. White. Yes. White like the lady in white. Lady in white? Connor had said that. Even Nick had made mention of a lady in white.

Nick. He had seen Nick, his long-lost son. Where was he?

"Jeremy, can you help us understand what happened?"

His eyes drifted until they landed on Biatta's stunning, smooth face. He smiled at the warm sensation the sight brought him. Like a China doll. Porcelain. "So beautiful," he muttered. She was dressed in white. White. Wait. Biatta was the lady in white. White owl. Black wolf. Wolf at the door.

The memory burst into his head, causing a lance of pain behind his eyes. He winced and squeezed his eyes tight.

"You do remember, don't you?"

He let the image settle and the pain ebb. "Yes. While you were unconscious, a massive wolf came to the door. He sniffed around, as if seeking a certain scent." His eyes shot open. "You. He was hunting for you. He came into the room. I couldn't let him take you." He stopped, his memory hitting a wall.

"Then what, Jeremy?"

"I don't know."

"This is important. Please try."

"There was an explosion. I went flying." He shook his head. "I'm sorry. That's all I can remember."

Rowan leaned down. "Was there anyone else in the room beside you, Biatta, and the wolf."

"I-I don't know. I don't think so, but then the wolf was too large for me to see if anyone was behind him."

Wilden asked, "Do you remember saying anything? Anything at all?"

"No. I think I was too frightened to even scream."

"What about that?" Biatta said. "You were frightened, but how did that make you feel? How did your body react? Did your muscles flex? Did you feel pressure in your head or chest?"

Jeremy just kept shaking his head.

"I'm sorry. I don't know what you want me to say. If anything else happened, I am unaware. Most likely someone was behind the wolf and caused the explosion."

They all exchanged glances as if seeking answers from each other. If anyone had answers, they didn't voice them. Biatta patted Jeremy's hand and they all moved away from him. He was curious and annoyed that they seemed to blame him for something he had no knowledge of, but his need for rest won out and he closed his eyes.

Without them hovering over him and as his mind cleared, something did begin to crawl back into focus. He *had* felt pressure, not just in his head or chest, but through his entire body. It felt like he was about to explode. Had that been what he heard? A loud popping in his brain? Perhaps he'd had an aneurism. No, that didn't make sense. He'd be dead already.

Should he tell them? He decided not to. Not until he knew more. Perhaps more of his memory would return and make the events in that room clearer. Besides, he hated the way they hovered over him searching for answers. What if he had been the cause of the explosion? They might try to bill him for the repairs, or worse, treat him like a lab rat.

But as his mind settled down again, he recalled the discussion they were having before the attack. Magic. Did he possess magic? That was impossible. Wasn't it? He had been able to create tiny sparks in his hands, but scientists could probably prove that was nothing more than static electricity.

His brain hurt. Too much was going on and he had too much to think about, not the least of which was how his son was. He'd had enough of all this nonsense and excitement. It was time to go home.

He pushed his feet down to lower the footrest, then stood. The group had their heads together in an intense whispered conversation. They stopped and looked at him as he rose.

"I'm done. I want to go home. Either take me or point me in the right direction."

"Jeremy, no," Biatta said, moving toward him. "It is not safe for you."

"I don't care. I'm going with or without your help. Besides, it isn't any safer here."

Someone knocked at the door.

"Enter," Rowan said.

A woman came in, her face flushed with adrenaline.

"Sir, our people just reported a lot of activity around the portal. They think Bradenbaugh is marshalling his people for a crossing into the other world.

Their exchanged glances held deeper concern this time.

"Gather whoever is available," he said to the woman.

She hurried out.

Biatta put a hand to her face. "Oh, Gwynedd. They broke her, Rowan. That poor child."

Silence fell over the room then Rowan turned to Jeremy.

"Well, I have good news for you. Looks like you *are* going home."

Chapter Thirty-Six

The base was alive with last minute preparations. Rowan, Tarney, and Wilden stood over a map discussing best approaches to the portal.

"There is no doubt in my mind," Tarney said. "Bradenbaugh left someone or something to guard the entrance. We've already learned that a few well-placed marksmen can control who comes and goes. He will want to ensure his return once he has finished whatever diabolical plan he has bouncing around that evil mind."

Wilden said, "I think we know all too well what his plan is. He is using that captured student to guide him to the others. Once he has them, he will kill the staff and leverage the students to get us."

"If that does happen, you two need to retreat and regroup," said Rowan.

Wilden said, "What is that supposed to mean?"

"It means," Tarney said, "our illustrious leader is going to give himself up to save the students."

"Rowan!" Wilden protested. "You can't."

"I can and I will. I will not let him torture those children to get at me. I will offer myself for the complete release of every student."

"He will kill you."

"Better me than students who have been placed in this situation through no cause of their own. Their safety has been entrusted to me. I will not see harm come to them." He smiled at Wilden. "Besides, old friend, I have two advantages Bradenbaugh will not see coming. He underestimates your power and ability to lead without me."

"And?" Tarney prompted.

"And I plan on collapsing the portal and trapping him in that world."

"Are you mad?" Wilden asked.

Brilliant," said Tarney.

"If he is trapped in that other world, he is no longer a threat to this one. If we do this right I will have a device to reopen the portal on a one time basis before it vanishes for good. That will allow you to get the students through to safety. Once the exchange is made, you leave immediately. I cannot stress that enough. You will need a head start to get through and close the portal before Bradenbaugh gets to it. He will already be suspicious since we are on that side of the portal. He will know we eliminated whoever he left there to protect it, meaning we control the other side. He will not think his path has been sealed off."

Tarney said, "That brings to mind another potential problem. We should assume Bradenbaugh has someone protecting the exit as well."

"Yes," Rowan said. "Good point. I will leave it to your strategic military mind to find a way past."

He faced the professor.

"I will need your superior research and technical skills to develop whatever is needed to close and open the portal."

Someone knocked on the door. Without looking up, Rowan said, "Come."

The door opened and Rhylie entered.

"Rhylie, old boy," Wilden said with enthusiasm. "How are you? Where have you been. You've missed a lot of excitement."

"While his injuries were healing, I had him on a special assignment," Rowan said. "You remember how we were ambushed on our expedition to find wild magicians?"

"Yes, of course," Wilden said.

"It has been my opinion and my concern that we have a mole within our ranks."

"A mole?" Wilden said, astonished that such a thing could happen.

"I dispatched Rhylie to work from a list I made to eliminate possibilities." He turned to Rhylie. "The fact that you are here tells me you have completed your mission?"

"Yes sir." He handed a folded sheet of paper to Rowan. "I have all my work recorded, should you want to see how I reached my conclusion but despite the name you will read, I stand by my finding."

Rowan stared at the paper, knowing the name he would see and not wanting verification. He took a deep breath as if steeling his body against pain and unfolded the sheet. Speculation verified, his hand dropped to his side and his head hung.

"Don't leave us in suspense, Rowan," Wilden said. "Who is the traitor?"

Tarney did not wait to be told. He moved to Rowan's side and removed the sheet from his hand. He read the name.

"Sweet Heaven and all the angels."

"Damn you, man," Wilden said. "Who is it?"

As if speaking the name made it more real, Tarney held up the sheet for Wilden to see.

"This can't be." He turned on Rhylie. "You have made a mistake. Your research is faulty."

"No sir. My research will bear out."

"Kanter. Of all people. But why?"

"You will have a chance to ask him, sir," Rhylie said. "He is on the way here."

"By God," Wilden said, "he will pay for this treason."

Tarney was remarkably calm. "What will you do?"

Rowan said, "I will meet and confront him. The next move is up to him."

"You're hoping there is an explanation you can accept," Tarney said.

Rowan nodded.

"That's something I want to hear."

"No," Rowan said. "I will meet with him alone."

"But Rowan!" Wilden objected.

"That is the way it has to be, and that is the way I want it." He turned to Rhylie. "When he arrives, escort him in and do not mention a word or display any emotion. Everything as usual."

Ten minutes later, Kanter, perhaps the most powerful wizard alive, was ushered into the room. Tarney and Wilden were gone. Rowan didn't want to even speculate on how that was going.

He sat in a large cushioned chair in front of a dying fire. A matching chair had been set next to his with a small round wooden table between them. On the table was a decanter of Rowan's favorite Scotch. If something happened in the other world and he did not return, he wanted to enjoy one last drink.

Kanter walked toward him, his posture erect as always; his stride and demeanor confident but low key.

"It's been a while, my friend. Have a seat and a drink."

Kanter halted for a moment. He was no fool and perhaps recognized the somber tone. He poured the drink, swished the amber liquid around the glass, and inhaled before taking the tiniest of sips.

Rowan smiled. "It is not poisoned or laced with anything."

"I wouldn't think so. That is not your way."

"Please, sit. I have little time before I must leave."

Kanter sat and pressed back into the chair until he was comfortable.

"Where is it you are going?"

"Forgive me, but for the moment I will keep that to myself."

They both took another sip. Rowan was disappointed he was not getting the usual pleasure from the drink that he wanted.

"Do you wish an explanation?"

"Very much so."

Kanter's smile bore a touch of sadness. "First, let me offer an apology for the loss of life and the injuries. That was not my intent. I pray you believe that, if nothing else. I didn't want anyone hurt. My hope was that the mere presence of the enemy was enough deterrent to keep you from your goal. I didn't count on the foolishness of the opposing force to actually attack."

"No, but they did, and as you say, people died. Our people. People I have known for years."

"But there lies the point. We are alike, but they are not *my* people."

"The wildlings."

"Yes."

"Tell me, Kanter, when you say enemy, which side do you see?"

He sighed. "I am not your enemy, Rowan. I couldn't let you use the wildlings as pawns to be placed on a board and moved about with no say in their fate. Yes, I leaked that a party would be there, but I did not disclose the purpose."

"But that wasn't for our benefit, was it? It was to keep Bradenbaugh's people from doing the same as you thought I was going to do. Use them. I'm sorry you don't know me better."

"My decision was not personal."

"Wasn't it?" Rowan's voice rose. "Tell that to those who died that day. It was extremely personal to them. To their families and friends." He fought for calm and brought his anger down. "I would not have hurt *your* people. I needed help. That was all. If any were willing great. If not, so be it."

He looked into his drink. Disgusted, he set it down on the table. "You can't possibly want Bradenbaugh to succeed."

"Of course not, but in truth, it is not our fight."

"How is this any different than the last time we fought the dark one?"

"I was younger then and not as wise. Many of the wildlings fought and died back then. Our numbers were thinned almost to elimination, but when the fighting was over and the battle won, no one reached out to them to offer a thank you or a condolence for the losses. No one offered to help them recover, rebuild, or join their—your precious school. You only cared about your own people. It was then I decided if you wanted us separated, then we would stay that way."

"I am sorry you feel that way and sorry for what befell your people before, but I was not in charge back then. I am now. If you had concerns you could have—*should* have brought them to me. I do not differentiate between yours and mine. I only see our. And right now, *our* community needs help."

"I understand, but again I say it is not our fight."

"What do you think will happen if we fall? You think Bradenbaugh and the dark one will leave you alone? Forget you exist? They will always see you as a potential threat."

"I will work to ensure them we are not and leaving us alone is in their best interest."

"That's how you want it?"

"Yes. It is the only way it can be."

"Then I am truly sorry for the loss of your friendship and your council. I am sorry for the losses our people will incur, and I'm sorry you have lost your heart and soul."

Chapter Thirty-Seven

They sat in silence for a long moment while Rowan settled his emotions. Then he changed subjects.

"What about Daria? It was you who took her, right?"

He nodded. "She is safe."

"She is one of my students. I want her back."

"She is one of us even if she doesn't know it."

"She was entrusted to my care. I cannot let her go. She must be returned."

"No. She is no longer your concern. She is being cared for, educated, and trained. The girl has a lot of natural ability. She may never reach her full potential under the strict structure of your school."

"You don't have the right to decide that for her."

"As much right as you do."

"Kanter. This is wrong. I can overlook everything else, but not this. She must be returned."

"I do not care what you overlook or don't. She stays."

Rowan wanted to debate this more, but his time was limited. The one saving thought about Daria was whatever happened, at least she'd be safe.

Kanter took the last sip of his Scotch and set the glass down.

"For what it's worth, I always thought of you as fair and honest, and a friend."

"Well, since the likelihood of me surviving what I am about to do is almost nil, I guess we'll have to leave it at that. My predecessor, if there is one, will have to deal with you."

Kanter eyed him, then stood.

"I wish you well, Rowan Vandalue."

With that he turned and left the room.

Rowan had little time to waste thinking about Kanter and refused to discuss the meeting with Tarney and Wilden. With everything ready, the group of twenty-three wizards and support personnel, including Jeremy, set out for the portal.

It was predawn as they traveled, arriving as the sun crested the horizon. They stopped two blocks from the alley where the portal was positioned and met with the advance scouts.

"Sir, Bradenbaugh led a party of more than thirty through the portal ten minutes ago. He left two shapeshifters to guard the entrance."

"Do we know what they shift into?" Tarney asked.

"Yes sir," the man replied. "Wolves."

"Of course, they would be," Wilden said. "Wish we knew what scorched that last one."

Both Tarney and Wilden flicked glances at Jeremy.

Rowan said, "We need to strike fast before they have a chance to shift. It won't kill them but it will delay the transformation. We need to be on them before that happens to have a chance to come away without losses."

"If I may," Tarney said. "You and a few others light them up and keep the pressure on. While they are dealing with you, another shifter and myself will pounce on them."

Biatta frowned. "You're talking about me as the second shifter, aren't you?"

"If the skin fits," Tarney said with a shrug.

"Will you do it?" Rowan asked.

"*Can* you do it?" asked Wilden.

She gave him an *Oh, please* look.

"What do you want me to do?"

"In our alternate forms we have the best chance of reaching them before they transform. I'll bound down the alley. You drop from above."

"I will not be able to use magic strong enough to harm them in that form."

"That will take brute force," Rowan said. "We will have to get to you fast. Before we go I need to know if you can handle yours. I don't want to get trapped down there having to deal with two."

"You take care of your part. I'll do mine." Without another word, Biatta ran behind a building. A minute later, a large white owl flew overhead.

Tarney took off at a run and transformed on the move into the big black dog. The rest of the group moved into position.

Once ready, Rowan said, "Wilden, you and Ravena take the one on the left. Precious, you and I have the one on the right. Everyone ready?"

He received three nods.

They stepped from behind the building across the street from the alley. The two werewolves in human form did not notice at first, giving the energy bolts a chance to hit and knock them backward. One went down but the other withstood the blast. It was already morphing into wolf form when Tarney bolted down the alley.

He leaped at the wolf, snapping fangs at its throat. He nipped the skin but did no real damage before the wolf slapped him away. With Tarney out of the picture, Rowan ordered the renewed attack of energy bolts, this time having all four attackers focus on the standing wolf.

Biatta flew into the alley from a rooftop. She targeted the prone man who had yet to transform. She had not counted on the narrow space to use her wings. Her only choice was to dive, but that maneuver meant she had little chance of stopping if the wolf form appeared. She aimed the sharp points of her talons at the man's chest. Ten feet before contact, the shimmering began. With little chance of attacking before the wolf appeared, she pushed more speed from her sleek form.

She struck the wolf hard as it was rising, driving it back to the concrete alley. It smacked its head and was stunned for an instant, allowing Biatta to sink her talons into the beast's chest. The werewolves' ability to heal was legendary. No sooner had her claws penetrated the skin than she felt it solidify around her. She fought back the rising panic and clawed deeper. The hard ribs pushed against the pad under her claw. She unfolded her wings and flapped hard, driving into the bone. One rib cracked. The wolf howled and swatted at her. The blow dazed her but still she pressed on. A talon pierced the heart as the wolf fought to its feet and grabbed her body. The pain tore through her as it compacted her wings.

She needed more time and several more inches to complete her task. To fail was to die. With a violent headbutt she plowed her beak into the wolf's eye. It whipped its massive head back and to the side to dislodge her as it howled in pain. It might heal fast, but it could still feel pain. She opened her beak, tearing through the eyeball, then clamped against the attached nerves and yanked upward. With a snap, the eyeball came free. The pitch of the howl rose several octaves.

She spit the eye out. The distracted wolf watched it fall and moved to catch it, relaxing its crushing hold on Biatta. The brief reprieve gave her the time and chance to drive into the wolf. Off balance, it fell as it reached for its falling eye. They hit the ground. The force of contact and Biatta's downward momentum gave her the distance she needed to wrap her claw around the heart and pull.

Her wings beat furiously to gain height and dislodge from the enclosed flesh holding her in place. The wolf, now aware of its own mortality, forgot about the eye and grabbed Biatta on both sides. It first tried to wrench her away from him but realizing how deadly that would be, moved to batter her into unconsciousness. Each blow brought her closer to that reality, but after each strike she regrouped, knowing to black out for even a second meant the end of her life.

With all her strength she whipped her wings in short, powerful strokes until they began to rise from the alley. Once in the air, the wolf's attacks faltered. Biatta bounced the wolf up and down in an effort to tear free from its chest. With each bounce the wolf howled anew. In desperation, it attacked her again with brutal and violent strikes, but Biatta did not cease. She could feel the heart pulling against its connecting veins and arteries, pushing against the ribs.

She brought her free talon up and punched it into the wolf's chest to create contrasting force. Once, twice, three times she rammed her claw into the chest. On the fourth fierce attempt, an audible tearing was followed by a pop, and the wolf fell.

Exhausted, Biatta managed to reach the rooftop. She landed, smashing the still-beating heart under her weight and ground it into a red pulp. With that done, she staggered backward and collapsed against a brick chimney. She transformed, gasping from the effort and the damage caused to her human form, and passed out.

Jeremy watched in awe as Biatta fought the werewolf. Never in his life would he have believed such things existed, yet here he was witnessing it. How could this entire world be real? He stayed back as a group of Biatta's friends moved forward, shooting some sort of beam into the second beast. They kept it up all the way across the street and into the mouth of the alley.

The white owl was taking a severe beating from the frenzied and powerful creature. He feared for her safety. Her wings extended and whipped the air. She left the ground hauling the wolf with her. He marveled at her strength and prayed for her safety. Then she rose to the level of the roof and the beast fell. But what was that clutched in her claw?

My God! Is that a heart? The sight made hum queasy.

He turned his attention to the battle raging before him. The beast roared and thrashed, trying to bat away the unending stream of invisible power that drove it back. A black blur leaped at the wolf and gnashed at its throat. Blood splattered around the alley. Wolf and dog fought with ferocity.

As soon as the dog struck, the group of attackers rushed forward. As the wolf attempted to crush the dog, they grabbed the wolf's limbs and held it down. The dog continued its attack with violent shakes of its head to rip the wound in the neck wider. It broke free with a mouthful of bloody flesh. Then, two of the arriving force drove knives into the throat and sawed in opposite directions until one lifted the head from the body. It thrashed long after the head was severed.

Rowan urged everyone on. "Hurry. Grab the bodies and drag them through the portal. Wilden, take care of the head. One of you get up on that roof and make sure Biatta is all right. Go. Go. We have to get through fast. Tarney, are you all right?"

Now in human form, Tarney looked battered, but if he was injured, he gave no indication.

"I'm fine. Press on."

"Then you take the lead with Precious and Ravena. I'm sure there will be guards waiting on the other side."

The trio of wizards moved into the portal. The others followed, dragging the bodies of the now transformed men.

"Come, my friend," Rowan motioned for Jeremy. "We must get through."

Jeremy shook his head.

"I'll wait."

"You were the one so anxious to get home. Go." He pointed into the spinning vortex.

"I want to make sure Biatta is okay first."

Rowan nodded but moved to Jeremy's side, placed fingers at his temple and said, "Sleep."

Jeremy went limp. Rowan bent to catch him and with a grunt, lifted Jeremy over his shoulder. He stepped into the portal and traveled through.

Chapter Thirty-Eight

"Child!" Oli raged. "This obstinance will not be tolerated."

The room darkened like her mood, but the effect was wasted on Daria. If the woman sought to cow her into obedience, she was going to be more upset than she already was. Daria refused to eat. When that had been taken away as punishment for her disobedience, she was told it was time for chores. Again she refused.

"I am not playing with you. You will do as I say, or your punishment will be severe. You cannot stand against me for long."

"Do whatever you want. I will not be forced to do anything."

Delphina moved up beside her sister.

"Child. Daria. Can't you see this is for your own good? We are trying to help you."

"Making me a prisoner and stealing me away from my friends is not helping me. You are my enemies. I will not comply with anything you want me to do."

"Then you are in for a long, unpleasant stay," Oli said. "You will comply. It may take some time, but eventually you will give in."

"Not going to happen. Any chance I get, I will run. You may be able to force me to stay here, but you can never force me to do what you want."

Pressure built around her. She was getting experienced enough now to know when magic was being used, and in this case, it was against her. She was lifted off her cot and pushed against the wall. Not hard enough to do damage, but to a point of pain. She gasped, kicked her legs futilely against the wall, and clutched at the invisible fingers squeezing her throat.

"Oli, you're hurting her."

"If that's what it takes to gain her cooperation, then so be it."

Blackness formed around the edges of her vision. With a sudden calm, she lowered her hands and stopped kicking, resolved to allow whatever was going to happen to happen.

Oli said, "What-what is she doing?"

"She's letting you kill her."

"What?"

She released her hold on Daria and she fell to the bed. She couldn't help but rub her neck and felt weak for doing so.

"Daria, please. It doesn't have to be this way," Delphina said in a pleading voice.

"It does for me. I would rather die than be your prisoner."

"But you don't have to be a prisoner. Can't you understand that? You are the one doing this. We only want to help you. To teach and train you."

"I have a teacher. I don't need another."

"What they teach you at that school is very structured and limited. We will open entire realms of magic you will never learn about in school. You will not have to follow rules or listen to anyone else's interpretation of what is good or bad magic. You will be free to choose."

"You mean like I'm free to choose now? It sounds a little contradictory to me. What good is having all this training if you are just going to hide away on a mountain while the world is threatened? I have friends out there standing against the evil that is rising; friends who understand the difference between right and wrong and are willing to die for that belief. I may not have your skill or power, but I have friends, and to me that's the greatest power in the world."

"Why, you ungrateful brat!" Oli said, her voice rising to a roar. "We didn't ask to be your mentors. That was a job assigned to us. Why should we care what happens to you? You want to be an ignorant practitioner? Fine by me."

"Then let me go."

"No!" she shouted. "I will not give in to a stupid little girl."

Her anger flared and Daria was lifted again. This time when she hit the wall, it was with force that stunned her and drove the air from her lungs.

"Oli, stop this madness at once."

"Don't get in my way, sister. This child will learn to comply."

"Or what? You going to thrash her on a daily basis?"

"If that's what it takes."

While the sisters argued, Daria struggled against the grip on her throat. This time it was more severe, not only cutting off her air, but beginning to crush her throat. Panic came easily but would not fade as before. She was actually going to die. This monster was going to kill her.

Then the fires inside her lit hot. She felt the energy rise within her and that same pressure she felt before pushed against every inch of her skin. Her eyes bulged but once she got the rising panic under control, she saw clearly.

A deep rumbling was the first sign that her power was being unleashed. She had no spell to direct the flow into. It was operating as if it had a mind of its own. The walls began to shake.

Oli said, "What the—"

"Have you ever seen so much power in a child?" Delphina asked. "Daddy was right about her."

The grip on her throat released. Instead of falling to the cot, Daria floated. Her vision altered, allowing her to see the streams of raw power emanating from her body. The streams licked at the magical bars of her prison and began to eat through them like acid on metal.

"What is she doing?"

Daria thought she heard a note of concern in Oli's voice. That pleased her. She pushed to the next level. The bars vanished one by one.

Delphina said, "She's escaping." Her voice was surprisingly calm.

Damn right I am, sisters.

Fire exploded from her hands and spread around the room.

"Del!" Oli exclaimed. "She's going to burn the house down!"

The sisters worked together to combat Daria's attack. Daria met their counter spells with raw magic. She gained confidence every second she held them at bay.

"You will not keep me here!" Daria shouted above the roar of the fire.

An explosion occurred and the sisters were pushed back, temporarily disrupting their spells. They attacked with renewed vigor, showing power of their own. Their superior knowledge and skill began to tell. The sudden expenditure of that much power drained Daria fast. She could not hope to maintain so much usage. The thought of succumbing spurred her on, kicking to the next level of adrenaline.

She stepped down from the cot and despite the strength of the force leveled against her, she made ground against her opponents. Then, a new burst of energy was added to their stream more powerful than the two sisters combined, and Daria was pushed back. With the last bit of energy exhausted, she was thrust back into the wall, smacking her head. As she slid down the wall on the way to unconsciousness, a small black man stepped forward. Her last thought was that he didn't look happy.

Bradenbaugh was excited. The chance to end the war in victory was within his grasp. The little girl was in a magic trance under the control of Madelyn. He had no concern for whatever games she was playing inside the girl's head, as long as it didn't interfere. Periodically, the girl lifted an arm and pointed a finger in the direction they needed to go.

She was unable to tell him the distance they needed to travel to reach the students but as long as they were moving, that didn't matter. He looked around at his small army as it moved through a forest. All his planning was about to reach fruition. With Vandalue and his followers rendered powerless, raising the dark one would be a simple matter. But lately, Bradenbaugh had come to wonder if doing so was a good idea. With the dark one roaming the world, Bradenbaugh would be relegated to second in command. That might be fine in normal circumstances, but the dark one was far from normal. One small mistake on Bradenbaugh's part and he might cease to exist.

Perhaps there was a better way to handle things. In fact, two options came to mind. The first, that he didn't raise the dark one, and ruled the world himself. That idea pleased him. He liked being in charge. The drawback was if one of his ingrate followers took it upon himself to raise the dark one. Bradenbaugh would not survive his wrath.

The second option...the better and safer one was to disappear into this world once he raised the dark one. He would collapse the portal, then work to take over this world. That choice gave him as much pleasure as the first option and had the added benefit of longevity.

He scanned the land around him. Though he hadn't seen much of this world so far, he saw little difference between this world and the other. Once he had the students and maneuvered Vandalue into surrender, he might have to do some exploring here before he decided to raise the dark one.

Yes, he liked option number two much better.

Chapter Thirty-Nine

With the two watchers on the backside of the portal dispatched, Rowan's group was on the move. He passed Jeremy to two of his support staff and set a fast pace. Though Biatta had been led through before they collapsed the portal, she was too weak to keep up. She was left behind with one of the non-magic men until she was strong enough to catch up.

He should have left Jeremy with her, but he needed to know more about the man and feared he might disappear into this world if left behind. True, Biatta could track him but they could ill-afford the delay.

Tarney sent two wizards ahead to scout and ensure they continued on the right path and didn't stumble into an ambush. So far, Bradenbaugh's trail was easy to follow. The arrogant man probably saw no way Rowan would follow. That arrogance would be his undoing.

They seemed to make good time. This world looked no different from his but then so far, they had only seen trees. Rowan calculated how far ahead Bradenbaugh's army might be. If they left twenty minutes behind Bradenbaugh and it took another ten minutes to fight the werewolves, five minutes to eliminate the backend watchers, three more to wait for Biatta to be assisted through, then ten minutes to collapse the portal, Bradenbaugh had nearly a fifty-minute head start. Not insurmountable, but a lot depended on how far they had to travel to reach Jerricka and the students.

Though he didn't have a destination, he knew Jerricka well enough to know she would not settle the students close to the portal. Wherever they were, he was positive steps had been taken to protect the area. She would have advance warning and be prepared for Bradenbaugh's army. Whatever time she bought them only shortened the journey to get there. With luck, Bradenbaugh would be so focused on getting the students that he'd leave his rear exposed. If Jerricka was able to hold Bradenbaugh off, Rowan's reinforcements might just end the war. He was also smart enough to know the easy way never happened. There was going to be a battle, and some of his people were going to die.

His people. Those two words brought back his discussion with Kanter. As brilliant as he was, Kanter only saw that joining with them to combat the evil threat to their world was the best way to bring everyone together, unified and equal. With Kanter on their side, this war would end in a blink.

"Sir," one of the men carrying Jeremy called. "He's waking."

"What? Impossible." Rowan moved to the man. The spell he cast should have lasted another three or four hours at least. "Set him down." He turned to the group. "The rest of you, keep moving. We can't afford delays."

Rowan squatted next to Jeremy. He wished he had more time to delve into the mystery behind this man. Whether he proved to be a long-lost descendant or just some oddity of this world intrigued him, but not at the expense of winning the war.

Jeremy's eyes fluttered open and at once he was aware. He narrowed his eyes in a stern gaze.

"What did you do to me?" With ice in his voice he asked, "And where is Biatta?"

The tone made Rowan flinch. *Was this man more formidable than expected?* "She is behind us. She was too drained to travel with the group. She will join us when she can."

"Why didn't you leave me behind as well?"

Rowan hesitated before answering. That hesitation told Jeremy a lot.

"You want something from me."

"Yes and no. Your knowledge of the area might prove helpful, but I expect nothing more. Will you help us?"

Jeremy got to his feet and brushed off his pants.

"No. Not until I see that Biatta is all right."

"We don't have time for that. Children's lives are at stake. Please. Help us save them." Though his tone was pleading, Jeremy got the feeling the man was playing him. How much of what he said was true and how much was for Jeremy's benefit to illicit his aid?

"My decision has been made. I'll wait for her to catch up."

Rowan eyed him with less friendly eyes. "I could make you."

"Go ahead. See how well that works out for you."

"I can't believe you won't help, knowing children's lives are at stake."

"And I can't believe you would use children's lives to motivate me. The simple truth is that I don't know you or trust you. Like a politician, you'll say anything to get what you want."

Frustrated and without the time to force the issue or convince him otherwise, Rowan said to the two men, "Bring him with you in whatever manner you see fit."

He pivoted and strode away.

"You heard the man," the taller of the two men said, "Move or we'll move you. One way or another, you're going."

Connor looked up from his Lego construction. He was sitting on a chair facing the window in his uncle's hospital room. Harper sat next to him. For a moment his eyes went unfocused. When they cleared, he resumed his work and said, "Pe-pop's back."

Harper said, "Yeah, Pe-pop's back."

Chandra looked up from her phone.

"What do you mean, he's back?" She stood and walked to the window, scanning the grounds below. "Do you see him?"

"Yep."

"Yep."

"Where?"

Without looking up he said, "In my head."

"Yeah, my head too."

Chandra stared at her children, thinking not for the first time lately that they were both a little strange.

Nick spoke suddenly, and Chandra jumped. "Lady in white. Lady in white. Lady in white." His eyes never opened but he kept repeating the phrase.

Unsure what to do and feeling unsettled by her brother and the kids, she said, "Don't move, you two."

She ran out of the room to get the nurse.

"Mom's acting strange again," Connor said.

"Yeah, so strange," said Harper.

Biatta sat up. She had been dreaming. Or had she?

"Nick," she said in a soft voice. "Can you see me?"

In her mind, she heard a voice say, "Lady in white. Lady in white."

"Nick, where is your father?"

"Lady in white. Safe. Lady in white. Ahead."

"Can you see the children?"

"Lady in white. Trouble. Lady in white."

"Can you reach your father?"

"Lady in white. Yes. Lady in white."

"Tell him I'm coming."

"Lady in white. Yes. Coming. Lady in white."

"Lady in white?" the nurse said. "Why does he keep saying that?"

"You don't think he sees an angel, do you?" Chandra asked.

The nurse evidently hadn't considered that possibility. The color drained from her face and she made the sign of the cross.

"Dad." Nick said. "Dad. She's coming. Lady in white. She's coming." Then Nick seemed to sink into the mattress.

Chandra said, "Oh God, no. Is he dying?"

The nurse reached for his wrist to check for a pulse.

"No, Mommy," said Connor. "He's sleeping."

"Sleeping," Harper repeated, then made several snoring sounds.

"Dear God, I'm going crazy," Chandra said to herself.

"Got that right," Connor said.

Harper said, "Yep."

Jeremy walked. He didn't fight the two men or work to slow them down, but he was far from cooperative. Then a voice spoke to him. At first he thought it was one of the men but neither was paying him any attention. The voice came again.

"Dad."

The voice was familiar. It came to him fast.

"Nick," he said aloud.

The man on the left looked at him.

"She's coming. Lady in white. She's coming."

Nick was telling him that Biatta was on her way. Was that true, or was the voice just a creation of his mind to reassure him she and Nick were okay? He glanced over his shoulder. If Biatta was coming, she wasn't close enough to see.

The man on the right said, "Keep moving."

Biatta stood and brushed herself off.

"Are you feeling better?" her minder asked.

"Yes, I'm fine. Or I will be. She pulled out a small pouch she wore around her neck from inside her dress and opened it. Inside were several objects. She plucked out one of three tiny vials. She uncorked the stopper and tipped the liquid inside down her throat. Within thirty seconds she could feel the effects. Yes, now she was quite fine as the rejuvenating potion spread warmth through her body.

"If you will forgive me, I must be off."

"Off?" the man asked, concerned.

She smiled. "I mean to go…well, you understand. I shall just be a minute."

She ducked behind a tree, took out her owl icon, and spoke the transformation words. As she pushed off and rose skyward, she could hear the man calling from below.

"Please don't go! The headmaster will be angry with me."

She felt sorry for the man but she had things to do and he would only slow her down.

Within minutes, her powerful wings brought her over Jeremy and the two men escorting him. She recognized the men and knew neither possessed any magic, though they may have magically infused items. Knowing what she did next would not be challenged, she dove. No one noticed her until she was right on top of them. By then, it was too late to prevent her from snatching Jeremy up and soaring over the treetops with him screaming in her grasp.

Chapter Forty

The girl shrieked, slapped her hands to her head, and collapsed, writing on the ground. Bradenbaugh looked from the child to Madelyn. The attempt at an innocent look from mad woman told him all he needed to know.

"Madelyn, stop messing with the girl's mind. I need her sane to lead us to the others. If you destroy her mind, we may never find them."

She gave a mocking curtesy. "As you wish, my master."

Though she said the words without a sneer or display of malice, he knew she did not consider him her master. Not for the first time he thought she had to be dealt with, though not yet. He still needed her skill, and in a fight, her sheer brutality was worth ten of the others he had assembled.

"We are coming to a more populated area. Her screams will draw attention we don't need. Once we find and finish the other students, you can play with her all you want."

"My apologies, master. This trip is boring and I needed a momentary diversion. It won't happen again."

She smiled sweetly. It was not a sight that transferred warmth to the receiver.

Before he moved again, one of his scouts joined them. "There is a road up ahead with a lot of traffic. If we continue straight, we will have to cross it."

"Probe the girl's mind," he said to Madelyn. "Make sure we are on the right path." To the scout, he said, "Show me."

They walked for ten minutes before reaching the edge of the forest. A street ran east and west and had many vehicles traveling in both directions. It was more traffic than he ever saw back in their world. Across the street was a row of trees but not a forest. Between the trunks was a line of buildings. Some sort of shopping center. People moved about, making the job of remaining unseen difficult.

Bradenbaugh scanned the road in both directions and settled on moving east. They ducked back into the woods to stay out of view, yet close enough that he could see the road and what was behind it. They came to a creek with a bridge running over it. Though not wide, to cross they needed to go over the bridge. They stopped.

As Bradenbaugh studied the immediate surroundings, he spied a delivery truck unloading behind a building on the far side of the creek. He turned to his scout.

"Get the others and meet me here."

Once his scout left, Bradenbaugh crossed the bridge and moved toward the truck. He slowed his approach when he realized the driver was not alone. Two people from inside the establishment were lending a hand. He stopped at the back end of a parked car, squatted, and watched.

The truck appeared to be carrying food. *The business must be a restaurant*, he thought. That could offer some additional benefits. Minutes later, the driver pulled the roll down door closed, waved to the other two, and got inside the cab. There was beeping as the truck reversed. Bradenbaugh stepped out behind the truck and smacked the tail with the palm of his hand loud enough to be heard.

Instantly, the beeping ceased and the truck jerked to a stop. He heard the door open. The man rounded the rear of the truck and pulled up short seeing Bradenbaugh standing there.

"You think that's funny? I thought I ran you over. Get out of the way."

Bradenbaugh smiled. "Sleep," he said, waving his hand at the man. The man took a step and fell smacking his face on the blacktop.

"Oops!" Bradenbaugh said.

He moved forward, dragged the man behind the truck, then rolled the door part way up. He hoisted the body into the truck but left the door partially open. Then, he got into the driver's seat and moved the truck to the street. He waited there for a few minutes, looking for his group. When they appeared, he motioned through the window for them to come. They would be crowded, but it beat walking the entire way.

Gwynedd was getting weaker. She had held up her defenses so far but the crazy woman was so much stronger and if she suspected Gwynedd was faking, she had little doubt her retribution would be quick and painful.

Though only in her first year at school, she did know some things. Her natural ability was much like the crazy woman's. She could work a person's mind. Early on in her young life, she heard voices and thought she was going as insane as the woman who controlled her. She dared not tell her parents, siblings, or friends, but they knew something was bothering her by the constant pained expression on her face. It was a while before she discovered the cause. She had the ability to read minds. One of the first lessons she learned at school had to do with the ethics of listening in on a person's thoughts. She learned how to block the voices, how to pinpoint just one voice, and the most important skill, to block other people's probes.

She had to let the crazy woman in or she might suspect what Gwynedd was doing, but she was able to direct her probe to where Gwynedd had control and only gave her the information Gwynedd allowed. So far, her ruse had gone undetected and she was leading them to a small town she had seen once when they lived at the village in the forest. But eventually they would get suspicious or her power would deplete, granting the crazy woman complete access to her mind.

She had already felt how cruel her torturer could be, though not nearly as painful as she let on, she still caused damage. If she ever found out Gwynedd had been misleading them, she would not be able to fend off the assault unleashed upon her brain. Each new minor attack drained her. She prayed the others rescued her before the crazy woman shredded her mind.

Nick's eyes opened. He scanned the room. Chandra and the kids were there, all absorbed in whatever they were working on. The kids were working on projects. Chandra had her face in her phone. He needed to get out of the hospital room without causing a scene. His father needed his help. Did he dare confide in Chandra? She had made it clear on several occasions she was not one of his fans. She'd never believe him.

Hi, Uncle Nick.

Startled, Nick glanced at Connor. The boy was looking at him and flashing a big grin. Had the greeting been verbal or only in his head? Connor pointed a finger at his own head as if in answer. Nick felt his eyes widen in surprise. Had Connor just replied to his thought?

Connor seemed to be thinking, then he nodded.

No way.

"Yes way."

This time, he knew the words were spoken.

"What's that, honey?" Chandra asked without looking up.

Nick gave a quick shake of his head and closed his eyes.

"Nothing, Mommy."

"He's just being weird again," Harper said. She rolled her eyes and shook her head.

"That's good," said Chandra, only half listening.

Starting from about age sixteen, Nick had to deal with the constant voices. He always thought he was unique and that it was some form of mental illness. Connor apparently had the same curse, and at a lot younger age. He did not want to see his nephew go through the same things he had. The voices would eventually drive him nuts. He knew from firsthand experience. His own parents thought so and thought he was on drugs. If he was being honest, he was on drugs, but only after they accused him and only because it was the only way he found to keep the voices contained.

He tested the connection between Connor and himself. *Connor.*

The boy set his Legos down and turned to face him. He smiled broadly. He was such a good looking kid and his smile was infectious. He smiled back and Connor gave him a quick wave.

Listen, buddy, I have to get out of here.

Before he finished his thought, Connor was getting down off his chair.

No. No. Don't tell your mother. I want to play a hide and seek game with her. Can you get her out of the room without telling her so I can hide?

He nodded. "Mommy?"

Nick barely had time to close his eyes.

"Yes, honey?"

"I have to go potty."

Harper tossed her crayon down and hopped from her chair. "Me too, Mommy."

"Okay. Connor, you go first. It's right behind that door."

The boy stood wavering. Evidently, he hadn't known about the bathroom inside the room, Nick thought. Nick heard, *Uh-oh,* in his head.

"I'm hungry too. Afterward, can we get something to eat?"

"Yeah, that's a good idea. Go to the bathroom and I'll tell the nurse we're stepping out for a bit."

Chandra's heels clacked across the tiled floor as she left the room. Nick sent his thoughts to Connor.

Nice job.

I know.

Nick waited until he no longer heard Chandra's heels before making his move. After the kids used the bathroom, his sister took their little hands and led them from the room. Nick got up and wheeled the IV stand toward the closet, hoping his clothes were inside. To his relief, a hospital bag with his dirty clothes had been set at the bottom. He took it out and put his pants and shoes on. Once he took the IV out and tore off the monitor pads, beeping would start. He wanted to be ready to go by then.

He turned the power off, put his shirt on, and slid from the room. He closed the door behind him. One of the nurses looked up from her station.

He whispered, "He's sleeping."

She nodded.

He tried to appear casual as he walked but his legs wobbled a bit, forcing him to put out a hand to the wall to stabilize.

From behind, he heard, "Excuse me, sir."

Nick quickened his pace. He reached the elevators as someone else was exiting. He entered and pressed the button for the ground floor repeatedly. The tension built within him with each passing second until the doors closed. Even as they, did the nurse called, "Sir!"

He reached the ground floor and exited fast, keeping his head down. He didn't relax until he was out the hospital doors and a half mile down the street. Now came the hard part. Finding his father and the lady in white.

Chapter Forty-One

She settled at the old village. As soon as his feet touched ground, he pivoted and fought back what he considered an inappropriate urge to hug her. She didn't appear to have noticed.

"I'm too tired to fly us all the way, though in truth I'm not sure where all the way is. Can you drive us closer?"

"Sure. If I had a car and at least a general direction."

"What if I got you a vehicle?"

"You mean like steal one?"

"Let's say borrow."

"Well, if the question is if I can drive it, yeah. But would I? I just don't know. Stealing a car not only brings the law down on us, but it is an inconvenience to the car's owner. I'd rather just drive mine, but it's back at my house."

"Ah, actually..." Biatta said, "it's back near the portal."

He gazed at her, uncomprehending. "What?"

"Well, Daria and I needed to get here fast and I was too weak to fly, not to mention seeing a large owl carrying a girl might not have gone over well with the neighbors. I'm not sure I can get us there and I'm sure I can't do it without being seen. Here, at least we are in the woods."

"Can you get us to the street in that direction?" He pointed west.

"Yes. I can make it that far."

Biatta motioned for him to turn around, then took a few deep breaths and performed the transformation ritual. Jeremy was still awed by the process. How was it possible for a human to turn into an animal? In the movies, sure, but in real life? Yet here they were, flying. Now that he was used to being airborne, he had to admit it was exhilarating. But with little free space to use her full, wide wingspan, Biatta was forced to hug the treetops to prevent being seen, which made branches pass close to Jeremy.

She found a small clearing to land about fifty yards short of the road. They hiked from there until they heard a large crash ahead. They froze and Biatta motioned Jeremy to the side. They squatted in a thicket of bushes and waited. A short time later, they heard the heavy trampling of many footsteps approaching.

Biatta chanted something in a low voice, then swept her hands over their heads before bringing them down to the ground. It was like flinging a bed sheet into the air and letting it fall. She placed her lips at Jeremy's ear.

"Do not make a sound. Someone is coming, and my sense is they aren't good."

Thirty seconds later, a man broke through the undergrowth and strode passed them not twenty feet away. Ten seconds later, a group of people emerged and moved past. They were followed by a larger group, which included people Jeremy recognized. The man in black walked by himself, his hard eyes focused ahead.

He called out, "Madelyn, how much farther?"

Mad Madelyn McGrew came into view twenty feet behind Bradenbaugh. She walked next to a small dark-haired girl who appeared more zombielike than alive. Next to him, Biatta slapped her hands over her mouth. Jeremy thought something had happened to her. Large tears formed in her eyes and rolled down her cheeks.

Jeremy didn't know what was going on but was afraid they had been discovered and tensed. The wild-eyed woman with the dark-haired girl stopped for a moment as if aware of something. She scanned the area slowly, turning a circle, then stopped with her gaze almost directly on their small thicket.

"Madelyn!" the man in black yelled.

The sharpness of his tone snapped her head forward. She dug her hand into the girl's hair and yanked back.

"How much farther, girl?"

Though the girl didn't speak, the evil woman shouted a reply. "Twenty minutes!" They started moving again. "I can't wait to get there. You and I are going to have some fun."

Jeremy thought he heard a whimper as they passed from sight.

"My God! They have poor Gwynedd. That foul creature is torturing her." She wiped angrily at her tears. "Change of plans. You go find us a ride I'm going to rescue Gwynedd."

"Wait," Jeremy said. "Against that entire group? You won't stand a chance."

"I will not leave Gwynedd in the hands of that monster. I am going. It is not safe for you. Go. Do what I told you to and we will meet on the road."

She did not wait for a reply. She turned and loped away, taking a wider path to the side of Bradenbaugh's army.

Undecided whether to follow her orders or follow her, Jeremy hesitated. He knew she was trying to keep him safe and he appreciated that, but it felt wrong leaving her to face them on her own. How could he possibly help? He had no special superhero abilities or magical skill like Biatta. Superheroes? Magic? Had he bought into this fantasy world? Didn't this all have to be a dream? Perhaps he was in a coma in the hospital. Regardless, he had to do something. If he was in a coma, maybe this was his brain's way of reviving him. Solve the problem and wake up.

Jeremy turned to do as instructed. Maybe Biatta was his brain sending him on the best path for recovery. Did he really believe that?

As he walked, he called up all the strange things that occurred in the past, what? Three days? Week? He lost track. Another sign he wasn't all right. Daria, Biatta, the wild boars, the rat-faced men, an invisible village, a goat head man, being abducted, taken to another world, riding a wolf. What else? Good Lord, if he ever told that lineup of events and characters to anyone, they'd lock him away in a looney bin. Of course, he was dreaming.

Lost in thought, he tripped over a fallen branch and fell, catching his weight on his hands. Pain shot through his palm. He yelped and pushed back to his feet with one hand while looking at the other. A sliver of wood was embedded in the palm. He stared at it for a moment while his hand throbbed. If this was a dream, would he feel pain?

He removed the sliver. A tiny droplet of blood formed. He stared at it, seeing all the pain and loneliness in his life. Life was just so fragile. Miranda. God, he missed Miranda. He was suddenly extremely tired. Not for the first time in the past year, he thought maybe it was time to see Miranda.

Fresh images came to him. His mind fought back against the overwhelming urge to quit. Chandra. Nick. Connor. Harper. What about them? Weren't they worth living for? Wasn't seeing them a reason to fight back to consciousness? A random thought bloomed. He had missed Connor's birthday. The boy was six now. He owed him a present. He had to finish his task and get back to reality.

He was being the quitter he had always been. His failure as a husband, a father, a man. The only way to alter the ending to the story was to continue and vow to do better.

Jeremy cleared his mind and brought forth a new determination. If he was unconscious and this was the path for him to get back to his family, then he was going to do everything in his subconscious power to make that happen. With renewed vigor, Jeremy Kline moved to conquer his dream world.

Ahead of him, a delivery truck had bounced over the curb and into the trees. The street was forty feet beyond the truck. *Of course*, he thought. His brain was making it easier for him since he decided to go all in on his recovery.

He raced around the side to the driver's door, ready to enter when he heard, "Stop right there."

He jumped backward, surprised to hear a voice and find that he wasn't alone. A policeman was there with one hand pointing at him and the other on his holstered weapon.

"Is this your truck?"

"Uh, no, Officer. I just found it here."

"Then why were you getting in?"

"I, uh, wanted to make sure no one was hurt inside."

"You didn't drive this truck up here?"

"No. I came from the woods." He looked deeper into the trees, remembering he had a job to do. Was the officer there to assist him, or was he having a setback? He always respected the police and saw them as symbols for good. If this was a dream, his brain had created this man to help him.

"Officer, I saw something in the woods that I need your help with."

That statement made the man more wary. "What thing?"

"Look, I don't have time to explain. I can do that while we go."

"Buddy, I'm not going anywhere until you explain yourself."

The urgency of the situation agitated Jeremy. "Okay, look. I was walking through the woods with a friend. We saw a large group of people traipse through. I'm guessing they arrived in this truck. They had a little dark-haired girl with them. From the looks of her, I think she was abducted. She appeared to be drugged."

The officer straightened and hardened his eyes at the mention of the girl.

"Where is your friend?"

"Following them. She sent me to get help since neither of us has a phone. I saw the truck, thought that group came in it, and was hoping there might be a radio or phone. If not, then keys so I could drive for help. I'm not making this up. By appearances alone, this group did not look to be anything we wanted to confront."

"Are you on the level here?"

"I swear to you, I am. Officer, the girl wasn't older than maybe ten. What if they're using her as a sacrifice or something equally heinous?"

The officer was deep in thought, perhaps wondering if any of this was true. "Give me some ID." He motioned with his fingers.

Jeremy reached behind him for his wallet. It wasn't there. He patted both rear pockets. He had been taken from the house and didn't have his phone or wallet with him.

"I left it home."

"All right. You come with me while I call this in."

"That girl doesn't have long. We have to move now. Use the radio on your shoulder there to call in while we go." With that, Jeremy turned and bolted back into the trees.

"Hey! Come back here."

Though Jeremy had a head start, he had little doubt the officer could catch him. Still, he ran hoping to find Biatta and let her deal with the officer. Behind him, he could hear the officer calling in for backup. "White male. Six foot. In his sixties. Says a girl has been abducted and carried into the woods. I'm in pursuit."

Jeremy missed the rest as he heard a crash and a series of curses. *Officer down*, he thought. His brain was assisting his escape. With each obstacle the condition placing him in the coma had created, his brain and body rose to conquer it and move forward. He realized then he was fully onboard with the dreamworld explanation. None of this was real. With the images of his children and grandchildren dancing before him like a carrot on a string, Jeremy pushed his body to move faster.

Chapter Forty-Two

Biatta slowed and crouched when she heard the trampling of branches and undergrowth. Where were they going? It came to her in a flash. The village. Why would they go there? If they were tapping into Gwynedd's mind, they had to know the village was abandoned...unless one of them could track the students from the village. But wait. Something didn't add up. Gwynedd had gone to the new location and been dispatched from there to bring the message from Jerricka. Gwynedd knew where the new location was, yet still led Bradenbaugh here. Gwynedd was misleading them.

She was alert inside that pretty little head.

The thought gave new hope to the rescue attempt. If Biatta managed to get into Gwynedd's head without alerting Mad Madelyn to her presence, they may be able to derive some plan for Gwynedd's escape.

She sent a quick probe. Blocked. How was that possible? Unless Madelyn had created the block. But why would she? No one else in this world had the ability to enter another's mind, so who was she blocking against? Her? Did Madelyn know she was here? No. They'd have a wider perimeter with magic wielders on the outside for defense. But if not blocked against her, then who?

The answer formed as a small flicker of light and grew into a possibility. Did Gwynedd herself possess the skill to raise a mental barrier to wall off a portion of her thoughts? If so, that was quite an advanced ability. It was also eye opening to the direction of Gwynedd's talent. An individual's talent often didn't manifest until their teens. If the block was Gwynedd's work, she was ahead of normal development, which meant her power might be great. It also meant she had more control over her own actions than Madelyn knew. That might prove helpful in their escape attempt.

Biatta tried to reach her again. Nothing. She had to get a signal to Gwynedd that she was there. To do so she needed a line of sight, which would place her close to Bradenbaugh's group. With as much speed as caution allowed, Biatta moved farther away from the group before angling to get in front. The position she established was ten yards to the front and offered a clear view of the approaching assault team. As she waited for a view of Gwynedd, she prepared her spell. It had to be precise so only Gwynedd saw it. It would take extreme concentration. She calmed other brain activity and focused all efforts on directing the spell.

As Gwynedd approached, Biatta only had a partial view. Madelyn's body blocked all but her legs. Annoyed at the unforeseen obstacle, Biatta flashed a hand in anger and a small broken branch lying at the side of their path moved. It slid between Madelyn's feet, causing her to stumble.

Gwynedd reacted, showing a startled but aware expression. Biatta worked fast, casting her spell with less control than she wanted. A tiny starburst like the dancing sparks of a sparkler appeared in front of Gwynedd's chest. The girl's eyes widened, then she quickly cupped her hands over the starburst, vanishing its affects.

Madelyn caught her balance and glared at Gwynedd. "You little witch. What did you just do?"

The group stopped and Bradenbaugh moved angrily toward them.

"Why are we stopping?" he snapped.

"'Cause missy here tried to escape. I think she saw something."

Bradenbaugh whirled, casting his gaze around them.

"What?" He motioned for several members of the team to spread out and search for intruders.

Madelyn gripped Gwynedd by the shoulders and shook her hard.

"Easy," Bradenbaugh warned. "Do not damage her until we no longer need her."

"That can't be soon enough." She grabbed Gwynedd's hair and yanked back.

Unable to continue her ruse through the pain, Gwynedd screamed.

"Aha!" Madelyn said in triumph. "You were faking. There's more to this girl than we first thought. She has been blocking my probes. Well, let's see how well you do when I unleash my full power on you."

"Madelyn!" Bradenbaugh said, reaching for the woman.

A sudden crash drew the entire group's attention. Ten feet away Jeremy appeared. He stumbled to a stop when he saw who was facing him. His eyes went wide with fright.

"You!" Bradenbaugh and Jeremy said simultaneously.

Jeremy pivoted to run. More crashing from beyond Jeremy raised a more aggressive posture from Bradenbaugh's people.

The officer came into view. As soon as he saw the group before him, he stopped. Confusion crossed his face that clouded into suspicion.

Jeremy pointed. "There they are. Just like I told you."

The officer looked from Jeremy and back to the group, then keyed his mic as he pulled his weapon. Before he got more out than, "I need . . ." or cleared his gun from the holster, a large dart-like blade pierced his throat. His hands went to his neck as his legs buckled. Gagging, he dropped to his knees.

Jeremy moved to assist him. Bradenbaugh instructed his minions to grab Jeremy. The scene before Biatta quickly escalated out of control. Gwynedd, free from Madelyn's clutches for the moment, backed away ready to run. She needed cover, as did Jeremy. Biatta called up her heavy mist. It took a moment for the tendrils of smoke to rise from the forest ground. The advancing people running toward Jeremy ran through it, unaware of anything out of the ordinary. But Bradenbaugh, Madelyn, and two others recognized the occurrence for what it was.

Biatta threw all her energy into expediting and intensifying the spell. The result was a sudden whiteout that engulfed a large area. Biatta sent a mental message.

Run, Gwynedd!

As soon as she was obscured from sight, Biatta ran. Like a spirit, she moved through the thick billowing mist. As the creator, she alone had a clearer view. She dodged past several of Bradenbaugh's people, touching them as she passed. Using a magic she loathed and feared, she said, "Muertos," with each contact. Those touched fell to the ground, convulsing until their spirits fled their bodies.

Biatta reached the other side of the group and called to Gwynedd.

Here! came the mental reply.

Biatta veered to her, scooping her in her arms as she went.

Behind her she heard Madelyn shout, "The girl! She's gone!"

Bradenbaugh said, "Find her. Forget about the man. Find the girl."

As she ran, Biatta worked the owl icon from her pocket, but try as she might, she did not have the strength needed to activate the spell. After only a short run, Biatta was forced to set Gwynedd down. She took her hand and ran hard, forcing Gwynedd's shorter legs to keep up. The mist's duration was limited to the amount of energy put into it. Already weakened but desperate to make it work, Biatta used all remaining reserves to thicken and hurry the mist. It would not last long. She hoped to be much farther away by the time it faded enough for Bradenbaugh's people to give chase.

She thought about Jeremy. She hoped he was all right and got away in the chaos because she did not have the ability to perform another rescue. For now, she concentrated on getting distance from her pursuers. After that, she wasn't sure what to do. Perhaps their best chance of staying free was to mingle with the residents of this world. That was a huge gamble though, knowing Bradenbaugh's and Madelyn's disregard for life. They wouldn't hesitate to injure or kill anyone who stood in their path. Still, that option was the best she came up with, considering the situation.

"This way," she said pulling Gwynedd toward where she thought the street was. To her immediate right she could hear the sound of grunting, like someone exerting extreme effort. She motioned Gwynedd down. They crouched low and tried to peer through the branches at the source of the sound. She caught movement. Then a voice.

"It's not much farther. Stay with me. I'll get you help."

Biatta recognized the voice. Jeremy. She stood for a better view. Jeremy had the officer's arm draped over his shoulder and struggled to keep him moving. The officer had little strength left Jeremy was more dragging than carrying him. With a quick check to the right to listen for the sounds of pursuit, Biatta moved. She rushed to Jeremy's side, giving him a start. He cried out.

"Shh!" Biatta hissed. "Set him down. Hurry."

Jeremy laid the barely conscious man down. From the same pocket that contained the owl icon, Biatta removed a plain wooden ring wrapped with a tiny green vine. She slid it on a finger. The healing ring had stored energy with the spell ready to perform. She always kept a few magically infused tokens on her for just such a situation.

The officer tried to speak. Blood bubbled up from his mouth.

"He is drowning in his own blood. When I tell you, pull the blade out. Do it slow and steady. Do not jerk it or you might ruin what I'm doing."

The officer put a restraining hand on her arm and gave a slight shake.

"It is the only way. You will die long before help arrives. Trust me." She touched his forehead and a faint glow appeared and died out. "Can you do that?"

His eyeballs clouded as his eyelids began to close.

"Now, Jeremy."

She closed her eyes, mumbled the activation words, and placed her fingers loosely around the retracting knife. Blood pushed out, though not with force. The puckered flaps of skin meshed until only a thin line was visible.

"Turn him on his side," she instructed Jeremy. Batta ran her ring finger from the officer's belt, up his torso, over the wound, and to his mouth. The man coughed and vomited up a small pool of blood.

His radio came active. "Johnson. Joe. We're here. Where are you?"

Jeremy pushed the button on the shoulder mic. "Your officer is here deeper in the woods. He has been injured and needs immediate medical attention." He released the button.

The voice on the other end asked, "Who is this?"

Jeremy went to answer but Biatta stopped him. She shook her head.

"He will live. We have to go."

Something large crashed through the branches about twenty yards away. Gwynedd extended her arms to the side, chanted something in a whisper, then made a throwing motion with both arms. A sudden noise sounded twenty yards away in the opposite direction.

"Over there," a deep voice said. The approaching pursuers altered course.

Biatta gave Gwynedd an approving nod and the trio moved. Twenty minutes later, they reached the forest edge and the main street that ran through it. A fast-approaching siren had them ducking for cover. An ambulance raced past. Jeremy signaled them to move. After nearly an hour, they reached Jeremy's subdivision.

For the moment, they were safe.

Chapter Forty-Three

A deep heavy rumble shook Daria awake. She sat up and gazed around her. No one was in the room watching her. Dark black streaks along one wall and several support beams showed where the wood was charred from the fire she'd unleashed. The other damage and destruction she had caused had been cleaned up.

Spurred by the fact no one was watching her, Daria stretched out a tentative hand, surprised when it met no resistance or magical bars. Eager to be away before they returned, Daria hopped off the bed. She stood for a moment listening for sounds of anyone approaching. She took two more cautious steps and eyed the open front door, ready to bolt. Before her next step, the ground shook again, this time longer than the first time. She was thrown off balance and prevented a fall by clutching at the kitchen counter.

She held that position until the floor stopped shaking, then moved to the door. The black man was standing on the end of the wooden front porch looking out over the mountainside. She recognized him from the headmaster's office. He was the one who had smashed her against the wall. Why was he here? One of the women stood a few feet from him doing the same. The other woman sat in a rocking chair knitting. That had to be Delphina. She was the calmer of the two sisters. Knowing escape wasn't likely, Daria chose to make her presence known and hopefully get some information.

"What was that?"

They all turned to look at her as if they had expected her sooner.

The man said, "You felt that?"

The question surprised her. "How could I not? What was it? An earthquake?"

The man shook his head. Oli answered in a civil tone. "No, child. What you felt is not natural and can't be felt by everyone."

It took her a minute to understand the answer. "Magic?"

"Yes," the man said. "Long-buried dark magic. Someone is attempting to open the dark one's crypt."

"The dark one?"

"Yes, I'm afraid so. They shouldn't be able to break him free, at least not without the keys that were hidden around the world, but someone is trying anyway and by the feel of it, they're having some success."

"Who has magic powerful enough shake the ground?" Daria said.

Oli snorted. "No one on this world." She walked away and sat in a chair next to her sister.

"The dark one is awakening. The rumbling you feel is from him attacking his prison from the inside."

"Who is the dark one?"

Kanter exhaled a long breath before speaking. "An old acquaintance of mine and one time head master of the academy you attended. He experimented with dark magic and succumbed to its power and call. The evil that enveloped him was released o the world almost destroying much of it until he was stopped and locked away."

Daria had a sudden desire to wrap her arms around her body to protect against the chill settling over her. She had never heard that story before. "Shouldn't someone stop him?"

The black man gazed at her. "Someone should. But not us."

Daria came out onto the porch. "I don't understand. If this dark one is evil and has that kind of power, shouldn't everyone want to stop him?"

"No. It's not our fight. If we leave him alone, he will leave us alone."

"And what if he doesn't? How will you feel if working with the other wizards in the world could have stopped him? Seems to me that's not a good plan at all."

"It's not up to you, though, child," Oli said.

"Maybe not, but if needed, I'd at least try to lend a hand. I won't sit on a porch on a mountain top and hide."

"You talk so bravely now. If you ever faced that kind of raw evil power, you would run as fast as those spindles you call legs can carry you."

"Maybe I would, but unless I try, how will I know?"

Delphina spoke for the first time, her eyes never leaving her work. "Daria, we are doing you a favor by keeping you here away from the upcoming war."

"You may see it that way, but I don't. If you do nothing to prevent this evil from destroying the world, be they magic or normal, you are just as bad as this dark one. Doing nothing when the world is threatened is just…wrong. Cowardly."

Oli was on her feet and moving with haste and threat of violence toward Daria. Daria did not back up or even flinch. She held her ground and prepared to dish out as much as she got. She was done cowering from these people.

She felt the presence of the black man behind her. Olivianna pulled up short but did not take her angry glare from Daria. "You are fortunate my father is here to protect you."

"Father?" Daria glanced over her shoulder at the black man. His dark eyes gave nothing away.

Delphina said, "Are you sure she needs protecting, Father? Look at her posture. Look at her eyes. She has no fear of you, Oli."

"That's because she doesn't know any better."

"Perhaps, but I have a feeling you may bear the brunt of your actions by at least half of what you deal out."

Oli turned to her sister, aghast. "Are you serious right now, sister?"

"Absolutely. Can't you feel that? The air around us is stirring. Without trying, the energy rushes to her. Though she is unlearned now, if she is smart enough to accept our training, she may well be more powerful than the two of us together."

Daria said nothing but continued to look calmly into Oli's eyes. Oli studied her with curiosity, like seeing something new for the first time.

"It's a shame then that she is not smart enough. I'd very much like to see that." She backed away and returned to her seat.

Daria said, "Here's the situation. You want me here. I don't want to be here. You know I will fight you at every turn. You have to ask yourself if the damage and hassle I cause will be worth your efforts. Just look at the interior of your house to verify that statement."

"You have a point to make," the black man said as a statement.

"I have a deal to offer. Return me to my friends. Once I have established that they are all right and lend a hand to ensure they stay that way, I will return of my own free will. Less damage, less hassle, more cooperation. Should be an easy decision." She turned toward the door. "I'm hungry. Let me know what you decide."

Daria went inside, leaving them astounded.

After stealing a car, Nick found his way to the house. He could feel the lady in white's presence within. She was weak but alive. The house had taken some damage since he was last there. The front door was propped up in its frame. The garage door was destroyed.

It had taken him hours to arrive. No one was willing to pick him up when he put out his thumb. That didn't surprise him. Although he had hitched rides for a lot of years, he did not have the appearance that gave drivers a comforting feeling. In the end, he found a car with a running engine. Someone had popped in someplace for a quick stop. Police warn against doing that for this very reason. He hopped in.

He entered the house, ducking under the remnants of the crumpled garage door. The interior door was locked. He knocked. Inside, he heard footsteps. Someone stopped on the other side of the door. He assumed they were listening.

Sure it was his father, he called out, "Dad! It's me, Nick."

Inside, his father repeated the name. "Nick!" The door was unlocked and whipped open. His father stood in the doorway with a wondrous smile and watery eyes. He stepped down and embraced Nick, his emotions causing a momentary lack of oxygen. "I'm so glad you are here." He stepped back and ushered him inside. "I'm sorry I didn't make it to the hospital. Something came up and I was kind of unreachable. Are you all right?" He shut and locked the door before facing Nick. Without waiting for a response, he went on. "I assume you are, since they released you. You should have had one of the nurses contact me. I would have come to pick you up."

"Dad. Dad, relax. I'm all right. I need to speak to the lady in white."

The words stymied his father. "Nick, she has been through a lot and is resting. It's important she get some sleep."

"I understand that, Dad, but she has to know what's coming."

Jeremy stiffened and went to the front window. He pulled back the curtain to scan the outside.

"Coming? You don't mean now, do you?"

"No, Dad. Not now. Not here. But she has to be warned."

"Can it wait until she wakes?"

Nick sighed. He had come such a long way to speak with her, but perhaps it was for the best. After his long excursion he needed a rest and a shower. "Okay, Dad. I'm going to sleep a bit as well. Please wake me as soon as she wakes."

"Okay."

"No, Dad. Promise me. It's a life and death thing."

"I promise. Now go. Rest. Oh. Biatta's in your room and another girl is in your sister's old room. Take our room."

Nick nodded and walked toward the hallway.

"Nick," his father said.

He stopped and looked over his shoulder.

"It is so good to have you home."

"Thanks, Dad. It feels good to be here."

Chapter Forty-Four

Rowan was angry. His people had lost Jeremy and after walking for more than an hour, they were still no closer to finding Bradenbaugh. In fact, he was certain they were lost. With each step his anger increased.

Tarney's dog form raced toward them. It stopped, shimmered, and Tarney was there.

"There is an abandoned village ahead. I believe it is the one Jerricka and the students occupied."

Rowan nodded. That was good. At least he knew they were on the right track.

"Did she leave any tracking markers?"

"None that I noticed, but I did pick up a scent. It wasn't the students. I think Bradenbaugh has passed through. The scent is fresh, so I estimate they are not more than fifteen minutes ahead. I have two of our people following the trail. They were not careful about hiding their path."

"Do you sense a trap?"

"No, but it doesn't mean one isn't waiting for us."

"Return to your people. If there is a trap, you are more experienced at locating it before it springs. We are going to pick up our pace to close the gap. Do we have anyone who can get ahead of Bradenbaugh's army to warn Jerricka about what is coming?"

"No. Not unless I do it."

"I wish Biatta was here," Rowan muttered.

"But she's not, so let's deal with reality and use what we have available."

"Yes, of course. You are right. Stay on the trail. If things look clear or you are confident your people can handle what might be waiting for them, get ahead and warn

Jerricka. I'm sure she is prepared for an attack, but advance notice can't hurt."

As Tarney ran off morphing into dog form, Rowan called out. "We need to speed up. We are not far behind."

"Another runner arrived, this one from the west. "Sir, there is a lot of activity about a hundred yards in that direction." He pointed. "About twenty men and women in uniform like what our enforcement officers wear back home. They are heading this way searching for something or someone and have weapons drawn as if expecting trouble."

That was all they needed, another delay. They could not risk an engagement with local authorities. His guess was Bradenbaugh got into an exchange and reinforcements had been called in.

"Everyone move swiftly and quietly to the east. A large party of locals are heading this way. If possible, I want to avoid contact. Go."

To the runner, he said, "Keep an eye on their progress. Do not get involved. If anything changes, get back to us fast."

The man ran off, leaving Rowan to work out options, should they not be able to avoid the advancing officers. If they didn't handle this distraction right, the delay may prove costly. The most important question was what to do if a confrontation was imminent. Surrender and hope to explain their presence away? Fight? Or run and hope most of his people got away?

The worst-case scenario was to get caught between the officers and Bradenbaugh's army. Though he had no wish to harm any locals, Bradenbaugh would not have the same qualms. There would be bloodshed.

Their best course of action was to avoid contact completely. Unfortunately, the best course of action seldom turned out to be the actual course of action.

Things had been running smoothly over the past few days. The students had accepted their new daily routines and were making great progress with their studies. They had gathered most of the students they had housed in various places during their move and now all but a dozen students were once again together. Those were spread out in six houses where well-meaning and supportive locals had given them temporary shelter. The returned students also brought back Neveah and Gianna as well as Aric and Larrinan. That gave them strength and more defensive capabilities, should the need arise. Gone still were Allyra and Favyon, who were watching over the twelve sheltered away from the farm.

Jerricka could not be more pleased with their overall progress. Then why didn't she feel that way? It was when things were going well that bad things popped up. Perhaps that was negative, but she was unable to shake the feeling. It was better to listen to her internal concerns and be ready rather than taken by surprise.

Ever since Martine returned, Jerricka's thoughts and prayers were with Gwynedd. She berated herself daily for sending a child on such a dangerous mission, and one with so little training and life experience. A child, God forgive her, who was the most expendable of the students. Her hands rose to her face in distress and disgust. *What have I done?* Jerricka vowed that if Gwynedd survived her mission, she would step down as headmistress of the school. She did not deserve such a lofty position of power and respect, not after possibly sending a young girl to her death.

It was still too early for Gwynedd's return, but it didn't stop her stomach from doing nervous flips. If something happened to the girl, Jerricka would never forgive herself. A self-banishment was in store for her.

A knock on her door interrupted her anxious thoughts. She wiped at her eyes, sucked in a deep breath, and put on her business face.

"Enter."

Jno, strode in and stopped in front of her desk. "Headmistress."

She winced at the title.

"Someone has passed through the village."

Jerricka rose as excitement bubbled within her. "Someone? Any idea who?"

Her mind created an image of Gwynedd returning home. *Home.* How strange she now considered this world home.

"We do not know the identity, but it was more than one person."

"How many?"

"The wards were not set to give that information. The only thing we have to go on is the length of time the wards chimed."

"Give me an educated guess."

"A guess, Headmistress?"

He sounded as surprised as she was to hear the words come from her mouth. Guess was not in her vocabulary. She only dealt in facts.

"Yes. Give me your best estimate how many passed through the village."

"Judging by the length of time before the chimes shut down and taking into account if they stopped for a period in the village…"

"Jno, please. Your answer."

"Five to ten. Best guess."

Jerricka turned from him as she ran the answer around her thoughts. A group that small might be Gwynedd and an escort. It could also be an advance or hunting team sent by Bradenbaugh. Either way, she had to know. She pivoted.

"Send two of your best scouts toward the village. We need to know if anyone is coming, friend or foe."

"Headmistress, we only have two besides me. Others are away performing other duties."

Jerricka sighed. Numbers were a definite problem. "Send who you can."

Jno nodded and left.

Jerricka sat. She pushed away her hopes that Gwynedd was returning safely for more imperative matters. It might be time for the students to go on a field trip for the day until they knew for sure if danger was approaching. She checked the time. They would be moving toward their afternoon classes now.

She rose and left to put the trip in motion.

The front door was pulled back from the frame to reveal a stocky dark-haired man in the doorway. The man looked as surprised as Jeremy. Quick to react, Jeremy raced into the kitchen, snatched up a chef's knife, and whirled ready to fight.

"No you don't. Not this time."

After leaning the door against the outside wall, the man entered. He held one hand up as if signaling *Easy*, yet the other hand rested on a holstered gun at his hip.

"Get out of my house."

"Your house? *You're* Jeremy Kline?"

"Who wants to know?" The tension in Jeremy's chest built with each step the intruder took. He feigned a lunge with the knife even though they stood ten feet apart.

"You really don't want to do that, sir." He lifted the gun halfway out to emphasize his point.

"I do if you think you're taking me again."

"I'm not here to harm you or take you. I'm Detective Vasili. I'm working your case."

"My case? Why do I have a case?"

"Because your neighbors reported an altercation here and several saw you hauled away. Also, your daughter has given us information about two women that led us to believe you were kidnapped and possibly in danger."

Jeremy lowered the knife a few inches. "Let me see a badge."

"I'm reaching for it now. If you move toward me with that knife, I will shoot."

Jeremy swallowed hard, not doubting for a second the man would do just that.

He pulled a black wallet out, took a step forward, and set it on the island countertop. With a flick of his finger, he sent it sliding toward Jeremy. Not wanting to take his eyes off the supposed detective, he reached blindly for the wallet but kept missing.

"Oh, for God's sake," Vasili said. He took three steps back. "There. No way I can reach you now. Pick up the wallet."

Jeremy shot a glance at the wallet, then picked it up. He opened it and read. The man was who he said he was. Jeremy placed it back on the countertop and flicked it back. His flick sent the wallet flying off the end. It smacked onto the floor and Vasili gave an annoyed look.

"Satisfied now? Put the knife down so we can talk."

Jeremy hesitated but set the knife down in front of him, still within reach.

"Why don't you move over there and sit down?" Vasili motioned to a kitchen chair. "Get away from that knife. We'll both be safer."

"I prefer to stand right here."

"Okay. I've had enough of this." He pulled his gun. "Move to that chair. Now."

Jeremy raised his hands and sidestepped to the chair. Once seated, Vasili picked up the knife and set it in a drawer. Then he holstered his weapon.

"Now, we talk. Mister Kline, you have a lot of explaining to do." He waited for Jeremy to reply. When there was none, he continued. "Why don't you tell me what happened here. I don't see any injuries. Did anyone actually abduct you or did you stage the whole thing?"

"Stage? Do you think I would do this to my own—" A thought struck, stopping his sentence. If he admitted he had been taken, the investigation would continue. He didn't want that. "No, I wasn't abducted. I went a little crazy and made a mess of everything. I'm sorry. I feel much better now."

"Oh, do you?" Vasili said, an amused twinkle in his eyes. "So, you're telling me you did all this to your own home?"

"Yes."

"And staged an abduction to cover your temporary insanity?"

"No. No abduction. I don't know where you got that from. After I saw the damage I did, I was so upset with myself that I just left. I went for a long drive."

"Your car was still in the garage. It's gone now. Did you come back and get it? If so, where is it now? I see a different car in the driveway. Did you exchange it or is someone else here?"

"I walked. I'm old. I forget easily."

"Mister Kline, I don't know what went on here, but I know that story is BS. You want to try again?"

"No. I don't think so. I'm perfectly happy with this one."

"Even though it's a lie. You're lying to an officer of the law. That's a crime in itself."

"Dad?"

The two men looked up. Chandra stood in the doorway. Her mouth worked, trying to form words but nothing came out. Then she entered.

"I don't know whether to hug you or punch you." He stood as she approached and she started with the hug. "I was so worried. Where have you been? And what happened here?"

"Uh…well, it's a long story. One I'm embarrassed to tell, so why don't we wait until we're alone?"

"No," Vasili said. "That's not gonna work for me. You can tell your tale now or down at the station. If we go to the station, I promise it will be an all-day event. Your choice."

"Dad, just tell us. I can't take much more stress. First, you disappear, leaving the house destroyed. God, Mom would be so upset to see this place now. Then, I find Nick has returned, and then he disappears. I just can't do this anymore. It was those two women, wasn't it? They suckered you into something—you didn't give them money, did you? Oh, Dad. Talk to me."

Vasili said, "You know, he might if you took a breath and gave him a chance."

Chandra's cheeks colored. Jeremy could see the flare of anger light her eyes but she clammed up.

"Now, Mister Kline. Tell us a story, and this time make it the truth. Or at least believable."

Chapter Forty-Five

Biatta was awakened by the voices. She felt better but certainly could use more sleep. The constant morphing and use of heavy spells had taken its toll on her body. Judging by the tone of one voice, the discussion in the outer room was less than cordial. With as much stealth as the squeaking bed allowed, she rose and crept to the door. In slow increments, she opened the door to hear what was being said. She wanted to be ready in case Jeremy needed assistance.

She heard the stranger identify himself as a local enforcement officer. Evidently, someone had called him because of the recent events at the house. Once the voices sounded calmer, Biatta eased the door open and stalked across the hall to the room Gwynedd occupied. She opened the door with care. Though the door did creak, it wasn't loud. Biatta slipped through, closing the door behind her.

Gwynedd was still asleep. Her ordeal had drained her. Having that monster Madelyn in her head was enough to drain or warp the strongest of minds, let alone a child's. Biatta recalled the image of the girl casting her spell. She was impressed with Gwynedd, but not so much by the spell itself; that was a simple one to master. It was more for how quick she reacted and came up with a diversion on her own. Their students had been forced to grow up fast to survive. She was proud of all of them but especially Gwynedd, who had been alone with some completely evil people.

She watched her sleep for a few seconds, reveling in how peaceful she looked. If only she was allowed to stay that way and have the opportunity to enjoy her childhood. She wanted to talk with her but for now, sleep was more important.

Biatta rose and went to the door. As she cracked it open, she discovered a new element had been added to the already tense atmosphere in the front room. Jeremy's daughter Chandra had entered the house and the discussion. That was enough to raise anyone's anxiety. Biatta found the woman a little too tightly wound. Sure, she had a right to worry about her father. What child wouldn't, given the circumstances, but she was beyond that to the point of being controlling. She lectured and criticized Jeremy when instead she should be supportive.

It was best to avoid Chandra. Biatta knew the other woman disliked her, seeing Biatta as a threat to her father. If she ever relaxed, Biatta might convince her they meant Jeremy no harm and were there for his protection. She doubted Chandra was capable of believing anything Biatta said, so in the end, it was better not to be seen.

She slid into the hall to go back to her own room, but as she passed Jeremy's door, a whispered voice called to her.

"Lady in white. Lady in white," the tortured voice repeated.

Biatta pressed an ear to the door but only heard more of the same. She opened the door and entered. On the bed was Jeremy's son Nick. *Now that was interesting. How did he get here?*

She moved to the bed and watched him. His face was drawn like he was under great stress. The same three words streamed from his mouth. Something about the young man intrigued her. When she had healed him earlier, a strange raw power coursed through him. It attacked her as if in defense of his body, even as she tried to heal his fever. However, she had caught a glimpse of Nick's anguish. It was based in a deep-seated guilt that stemmed from his mother. He harbored resentment, sadness, and self-doubt ever since being banished from the house because of suspected drug abuse. It hadn't been drugs, though. It was his strange ability to see things in the future and the myriad voices that filled his mind.

Nick only started using drugs after his banishment to control the voices. The voices were driving him crazy. Biatta could feel that he was on the verge of a mental breakdown when she first touched him. She had pulled so much psychic poison from his mind the first time it took all her strength to ward it from infecting her. His thoughts were clearer now, uninfected. Now he seemed to have purpose, and whatever it was involved her.

She sat on the edge of the bed and studied the troubled face. If he ever allowed himself to relax, he might be a handsome young man. The years of constant strain had aged him beyond his years.

She lifted a tentative hand and placed her fingertips on his forehead. She only meant to enter his dreams but as soon as she made contact, his eyes shot open. He stared at her for a moment before relief washed over his face.

"Lady in white. You came."

"Yes. I am here, although I haven't had anything white to wear in a while." She smiled and glanced down at the jeans and sweater she had pulled on from Chandra's closet to replace her soiled and torn signature white dress.

He soaked in the warmth of her presence, smiling as if entering a happy dream. Then his eyes clouded and narrowed.

"Lady in white, he comes."

"*He* who?"

"The evil one. The dark one. He rises. You are in danger. Your entire world is in danger. You must not go back."

"If the dark one rises, I must go back."

"No!" he said loudly. "You cannot go back. You will die."

That announcement shocked her. Then the door opened and Chandra said, "I thought so. Here's the problem, Detective. As far as I'm concerned, she's been behind all the trouble around here. Ever since she showed up, my father has been out of control. If he's involved in something bad, it's her fault." Then she noticed who was on the bed. "Oh my God. Are you responsible for kidnapping Nick from the hospital too?"

"Chandra, stop!" Jeremy's voice was loud and authoritative. The tone shut Chandra up but her mouth fell open. "Biatta had nothing to do with Nick. He showed up here all on his own. In fact, he came looking for Biatta. You are out of line to accuse her of anything besides trying to help me."

With Chandra temporarily unable to speak, Vasili stepped between them and entered the bedroom.

"You are Biatta?"

Biatta saw no reason to deny her name. "I am."

"What's your last name?"

"Armstrong," she said without hesitation.

He jotted it down. "This woman." He pointed at Chandra.

Chandra got riled anew. *"This woman?"*

Vasili ignored her. "…has leveled some serious allegations at you. Do you wish to respond?"

"She believes I am here to take advantage of her father."

"And are you?"

"Of course not. Jeremy is a strong-minded, intelligent man who cannot be manipulated by a woman. He is still very much in love with his wife. He would never allow anyone to take advantage of him. We are friends. He offered me a room when I had no place to stay."

"What did you offer him in return?"

Chandra said, "Oh, I don't think I can listen to this." She backed from the room.

"Nothing," Jeremy said with too much force. "She does not do anything for me. She was in trouble. I helped her out. Simple as that. If you make anything more out of it, that's on you, not us. Now, if you don't mind, my son needs his rest and I think it's time for you to go. I have nothing more to say on the matter."

"That doesn't mean I'm done with you."

"For what purpose? Has there been a crime? No. I didn't call to report one. I can't help what my nosy neighbors say. Other than some damage to my house, which I admit to causing, there has been no crime."

"You lied to me."

"Oh, big deal. Who doesn't lie to the police?"

From the front room, Chandra said, "Dad!"

"I'm done with this. If you have a case to make or want to arrest me for something, go ahead. Otherwise, please leave."

Vasili eyed him more with curiosity than anger. "You are an interesting man, Mister Kline. I am going to keep an eye on you. I have a feeling this is a long way from being over." He started for the door. "Oh, by the way, I found your car. Did you drive it into that tree or was someone else driving?" he shook his head. "Doesn't matter. It's been ticketed and marked for towing. Just thought you'd want to know."

He walked down the hall. Jeremy could hear him speaking in low tones to Chandra.

On the bed, Nick grabbed Biatta's arm and pulled her back toward him. His eyes rolled up, showing only whites. His voice deepened and sounded otherworldly.

"He is almost free. They have all the keys but one and are weakening the prison in case they can't locate the last one. He will be free to roam your world soon. He has to be stopped." Nick squeezed her arm tighter. "But it can't be you. You will not survive the confrontation."

His eyes came back and held hers with an intense glare as if to emphasize the importance of his words. Then, he convulsed and slumped back on the bed.

Jeremy rushed to his side. "Nick!"

Biatta placed a hand on his forehead and closed her eyes. A minute later, as Jeremy looked on with anxious anticipation, she opened her eyes and stepped back. Her face paled and her knees buckled. She reached for the bed to prevent a fall. Jeremy looked from her to Nick, then he ran around the bed to give her support. He guided her to a chair. He wanted to bombard her with questions but knew she'd answer when ready.

Several minutes later, she looked up. Some color had returned to her cheeks.

"He is fine and resting. Whatever resides within him is powerful. I cannot discern if it is all him or if there is another directing him. Whatever the source, he must learn to control the power or it will destroy him."

Chandra had come to the door. "What? What do you mean, destroy him? Who are you? Or maybe I should ask *what* you are." She looked at her father. "Dad, you can't possibly be buying into her mad ravings."

Jeremy was about to respond when Chandra was pushed back against the wall. She slid upward until her feet dangled off the floor. Jeremy moved to help her but Biatta held up a hand. From her seat four feet away, Biatta said, "I have had enough of your verbal abuse. I do not care if you like me. I am here to protect your father. There is much more going on here than you understand. If you wish, give your father a chance to explain without doubting him or thinking him a senile fool. If you have no interest in understanding, you should leave. This hopefully will be over soon. Your father's life depends on my being here for him. If that's of no importance to you, then continue to make yourself a nuisance. Otherwise, get on board or disembark."

Biatta released her and Chandra dropped to the floor. She gasped and felt her chest where the force had pressed to hold her in place. Then her eyes watered and she shook her head. With a wild look at her father and Biatta, she ran from the room.

Chapter Forty-Six

"We're being watched," said Ivana, one of two shapeshifters in Bradenbaugh's small army.

"Where?" he replied.

"Fifty yards over my right shoulder."

"That means we're close." He motioned for Madelyn to come.

"What's up, boss man?"

He hated her flippant tone and the way she spoke to him. She would soon show him the respect he deserved. "We have company. Would you like to be the one to dispatch him?"

"I sure would," she said, rubbing her hands together. "Any particular way you want it done?"

"As long as he doesn't get away, I'll leave it to you."

"Oh, my favorite way." After getting directions from Ivana, Madelyn turned and ran back the way they came.

Bradenbaugh halted the group under the guise of taking a rest. "Any word from the scouts behind us?"

"None, but that's a good thing," Ivana said. "No one is following us."

"Unless they have been taken out, in which case we have no idea if someone is following us. Perhaps in your other form, you can go back and be sure."

"As you wish."

She left. He did not watch her transformation.

As they waited, he wondered if General Perva was performing his end of the plan. If anyone had followed them, Perva and his larger force would pin them between the two groups. He wanted to find and destroy the students but truth be told, his greater desire was to have

Vandalue and his bunch follow him. The war would end. If he finished it here, he might not complete his mission of breaking the dark one free. He'd be the king of the land then; perhaps even king of two lands. The idea quickened his pulse. The power he would wield excited him so much that he almost missed the scream.

His attention shifted in front of the group where Madelyn was strutting toward them with a wicked smile spread wide across her face.

He started them moving and met Madelyn on the way.

"That was fun, but way too quick."

"Did you question him first?"

"Of course. I asked him if he saw anything he liked. He said, *Huh?* I didn't like that answer, so I rammed my knife up through his jaw. He wasn't capable of answering then, so I drove it farther until he stopped squirming."

"Was he alone?"

"I didn't see anyone else, boss man. If I had, they'd be just as dead."

"With any luck, they won't know we're there until it's too late."

"I hope it's soon. Now that I am warmed up, I want more. A lot more." She cackled and skipped away.

Tarney morphed into human form and stood over the two corpses. If Bradenbaugh had people watching his back, it was because he expected someone to follow him. That bothered Tarney. If he thought someone was going to follow him, what other steps had he taken? No trap lay ahead; of that, he was sure. But why wasn't there? If he expected pursuit, he would be ready to defend. These two certainly hadn't been the trap. The most logical way was to set one. Where was it? An idea hit him like a physical blow. *Unless the trap was coming from behind...* Tarney turned and ran, morphing into dog form as he went.

He raced through the woods, fearing he might already be too late. He slowed as he reached the main group, grateful they appeared to be all right. He circled the group at a distance to ensure they were still alone, then broke off and sprinted back the way they came.

He traveled nearly a mile before slowing. He didn't have the stamina he once had to go farther. Panting hard, he lay down for a rest. Five minutes later, a noise perked up his ears. He listened more intently, then sniffed at the air. He didn't have a scent yet but was sure he'd heard something.

Staying low to the ground, he slinked forward until the noise not only became louder but multiplied. He crawled under a small thicket and watched as a horde moved toward him. That pretender Perva was leading. It was too late to move or he would be seen. He waited where he was, hoping they passed without discovery.

The line of people and beings went on for a long while. Some passed within a few feet of his hiding place. He kept a running total. The final number was staggering. As soon as they were past, Tarney crawled out and broke into a run. He kept a wide berth, but not wide enough. In his haste and with his mind occupied with the dire possibilities his party would face unaware, he missed the scouts.

Pain lanced through a haunch. He yelped and rolled as his leg gave out. He crashed into a tree and bounced off. Running footsteps and excited voices told him his attackers were coming. He was in too much pain to morph back and incapable of using magic in dog form. His only hope of surviving these next few minutes was to hide.

Before they got close enough to see his position, Tarney got to three legs and loped away. He spotted a small rise consisting mostly of large rocks and scampered to the top. That put him two feet above the height of an average man. His leg burned. An arrow jutted from a rear leg. He lay down and fought to calm the pain, his heavy breathing, and his rising heartbeat.

Two men approached with more caution now. Both were armed with handguns as well as bows and arrow. They were about the same height but one had brown hair and the other, black.

The black-haired one said, "You sure you hit it?"

"Positive. It was either a wolf or a large dog."

"I think it went behind those rocks. You go left. I'll take right."

The men separated. Tarney had only one chance. He had to take the first man by surprise, then make his getaway. He doubted he could take both. He crawled to the edge of the rock. The black-haired man was right below him. He was looking outward, expecting him to be behind the crop of rocks.

Tarney allowed him to get one step past him before leaping from his perch. As his front paws hit the man's shoulders and his weight bore the man down, Tarney sank his teeth into the back of his neck and tore a large chunk of flesh away. Without waiting to see the other man, Tarney spit out the meat and darted through the woods, leaving the brown-haired man to aid his partner.

Daria wasn't free but at least she was away from the cabin, the mountain, and most importantly, the sisters. She rode on the back of the large black bird, who turned out to be Kanter. Evidently he had been part of the team of wizards that had tracked, beaten, and imprisoned this dark one. That was a long time ago, which made Kanter older than he looked by a lot.

They flew a long way over a mountain range that wasn't even in sight of the one she had been on. These mountains were taller and had white caps and snow on their upper third. They soared over the highest peaks. The cold air assaulted her, sinking deep into her bones. Somewhere over the mountains they came upon open ground. A narrow rocky valley appeared beneath them. At the bottom of one side wall was a cave. They settled on a ledge across from the cave, where they had an angle to see if anyone was moving around in the area.

They were there almost an hour before the goat head man she had seen at Jeremy's emerged from the cave. The creature was tall enough to have to duck. It stood and scanned the mountain faces as if it knew they were there. They ducked back. Daria stayed hidden until Kanter, still in bird form, cawed it was all right to resume peeking.

"Someone is inside trying to open the crypt. What do we do next?"

Kanter morphed human. "Do? There is nothing to do. We confirmed my fears. Now we go."

"Are you going to tell someone, at least?"

He sighed. "Not sure."

"How can you say that? Even if you don't like people that aren't like you, a lot of innocents might die. Look, you've made it clear you don't want to get involved but the least we can do is tell someone."

"Okay, young miss, we will do that much. I will change but wait to mount until we are sure no one is watching. It will be best if they don't know they have been discovered."

As they flew away, Daria looked down. The large being with the goat head was staring up at them. Another creature that looked like the wolves she saw when rescuing Jeremy stood with him. She wondered if that was going to be a problem. She didn't see how. *It's not like he can catch us.* Still, knowing he had seen them nagged at her the rest of the flight.

Chapter Forty-Seven

The magical alarms went off, shocking Jerricka.
Someone had crossed through the wards she had set and
could only be heard by those attuned to the magic. She
bolted from the house and leaped down the stairs to find
Jno standing in the middle of the grounds scanning the
area left of property. He pointed.

"It's coming from that direction."

"Who did you send out there?"

"Chase. He has not come back or contacted me."

She didn't want to state the painful obvious. Chase was
not coming back. Jno was smart enough to understand the
implications.

"The students haven't left yet. We have to buy them
some time."

"Go. See to them. I'll hold here."

"No." She grabbed his arm. "You see to the students.
I'm better suited to hold off whoever is coming."

He started to argue. Anger flashed in her eyes and her
already dark skin became darker. Jno ran toward the barn.

Jerricka began her preparation, first, casting an illusion
of a dense forest, then setting energy bolt booby traps.
The wards had been set a quarter mile out in all
directions, which gave them perhaps five minutes. She
didn't have long to work. Unfortunately, the energy flow
of this world did not allow for full power or longevity of
creation depleting too soon. She did the best she could for
such a massive illusion. She paused to draw in more
energy and began the next part.

Running footsteps announced someone approaching
from behind but she could ill-afford a distracting glance.

She had a good idea who it was without looking. With fast moving hands and fingers accompanied by a long line of powerful words, Jerricka wove a wall of invisibility over the front of the house, barns, and outbuildings. She had neither the time nor the energy needed to vanish the entire property on all sides. All she could hope was that whoever was coming was delayed enough to allow the students a good head start before they realized the ruse. The only way to see through the spell was if the intruder was another magic user. The likelihood of that being friend rather than foe was slim.

Finished with her task and feeling weak, Jerricka put a hand out. Jno, her ever present protector, slid the hand around him and stepped closer to support her.

"You should go with the students," Jerricka said, resting her head on his shoulder.

"Yes, you are right."

She released a quick laugh. "But you are not going."

"You are right again."

"I don't want anything to happen to you, Jno. If you leave now, you will be safe and can help protect the students. If you stay…" She let the rest trail off. He knew what she meant.

"My place is here with you. We will face whatever comes together."

She gave him an affectionate squeeze, then pushed him away. "Go tell our benefactor the moment we warned her about has come and she should hide. Then, find a hiding place of your own until we know what we face."

Jno turned to go.

"Wait."

He stopped.

"Take this."

She handed him a ring. He gave her a quizzical look.

"It has several energy bolts stored within it. The simple command is *Relesio*."

He took the ring and mouthed the word, not wanting to accidentally discharge one of the bolts. They each held the ring and Jerricka looked deep into her longtime protector's eyes.

"I'm sorry."

He placed a hand on the side of her face. "Don't be. It has been my honor."

Then, he moved his face toward hers and kissed her for the first time in their long relationship. At any other time, the display of emotion or physical interaction would have been dealt with quickly and severely. However, perhaps surprised by her own passions and the knowledge their lives may well be ended, she not only allowed the improper action but willingly responded.

When their lips separated, there were no words or longing looks exchanged. They each went their own way with thoughts on the task ahead. The moment was over and may never happen again.

Bradenbaugh spread his arms out to the sides. "Do you sense that?" he asked.

The group stopped. He glanced at their faces to see if anyone else picked up on what he felt.

Madelyn stepped forward. "Yes. I sense it. Someone has used magic. It's close." She turned a wicked smile to Bradenbaugh. "*They* are close."

He nodded. "You six." He pointed to a group of followers. "Go left about fifty yards. You six go right. The rest of you, spread out. Be ready. If the magic we sense is an alarm, they will know we are coming."

He gave the two groups a few minutes to get into position, then started forward. Madelyn fell in at his side. She was giddy with bloody expectations. He watched her take a few skipping steps like a child ready to go out to play. Only her form of play resulted in bloodshed.

They moved on for five minutes before he raised a hand to stop. Something felt different about the woods in front of them.

"What?" Madelyn said.

"I'm not sure." He motioned for the two people on each end of the line to move forward. They did so. Nothing happened. Whatever he'd sensed had been wrong. Perhaps his heightened senses had reacted to expectation rather than an actual threat. He moved forward. Three steps later, sharp crackling sounds came from both sides. The four people he sent forward screamed, jerked in an eerie puppet-like dance, then fell to the ground with smoke rising from their bodies.

He ducked and the rest of his group followed suit.

"Do you see anyone?"

Madelyn said, "No, but it might have been a preset trap."

Whatever it was had cost him four people. He hated losing anyone. At least, until he knew what he faced. Staying crouched behind thick brush, Bradenbaugh drew in energy, then made circles with his hands and threw them forward with palms down.

"Dispelioso."

The air around them shimmered, then appeared to break apart in ragged pieces. Chunks of magically created scenery fell away, revealing open ground ahead. He moved forward, his senses emanating outward. Bradenbaugh stopped fifty feet farther when he picked up more magic. Once more he dispelled the illusion. A hundred yards away was a farm, complete with house, barn, and outbuildings. No one was in sight. He scanned the area for other traps or hiding places but if they existed, they were beyond his skill to find them.

He motioned his lines forward. Not wanting to appear cowardly, he made a show of advancing as well, though not as fast or as far as his people. Madelyn was smart enough to stay one step behind him. That did not offer him comfort. Accidental or otherwise, he might catch a deadly attack in the back.

His people reached the farmhouse. One woman climbed the wooden stairs but before she reached the door, a white energy beam hit and lifted her, tossing her off the porch. Her body hit the ground, bounced, and rolled, and did not rise. Immediately her partners responded, shouting activation words and aiming spells where the energy bolt had originated. The combined force of the spells blew up a small shed, sending a shower of splinters into the air.

From the opposite side of the farmhouse, another bolt ripped into one of the attacking wizards, almost tearing her in half. Two other wizards ran toward the house firing a variety of attacks. One used a wand while the other spoke spells and cast them from her hands. The corner of the house was torn away, exposing a portion of the interior.

By now most of his people were engaged in the assault, though he doubted many of them had a target to unleash upon. Madelyn was still slightly behind him cackling. He wasn't sure what unnerved him more, having her behind him or listening to that teeth-grinding, high pitched assault on his ears and nerves. Perhaps that was her attack on him. To prevent him from concentrating, rendering him unable to attack or defend.

The only way to avoid her was to move. Bradenbaugh ran for the barn. So far, nothing had happened from there. Did that mean it was unmanned or that whoever was inside had not yet made their presence known?

Bradenbaugh reached the large wooden door that slid on an overhead track. It was open about six inches on one end. He took a quick peek and ducked. Nothing happened. He pressed against the wall and sent the door rolling open with a wave of his hand. Nothing happened.

Two of his team ran up, taking positions on the opposite side of the door. He motioned for them to enter. When they did, a cone of fire engulfed them. Their screams were piercing. They fought to put out the magical blaze by dropping and rolling but neither survived long enough to douse the flame.

Bradenbaugh called up the same spell, but his had dark magic undertones. Without looking, he pushed both hands into the doorway and released the spell. Black fire shot from his fingers. In seconds, the entire barn was ablaze. He took another quick peek. When nothing happened, he gazed longer. The insides blazed too hot for anyone to have survived. Satisfied, he moved toward the house. As he walked, he searched for Madelyn. It was unlike her not to be first into the action. Something was going on with her, and that meant trouble.

Speaking of trouble, he glanced around the farm grounds. He had lost a substantial number of his force. He had to end this fight fast. For whoever his opponent was to be fighting so fiercely meant the students were close.

Professor Wilden said, "Oh my. Someone is expending a lot of magical energy."

Vandalue said, "That way. Come, we must hurry. The students may be under attack."

They picked up their pace. Forty yards ahead, multiple voices shouted.

"Freeze!"

"Stop!"

"Get your hands where I can see them!"

A line of eight men and women in the local constabulary uniforms stood facing them with weapons aimed. Their loud commands layered over each other.

His people froze, unsure how to respond. Vandalue pushed forward until he was in front of the line.

"Please. We are no threat. Some of our friends are under attack by another group just ahead. We must get to them before it is too late."

One man, possibly the person in charge, said, "No one's going anywhere until we know what is happening here."

"That may be too late. Our friends may be dead by then."

"We will check out your concerns, but not until we get more information."

A woman asked, "What is this, a retaliatory action against those you say are attacking your friends?"

Vandalue did not respond. This was a delay they could not afford. He turned his head and said to those closest, "Sleep."

Instantly, hands began to move and words were spoken. The abruptness of the movement had the officers on edge.

"Stop!"

"What are they doing?"

"Does anyone see a weapon?"

The man in charge shouted, "Do not fire!"

Then hands were shoved toward them. Unsure if they were under attack, several fired their weapons. As the bodies of their fellow officers began to fall to the ground, others fired until all of them were on the ground asleep.

Rowan turned to his people. Three of them were down; two with wounds. One dead. Damn! It was a gamble, and one that had cost a life. They may be at war, and in war, lives were lost. But this shouldn't have happened. Though anguished, Rowan Vandalue did not have time to grieve or shroud himself in guilt. They had to push forward. Leaving two people to tend to the wounded, he pressed the remaining members of his team forward.

Chapter Forty-Eight

They sat on the front porch of the cabin as Kanter told his daughters what they had witnessed. Finished, they sat in silence, absorbed in their own thoughts. A hawk landed on the railing and squawked at them. The air around the hawk shimmered and was replaced by a girl. Daria recognized her as the hawk-faced girl from the farm below.

"We are under attack," she said in a rush. "A large force of creatures and beings is attacking the farm and town."

In less than a minute, all four of them had morphed into birds of different colors and sizes and were beating wings down the mountain, and Daria was left alone. Though she couldn't fly, she was not going to be excluded. If the people below needed help, she wasn't going to sit around and do nothing. She bounded from the porch and ran as hard as the slope and the uneven ground allowed.

Unlike her ascent days before, she was able to use the path on the way down. It made the descent much faster. By the time she reached flat ground, it was nearly three hours later. She slowed to a fast walk as she entered the town. All around her was carnage and debris. Many of the buildings in the town had sustained damage. Several bodies littered the streets. Because the town had been made up of eclectic residents, Daria had trouble discerning friend from foe.

She found a young woman cradling a child. She rocked on her knees and moaned. Daria dropped to her knees. The woman barely noticed her through her grief. Though Daria did not possess the power or knowledge Biatta did, her mentor had taught her some things. She bent over the child and scanned first for life, then for wounds.

The child, a girl, had a faint life force and a nasty gash in her side that still pumped blood. Knowing the child's time was short, Daria drew in energy fast. Before she was full, she began reciting the minor heal spell Biatta had shown her. It might not be enough to save the girl, but Daria was going to give her best effort.

She felt the warmth deep within her as her hands began to glow bluish white. She swept the hands over the wound but nothing appeared to happen. Was she too late? She dug deep all the way to her core and pulled up every ounce of energy. Still no response. What was she doing wrong? As panic rose from desperation, she realized this was not a minor wound. Maybe it would take more than passing her hand over the injury.

The woman had stopped rocking and moaning and watched with hopeful eyes. The sight only increased Daria's anxiety. She had to make this work. She activated the spell again but this time, placed her hands on the wound, inserting the tips of her fingers inside.

Hands slick with the child's blood and feeling her own tears begin to roll free, Daria put everything she had into the spell. Beneath her glowing fingers, the wound began to dry and knit together. In slow increments, she pulled her fingers back to avoid having them sealed within the girl's flesh. Once her fingers were out of the wound, she held them on top of the skin to finish. When she could do no more, Daria collapsed to the side, exhausted.

The woman squeezed the girl to her chest and wailed. Daria was unsure if she'd succeeded or failed until the mother said, "Thank you. By the gods, thank you."

Unable to speak, Daria smiled and fell sleep.

She didn't know how long she'd been out but when she awoke, she was alone on a bed in an unfamiliar room. The murmur of voices came from someplace beyond the door. She got out of bed and found she was fully clothed but not wearing her shoes. She pressed an ear to the door. Multiple voices were clearer but none she recognized. She reached to open the door but was forced to jump backward to avoid being hit as it opened. She stared from the door to the doorway. No one was there. The door had opened on its own.

"Since you are awake," Oli said, "you might as well join us."

Daria stepped into a hallway and turned right. A few steps farther and she entered a cavernous room with twenty beings inside. Some were seated at a large rectangular table and others stood against the wall.

"As I was saying," said a large man with one eye centered on his forehead, "if this is a sign of what we can expect once the dark one has risen, I say we work to prevent that from happening. I mean, this wasn't some roaming band of marauders here to steal our food. They had a werewolf with them."

Instantly three others spoke over each other in opposition to the cyclops' words. As the din rose in volume, she caught Kanter's eye. He showed nothing on his face, which made his unblinking gaze unnerving. After a moment, his lips thinned into a straight line.

Daria stepped forward and said, "Did you say werewolf?"

The room went still.

"Yeah. Werewolf?" His tone was harsh as if he considered her as much enemy as the werewolf had been..

Others started talking ignoring her.

She talked over them addressing her words to Kanter. "There was a werewolf on the ledge with the gearhead man when we flew away."

Kanter cocked his head. "Are you sure?"

She nodded.

Upon hearing the exchange the room exploded in loud concerned shouting.

Kanter lifted a hand and the room went still.

"It has always been my opinion that the best thing for us to do is nothing."

An approving murmur came from about half the assembled group.

"However, after seeing the force attempting to resurrect this evil lord and this attack, I am having second thoughts on the matter."

This time, the other half of the residents agreed.

"I was reminded by our young friend over there that to do nothing is to be in agreeance with the dark one returning. I am definitely not in agreeance. She also stated that her friends were fighting his forces as we speak and has insisted on going to help. Her rationale is that they are her friends. You don't let friends face danger alone. Without friends, she feels she is nothing. Look around. We may not all be friends. We may not all agree. But we are a community. We have a bond. Many of our community were injured or lost their lives here today in a fight that isn't ours. Well, I say to you, the loss of those friends makes the fight ours. We will not know peace once the dark one rises. He will seek to bend our will to his. He will insist on our support and that we pay tribute. We will not be left alone to live our lives the way we see fit. In essence, I was wrong to think otherwise. My young friend over there has convinced me of the importance of standing together, not just with our community but with other communities to end this before it becomes a problem beyond our control."

He panned the room slowly meeting each being's eyes.

"You can do what you like and because we are a community, I will accept and respect your wishes. But also because we are a community, I ask that you stand with me to ensure our way of life continues for centuries to come."

He rose.

"I will not ask for a vote. I will not put you on the spot or make you feel pressured by my presence. I will take my leave, as there is much to be done. Have a peaceful discussion and make your choice. All I ask is that once that decision is made, you all stand together."

Kanter left. His daughters followed. Daria looked around the table, then at the door, wondering what she should do. Delphina poked her head back inside.

"Coming, little one?"

Daria brightened and ran after her.

Outside, she found Olivianna and Kanter already changed to their bird forms.

"Ride with my father. He has a plan he wants to put in motion. My sister and I will join you in a while."

Delphina lifted Daria onto Kanter's back.

"Hold tight. We wouldn't want you to fall off before you get to cause your chaos."

Kanter took off. They flew for more than two hours before settling on the roof of a building in the city. Once settled, Kanter changed.

"Do you know the location of the portal to the other world?"

Daria looked around at the buildings to get her bearings.

"Yes. It's that way." She pointed left.

"Direct us there."

Kanter stopped her with an arm from entering the alley. She knew better than to ask what was wrong. If he stopped her, he had good reason.

"Stay here," he said as he moved with caution into the alley. Several minutes later, he called, "Okay. Come."

Daria moved into the alley. Bodies had been set to one side out of sight from anyone peering down the alley.

Daria looked at the portal. Instead of a smooth and constant rotation, it bounced and writhed like a captured snake. The interior rotating circles did not keep the same speed but seemed to go faster, then slower, but nothing steady.

"What happened here? What's happened to the portal?" Daria asked.

"It appears there was a fight. I recognize one of the two bodies. They were with Vandalue. It looks like the portal was collapsed to prevent anyone from going through, however, someone with little skill and knowledge of such things reopened it and left it too dangerous to cross."

"But we have to try, right?"

"Do you know what happens if the portal shuts down with us inside?"

"No. What?"

He eyed her. "I don't know either, but I don't want to find out."

"Can't you stabilize it?"

"I'm afraid to try. I may shut it down completely."

"Well, stay here, then. I'll go through." She moved toward the opening.

"No," Kanter said, lunging for her. He missed as Daria ducked away.

Before he could utter another word or block her, Daria entered the portal and ran through. The uneven cadence of the portal threw her off balance. She fell and was caught up and around by the spinning circles.

She got to her knees as the portal bucked wildly. Daria crawled as fast as she could to the end and dove out. The portal wavered, whined, and blinked from existence, spitting Kanter out before it vanished. He hit the ground hard and grunted. He did not move for a long time as he took inventory of his body parts to check for injury.

He sat up and glared at Daria. "You realize you have gotten us trapped in this world, right?"

She shrugged. "Might as well make the best of it."

She turned and followed the freshly trampled ground, hoping her friends were all right.

Chapter Forty-Nine

A wisp of black smoke drifted through the trees. Something ahead was on fire.

"There's a battle going on ahead of us," Tarney said.

"Quick," said Rowan. "Position our people and let's move."

Rowan broke into a jog. Several others were on his flanks. They came to a clearing. A damaged farmhouse stood in the distance. The blackened husk of a barn was to the right. In front of the house, a battle raged. Jerricka was taking on eight opponents, one of which was Bradenbaugh. They worked to surround her.

Rowan's gaze was drawn to several forms on the ground. A few smoldered, telling him what had caused their demise. Another body near the house he recognized as Jno, Jerricka's right hand man. Rowan could not tell his condition from where he stood, but Jno did not move.

As soon as he broke into the clearing, he took aim and dropped one of Bradenbaugh's people from behind. As the woman fell, others swung around to engage the newcomers. Throwing up a haphazard shield, Rowan searched for Bradenbaugh, but the man had vanished. Since he was a wizard of significant power, vanishing was not beyond the realm of belief.

As the battle intensified, it looked certain that Rowan's reinforcements would end the fight quickly. However, as they engaged Bradenbaugh's people, another force arrived, trapping Rowan's force. If the battle had been wild before, it was an all-out blitz now. His people were forced to fight on two fronts. A magical lightshow lit the sky as attacks met shields, creating and cascading sparks in all directions. Wands, hands, and a variety of magic-infused items and icons came into play. Flashes of energy raced across the ground. Blasts of fire exploded in all directions. Lightning struck the ground several times. It was an unending blur of motion, like fencing multiple opponents at once from a distance.

Smoke rose and obscured all sides, making it impossible to determine friend from enemy. Rowan saw Jerricka go down on one knee. Unprotected and vulnerable for an attack, Rowan darted through the melee and dodged magical assaults to get to her side.

At least she was breathing. Blood seeped from a wound on her forehead and dripped down her arm from another. He scooped her up and ran. Once around the far corner of the farmhouse, he set her down to check on her condition.

"Just weak," she managed.

"Where are the students?"

"Sent ahead with Allyra and Neveah. Accompanied by Larrinan."

That was a relief. "Stay and get your strength back. I'm going out front."

Rowan raced around the farmhouse and caught one of Bradenbaugh's wizards with her back to him. He stopped, took aim, and lit her up with an energy beam spear. The bolt passed right through her. She crumbled to the ground.

A new sound rang out in the clearing. Gunshots. The new wave led by General Perva had men who used guns instead of magic. That meant protecting against different types of attacks or be cut down.

More gunfire came from the side. The officers had recovered and arrived on scene. They fired at anyone on the attack. Their presence created a dilemma. They were non-magic users. Normals. He did not want to kill any of them, but their bullets did not differentiate between his people and Bradenbaugh's. Though loathe to use magic on normals, even those from another world, he cast a wide-ranging spell. A lower powered sweeping blast crossed the open ground. It knocked four of the officers down. He didn't think any were seriously hurt, but he needed them out of the fight.

The combined might of Bradenbaugh's two forces was too much for his small band to counter, and they were forced to retreat. With enemy combatants on three sides, his survivors were funneled toward the cornfield beyond the house.

Gwynedd gasped, came awake, and scrambled from the bed.

"Biatta!" she wailed as she ran down the hall.

Biatta jumped to her feet. "What is it, child?"

"It's the headmistress. She's hurt and in trouble."

"How do you know?"

"She put something in my head so I could stay in contact with her. I heard her cry out in pain. Now I can't reach her. We have to go to her before it's too late."

"Do you know where they are?"

"Yes. The farm."

"Can you find this farm again?"

"Yes. She also put the directions in my head. I can see the path clearly."

"We have to go," Biatta said to Jeremy.

"We can take the car Nick drove." They started moving toward the garage. Behind them a door opened, then shut hard. Jeremy stopped to look as Nick ran out of the hallway.

"Trouble. They're all in trouble."

"Come on."

They ran outside. Chandra was in her minivan with her head down on the steering wheel. It blocked Nick's vehicle. Jeremy ran to the driver's side and rapped on the window. Her head shot up. When she saw it was Jeremy, she started the engine, shifted, and backed down the driveway.

"Chandra! No! Don't go!"

The engine coughed and shut down. The side door slid open. Chandra didn't know what was going on. Jeremy had his suspicions.

Biatta shoved Gwynedd into the rear seat and followed her in. Nick piled in behind them. Jeremy went around to the passenger side and got in, keeping his eyes on Chandra.

"Chandra, I'm sorry. I will explain everything to you. I know I've been promising to do that for a while now, but I will. Right now, we have an emergency and need you to drive us. Will you? Please?"

"Dad, I—" She paused, fumbling for words. The emotions of the moment compiled with those of everything that had happened over the past week threatened to send her into a breakdown.

The sliding door opened. Nick hopped out and ran to the driver's door. He opened it.

"Sorry, sis. This is too important to delay. Please climb into the back so I can drive."

Confused and scared, Jeremy unbuckled her seat belt, took her hand, and guided her between the seats to the next row. Nick jumped in, buckled up, and floored the pedal. The minivan leaped down the driveway. Nick slammed on the brakes, shifted, and the minivan shot forward.

"I have a general direction but I need someone to help me once we get close."

"I've got you," Gwynedd said.

They drove fast, ignoring stop signs and running lights whenever possible. The drive felt like it took hours but was in fact fifty minutes.

"Right here," Gwynedd said.

They drove down a long dirt road and kicked up a large dust cloud behind them.

"Left."

It was another dirt road. In the distance, dark smoke rose in the sky. Jeremy pointed it out. They all looked, having no doubt it was the site of the trouble. As they neared the farmhouse and burned barn, a series of lights and flashes lit the sky from the area of the cornfield. Nick braked to a stop, turning the wheel as he did. The van slid sideways, throwing up rocks and dirt.

Biatta stood and pushed past Gwynedd and Chandra.

"Everyone stays in the vehicle. Do not get out for any reason."

She stepped out as Jeremy got out of the passenger seat.

"No. That means you too," Biatta said.

Nick opened the door and Gwynedd stood to get out. Biatta's face flashed red and her eyes sparked.

"Is no one listening? I said no." She lifted her hands. The doors slammed shut and locked, preventing them from being opened from the inside.

She glared at Jeremy.

"Hey, I'm already out and the doors are locked." He turned to run. "We're wasting time. Let's go."

Exasperated by his failure to follow her directions, she took off after him.

They raced around the house. A *crack, crack, crack* caused Jeremy to stop. Biatta almost plowed into him.

"That was gunfire," he said. "Someone has a gun out there."

A black woman in a blue uniform limped out of the field. She spoke into her shoulder mic as she hobbled in obvious pain.

"I'm saying we have a war out here. We need every available unit. We've got several down and I'm wounded." She gasped and lowered to the ground. "It is so strange. Only a few have guns. They-they wave their arms and fire flies out of their hands like we're in some fantasy video game."

Jeremy ran to the wounded officer. She started and tried to raise her gun but it flew from her hand. Jeremy assumed that was Biatta's doing. He slowed and raised his hands.

"I'm here to help. That's all. Let me get you behind the house where you'll be safe." He pointed to her leg, which looked to be burned rather than shot. The blood had been cauterized. "Your leg looks bad. Let me help you."

She eyed him with suspicion as she fumbled her taser from its holder. He lifted her to a standing position and put his arm around her waist. She hopped more than walked but they made progress and reached the side of the house, away from the sounds of battle. He helped her sit.

Biatta was watching the fields and ignoring them.

Jeremy said, "Biatta, she's hurt. Can you help her?"

Biatta didn't respond.

"Biatta!" Jeremy pleaded.

When she turned, her face showed her annoyance. "Not a good idea."

"Helping someone is always a good idea," he said.

She frowned. "Very well. I'll ease the pain, but I can't do more."

She squatted next to the woman.

"Wait! What are you doing?"

She lifted the taser and aimed it at Biatta's chest. Biatta turned her head to Jeremy and gave him a *See? This is why* look.

Jeremy said to the officer. "She is not going to hurt you. She will take away your pain."

"And how is she gonna—oh, wow, uh—"

Biatta's palm glowed and hovered over the wound. In seconds, she was done and the officer had a dazed but euphoric look.

"Oh, that does feel better. How did you do that?" Then she became concerned. "You didn't give me drugs, did you?"

"No," Biatta said and stood. "We have to help our people now."

She moved around the corner and out of view.

Jeremy said, "You'll be all right now." He moved to follow.

"Wait! Who are you people?"

"I wish I could tell you. Suffice it to say, we are different but just like here, there are some bad and some good. I'd like to believe we're the good ones."

"Yeah, me too," she said.

Jeremy smiled and ran after Biatta.

Chapter Fifty

"There," Daria said, pointing to a cornfield below them. Fierce fighting occupied the entire field. It was difficult to determine if there were any sides or if it was one big free for all. She recognized some of the wizards as staff members or from around the academy but there appeared to be a lot more of the enemy. She also saw uniformed men and women she knew to be local law enforcement.

On her right she spotted Biatta running toward the cornfield. Jeremy trailed behind her. As Biatta entered the field in one spot, two black clad people exited twenty feet down. They stopped when they noticed Jeremy running toward them. Though he stopped and turned to run, he was no match for trained wizards. Not that she was either, but she had a better chance than he did.

"There." She pointed at Jeremy. "Hurry."

Kanter dove, taking an attack angle from behind the two enemy wizards. The wind buffeted her face but she narrowed her vision and prepared a spell. She prayed it worked and arrived in time. This far off the ground she had to draw energy from just the air, which she was woefully inexperienced at doing.

Kanter drew his wings tight to his sleek dark body, increasing their speed. Still forty feet away but out of time, Daria released her fireball spell. A small fiery ball the size of a tennis ball flew from her hands. It was smaller and slower than she had been trying for. As the female wizard set to release whatever spell she was casting at Jeremy, the ball of fire struck her in the back and propelled her to the ground, more stunned than damaged.

The second woman wizard cast her spell but was interrupted by the sudden catapulting of her partner. The ground in front of Jeremy upheaved and stopped, rising enough to trip him. He rolled several times before scrambling to his hands and knees.

Before the second wizard regrouped, Kanter snatched her from the earth, soared upward, and flung her. She flipped head over heels a few times before thudding to the ground. She did not rise, but the first woman did, firing a bolt of something unseen into Kanter's breast. He pulled up short as if striking an invisible wall, then plummeted.

Daria had no choice but to hang on. She patted Kanter's neck a few times, hoping to revive him but he continued to fall. Daria braced for impact, then noticed Jeremy running toward them. Was he hoping to catch them? With a sudden jerk, Kanter leveled out and soared upward. The suddenness of the move pitched Daria from his back. She flew, still thirty feet off the ground. Before she went into a wild scream, she realized her trajectory was taking her straight at Jeremy.

His eyes widened. As he realized there was no avoiding cannonball Daria, he added his scream to hers. He threw up his hands, though whether to catch her or defend against her, she could not tell. Then she made an abrupt stop. She looked around. She had not hit the ground but instead, floated above it. As Jeremy lowered his hands with an astonished look matching hers, Daria lowered as well. She touched gently to the ground and looked around, thrilled she was still alive, then ran into Jeremy's arms.

"You saved me. How did you do it?"

"I-I didn't do anything…did I?"

"I'm so glad to see you."

"I'm glad you are all right."

"Aw, how touching."

They looked to see the first woman wizard approaching with a spell already in the works.

"I'm glad you're reunited too, so I can kill you both at once."

Each with an arm around the other, they only had one to throw up in front of them. Though Jeremy did not speak, Daria said, *"Deflectous."*

The spell cast at them hit an invisible barrier and coursed around them. However, they had done it, their two forcefields had meshed at just the right time.

The woman was not giving up. She released a second beam and a third. The strain was too much to hold for either of them. The shield fluttered, then faltered, leaving them exposed and vulnerable.

A wicked smile spread across the woman's face as she must have realized they were unprotected. She called up her next spell. Jeremy stepped in front of Daria and held her behind him.

Before the woman could release her deadly spell, Kanter swooped down and snatched her from the ground. His sharp claws dug deep into her. She shrieked. Then with a twist and a pull, two halves were tossed into the air before they fell back to Earth.

Daria stepped out from behind Jeremy, then reached to hold him upright as his legs seemed to give way.

"You all right?" she asked.

"Yes. Just a little shaken."

"You protected me with your body."

"I couldn't let her hurt you."

She embraced him again, this time with more ferocity.

They felt the air flutter about them and broke the embrace to see Kanter in bird form settle to the ground. The body shimmered and seconds later, Kanter stood there. He bent at the waist and groaned. Jeremy and Daria rushed to his side.

"Let's get him behind the house where it's safe."

Each taking a side, they guided him behind the house and sat him down. The policewoman was gone.

"I'll be all right," Kanter said. "Just give me a moment to do a self-heal. That woman caught me by surprise." He glanced up at Jeremy, his black eyes boring into him, searching for something. "So, you are a member of the supposed lost tribe of Salemnon?"

"I have no idea. I've been told some things but can't believe any of it is true. In fact, I believe this is all a dream."

"Is that so?"

"Yes. Since it has been going on for a while, I'm most likely in a coma and getting ready to die."

"Whatever you are, you are an enigma. I see you have some magical ability."

"I'm not sure that's what you call it. Regardless, it is recent. Again, probably a creation of my brain helping me fit in with this storyline."

The battle sounded like it had lost much of its intensity. Daria went to look around the corner. "I think the fight is over. A lot of people are running."

Kanter raised an arm. "Help me up."

Once on his feet, Kanter studied Jeremy from inches away. He felt a tingling deep within his chest, like being probed by an electric current. Then it was gone. Kanter moved to the edge of the house, leaving Jeremy alone to wonder what just happened.

"It is over," Kanter said. "Let us see who needs our help."

Daria and Kanter moved around the corner. Jeremy stayed behind.

As they approached the cornfield, Biatta guided Jerricka out of the cornfield. The tall black woman looked slightly dazed but when she spotted Daria, a wide smile lit her face. "I am so glad you are all right."

"Thank you, Headmistress. Is there anything I can do to help you?"

Biatta answered, "Take her. I am going back to assist others."

Jerricka was passed off and Daria walked her toward the farmhouse.

"Have you been able to keep up with your studies?" Jerricka asked.

"Yeah, I guess."

"What does that mean?"

"I've learned a lot, but not in traditional ways."

"I see Kanter. Has he been instructing you?"

"No, but he wants me to learn from his daughters."

"Ah, wildling magic. It does have its uses, I'll grant that, but it also has many limitations. I hope once this conflict has been resolved that you'll come back to the school. Get a good solid base. Then if you want, you can go off and learn variants. That will only make you stronger and more well-rounded."

"Thank you, Headmistress. I will keep that in mind."

They reached the house.

"Just set me down here on the steps. The local authorities are on the way and we will need to be long gone by then." Once seated, Jerricka said, "Daria, you have much potential. I knew that from the first, but it is important you are trained properly to avoid being drawn into a world of magic that will never release you from its hold. That will change you forever. Now go help the others."

"Yes, Headmistress." Daria ran off with Jerricka's words running through her head. It was one of only a few times the headmistress had spoken to her and perhaps the only time she had said anything positive. It gave her a lot to think about.

Daria entered the cornfield and moved toward the sound of pain.

Chapter Fifty-One

As Jeremy drove down the dirt driveway from the farm, a multitude of wailing sirens approached. The minivan was full to the max. Being so weighted down gave them even less chance to avoid being pulled over.

"What are we going to do?" Jeremy asked with a touch of panic in his voice.

"Stay calm," Biatta said from the passenger seat. Her gaze swept the area around the driveway. The immediate terrain offered scant opportunity to hide.

They were closing in on the dirt road that ran in front of the driveway. In the distance to the left, Jeremy caught the flash of a blue light between branches. Even if they reached the road and turned right, the police were too close to avoid.

"We have to come up with a story to avoid being detained," he said.

Biatta pointed. "There. Pull up behind those trees."

Jeremy looked and saw three trees in a straight line. It was nowhere near enough cover to hide them.

"But—"

"Don't argue. Do it. Now." Her voice was commanding.

Jeremy responded immediately. The overburdened minivan bounced over the rough terrain, the weight bottoming the suspension. He maneuvered behind the middle tree and braked.

"Shut it off," Biatta instructed. Her hands were doing their weaving thing.

Jeremy turned the engine off and noticed Jerricka sitting up on the floor doing the same as Biatta. He looked outside but didn't notice any change. The magic or whatever it was they were doing was not affecting anything he could see.

A host of lights came into view. A train of vehicles led by a half dozen police cars turned up the driveway. They were followed by ambulances, firetrucks, more police cars, and a large black vehicle with the letters S.W.A.T. painted on the side.

Jeremy held his breath as the vehicles approached. He expected them to pull off the road and surround them but as the vehicles drove past, he began to relax. He looked at Biatta then at Jerricka. They each sat still, eyes slightly rolled back and hands extended with palms out and the ring and pinkie fingers curled inward. Amid the silence in the van, a low two-tone hum was barely audible. He realized the harmony was coming from the two women.

He glanced up to see Chandra staring at them with her jaw slack. It was a look she had maintained throughout the ordeal. Nick sat next to her, a satisfied smile playing across his calm face. Daria and Gwynedd watched from the cargo area. An injured woman Jeremy did not know slumped unconscious next to Nick. A body lay on the floor at their feet.

The last car raced past and Jeremy reached for the key.

"Hold," Biatta said, looking like her normal self now.

A minute later, two more police cars and another ambulance turned up the driveway. They waited until they were well past before Biatta nodded. Jeremy drove to the dirt road and turned right, having no idea where it went. He was still shocked they had not been discovered and taken into custody.

Biatta turned to Jerricka. The woman had her eyes down looking at the body. Biatta placed a tender hand on Jerricka's arm.

"I am so sorry for your loss. Jno was an invaluable friend."

Jerricka met her eyes, swallowing the emotional lump, and gave a quick nod. Her eyes filled with tears that a moment later appeared to evaporate, leaving a steely-eyed glare.

"There will be retribution for his death."

The inside of the van chilled noticeably.

Biatta said, "Yes, there will, but not now."

Jerricka's eyes narrowed. Then with a deep exhalation, the temperature inside the van returned to normal.

"Where should I go?" Jeremy asked.

Biatta did not respond at first. "We need to drop you and your family off."

"Why? Where are you going?"

"Do not concern yourself. It is time for you to return to your life. Your children need a break from all this excitement."

"Does that mean we're safe?"

"You should be fine. Rowan is going to collapse the portal so no one can get back through."

"But don't you still have students here?"

"We will bring them back once the threat is ended."

"So, you can still reopen the portal?"

"No. A new one will most likely need to be opened."

"If you can open a new one, can't the other side do so as well?"

She sighed. "Technically, yes, but you should not worry. We have them on the run now. They will be fighting for survival and won't have time to open a portal."

"But it is possible, right?"

Biatta faced him. "Jeremy, it is time for you and your family to forget about all of this and go back to your lives."

"Does that mean I won't see you…uh…or Daria again? What if something happens? How can I contact you?"

"You can't."

"But I thought you wanted to study me."

"I'm sorry, Jeremy. It's over. Perhaps sometime in the future we can reconnect, but for now it is not a good idea."

The van fell silent until Chandra said, "I, for one, will welcome the return to normalcy."

Biatta gave her a warm smile. "I'm sure you will. I apologize for the upheaval our presence has caused."

Jeremy glanced in the mirror, expecting a sharp retort from his daughter. Instead, he saw the words form in her narrowed eyes, then get swallowed. He breathed a sigh of relief.

Nick spoke up to break the tension. "How do you think the authorities will respond when they see all the bodies left behind?"

"That's a good question," said Jeremy. "Hopefully none of it will lead back to us. That would be difficult to explain."

The bodies of our fallen have been taken away," Biatta said. "Only Bradenbaugh's people remain. He turned onto their street. As they approached his house, he noticed a car parked across the street. He leaned forward over the wheel. Too late, he realized it was an unmarked police car. He slowed.

"What are you doing, Dad?" Chandra asked. "Let's get home so I can get out of here."

"Does that car belong to that detective?"

She sat forward to get a better look out the windshield. "Who? Vasili?" She blew out an exasperated breath. "What does he want now?"

Jeremy turned up the driveway but kept the engine running.

"We have to cover the body or none of us are going anywhere."

In her haste to get out, Chandra opened the sliding door. She stepped out as Vasili was crossing the street. Ready to unleash her pent frustration and anger, she strode straight at him. "What are you doing here. Haven't you harassed us enough?" She squared off in front of him, spreading her legs and planting fists on hips. "If you don't leave us alone, I'm going to file a harassment complaint then get an attorney."

"Lady, you need to calm yourself now or things will go very bad for you."

"Is that a threat?"

"Yes."

They eyed each other with matched fierceness.

"I'm so beyond caring what you do. Go ahead. Arrest me. That will look great for the case I bring against you. Well-respected mother of two involved in the community arrested by over-zealous policeman."

"That's over-zealous detective, and I have my doubts as to the well-respected tag you place on yourself."

Nick and Jeremy came up behind Chandra.

Jeremy said, "What's this about, Detective?"

Though he kept his hard glare on Chandra, he replied, "Where were you over the past three hours?"

"We went for a drive with some friends."

"What friends? Who are those people in your van?"

"Friends. If there's a problem, it does not concern them."

"I'll be the judge of that." He moved to the side of Chandra. "You in the van, come out of there."

Chandra moved to block him.

"Lady, you're playing a dangerous game. I will arrest you for obstruction."

Biatta exited and moved toward them. "There is no need for that, Officer. She placed a hand on Chandra's shoulder. "No need to escalate things, sister."

Behind her, Jerricka came out full of fire.

"I have no patience left for these niceties."

With a wave of her hand, Vasili took a step back, reached for his weapon, then fell. He hit the ground hard, smacking his head.

Jeremy and Chandra whirled on Jerricka.

"What did you do?" Chandra shrieked.

"Jerricka," Jeremy said. "You're leaving here, but we live here. When he wakes, we will be in serious trouble."

"Then perhaps he shouldn't wake," Jerricka said, her eyes turning black.

Chandra rushed at her. "No!"

Biatta stepped in front to block her. "No, Jerricka. Do not do this. Release that type of magic before it takes control of you and causes real damage."

Jerricka's eyes flashed with violent intent. Biatta remained calm and stepped closer. "Do not allow it to control you, sister. You are far better than to submit to its call." She placed a hand on Jerricka's arm. Her body convulsed and then she slumped into Biatta's arms. She looked up.

"Biatta, Help me."

"I am here for you, sister. Sleep now. We will work on this together once we cross over."

Nick, who had squatted next to the fallen detective said, "Hey, I think he needs immediate help."

Jeremy said, "Help me carry him inside." Nick and Jeremy hoisted Vasili. As they moved toward the house, he said, "Chandra, call an ambulance. The rest of you get back in the van. I'll drive you closer to the portal."

Once inside, they laid the detective on the sofa where recently so many other unconscious people had lain. Biatta pushed past them and knelt at his side, as she had done for Nick mere days before. She placed a hand on Vasili's head and the now-familiar glow appeared. Seconds later, she stood.

"I have done what I can for now, but he will need medical attention. Jeremy, we have to go."

They left Chandra and Nick to care for Vasili. As the minivan backed down the driveway, sirens screamed in the distance. They drove away with Jeremy suddenly thankful this wild and crazy adventure was coming to an end.

Chapter Fifty-Two

"Rowan, we can't wait any longer," Tarney said. "I know you want to get all our people across, but we need to collapse the portal before Bradenbaugh's people get here."

When they arrived, they found the portal collapsed but not gone. Someone with lesser skills had attempted to reopen the portal from the other end leaving it weakened and unstable. They were forced to shore it up if only on a temporary basis.

"I know. I'm just not sure it's the best course of action to trap such an evil entity in this world. Besides, we don't even know they're still here. They retreated before we did. They may already be across."

"Perhaps, but if that is true, the longer we wait, the more time they have to set up an ambush."

"Mister Tarney is right, Rowan. Crossing now is the best course of action. All our people are through except for us."

Rowan cast a curious eye at Kanter. "Our people? I thought you were sitting this action out."

Kanter glanced away. "Perhaps I was hasty in my decision."

"What changed?"

The flicker of a smile touched his lips. "Your little friend Daria can be quite persuasive."

"No doubt."

"You realize she has the potential for world-changing power and great things if she is taught properly."

Tarney scoffed, "You mean by you?"

Kanter shrugged. "That might be for the best. Let her learn in an environment that allows her freedom in her educational choices."

"That also allows her the freedom to become another Bradenbaugh," Tarney countered.

"There is that possibility without the proper guidance," Kanter conceded. "However, under my daughters' watchful eyes, it's doubtful. And she will be much more powerful than Bradenbaugh ever dreamed of being."

"That is the concern," Rowan said. "That is why I think a more structured approach to her training is called for."

"Well, I guess we'll just have to agree to disagree on this point."

"Yes, we will, but perhaps in the end we should allow Daria to make the choice for herself. We each make our case and let her choose. However, perhaps you will be open to a shared experience."

"Go on."

"I agree, she has boundless potential. My fear is that without proper grounding, that power may draw her irrevocably into a dark place where we will have to do something about her. If you are agreeable, allow her to ger her base training with us to root her in a belief of helping her fellow people; one that draws on friendships and peace. Once that is accomplished, I will gladly turn her over to you and your daughters to finish out her education. Between us maybe we can block any negative energies from seducing her to a darker existence."

"Otherwise," Tarney said, "it is better to deal with her now before she realizes her full power."

Kanter's eyebrows lifted. "You would end the girl?"

"I'd rather do it while we still have the ability to do so rather than face her might once she comes of age."

"That's rather harsh, Mister Tarney, even for you."

"Just being proactive."

"There is still a long way to go before any of this is relevant. As far as her education goes we must also consider Daria's wishes in this matter. However, if we can reach an accord, we have no need for her wishes to be part of the deal."

"As you say, we have a long way to go before that comes to fruition."

"Am I to assume you are now standing with us in this final battle?"

"Yes."

Rowan eyed the older man, waiting for further explanation.

Kanter did not continue but altered course, hoping Rowan took it as such. "Bradenbaugh's people know where the dark one is imprisoned."

The news did not appear to surprise Rowan.

"You knew."

Rowan nodded. "Word reached us that the first key had been discovered. It was a matter of time."

"But they must know that without all four keys, breaking him free is impossible."

"What were they doing at the site?"

"Casting heavy spells to weaken the wards."

Rowan narrowed his eyes as he thought. "They would have to know it was a waste of time and effort..." His eyes widened. "Unless..."

Kanter finished the thought. "They have discovered other keys. Depending on how many they possess the task is incrementally easier. If they have three— he allowed the thought to trail off.

"With enough time and force," Rowan said. "The fourth key may be weakened enough for the dark one to break free."

"Doubtful," Kanter said. "I was there and helped set the wards. A different form of magic was used for each key. Mine was based on a long-forgotten sect of now extinct power. The knowledge has been lost in time. I may be the last person to have specific memory."

"Do you know where the fourth key was hidden?"

"No. Salemnon took it upon himself to hide it and would not permit anyone to accompany him, thus being the only person with the knowledge."

"Kanter, we must find that last key before Bradenbaugh does."

Just then, a rustling of branches drew their attention. They all prepared offensive spells. Biatta, Daria, and Gwynedd emerged. Jerricka and Jeremy carried Jno's body. A dazed Precious followed.

"I am relieved to see you," Rowan said.

"And we you," said Biatta. "Is this all of us?"

"No. We sent the others ahead to secure the other end. We need to go. Bradenbaugh may still be here."

They watched in mournful silence as Jno's body was passed from Jeremy to Tarney, then carted through the portal. Gwynedd followed Jerricka. Daria stopped.

Kanter asked, "Are you all right, child?"

"I'm fine, but after all I've been through, I wish people would stop calling me child."

Kanter smiled. "Do not be in such a rush to be older than your years, Daria. Despite all you have seen, compared to the rest of us, you may always be a child."

She shrugged. "I guess."

"Go now, Daria," Rowan said.

She started to move, then turned to Jeremy. She rushed forward and embraced him.

"Goodbye, Jeremy. I will miss you."

"And I you, Daria. You being here was like having my own child home again. Although a little more destructive."

She gave him a final squeeze and stepped through the portal.

Biatta took his hand. He pushed it aside and stepped in for a hug.

Her exchange was tentative.

"Thank you for all you have done for us, Jeremy. I will never forget you."

"Stay safe, Biatta. Perhaps we will meet again."

She pushed back and smiled. "Perhaps. Someday." She stepped toward the portal. "You should go now before that detective awakens."

Then she was gone.

Jeremy looked at the remaining two men. He nodded at them.

"Thank you for looking after our people, Jeremy," Rowan said. "You have been a good friend."

"I'd say anytime, but I'm not sure my house, my children, or my health can bear much more." He offered his hand and they shook, then he walked back through the trees.

"He is quite an enigma," Rowan said.

"Yes, quite."

"Do you believe the theory that he is from the lost tribe of Salemnon?"

"I do not," Kanter said.

Surprised at the conviction in those few words, Rowan asked, "Weren't you the one who postulated the theory in the first place?"

"I was."

"And?"

"It was a ruse."

They moved to the opening of the portal.

"Explain."

"I suggested it to throw everyone off track."

"I don't understand. You don't believe he could be part of the lost tribe?"

"I am sure he is not."

"Why?"

"Because I am the last original survivor of Salemnon's tribe."

The statement drew Rowan up short.

"We never went through the portal. Salemnon did not want to lead others to explore an innocent world in search of our people. Salemnon faked going through to the point of leaving witnesses to the event, but they were planted. We settled in the area where my daughters live now and have been there ever since."

He paused. Then as if speaking to himself. "He was intrigued by the portal and the idea of visiting other worlds. After seeing us settled he disappeared for a time. I always wondered where he went."

Rowan puzzled on this new information for a while before speaking. "If that is true and Salemnon's tribe did not go through to this world, then who is Jeremy?"

"That is a good question, and one I sense will need to be answered before our current threat is over."

With that the two men passed through the portal to their world. Once on the other side, Rowan, Kanter, and Tarney worked a spell to collapse the portal forever.

As they walked away to face the new threats the dark one's forces had in store, Kanter flicked a finger and a small spark flew. It struck where the portal had once been and hung there as an invisible beacon that would allow him to return to this spot. Though Rowan might be ready to dismiss Jeremy as non-important, Kanter felt the man a threat. He wanted the option to go back and deal with him, should the need arise. For now, they had more important matters to contend with.

The End

Jeremy Kline will return soon in Jeremy Kline and the Keys of Power.

ABOUT THE AUTHOR

Ray Wenck taught elementary school for 36 years. He was also the chef/owner of DeSimone's Italian restaurant for more than 25 years. After retiring he became a lead cook for Hollywood Casinos and then the kitchen manager for the Toledo Mud Hens AAA baseball team. Now he spends most of his time writing, doing book tours and meeting old and new fans and friends around the country.

Ray is the author of forty-four novels including the Amazon Top 20 post-apocalyptic, Random Survival series, the paranormal thriller, Ghost of a Chance, the mystery/suspense Danny Roth series and the ever popular choose your own adventure, Pick-A-Path: Apocalypse. A list of his other novels can be viewed at raywenck.com.

His hobbies include reading, hiking, cooking, baseball and playing the harmonica with any band brave enough to allow him to sit in.

You can find his books all your favorite sites.

You can reach Ray or sign up for his newsletter at raywenck.com or authorraywenck on Facebook

For a free book, visit raywenck.com and sign up for the newsletter.

Other Titles

Random Survival Series
Random Survival
The Long Search for Home
The Endless Struggle
A Journey to Normal
Then There'll Be None
In Defense of Home
Soon: A Life Worth Dying For

Danny Roth Series
Teammates
Teamwork
Home Team
Stealing Home
Group Therapy
Double Play
Playing Through Errors
Pitch Count

The Dead Series
Tower of the Dead
Island of the Dead
Escaping the Dead

Pick-A-Path Series
Pick-A-Path: Apocalypse 1
Pick-A-Path: Apocalypse 2
Pick-A-Path: Apocalypse 3

Stand Alone Titles
Warriors of the Court
Live to Die Again
The Eliminator
Reclamation
Dimensions

Ghost of a Chance
Mischief Magic
Twins In Time
When the Cheering Stops

Short Stories

The Con   Short Stop-A Danny Roth short

Super Me   Super Me, Too

Co-authored with Jason J. Nugent

Escape: The Seam Travelers Book 1

Capture: The Seam Travelers Book 2

Conquest: The Seam Travelers Book 3

The Historian Series

The Historian: Life Before and After

The Historian: The Wilds

The Historian: Invasion

Jeremy Kline

The Invisible Village

The Lost Tribe

Bridgett Conroy Series

A Second Chance at Death

Traveling Trouble

Ray Wenck